ARROGANT
Bastard

ARROGANT
Bastard

ZARA COX

FOREVER

New York Boston

Copyright © 2017 by Zara Cox
Excerpt from *Black Sheep* © 2017 by Zara Cox
Cover design by Elizabeth Turner
Cover copyright © 2017 by Hachette Book Group, Inc.
Hachette Book Group supports the right to free expression and the value of copyright. The purpose of copyright is to encourage writers and artists to produce the creative works that enrich our culture.

The scanning, uploading, and distribution of this book without permission is a theft of the author's intellectual property. If you would like permission to use material from the book (other than for review purposes), please contact permissions@hbgusa.com. Thank you for your support of the author's rights.

Forever
Hachette Book Group
1290 Avenue of the Americas
New York, NY 10104
hachettebookgroup.com
twitter.com/foreverromance

First published as an ebook in 2017
First trade paperback edition: February 2018

Forever is an imprint of Grand Central Publishing.
The Forever name and logo are trademarks of Hachette Book Group, Inc.

The Hachette Speakers Bureau provides a wide range of authors for speaking events. To find out more, go to www.hachettespeakersbureau.com or call (866) 376-6591.

The publisher is not responsible for websites (or their content) that are not owned by the publisher.

Library of Congress Control Number: 2017961072

ISBN 978-1-4789-7023-1(ebook)
ISBN 978-1-4789-7024-8 (trade paperback)

Printed in the United States of America

LSC-C

10 9 8 7 6 5 4 3 2 1

To Tony. For Love. For Everything.

ARROGANT
Bastard

PART ONE

Chapter One

KILLIAN

Present Day

I've found her.

After four years and two months.

I stare at the screen, my blood pumping relief and shock and fury and joy through my veins. The cocktail of emotions paralyzes me for several minutes.

Then I force myself to analyze what I'm seeing.

Her hair is different. Longer. Darker. Pin-straight and rigid where soft, friendly waves used to be. The curve of her jaw captured by the camera lens also shows the difference. She's leaner. Meaner. Even from this obscure angle, I can tell any trace of gentleness has been wiped clean. Eroded by sin and tragedy and horror. The change was probably inevitable, but I still don't want to see the evidence.

To anyone else, the picture would seem ridiculously vague, the image nothing more than a blurred black-and-white pixelation of hair, chin, and shoulder.

It's the reason my algorithm spat it out almost reluctantly, a last batch of possibilities in the dregs of to-be-discarded possibilities, and then dumped it in my supercomputer's equivalent of a spam folder, the code scrolling impatiently as it waited my command to delete, delete, delete.

But I know it's her. Despite the dark leather cap pulled low over her forehead. Despite the bulky jacket designed to hide her true shape. Her stealth speaks volumes. Besides, she's in my blood, in my heartbeat. After so many years of dead ends and fruitless hoping, of agonizing disappointment and withering despair, this time I simply…know.

It's her. The Widow.

My hand shakes as I hit the *zoom-in* key. My gut churns, and I feel a little sick as my ever-helpful brain cheerfully supplies me with all the ways she could've continued to elude me—if I'd turned away, for a second, to stare at one of the other three screens on my desk. If I'd trusted my supersmart computer and accepted the prompt to delete without reviewing this particular needle in my mountain of haystacks. If I hadn't tweaked the code yet again last night to capture just such an obscure image.

Hell, if I'd blinked at the wrong time…I torture myself with infinite possibilities as I stare at that mesmerizing angle of chin and shoulder.

A chin I've trailed my treacherous fingers over many times in helpless wonder.

A shoulder I've rested my guilty but secretly unrepentant head on.

There's so much more to her. And I treasured every single inch of her forbidden body, fucked her at every opportunity she granted me. Until she systematically erased herself from my life.

But why New York? And why now?

I know how good she is. Hell, she's the best or she wouldn't have evaded me for this long. The thought of another four years without her punches a cold fist through my gut. With it comes the certainty that I wouldn't have survived those next four years. That I've been clinging on with the very last dregs of my endurance to make it this far.

But here she is…

The Widow.

I can't see her eyes, but I don't fool myself into thinking they'll hold an ounce of softness. What we did changed us forever. And not for the better.

I lean back in my chair. Exhale slowly. Terrified of blinking in case she disappears from my screen. It doesn't matter that I've copied and stored the longitude and latitude of her location in a dozen vaults on my server and memorized every single piece of data on the screen.

New York City. East Fifty-Third Street. CCTV camera. A one-in-a-billion shot.

Without taking my eyes off her, I reach for my phone and press the voice activation app. "Good evening, Mr. Knight."

"Nala, how many times do I need to tell you to call me Killian?"

"You have yet to change my default settings, Mr. Knight."

My lips twitch but a smile doesn't quite form. My eyes water with the need to blink. But I resist. "I changed them last week. You reset them again, didn't you?"

"I assure you, I'm quite incapable of doing that."

"Yeah, right. Fine. Place a call for me. Pilot. Home."

"Dialing Pilot. Home," the female AI obliges me.

Nelson Whittaker, my LA-based English pilot, picks up on the second ring. It's three a.m. but he answers as if it's normal working hours. Which it is, to be fair. Everything is normal for me in my line of work.

"Good morning, sir."

"How soon can you get to the airport?" I snap.

"As soon as I put on my trousers and chuck a bucket of water over my son to wake him up," he replies with a dark chuckle.

My fingers fly over the keyboard as I save her information in a few more electronic vaults. "Give William my apologies," I say.

"No need. He's been champing at the bit to take the new girl for another spin." The new girl being the Bombardier Global 8000 I added to my collection of private jets last month.

"In that case, I expect to see you at Van Nuys within the hour."
At this time of the morning, traffic from their Santa Monica apartment should be light enough to get them there fast.

"We'll be there." He clears his throat. "I expect the paperwork re-
garding out-of-curfew flights—"

"Will be taken care of. I'll text you the details but we won't be
straying far from the usual parameters."

"Very good, sir. Destination?" he asks crisply.

My gaze tracks that chin. That shoulder. The hair. Four years'
worth of turbulent emotion threatens to rip free. My chest burns
with it, but I contain it. "New York."

"And do I need to file a return flight?" Nelson asks.

"Not yet. I anticipate being there for a while." Until I find her.
Until she's back in my arms. She won't come willingly, but that's another problem for another day.

"Got it."

I disconnect the call and stare at the picture for another minute
before I blink and turn to the next screen. It takes less than five
minutes to hack the aviation database I need and input the relevant
information.

Russell, my driver, is waiting when I sprint downstairs. One advantage of owning homes around the world is the ability to pick up
and go at a moment's notice without the need to pack a suitcase. All
I need are the clothes on my back, my computer, and other clandestine electronics.

"All set to go, sir?"

I nod, hand over the extra computer bag, and slide into the backseat. I'm already itching to power up my computer again to make
sure her picture is still on my home screen. When it flares to life,
and I see her again, I breathe easier. I note that the shock is wearing
off, and anticipation is filling its place. As is the growing bewilderment. But also…I'm angry. It's one thing to have your insides
ripped out when a relationship, or whatever the fuck we had, ends.
It's another to be eviscerated without explanation and left bleeding
and half-dead.

It's what she's done to me. As much as I want her back in my arms, I have a lot of volatile emotions to resolve. My body immediately supplies me with one avenue of resolution, and my cock jerks to life in my pants. Like an eager bloodhound straining at the leash, it flexes with very little heed to my gritted jaw or angry intake of breath. It wants what it wants. And I can't really blame it. This has been a very long time coming. And I haven't even truly gotten her back yet.

I breathe through my angst and resist the urge to stroke off to her image. I've done enough of that since she's been gone.

The next time I come, it'll be with her in front of me, on her knees or on her back…or whichever way the fuck I please, I silently promise my raging dick.

There's very little traffic at this time of night, but I stare at the screen for the short drive to the airport. The photo has got me whipped. I can't look away from it. Just like I couldn't look away from her the first time I saw her.

God, was that only five years ago when I almost didn't make it to her fateful birthday party? When I dragged my darkness through the side gate of a house in the middle of Xanaxville under completely false pretenses and felt the earth shift beneath my feet?

I feel like I've desired her and lost her through several lifetimes. She wishes she'd never met me in any of them, I know. But that matters very little now.

It happened. We happened. And this time…I don't plan to lose her again. My fists clench as I debate the lengths I'm prepared to go to make it that way. She'll fight me. That's her nature. I might even lose this particular fight. But there's a reason the term *or die trying* is more than mere words to me. To us.

"Another medical emergency, Mr. Knight?"

I look up from the screen and frown. I have no recollection of leaving the car and entering the VIP terminal building reserved for private flights.

"Unfortunately, yes," I respond, my gaze already sliding away from the uniformed officials gathered around, and back to the screen.

"Damn, you must have the worst luck in the world, huh?" The customs guy is standing next to the immigration guy. They're both staring at me. Because what? They think I'm going to fuck up and confess that I hacked into their system to input the information that is allowing me to fly outside the aviation curfew? Right.

"I go where I'm needed. These things can't be helped," I reply insincerely.

He laughs, and we both shrug. He follows me across the carpeted reception area, and I slip him a couple of hundred-dollar bills although he's getting paid triple time for the half an hour's work it'll take for my flight to be cleared for takeoff.

We part ways, each feeling marginally satisfied but a little screwed over and a little dirty. The money means less than nothing to me, and although very little would make me feel bad about faking an excuse to fly outside curfew hours tonight of all nights, I detest the extraneous lies I have to tell to achieve what I want.

Which is beyond laughable considering what my chosen profession is.

I hurry toward my plane, the grip of anticipation getting tighter with each step. Nelson, trim and tall and much younger looking than the sixty-three years he is, emerges from the plane first, followed by Will. The father-and-son piloting team have been in my employ for three years. Between them, they have forty years of aviation experience, which gives me one less thing to worry about in the grand, fucked-up landscape of my life.

"We're ready to hit the skies as soon as you are," Nelson says as he signs the requisite preflight papers and hands the clipboard back to the official. "I've been informed your doctor will be on standby at Teterboro," he adds, tongue firmly in cheek.

"That's excellent news, Nelson. I'm assuming my doctor is also capable of doubling as my driver?" I ask as I follow him up the steps into the plane.

"He's willing to be whatever you need him to be, sir. He has a helicopter license if you want him to be your chopper pilot. He's very versatile that way."

"Remind me to add a little extra to your Christmas bonus this year, Nelson."

"Don't worry, sir, my reminder email will be right on time."

I allow myself a little smile, but it's soon eaten away by razor-sharp memories, acid guilt, and churning anticipation. I wave the flight attendant away as she arrives beside me with my usual pre-flight shot of Hine cognac.

She quietly retreats, and when I'm finally alone, I dare to glide my finger over the screen, across her cheek. One artificial touch and my insides go into free fall.

The shaking could be from the power of the engines thrusting me and my crew into the sky. Or it could be the cataclysmic chain reaction that has only ever come from her.

It's a universally held belief that you can't help who you fall in love with. There are a fuck-load of books expounding on that theory.

I call bullshit.

I could've walked away that day, got someone else to do what I went there to do. My superiors were already whining about the conflict of interest before I made that trip to Arkansas. I could've waited another three years to see the brother who hated my guts twice as much as I hated his.

I should've walked away when the crackle and flash and roar of flames warned me the fires of hell were consuming what remained of my pathetic soul.

I could've stopped myself from soiling her goodness. From falling ass over feet in love. But I carried on walking. And with each step I took, I knew we were doomed. Because with each step, I glimpsed her potential, absorbed her genius and her beauty and her flaws.

She was everything I'd been waiting for without even knowing it.

And somewhere between the sparkling pool and the shitty Tupperware strewn on the floral-clothed table where she stood cutting her birthday cake, I decided to just…take.

The only problem was that Faith Carson, the woman I eventually turned into the Widow, the woman who fucking conquered the world, wasn't mine to take.

She belonged, legally, according to the laws of Arkansas anyway, to another man.

Did I change course? Retreat? Accept that the conflict of interest wasn't professional but viscerally, irrefutably personal?

Fuck, no.

Chapter Two

KILLIAN

The first step was easy.

I'm a spy. Albeit a reluctant one. I never asked for this role, but I eventually accepted it. Also...turns out I'm fucking great at it. Or I was. Until I met Faith. She made me think recruiting her was easy. I soon discovered the truth.

She was way better than I was.

I wasn't even upset when I found out how good she was on our first assignment together. Beauty and brains are an insane combination in any given scenario. With her it was lethal. When she wasn't slaying me with her mind, all I thought of was her killer body and the new and inventive ways I could fuck it.

That day, in the house I grew up in, even while I walked by her side and responded to introductions to people I would never willingly mingle with again, even before I finished the slice of too-dry chocolate cake I didn't want, I knew our destinies were already aligned. And it wasn't because my utter preoccupation with her insulated me against the quiet vitriol spilling from my older brother's smiling lips. Before I became a spy, I often wondered how he could do that—smile so affably to everyone else while ripping me to shreds with his words every chance he got. I wondered why he bothered when anyone with a lick of sense could tell we hated each other with a vengeance.

Two things became clear soon enough. Matthew Knight was a born politician, right down to the sleaze running through his veins. And becoming a spy opened my eyes to the existence of smiling assassins.

But I digress.

The Widow. She was the only recruit I actively campaigned for, gleefully ignoring the shrieking alarm bells that basic espionage training taught you to heed. I had no problem ignoring them. I was getting out. The powers that be knew I was done but greedily accepted my recommendation to recruit her. She was supposed to be my last, my reluctant victory lap before I retreated into the contented coding cave the government had dug me out of. At the ripe old age of twenty-nine, I was done serving my country or, more accurately, letting it chew me up and spit me out while leaching my talent every chance it got.

Hell, who am I kidding? She was supposed to be the present I gave to myself.

Until it all went wrong. Until we went too far.

Still, we were supposed to pay whatever penance we owed together. Not apart. And not in silent darkness.

My shaking finger drops from the screen. The deep breath I take barely hits my lungs before it ejects itself back up again. Agitation spikes through me, and I finally release my death grip on the laptop long enough to dump it on the sofa beside me. I stand and head for the cockpit.

Father and son glance over their shoulders when I enter, a little startled by my presence. In all the time they've worked for me, I've entered their domain probably once. I should say something boss-like and reassuring.

Fuck it.

"How long before we land?" I snap.

They exchange glances. "We took off forty-five minutes ago, sir," William says.

I raise an eyebrow.

He clears his throat. "Not for another four and a half hours, sir."

Way too long. "Is there any way to shave some time off that estimate?"

Will frowns. "Uh…"

"Are you sure we can't get this tin can to go a little faster?" I look down at the controls, making some quick calculations. "We're not doing anywhere near our top speed."

"That's correct, but we need permission from the aviation authorities for that."

"Get the permission. Bribe someone if you need to."

Nelson stares at me for a beat before he shakes his head. "I don't advise doing that, sir. Not without getting our knuckles severely rapped. And frankly, I'd much rather not rekindle memories of Mrs. Butterworth and her wooden ruler."

Will sniggers under his breath. The look I send him dries up the sound, and he clears his throat.

"But you are welcome to keep us company if you wish," Nelson offers after an uncomfortable few seconds.

I drop into the jump seat behind the copilot even though every particle in my body is straining to return to my laptop.

"Can I get Stacy to bring you something to eat or drink?" Will asks.

"No, but you know what I'd like?"

"No, sir."

"For you to nudge that throttle lever up a fraction. Think you can do that?"

Father and son eye each other again and then turn resolutely to face forward without replying.

I close my eyes, slam my head back against the wall, and grit my teeth to keep from unleashing the demons of frustration running rampant through me.

Five hours. New York City.

The Widow needs to be there when I land.

Any other scenario besides her in my arms at the earliest fucking opportunity is more than I can bear right now.

She needs to know that a small part of me never meant to drag her to hell with me. I won't be insincere and confess a whole-hearted regret I don't feel. But maybe that small admission might achieve...fuck knows. Something. Enough for her to let me in? Enough for me to touch that goodness again, to calm the ravaging nightmares that are eating me alive?

Or just drag her back down because hell wasn't such a lonely place when she was right there beside me? The truth doesn't cause me discomfort. There has to be a degree of moral bankruptcy to do what I do, achieve what I have achieved.

And if I need to exploit it for the sake of getting her back? Well...fuck it, I'm already damned.

Chapter Three

BLACK WIDOW

Run.

The word stabs through my brain and then echoes in the literal kick to my midriff and another one to the side of my head seconds later. My breath puffs out, half in surprise, half in pain, and I land with a hard bump on my ass.

Run.

I need to get up, grab that black emergency bag that's been waiting patiently at the back of my closet for three weeks now, and get the hell out of town. The out-of-the-blue phone call was bad enough. Ignoring my instincts after coming face-to-face with the shadow that should've stayed in the shadows? Yeah, I need a kick upside the head.

So why aren't you listening to your own advice? The voice in my head mocks me as I struggle to catch my breath.

"You ready to go again?"

I blink away the streams of sweat sliding into my eyes but welcome the salty sting on my membranes. Weirdly, it, more than the pain throbbing in my ribs and shoulders, tells me I'm alive. Maybe it's even forcing me to open my damn eyes and face reality? My cover is blown—

"Yo, B? Are you awake in there? That head kick didn't dislodge your brain, did it?" My Muay Thai instructor stares at me with his head tilted and a smirk on his face. He's not my usual sparring partner. Kevin, the owner of the Soho fight club and my regular trainer, is away for some MMA contest in Chicago, which is why I'm stuck with this joker.

I roll my eyes as I straighten up from my hunched-over position. "It'll take a hell of a lot more than your feeble-ass kicks to dislodge anything on my body."

I grit my teeth as his gaze slides, predictably, over me. At least he doesn't linger. I get a quick hit of blatant male appreciation before he attempts to resume his professionalism. "You had a dazed look in your eyes that told me to go easy on you."

"Please. We've sparred twice before, Anwat. I beat your pathetic ass both times, even though you allegedly brought your A-game." I infuse as much sneering into my voice as possible. Hopefully it'll dissuade him from doing what he wants to do, which is to find a way to promote his own interest.

Predictably, his eyes gleam at the direct challenge to his ego. "So you wanna put your money where your smart mouth is and go again or what?"

I toss the idea around, and I watch him prowl back and forth on the black rubber mat as I toy with the Velcro strip on my glove. Maybe I should go another round. There's nothing like blinding pain to wipe out thoughts of everything else, especially the thought projected in neon lights that tells me that choosing fight over fight won't end well.

Anwat slowly approaches, eyes narrowed, and positions himself before me with intent. I want to laugh. I can break every major bone in his body and severely compromise several organs in two minutes. I haven't used my skills in years, but once learned, that knowledge never goes away. Especially when the threat of danger is ever-present, like a second skin I've never been able to shed.

Anwat beckons me with a jerk of his chin. The urge to punch the shit out of it ripples through me. That's certainly another avenue I can take. But that sort of action I reserve for those who deserve it, and pay for the privilege, at the Punishment Club. So I step back from the temptation. "Sorry, sunshine. Maybe one day I'll give you the chance to impress me."

He slowly lowers his hands, irritation stamped on his face. "What the fuck, B? You booked me for two hours. It's only been twenty minutes."

I shrug. "No need to crap your pants, Anwat. I'm not going to demand a refund. Go have a beer on me."

He yanks off one glove with a little more force than necessary. "I don't drink beer."

I sigh, finish removing my gloves, and drop them at his feet. "Have an iced tea then. God, you always this annoying?" I say as I walk past him.

"You always such a bitch?"

I whip around, once again dying for a fight to displace the fear crawling through me. "What did you just call me?" I snap.

To his credit, he immediately steps back, hands raised in apology and surrender. "S'all good, B. S'all good."

A tiny bit of regret for his cowardice lingers as I step out of the ring and head for the shower. For several minutes I stand beneath the hot spray, accepting what I can't hide from anymore.

This can't go on.

Fight or flight. I need to pick one and get the hell on with it. Except the fight went out of me a long time ago. In a cold, dark room in Cairo four years ago, my heart stopped beating, and it took everything else with it. No, not everything. Raw, eviscerating guilt remained. For a long time, it was the only emotion to cheerfully take root and nurture itself with absolutely no help from me at all. But slowly, other emotions invited themselves to the party.

Fear. Anxiety. Apathy.

Craving. At times that was the worst of all, that dark, merciless, gouge-your-soul-out craving. For him.

My nightmares are filled with him. My lustful dreams too. My waking hours are spent fighting the thought of him. But he never goes away. Always lingering. Always taunting.

The memory of him pulses through me so vividly that it's almost as if he lives inside me. In my darkest nights, I toy with the possibility that he left something inside me on that last assignment in Cairo. It's not outside the realm of possibility. It was why I paid a few thousand dollars to undergo a thorough body scan in a black site lab just to find out. The evidence that I wasn't carrying a metal tagging chip that would lead him to me didn't dispel the notion that the object of my craving still had a hold over me, even if it was all in my head.

The piece of my wasted soul that I sacrificed on the altar of my forbidden desire will forever be its own testament to how far gone I was by the time I left him behind.

Perhaps it's the reason I've thrived as manageress at the Punishment Club. It was supposed to be a six-month gig. It's been four years. At first I imagined I could find salvation for my own sins within the walls of the private club. After all, it's the place I created for other people who wanted to atone for their sins. As a moneymaking venture, it's been obscenely successful. But I quickly accepted there would be no such salvation for me. There was no going back for the person I'd become. So I embraced my role as the punisher.

And then I became complacent. I even attempted a friendship.

Until the first phone call came three weeks ago.

Fight or flight.

I turn off the faucet and step out of the shower, my thoughts still turned inward. I dress in my customary black getup of yoga pants, tank top, and zip-up hoodie, stuff my damp hair under a nondescript black cap, and shrug on my backpack. I pause with my hand on the door handle, my heart hammering its urgency about what I know I should do. I take a few breaths to center myself, slow down my heartbeat. Solidify my decision.

Flight.

After four years of leading a near-stagnant life, acceptance that I'm about to run again is easier than I thought it would be. Maybe it's because I know Axel Rutherford, my boss, will understand. Against all odds, he's finding his own shaky salvation with Cleo McCarthy. I've learned a few things about him that tells me he could make my life difficult if he wants to, but I know he won't prevent me from disappearing as quietly as I arrived.

Flight. Okay.

I leave the twenty-four-hour fitness club, stepping out after a quick, customary surveillance of the quiet streets. I picked this club purely because it was located in the most unsavory part of Soho. Some helpful soul also disabled a couple of street cameras a while back, and the city authorities didn't replace them after the third vandalism.

That has worked in my favor, although I have to carefully navigate about a dozen more between here and my apartment six blocks away. I pull my hoodie over my cap for added protection and quicken my footsteps. I'm itching to add sunglasses to my disguise, but that'll draw too much attention at this time of night, so I pull out my phone and adopt the universal fuck-with-my-phone-time-at-your-peril position.

Three blocks from home, I feel it. I don't recognize the tingle at first because it's been a while since I last experienced the unmistakable sensation. Or perhaps I resist it because I don't want this, like the phone call three weeks ago, to be true.

The sensation spreads fast and hard and real. I'm being tailed. Shock punches through me. It's enough to weaken my knees, almost making me stumble. Enough to drag a set of icy claws through my gut. I snatch in a breath, gauge my surroundings without looking over my shoulder, and mentally zip through escape possibilities.

There's no way I can go back home now without leading them right to my door. The subway is out of the question. Too many cameras. Same goes for other forms of public transportation, even at this time of night.

Without hesitation, I break into a sprint, heading north. Luckily,

this being New York City, no one raises an eyebrow at a woman fleeing her demons at one o'clock in the morning.

Within five seconds, I know this ploy isn't going to work. The dis-
tinct sound of a large engine—possibly a van or an SUV—speeding
up confirms my tail has backup on four wheels. Maybe more than
just one.

My heart leaps into my throat.

I'm fit enough to keep running all night if I have to. But I get
the feeling my pursuers have other ideas. I can't hear the ones on
foot yet, and stopping to check behind me will slow me down, but
I know they're there. And I don't fool myself into thinking they're
not as well trained as I once was.

Shit. I need to get off the streets. I check out the restaurants and
open establishments a block away, wondering if I can slip inside and
out the back of any of them. But I'll still be on the street, possibly
cornered in an alley. I rule it out and sprint across another street. I
spot a familiar monument up ahead to my left.

Washington Square Park.

Too many open spaces but with enough tree cover at this time of
night for it to be a better bet than the street. The pedestrian crossing
sign lights up, and I dare to hope it's an omen that I'm headed the
right way.

The sound of the revving engine smashes that hope to shit a second later. They're no longer making an attempt at stealth. This is
full-on pursuit.

I still can't make out footsteps behind me, but I run into the park,
through the marble arch, and veer left into the nearest clutch of
trees. I get a little bit of that smashed hope back when I see that the
early summer foliage will provide even better cover than I'd hoped
for. Enough to hug the edges of the park's perimeter until it's safe to
return to the street.

Halfway across the park, in the middle of the small wood, I
force myself to stop behind a large beech tree. My pounding heart
makes it difficult to hear, but I take shallow breaths and force myself to listen.

Nothing. Not beyond sounds of humanity recycling itself in a never-sleeping city anyway.

I turn my cap backward so it doesn't give me away when I tentatively peer out from behind the tree.

I don't fool myself into thinking I'm safe. They're still out there. And my position is also a prime spot for a mugging by some drug addict desperate to fund his next hit. Or worse. I double-check my surroundings to make sure I'm truly alone. Then, as silently as I can, I reach for the side pocket of my backpack. The sound of the zipper opening rips through the silence like a jet engine, and I grit my teeth as fear climbs higher.

My hand closes over the compact Ruger I've been carrying since I got that unwanted phone call three weeks ago. The gun's cold metal brings no reassurance, but I'm grateful for the false protection it provides. As much as I hate them, guns will make even the meanest bastard hesitate for a second before—

"Are you going to shoot me with that thing, Faith?"

My mind goes blank for a damning few seconds before it attempts to grapple with the detonation at its epicenter.

The voice. *That voice!* Oh God.

Icy shivers drench my body, followed immediately by a furnace-hot craving so sinful and monumental that I stagger back on my heels and sag against the tree. I'm aware my mouth is open on a wordless, stupefied gasp, but I can't get it to close.

He's here.

Killian Knight.

The gravity of his presence pulls mercilessly at me, as if it's determined to yank me straight into his orbit. My free hand grips the bark of the tree. For support? Resistance against the need pounding through me? I have no idea.

Somehow I fooled myself into thinking he's forgotten about me. That he pushed me into his past and moved on after Cairo. Every thought I try to form fractures. The reality that he's here, with the sort of manpower he always commands, blocks out everything else until only his name reverberates through my head.

Killian.

"Yes, it's me, baby," he answers, exhibiting that unnerving decoding of my thoughts that always freaked me out.

Oh God…

"No," I manage to croak.

"Yes," he counters. Then he steps out from behind the nearest tree. A dark shadow in a world of sinister shadows. The description is so apt that I swallow hard.

Run.

I can't move. I'm frozen in place as he closes in on me. Half a dozen feet away, he stops. His gaze is hooked into me, his eyes probing me in the near darkness.

"Have you forgotten what I taught you?" His voice is deep. Smooth. As dark and decadent as the inner sanctum of a club he once took me to in Morocco. And hypnotic enough to make me fall off the edge of the world with him.

"I…what?"

"Aim for the head, sweetheart. That is, of course, if you're planning to shoot." He's shrouded in darkness, his attire as dark as my own.

I can't see his face clearly enough to ascertain whether he's undergone as much change as I have. But I don't need to. Killian Knight represents danger in every form. But it was my raw addiction to him that I feared the most. And like every recovering addict, the terror of a relapse is never far away. In my case, it's a mere six feet away.

Run.

"You think I won't shoot?" I challenge, instead of doing what my instinct is screaming for me to do. Logically, running is no longer an option. He'll catch me before I make it to the next tree. It'll be a waste of time to try.

"No, on the contrary, I think you very much want to. Which is why I'm telling you to aim for the head," he states evenly. His advice doesn't stop him from taking another step toward me.

My gut clenches as I catch the first faint scent of him. I stop breathing because I don't want his intensely intoxicating smell in my head. "What the hell do you want?" My voice is nowhere near steady, but I don't care.

"What I've wanted since that day five years ago. August twenty-fifth, wasn't it?" There's a hell of a lot more feeling in his voice now.

It evokes. It churns. It burns.

August twenty-fifth. My birthday. Maybe karma designed it that way so I'll never forget. But I have a feeling had we met on any other day of the year, that date too would be seared in my memory just as vividly. Just like the days that followed have been.

The guns trembles wildly, and I'm scared I'm going to drop it. My left hand leaves the tree so I can cup my right hand to keep the weapon steady. "Well, you can't have it. Whatever it is. So do yourself a favor. Turn around and disappear back to wherever you came from."

"Oh, sweetheart. You know as well as I do that I can't do that." There's a hint of pity in his voice, maybe even regret. But the remaining ninety-nine percent is all cold, steel-hard determination.

A disturbing sensation jerks inside me. Dread? Anticipation? I reject both. "Why not?"

He doesn't answer. I don't push him because I don't really want to know.

"How the hell did you find me?"

He takes another step, and he's close enough for me to catch the naked resolve gleaming in his eyes. "With great difficulty. But know this, baby. I *never* stopped looking."

"I really wish you had."

A hint of movement as he shakes his head. "No, you don't. If you did, the safety would be off that gun and I'd be taking my last breath at your feet."

Dammit. "I'm hoping you see sense and walk away before I'm forced to use it."

"And I'm hoping you get rid of it so I can take you in my arms and kiss the hell out of you. You have no fucking idea how much I've missed tasting those lips, baby. Hell, I'll even allow you to shoot me if you promise to kiss me first."

This time a gasp releases itself from my throat. "You can't be serious—"

"Oh, I am, sweetheart. Deadly. Fucking. Serious." The raw edge in his tone delivers the inescapable message my brain has been refusing to accept.

Killian Knight is here for me. And neither my gun nor my words are going to sway him from his purpose.

So I take the only option left to me. The one I discarded a couple of minutes ago.

I turn and run.

Predictably, he catches me within five seconds. Predictably, I fight with everything I have. But within one breath and the next, he disarms me, and I'm trapped, my back to his front, against him.

From shoulder to thigh, our bodies are imprinted against each other.

God. His body. His smell. The feel of his steady exhalations against my nape. The electrifying reality of his body against mine is too much to bear. I'm dying.

So I struggle harder. Arms claw. Legs tangle. All in a silent battle because my screams will attract attention I don't want. I need to get rid of him without drawing attention to myself.

Once a spy, always a spy.

"Stop. I'm much stronger than you. I don't want to hurt you," he breathes in my ear.

"Then leave me the hell alone!" I hiss back.

He sighs. "Faith—"

"Jesus. Don't call me that!" My reaction to the name is visceral. I can't stand the reminder of the woman I once was. Wife, devoted churchgoer, chairperson of the Little Leaders Fundraising Club. Sundresses and blinding smiles and bouncy chestnut curls and all things nice.

Dying, dying, dying.

The arm clamped around my waist binds me tighter. "I've come for you, Faith."

I can't stop my trembling or the dangerous rush of forbidden excitement that comes with it. I simply *cannot* feel like this. "No."

"Yes." He whips us both around and presses my body into the nearest tree. The sensation of his hard, muscle-packed body against me sends every atom of my being into fiery free fall. Memories rush to the fore of us like this—in combat training, dancing to the rhythm of a salsa beat in Mexico, and fucking…God, how I loved him taking me like this—and I want to do the unthinkable and weep.

Killian Knight is everything I should've run away from the day he walked into my life. Everything I should've gotten on my knees and prayed to be delivered from. His brother called him the devil long before I met him. I shouldn't have laughed at what I thought was gross exaggeration. I should've crossed myself and said a few more Hail Marys.

Because what came after guaranteed me a front-and-center place in hell.

"Let me go, Killian. Please."

I don't know whether it's the sound of his name on my lips that drives the shiver through him. Or the naked plea in my voice. Either way, I then feel his lips brush a kiss on the top of my head before he exhales. "No. Never."

Fight kicks in. I use my purchase on the tree to attempt to dislodge him. He's an immovable mountain. He whips my cap off and slides his fingers into my hair, holding me even more immobile. His body presses harder into mine, and I feel the rigid outline of his cock in the crease of my ass.

The sound that emerges from my throat is a cross between a growl of fury and a whimper of desire. The memory of him, hard and huge and deep inside me, rocking me to the fieriest depths of pleasure, isn't one I want to recall. Nor do I want to recall the guttural, dirty words that tumble from Killian's lips from the moment we get naked. But they're blazing a path of unstoppable destruction through my head, and I want to kick my own ass ten ways to Sunday.

"Shh, baby, it's okay to remember," he says soothingly, so in tune with my feelings it's scary.

"Fuck you. It's not okay. I'll never be okay."

"I know. But this is still happening. I've come for you, and I'm not leaving without you."

"If you think I've turned meek and mild since you last saw me, you're in for a hell of a surprise."

I feel the slide of his finger against my neck, brushing my hair away, exposing my nape. I can't stop my body's tremble at his touch, much as I'm dying to.

"I know you haven't. But I need you to come with me. So I apologize in advance for this."

"I...what?" I start to turn my head. The touch of something cold and damp against my neck sends a bolt of shock through me. Ice-cold dread rolls through me even as I start to lose sensation in my extremities. "Killiarrrr..." The second part of his name thickens in a slur on my tongue as I feel another kiss against my temple.

"You're mine, Faith. You'll always be mine. And I'm sorry, but this part is nonnegotiable."

Those are the last words I hear before sweet oblivion sweeps me away.

Chapter Four

BLACK WIDOW

My head is filled with cotton wool, and my mouth feels like every grain of sand in the Gobi desert has been stuffed in it.

Even before I'm fully awake, I know I've been drugged. Unfortunately, it's not the first time I've had chemicals pumped into my bloodstream to keep me subdued. It's the consequence of the life I've led. The life I've been hiding from these past four years.

I can't exactly hear my heartbeat, but with the absence of any foreign tubes in my mouth, I know at least I'm breathing on my own and not with the aid of intubation like the last time. That's a good start.

The lights are thankfully low when I attempt to open my eyes. I'm in a room, on a sofa, in an apartment. Shit.

Memories of the evening's events take precious few minutes to return, and when they do, they're a touch sketchy. But his presence registers almost immediately.

For a single moment, I wish for the harsher lights of a hospital, the rushed voices of an emergency room providing a soundtrack that tells me I'm not in the deepest, darkest shit. But of course, that's impossible. A hospital means names, records, and pushy doctors demanding to know every last thing about me. And nosy computers in black sites ready to pounce on the tiniest morsel resulting from a misstep.

I've already fucked up by not acting and running when I should have. It's stupid to even wish for anything that'll compound that problem. So I tackle the one immediately confronting me.

I take a breath, and I'm surrounded by his scent. God, he smells so good. I want to close my eyes and block out the inevitable. I want to take a deeper hit even as another part of me clamors to stop breathing altogether so I don't have to face what's coming. I choose the former option and shut my eyes. I can't face him again. Not yet.

Killian.

"You've been awake for five minutes. How long are you going to ignore me?" the deep, solemn voice asks.

I'm not sure if my shiver is real or in my imagination. "You…" I stop when my tongue refuses to cooperate. I wriggle my jaw and try again. "You drugged…me." I sound like I've downed a full bottle of vodka and chased it with two dozen shots of Jägermeister while high on E.

"It was the only way I could ensure you'd come quietly."

The last moments in the park remain hazy, but I know enough to arrive at an accurate assessment. "You're an…asshole."

"Yes."

That he's not even attempting to deny it pisses me off. "Don't…fucking do that."

"Agree with you? Why not? It's true."

I grit my teeth, only it feels like I'm gnashing a row of marshmallows. Whatever he gave me is taking its sweet time to wear off. It's keeping my physical responses slow but keeping my brain sharp. "What…did you give me?"

"There's no official name for it yet. We can come up with a name together when you're better if you want."

I ignore that simply because my mouth is too dry to waste my time on unnecessary conversation. Besides, I don't intend to stick around long enough to do anything Killian Knight suggests in that hypnotic voice of his.

I take a deep breath, curbing the urge to scream. Will I even manage to scream? "How long…have I been…out?" I ask.

"A little under three hours. You're probably thirsty. I'm sorry but I can't give you any water just yet. I've spent too long looking for you to have you choke on me now. The drug's effects will wear off in about ten minutes. I have a glass of water waiting right here next to me. Or I can get the champagne chilling in the kitchen if you prefer. We can celebrate however you want," he offers magnanimously.

You're insane, I want to say. I want to call him a dozen different derogatory names. Challenge his state of mind. But they would all be true. I know because we have that in common. No, we *had* that in common. Back when the thrill of an op was a high, that came second only to the fact that I was chasing it with Killian. And every success drew us deeper into our own dark vortex of obsessional sex and guilt-fueled destruction that eventually broke us.

The Bonnie and Clyde of the espionage world, one team member labeled us. And he wasn't far off. The only thing is that we haven't perished in a blaze of glory. Yet. But we stroked that edge too many times for fate not to have one eye on payback where we're concerned. It's already taken a giant chunk of my heart. I'm almost amused by how very little else there is to take.

Almost. Because I know better than to issue fate that challenge.

"Why?" I ask instead because it's the only question that might get me some answers.

"I told you in the park. You belong to me. Now that I've found you, I'm not letting you go."

This time I feel the shiver a little more. More snippets coalesce into solid memories. I attempt to shake my head, but it barely moves a fraction. "No. There's…more."

There has to be. The Killian I knew was ruthless when he needed to be. It's a prerequisite of the nature of being a spy. In that world, there was no black or white, only an endless, all-encompassing gray.

But unless something's gone very wrong, I know he would never turn the darker side of his considerable skills on me.

But then we haven't seen each other in four years. I ran from him without saying goodbye, suspecting he would come after me. Maybe I was too good at hiding. Maybe what happened in Cairo affected him almost as much as it did me.

I have no doubt I'll find out soon enough, so I push those particular memories to one side and attempt to read the tone of the silence.

"You're right, there's more. But we have time for that."

My heart lurches. "I want…to know. Now."

"And I want to know why you left me," he replies, that hard edge back in his tone.

"You know why. It…we should never have happened."

He laughs, a deep sound filled with bitterness that's nevertheless the sexiest thing I've heard in a long time. I'm flat on my back, as helpless as a goddamn baby lamb; the sound attacks my sensitive, needy parts with merciless disregard for my well-being. My nipples tighten and peak. Heat rushes between my legs and gleefully strokes my clit.

"You say that as if you have a choice as to whether the sun rises in the morning or not. Do you really want to waste time on that nonsense?"

"It's…my life wasn't…nonsense."

"I'm not talking about your life before we met. I'm talking about what came after you left that excuse for an existence you were living. Wishing we didn't happen is useless bullshit. I was yours the moment you looked at me. And you were ready and willing to take me. It's a waste of time to feel guilt about any of it now."

"Don't tell me what to feel." *Yeah, that's a really powerful comeback.*

He sighs after a minute. I hear him move somewhere behind me. He's probably sitting forward, propping his elbows on his knees like he does when he's about to tackle a problem with his scarily sharp intellect. I'm almost afraid of what's coming. But I'm tired of being afraid of every little thing. And yes, I'm also tired of the guilt. If only I could shed it as easily as Killian seems to have shed his.

He was already halfway to dropping that particular set of baggage when I left him four years ago. It was partly why my resentment toward him reached unbearable proportions. He managed to put our iniquities behind him far too easily, whereas I was stuck with the seeds of my sins growing inside me like a living thing.

"After all this time, you still want me. I know you do. Until that belief goes away, nothing is going to stop me from coming after you and keeping you *if* you manage to get away from me again."

"You're...wrong. I don't want you," I lie. "I haven't wanted you for over four years. Let me go, leave New York, and I'll happily spend another four years proving how I haven't spent a minute thinking about you."

He doesn't respond for a handful of seconds, but he exhales heavily. "That's going to happen over my dead body." It's a low-voiced, lethal vow that resonates deep in my belly.

"I can arrange that too," I reply, despite the shakiness taking root inside me.

He chuckles. "Okay, have at it. The gun is right there next to you. Pick it up and shoot me if you feel that strongly about living without me."

"What?"

"Your speech is clearer now. You can probably move now too. Give it another minute and you can sit up and grab the gun."

My breath catches a little as another cold memory slides into place. That of taking a life. "That's how you want me to prove I don't want you? For me to commit murder?" *Again?*

"It's certainly a definitive way to end this," he replies. "You can put us both out of our misery."

There's no humor in his voice. A weird sensation grips my nape. Jesus, he can't mean it, can he? I shake my head to clear the last of the fuzziness. The expanded range of motion confirms that whatever he gave me is leaving my system.

My temple throbs a little as I raise my head and look around properly. I take my time, delaying the moment I have to look at him again. The gun is where he said it was, sitting on a low, expensive-looking coffee table made of solid dark wood and glass. Across from me, a long sectional sofa like the one I'm lying on sits beneath a wide glass window. From the angle of the lights outside, I can tell we're high up. Damn, that means my chances of getting out of here are limited. I try not to show the dread that morsel of information brings me.

I take in the sleek, suspended marble fireplace, the plush carpeting, the tasteful pieces of art and expensive furniture. The space may be minimalist, but it's the type that screams class and money.

I'm not surprised. Killian Knight was seriously loaded long before I met him. A technology-genius-and-coder-turned-spy, he was amply rewarded by a government eager to win the espionage war, and pounced on his every invention.

He was twenty-nine when we met and ready to retire. Or so he said. It may have been a lie. We excelled at those too. Especially the ones we fed ourselves.

What has time done to him? In the shadows of the park, I didn't get the chance to see him as clearly as I wanted to. I'm still not sure I want to. But I can't stay on this damn sofa forever.

Stomach clenched tight, I tentatively sit up and swing my legs to the floor. Only then do I notice my hoodie is gone, and so is my cap.

"Where are my things?" I demand with my eyes trained on the fireplace.

"You can't avoid me forever, sweetheart. Look at me," he commands.

Self-preservation urges me to scream *no*. But enough of this shit. Making grown men cry is literally part of my job description. Time to take this bull by its horns.

I turn my head slowly to the left and set eyes properly on Killian Knight for the first time in over four years. As predicted, and as I vainly hoped wouldn't be the case, I lose the ability to breathe the moment our gazes lock.

Cobalt-blue eyes cut through the armor I've erected around myself like a hot knife through butter. Eyebrows a couple of shades darker than his brown hair rest broodingly over his watchful eyes.

His face is leaner and his cheekbones a little sharper than I remember. The meaner look is heightened by the square, stubble-shadowed jaw and longer hairstyle. But it's his mouth that captures my attention. Nothing about Killian's lips has changed. His upper lip is a harsh, curved line that always hints at darkness and cruelty. Whereas his fuller bottom lip is the last word in carnal temptation. The memory of what those lips have done to me, how they've made me scream and beg and claw in ecstasy, glides right through the crack he's opened with his potent stare.

That silent, deadly scrutiny rakes my face, taking in every inch of my skin before he looks into my eyes again. "Hey, baby," he murmurs, his voice deep and rough with whatever emotions he's experiencing. The sexiest sound known to woman. Aimed straight at my core.

I snatch my gaze away before the sound weakens me further, and I gulp in a deep breath. Desperately, I focus on something other than the man sitting a few feet away, watching me with a single-minded concentration that is freaking me out.

He's sitting in a black leather armchair. The type that squats low on the floor and looks expensive enough to cost a whole month's rent in the Gramercy Park apartment I call home. Next to him is a smaller coffee table with the glass of water he promised me. Beside the glass is a bowl of ice chips, a towel, and a straw.

He has no weapon, which means with my gun I'll have the upper hand. But I'm not going to shoot Killian Knight. We both know that. However, I'm not above disabling him to make my escape if I have to.

"Whatever you're planning in that gorgeous head of yours, have mercy on me and make it lethal?"

The casually murmured words ramp up my agitation. "God, could you please stop talking like that? I'm not going to shoot you."

One corner of his mouth lifts. "Okay. I'm glad we've got that cleared up. Can we talk about us now?" he suggests.

I jerk to my feet and grimace when I sway a little. "There's nothing to talk about. Whatever us there was before is over and done with. Where are my things?" I look around while studiously avoiding looking at him.

"You'll get them back when you need them. Sit down. You shouldn't be on your feet just yet."

"I'm fine," I snap, just before a particularly heavy throb pounds my temples. I lift my hand to massage the area before the weakness of the action registers. I drop my hand but it's too late.

He stands and I can't help myself. I watch him walk over with the glass of water in his hand. Killian has kept himself fit. I knew that from the park when I was pressed against his hard body. But seeing him now, watching his broad shoulders and his long-legged, sexy swagger that used to draw immediate attention when he walked into a room, I feel decidedly, shamefully frailer.

He reaches me and holds out the glass. "Sit down and drink this."

I slide my gaze from his body, turn away, and shake my head. "I'm not accepting anything from you. How do I know you're not going to drug me again?"

"Because I want to have a conversation with you. And to do that, I need you awake and alert."

"At the risk of sounding like a broken record, we have nothing more to say to each other."

"If you're sure we've exhausted conversation, may I suggest other activities?" he says, his voice a fraction deeper.

I know what that means. And, God, I can't entertain that suggestion. Even a little bit. "You may not."

He sighs heavily. A familiar, melodramatic sound that used to make me laugh. The memory tugs hard at me. I shift my gaze back to the window. Dawn is fast approaching. I don't need to be back at the Punishment Club for another several hours. But the reminder that I have a life out there, one that's been violently interrupted by my past, rams home.

"I can't stay here," I say without looking at him.

He doesn't reply.

"Whatever you've planned by kidnapping me, it's not going to work," I stress.

More silence. Against my will, my attention is drawn back to him. The glass is on the coffee table, and his gaze is on my body. I open my mouth to say God knows what, but the look in his eyes stops me.

He inhales raggedly as his eyes slide all over me. "I didn't forget how beautiful you were, but, God, having you right here, in front of me, you're even more beautiful than I remember." His voice is gravel-rough, filled with the same churning hunger dredging through me.

And just like that I'm trapped. By his words. By his eyes. By every essence of the man in front of me. His hold on me was shamefully effortless right from the start. Against my will, I allow myself a small sliver of him, and let my gaze feast on him too.

Time has given Killian's fallen-angel looks an even more lethal edge. The air around him bristles with danger and something else I can't place my finger on.

"You've changed," I say, more than a little distracted by the shift of cotton moving over his shoulders and torso as he withstands my scrutiny. "You seem…harder." Not that he was soft before.

"It's been hell without you," he responds simply.

Killian's ability to disarm me with words had knocked me off my feet within a few minutes of first meeting him. The deadly effect hasn't worn off. "You say that like it was paradise before."

"Then let me rephrase. It's been a different kind of hell without you. I've discovered there are several layers of hell since you left me."

Every breath I take rattles its way weakly into my lungs. "You can't hold me responsible for your suffering."

He steps closer into my personal space. Until we're almost sharing oxygen. My tingling intensifies until my whole body is vibrating on a fine frequency only Killian Knight has been able to strike. "Can't I? I may have failed at many things, but I know I didn't fail to tell you or show you how much you meant to me. You knew exactly what leaving would do to me," he says with more than a hint of a chill in his voice.

"Killian…" I stop and clear my throat when my voice sounds like I'm in the middle of a porn movie. I see its effect on him when his eyes darken.

"God, do you have any idea how many times I've heard you say my name like that in my dreams?"

"Killian—"

A rough sound rumbles out of him. "You keep saying my name like that and it'll make me forget about the conversation we need to have. Instead I'll make it my mission to strip those clothes off your body and reintroduce myself to this lean, mean new you. I like it, by the way. Not that there was anything wrong with the old you. I'm not entirely convinced about the hair color though, but I can come around to—"

"Stop! For the love of God, you're driving me nuts."

A half smile twitches his lips as he stares at me. But there's no humor in his eyes. He's watching me like a hawk. Enough that I know he'll capture me in a second if I follow my instinct and try to flee again.

"I'm still very much open to trying other forms of communication," he says gruffly. His eyes are twin fires of blazing hunger as they latch onto my mouth.

The fierce tingling that starts where his eyes remain makes me want to lick my lips. Over and over. Just to see if the memory of his kiss is as mind-blowing as I remember. God, I can't take much more of this. I retreat a couple of steps away from him, and I nod at the glass on the table. "Can I have the water now?"

His gaze slowly rises to meet mine. "Of course."

The moment he turns away to grab the glass, I bolt for the only opening that leads out of the living room. It's a wide entryway with two hallways branching out on either side. Behind me, I hear the glass hit the table right before he curses under his breath.

I mutter a quick, desperate prayer to a God I know no longer takes petitions from me, and I vault down the right hallway. Relief floods me as I see a foyer and wide double doors. I reach them and then realize why Killian sounded more exasperated than alarmed by my attempted escape.

The doors in front of me are no ordinary ones. For a start, there's no handle. I search valiantly for an opening anyway as I hear him approaching.

"Don't waste your time. I've been in town for four days. I've had more than enough time to put a few contingencies in place for when I found you. That front door for instance." He strolls toward me as I slide my hand along the very thin edge where the door meets the frame. Nothing. I'm still searching when he leans in close like he did at the tree in the park and plants his hands on either side of my head. I don't turn around. "To your left," he says softly in my ear after the silence stretches out for a tense moment.

I reluctantly turn my head and see a slim panel set into the wall. He reaches out and touches a button, and the sleek glass surface lights up in neon blue. "Alphanumeric code, a warm palm print that registers my heartbeat, and a retina scan. And that's just for starters. If by some miracle you manage to leave the apartment—and I don't underestimate your ability to do so—there's another door before you reach the elevator. That one needs a different set of commands. As for this door, it may look like wood, but there's a titanium panel inserted between the two outer layers, just in case you happen to carry an ax in that backpack of yours and you think of hacking at it. We're on the twenty-eighth floor. The fire escape is temporarily out of commission, and the windows are sealed tight."

With each bullet point of precautions he's taken to prevent me from leaving, my heart drops lower into my belly.

"The only other occupant on this floor accepted a very generous offer to vacate his apartment for a while, so we have the whole floor to ourselves."

"Stop acting like we're on a vacation, Killian. You've kidnapped me."

"I'm keeping you safe."

"God, you're deluded. You must also be really desperate to go to these lengths to imprison a woman who doesn't want you."

"You don't want me? Then why are you shaking, baby?" His breath washes over me right before his lips graze the sensitive skin beneath my ear.

"In case you can't tell, I'm shaking because I'm fucking pissed."

His chest brushes against my back as he slowly closes the gap between us. "I know you are. And I'm right here. Feel free to work out your frustrations on me any way you want. But you're not leaving this apartment."

I slam my hand against the door, more than a little panicked at the weakness infusing my body from his proximity. "This is nuts. You can't keep me here forever."

He doesn't say anything, and my trepidation grows. I know how blind to everything our obsession made us in the past. If Killian has retained even a fraction of that, I'm in deep trouble. I also know that when Killian doesn't speak, it's because he believes his silence will express his feelings.

His mouth skims the top of my spine and then returns for a firmer, longer kiss. I press myself against the door in a vain attempt to escape him. "Killian, no."

"Yes. With every breath in my body, yes," he insists gruffly.

I fight the melting in my brain and struggle to retain an ounce of sanity. "You…you said there was more to why you've brought me here."

He exhales harshly. "There is, but dear God, how the hell do you expect me to think straight enough to talk to you when you're this close? When I'm dying to be inside you again? Do you have any idea how much I need you right now?"

I don't respond in the vain hope that he'll stop talking. Stop evoking a thousand shards of memories.

"Turn around, baby," he insists. "Kiss me."

I shake my head and try to pull away, but there's nowhere to go. "Tell me why you think I'm in danger."

"I don't think. I know."

The unwavering certainty in his voice. The locked door. The extra manpower in the park. Knocking me out to ensure my compliance.

He may have his own intensely personal reasons for tracking me down and kidnapping me, but the tightening in my gut tells me that the *more* that's coming will alter my reality. Possibly in the long term. But there's no hiding from this. Not anymore. And if a ghost is reawakening, I want to know which one it is.

"Who?" I force the word out through a throat fighting to stay closed.

He inhales slowly. My heart is trying to beat itself out of my chest when I feel his breath on my neck. "Cairo."

Chapter Five

BLACK WIDOW

Cairo. Oh God.

"No. That's impossible."

"It's not. I didn't want to believe it either. But the monsters we slayed are no longer happy to stay dead."

The quiet gravity of his answer freezes everything inside me. Long enough for Killian to place his hands on my shoulders and draw his fingers down my bare arms.

"How…when…why?" I don't know where to start. Cairo was supposed to be our last assignment together before we sailed off into the sunset. Or wherever people go with the kind of toxic baggage we carry. Instead I ended up sacrificing what precious little I'd managed to wrest of my soul from eternal damnation. And still that hadn't been enough. By the time I crawled away, broken and bleeding, I was less than nothing.

While I'm grappling with the connotations of the bombshell he's dropped at my feet, his fingers shackle my wrists. The unbreakable hold and the unspoken command to submit in that act grounds my fraying senses and shifts my attention from one nightmare to another. A second later, he presses his body into mine. I'm too shocked to be pissed at the fact that he's restraining me again, exerting his dominance.

These days, the role I've taken for myself includes six-inch heels and head-to-toe leather, with the odd exception when a client demands a specific outfit. But in my sneakers, I'm more than a foot shorter than Killian. I may be small but no man has made me feel vulnerable in a long time. No man except Killian. And it's the kind of vulnerable that has always turned me on. He knew it then. He's counting on it now. Before I can demand to be freed, he widens his stance and brackets my hips with his thighs, using his body to dominate me even more.

"I'll tell you everything," he mutters in my ear, his voice so rough it's nearly incoherent. "I promise. But it's been over four years, baby. I'm fucking dying here. You have to give me something." He rocks his hips into me, firmly imprinting the rod of his cock in the small of my back.

Dear God, he's even thicker than I remember, and I pride myself on the sharpness of my memory. It's saved my life more than a few times.

My pussy clenches, even as I force myself to shake my head. "I'm not going to fuck you, Killian." I'm pleased with the delivery. Firm. Succinct.

His strained groan turns into a laugh against my neck as his fingers tighten around my wrists. "I'm aware of that. For reasons I still don't know, you need to twist the knife in a little more. But I need something. Dammit, I need you," he pleads.

My insides threaten to turn to jelly. "Blow jobs and hand jobs are off the table too," I snap.

His thumbs caress the insides of my wrists, linger over my racing pulse. "Fair enough. I'd probably make a damn fool of myself if you put those beautiful lips on my cock right now anyway."

"You act like we're negotiating. This isn't a negotiation. This is me telling you everything you want is off the table."

"I'm sorry, sweetheart. That's not going to work for me."

"Killian—"

"I'm going to let go of your wrists now," he interrupts. The edge is back in his voice. Sharper. Rougher. "Stay put. I'm not chasing you around the apartment again."

"You—"

"Shh. You've stated your terms. I've heard you out. Now you hear me out." He releases one wrist, and I feel his hand on my hair. He tackles the knot, and the band holding my ponytail is tugged out a moment later. Impatient fingers slide through the tresses, and he makes a gruff sound under his breath as he grips a handful and imprisons me again. "I've barely been able to eat or sleep these past four days, knowing you were here within reach. I told you the years have been hell. These past days have been beyond pure fucking torture. A lesser bastard would be content with having you in his arms, alive and so fucking beautiful, once again."

His mouth trails my jaw and cheek, and I shudder at the brush of his rough stubble. I close my eyes and desperately try not to think of the other places I want that stubble to rub.

"But this bastard, *your* bastard, is going out of his mind with the need to taste you again. If fucking you is off the table, I'll take the next best thing."

My body goes furnace-hot, and my mouth drops open. "No…that's not…you can't—"

He whirls me around and slams his mouth on mine. Like two meteors colliding, the explosion is cataclysmic and intense enough to stop my heart for a second. Then he slides his tongue across my lower lip, and everything goes into free fall. Killian devours my mouth with an intensity that makes me almost fear how close to the edge he is. But with my own hunger clawing right up the crazy peak to join his, I chase the sensation with a rabid ferocity I know I will be ashamed of once this ends.

And it has to end. I didn't run for this long only to be sucked back into his dark, addictive world where living on the edge became the norm. That world broke me, and I'm sure the pieces I managed to pick up are a poor, pathetic mosaic of the person I used to be. But she's all I have. And I'm not giving her up that easily.

No matter how devastatingly divine his kiss feels.

His tongue strokes against mine in a slow, filthy dance that makes my knees sag in a response totally out of my control. He groans in mutual pleasure, and his cock jumps against my belly. And simply because this feeling, once birthed, demands nurturing, he repeats the move. Over and over until I'm hopelessly wet, and the hands I don't remember wrapping around his waist are digging into his back.

We're both struggling to suck in enough oxygen when Killian rips his mouth from mine and leans back. Eyes turned a dark, turbulent blue rake my face before they settle on my tingling mouth. "Jesus, baby, your fucking lips. This gorgeous, insane, fucking mouth."

Before I can scramble enough brain matter to respond, he groans again, dips his head, and begins the assault all over again. My lips are on fire. My breasts are screaming for attention, and my nipples are as hard as diamonds. And that's just what's happening up north.

Down south, my clit feels like three times its normal size, and my pussy is clenching and unclenching with furious spasms that make me scared it's going to permanently damage itself if I don't fill it with a cock. With Killian's cock. Like, right now. Before it shames me into a premature orgasm like that time when Killian challenged me to orgasm just by kissing. And I hopelessly, gloriously lost the bet.

No. God, no. I don't want that reminder anywhere near my treacherous body. But Killian's hands have joined in the mind-altering torture. His fingers trace my neck, lingering on the pulse hammering at my throat. Then down my collarbone to follow the neckline of my tank top. He lingers there for the longest time, drawing out the time when he shifts lower. I barely manage to contain my scream when he bypasses my breasts to slide his hands down my rib cage. He grabs my waist and lifts me off my feet, and his mouth fuses with mine for another carnal kiss before he sets me back down.

And then he lifts his head. "Are you ready?" he growls against my mouth.

My brain scrambles for a few seconds, my functioning senses focused on where he *hasn't* touched me yet. "Am I...? Kissing me wasn't what you meant by the next best thing, was it?"

He nips at my bottom lip before answering. "Kissing you is a joy I'll happily chop off a limb for. But no, that's not what I meant. Not this time anyway."

His thumbs trace the area just below the curves of my breasts, turning me further into a delirious wreck. "I...you..."

"I can't wait any longer, baby."

I become painfully aware of his destination a moment later when he shoves his fingers into the waistband of my yoga pants and tugs down with a decisive motion. Lycra and satin roll halfway down my thighs before I suck in my next breath. The fiery protest that rises to my lips dies when I catch a glimpse of Killian's face as he stares at what he's unveiled.

It's a twisted mess of voracious hunger and intense pain. Of gnarled joy and censure. His color heightens as his nostrils flare slightly. "You kept it shaved," he finally rasps. His eyes haven't moved from my pussy. He seems incapable of looking away.

"Not..." I barely stop myself from saying *not for you*. Regardless of how I feel, those words seem petty somehow. Besides, they would also be a lie. The reminder that no other man has seen me like this since I walked away from Killian pierces through my fog of lust. I move my hands but they never make it to their destination.

Killian recaptures my wrists. "Stay," he commands gruffly.

"Don't tell me what to do." My response is pathetically feeble this time. And he doesn't dignify it with a response, save to slide his thumbs into my palms, straightening out my fingers before nudging them flat against the door. His fingers splay over mine for a second before he drops his hands.

Stay.

It takes every ounce of strength in me to drop my hands and utter the word. "No. This...is as far it goes."

His chest expands as he sucks in a deep breath. I know he's about to talk me around. And, God, a part of me wants to. But this is ten kinds of fucked up. I remind myself of the reasons I left him in the first place. Because of where our type of combustible sex leads to. Insanity and ripped souls.

"Baby—"

"No!"

He steps back immediately but his eyes remain pinned on me.

Legs shaky, I reach for my clothes. There ought to be something faintly undignified in digging for your panties among the tangled elastic of your yoga pants while the man whose face you're dying to ride watches you with unwavering intensity. Especially when all your fingers turn into useless thumbs.

My face is burning by the time I struggle into my panties. And when Killian silently steps forward again, tugs the pants out of my hands, and takes over the task of helping me put them back on, I'm so disgusted with myself that I remain silent and let him do it.

My hair band is nowhere in sight, so I make do with shoving the mess over my shoulders and behind my ears. "Now that you've…that we…" *Oh, fuck off, brain. Get your pathetic self together. I need you.*

"Now that I've reacquainted myself with how beautiful your lips taste? How you still get as wet as fuck just from kissing me?"

My face burns a fresh shade of *what have I done?* "Can we just get on with it?"

"Of course." He steps close, places his hand on my back like we're about to take our seats at a state banquet and not as if I've just clawed at his hair while kissing the hell out of him. "Let me show you the rest of the apartment. Then we'll talk."

I want to refuse. I want to demand that he open the door so I can leave. But the intensity of the orgasm I've just denied myself has fried enough brain cells to keep me mute. Plus, if he's correct—and unfortunately Killian, when it comes to this part of his life, is rarely wrong—and it really is the monsters from our last assignment that have reared their respective heads, I'll need every scrap of intel at my fingertips. And the man who once embodied my every obsession and darkest nightmare is the person to provide it.

So I nod. But when he goes to take my hand, I pull away. It's either that or beg for him to finish what he started.

Sad amusement flickers over his face before he shoves his hand in his pocket. I avoid looking at the huge erection in his pants as we walk back into the living room. Jesus, he must be suffering. Killian is a master at delayed gratification, but I know what four years without sex feels like. I've just come within a whisker of demonstrating it in reckless abandon.

No matter how badass he is about it, it can't be easy. Except I'm pulled up short by my line of reasoning a second later when it occurs to me that Killian may not be as hard up as I've been in the sex stakes. Unlike me, he may not have been as picky to the point of complete abstinence. Hell, he may not have held back at all.

He wasn't exactly a monk when we met. Far from it. I witnessed a few awkward conversations with various women before his electronic black book was deleted. But had it remained deleted?

I shut off the part of my brain that threatens to become obsessed with that question, and focus on my surroundings. The living room is much larger than I initially thought. There's a bar at the end of the open space with a wide range of bottled liquor displayed on the mirrored shelves behind it. Another smaller grouping of sofas next to the bar looks out onto a stunning view of the East River, where the sun is putting in a tentative appearance on the horizon. The soft, warm tones complement the art and make the room a stunning masterpiece, but I'm not here to admire the real estate.

"Okay, living room. Check." My brisk tone earns me another barely there smile.

"Kitchen next." He leads the way to the foyer but takes the left hallway this time. The kitchen, like the living room, reeks of money, taste, and class. Futuristic-looking appliances gleam on spotless surfaces, and a sleek breakfast island and stools are perfect for after-marathon-sex snacking. I try very hard not to picture another woman standing at the breakfast counter, making Killian's favorite coffee while wearing absolutely nothing. Like I used to.

"Kitchen. Check."

"Wait."

I grit my teeth and turn to find him pouring a fresh glass of water from a jug in the fridge. "You never had that glass of water. You need to hydrate." He walks over and holds out the glass.

I take it with the fresh reminder of everything that's happened this evening. God. Was it only a few short hours ago that I left the martial arts studio in Soho, convinced I knew what my next move was?

I feel as if a lifetime has passed since then. I drink the water, mildly surprised when I drain every last drop. He takes the glass from me, and we continue with the tour. By mutual consent we don't linger in the bedrooms, of which there are three with a master bigger than my apartment.

The last room is the study. Killian gives me no warning as to what to expect when I walk in. Probably because he expects me to take the sight of my picture reproduced a couple of dozen times on the walls in stride. I stop in the middle of the room and stare at the shadowed image.

Supersize, small, and in between. All showing the same single picture of my cheek and jaw. My shock passes, and I face him.

"This is how you found me?" That question had crossed my mind more than a few times tonight.

He gives a watchful nod.

I hide a grimace. It was the day I let my concern get the better of me and took the more direct route to the Upper East Side instead of my usual circuitous one. It didn't matter that Axel Rutherford, my boss, had demanded the punishment that put severe bruises and lacerations on his wrists after a session in the Punishment Club. The man I've come to see as more than a boss was going through a hell I vaguely recognized, so I set aside our strict boss/employee relationship and went to his Upper East Side apartment.

"You were sloppy," Killian says in the voice I remember from when he was my trainer.

I shrug.

"Where were you going?" he presses, his voice growing a little more abrasive.

"Does it matter?"

His piercing eyes narrow a fraction. "Not immediately, no."

Which means the third degree is coming. If I stick around. Which I won't be. "Tell me about Cairo. How sure are you?" A small part of me remains hopeful that he's got this wrong.

He remains silent for a few seconds, and then he jerks his chin at the two high-backed leather chairs behind his desk. He pulls out a seat for me, and I sit before a bank of state-of-the-art screens. I catch his wince as he sits, and my gaze drops to the erection that shows no signs of abating. My internal muscles clench in an empty muscle memory reflex, and I hate myself just that little bit more.

He activates an electronic keyboard, taps a button, and Killian Knight morphs into someone else. Computer genius extraordinaire.

He was famous for his coding skills long before he became a spy. And while adding such a dangerous profession to his résumé may have been a very risky thing, considering he was a tech god and therefore worshipped by nerds with social media hacking and surveillance skills at their fingertips, his ability to manipulate technology was the very thing that made him a genius spy too.

I watch his fingers fly over the keyboard for a minute. Three pictures flash onto the screen. My breath locks in my throat, and icy fingers crawl down my neck. Two of the four people are known to me. Ted Milton and Shane Richards. Faces from another life I don't want to return to. Faces staring at the screen with lifeless eyes. "Oh my God. When did this happen?" I whisper.

"Over the past month. Ted was the first. He disappeared from his hotel room in London three weeks ago. They found his body four days later in an abandoned warehouse in the East End. Shane was taken the day after Ted's body was found. He was booked on a flight from Dubai to DC. He never made it. He was also found a few days later."

I struggle to digest the news, and the glaring connection I can't hide from. "How…did they die?"

Killian's jaw tightens. "They were tortured."

My heart drops. Spies are primarily tortured for one thing only. Information.

"Do you get the picture now?"

I shake my head, still wanting to live in denial. "Were they still active?"

He frowns. "Yes, but what the fuck does that matter?"

"I'm no longer active. I'm out of the game, remember?"

His face hardens as his fingers fly over the keyboard again. Pages and pages of mumbo jumbo scroll across the screens, with the occasional fuzzy picture flashing past. He hits one key and the screen freezes. Through the jumble of code, I spot the name *KNIGHT WIDOW* several times. I'm almost too afraid to ask. "What am I looking at?"

"The number of times our code name and images have been searched for in the last six months by someone other than me."

Dread punches me in the gut. "I...that doesn't mean..."

"Yes, it does. It's time to wake up, Faith. We're being hunted."

Chapter Six

BLACK WIDOW

Cairo was supposed to be the end stage of a five-year-long operation to dismantle a powerful sex trafficking ring spanning the globe. The agency I worked for—an offshoot of an offshoot of a clandestine government organization nonthreateningly named the Fallhurst Institute—got involved in the operation when they unearthed evidence of root-deep involvement of key political figures in over a dozen countries. The words *international incident of fucked-up proportions* were bandied around frequently, putting everyone in the agency on permanent tenterhooks.

It wasn't surprising therefore that things started to go wrong almost immediately once the final team was put together.

Ted Milton despised me from the moment we met. A middle-aged old-school spook straight out of *Tinker Tailor Soldier Spy*, he was an unapologetic sexist pig who made no bones about the fact that he considered me a worthless slut for sleeping with my boss. The fact that Killian and I were supposed to be lovers as part of our cover didn't mean a damn to him. It didn't help that we made it blatantly clear that we were involved both on and off assignment.

Ted continued to actively despise me in the five months we worked together. Right until I saved his life on an op in Rome. Then he thawed to barely tolerating me. But not once did he fail to let me know how much he wished I wasn't part of the team. And when we ultimately failed, he laid the blame for all of it at my feet.

Unfortunately, he wasn't far off from the truth. "You think it was Ted?"

"Who gave you up?" Killian asks.

I nod.

Killian's jaw clenches. "The thought crossed my mind. He hated your guts, and mine, but his whole life was dedicated to serving his country. That said, I get it. I would give up everything that means half a damn too, if it means protecting something I value. He may have been twisted enough to believe giving us up and getting us out of the way might protect Fallhurst and its agents in the long run."

"So he may have thrown us under the bus for the greater good?" I know how fucked up life can be, so I'm not surprised that Ted is capable of this.

Killian shrugs and continues tapping on the keyboard. "Like I said, I know I'd throw the whole fucking world under a bus to have you, so yeah," he states without taking his eyes off the screen.

This time my breath strangles for an entirely different reason. Before his words can seep into my blood and disarm me further, I shift my gaze to the screen. "Shane?" Unlike Ted, the possibility that we were betrayed by Shane makes my chest ache. So I'm relieved when Killian shakes his head.

"It's not him."

"Why? Because he worshipped you?" The waspish snap in my voice makes me cringe inside.

"Because he worshipped *you*."

"Only because you were with me." The analyst is...*was* gay. A typical bespectacled nerd who barely held himself together in Killian's presence during briefings. His saving grace was that he didn't hold a grudge against me because Killian was mine. At least not as far as I could tell. He'd been happy to bask in the glow of his idol's magnificence no matter who Killian was with. I learned to live with it. Barely.

I stare at his photo now, struck by how young and innocent he looks. "How old was he?" I ask.

Killian sighs and stops typing. "Twenty-seven. Cairo was his first assignment. I was against him joining us in the first place. I recommended he not be placed in the field again after that. Obviously someone disagreed because they kept sending him out on ops."

I thought I was inured against softer feelings, but I can't seem to fight the sadness that wells up inside me. I close my eyes, regretting my momentary bite of resentment. "God."

Firm hands grip mine. I open my eyes to see that Killian has moved his chair directly in front of me. He lifts my hands and kisses my knuckles, then each palm. I shouldn't allow my senses to fire up like this. Not right now. But I can't stop my breath from catching. From wishing for more of that contact.

"Now that you know what's going on, you get why I can't let you leave, don't you?"

I get that that's partly why. A huge remaining part of why I'm here is blazing at me in his eyes. But I don't have the head space to deal with it right now. Without answering, I look back at the nearest screen, and the unfamiliar face. "Who's the woman?"

His thumbs move to my wrists, sweeping back and forth over my pulse. It's distracting as hell, but I try to breathe through it.

"Her name is Lisa Channing. She debriefed me. After you left."

There's a guardedness about him that spikes my antenna. "So she works for the Fallhurst Institute?"

A half shrug. "In a sense."

"What does that mean?"

"She had the right clearance but she was an independent contractor of sorts. Also she was more of a shrink than anything else."

I frown. "You spoke to a shrink, not your handler?"

His mouth twists, but I can tell he's not coming from a place of amusement. "It was part of the deeper defrag process, apparently."

"Defrag?"

He flashes me a half grin. Again, barely amused. "Sorry. Tech speak. They needed to tick a box to say I wasn't permanently traumatized after the op. She was sent to help me off-load a few things."

Right. "And did you?"

He shrugs. "The box wasn't checked for three years so I guess my level of fucked-up-ness was rather epic."

My hearts starts to bang urgently against my ribs. "And during your off-loading, did you...was there...?"

"Full disclosure?" he supplies gently.

The secret that has become part of my DNA rises like a stone and wedges in my throat, preventing me from speaking. So I nod.

Killian leans forward until his face is right up in front of mine. Startlingly direct eyes bore into me. "What do you think?" The question contains a steely edge. As if he's offended that I would ask that.

"I don't know," I answer truthfully. "If you were as fucked up as you say you were then—"

"I may have been off my head a little. Or, okay, a whole fucking lot, but some transgressions I will take to my grave. You know that. Our secret is ours to keep. No one else will ever know."

I don't want to think about the series of epic fuckups that occurred in Cairo. Not now. Not ever. So I return my attention to the woman. She's beautiful, with bright gray eyes and an attention-seeking mouth. The kind that seems to be a hint away from curving in a sultry, I'm-great-at-blow-jobs way. And that's not all. She's blessed with the type of flaming red hair that could either be expensively fake or real. I can't tell from the head shot, and that pisses me off a little.

I wonder if her prettiness is the cause of Killian's caginess. Did he off-load on Lisa Channing in more ways than one?

"How long did you see her for?" I ask, jerking my gaze from the screen to stare down at our hands. Our still-joined hands. I try to pull away. His fingers circle my wrists in a definitive hold. I let him keep me prisoner. Just for now.

"On and off for two years. The first shrink didn't work out."

Something tightens inside me. "You needed that long to *off-load*?" Okay, I officially hate that word.

"I wasn't feeling inclined to cooperate."

"Why not?"

"They wanted to check their box and put me back in the field. I had other priorities."

"Which were?"

"Finding you." He leans even closer and ghosts his lips over mine. "I've looked for you every day since you left."

At my soft gasp, his eyes turn dark. The fierce need to plaster my mouth to his makes me pull back in self-preservation.

"The first time they sent her, I threatened to set fire to the world if they attempted to put me back in it. The threat didn't go down well and...let's just say things got progressively worse after that. When it became clear they wouldn't back down, we eventually reached a compromise."

My tiny snort of disbelief earns me a raised eyebrow. "I didn't think you were familiar with that word."

"I had to learn to be. I figured it was better to get her off my back so I could focus all my energy on locating you."

"But still, two years is a long time."

"There was one subject she wanted me to open up about and I was...resistant."

The hairs on my nape stand to attention. "What subject?"

"You. Me. And Matt."

I yank my wrists from his hold. He lets me go, and I push my chair back from him. He leans on his elbows and watches me as I fold my arms around my middle in a defensive gesture that projects vulnerability, but I don't care. "You told her to go fuck herself, right?" I snap, knowing my guilt is what's making me lash out.

"Many, many times."

"And did she?" The idea that some stranger was digging into this particular subject makes my skin crawl with guilt and shame and anger.

Killian remains silent for a very long time. "Eventually she got the message," he finally says.

That caginess is back again. I want to probe it, but the mention of Matt's name is triggering all my self-loathing buttons, of which there are many. I jump to my feet and pace for a minute. When I turn back, Killian is on his feet too, leaning against his desk and watching me with those piercing eyes.

"Okay, is this all you have?" I wave my hand at the screen.

"You need more evidence?"

My laugh scrapes my throat. "I get the picture. But I'm capable of keeping myself safe."

"I found you the first time you slipped up. Be thankful it was me. For all you know, the bastards could have this same picture of you."

"I won't slip up again. Anyway, this could all be one giant coincidence," I reply with more hope than certainty.

His face tightens, and a muscle ticks in his jaw. "Come on. You don't have a naïve bone in your body. Don't insult us both by pretending otherwise, especially when you know dropping your guard can get you killed. You know a hell of a lot about Cairo that's just as relevant now as it was four years ago. The case is still open. They've sent two teams since we were there, and they've done fuck-all at shutting those bastards down."

"What about you? Is hiding in plain sight still working for you?"

"I'm taking extra precautions but, so far, yes."

Frustration bites hard. "But for all we know, Ted and Shane didn't give me up. I can't look over my shoulder forever. I won't."

"You don't have to. I'll do it for you. All you have to do is stay put for a while."

"No, that's not going to work for me."

His whole body tightens with a pre-warning that makes my stomach sink to my soles. I'm more than familiar with that look. It's the arrogant-alpha-bastard look that used to drive me completely nuts, while shamelessly turning me on.

"I prefer we do this without any more…coercion," he says softly.

"You didn't say you were permanently out of the game. I assume coercion of a different sort is what you're doing these days? Like testing drugs on unwitting victims?"

"No. Before you, I only tested that drug three times. All on myself," he states matter-of-factly.

My arms drop in shock. "What? For a man with the staggering IQ you're purported to have, that was exceedingly stupid, don't you think?"

"You think I would use something like this on you before I knew whether it was harmful or not?"

I turn away, slicing my fingers through my hair. "So you tested it on yourself? Jesus. You're insane."

"When it comes to you, there's almost nothing I wouldn't do."

I whirl around to face him. "Do you hear yourself? What if something had happened to you? How can you ask me…anyone to bear that kind of burden?"

He gives me that look. The one that holds equal parts determination and sadness. "You would never have known if I hadn't told you."

"But you did, and now I can't not think about you using yourself as some sort of guinea pig."

"You're thinking about me. That's enough for me."

The ease with which he drops those bombs at me makes my head spin. "Killian…"

"When are you going to get it through your head that I exist just for you?"

My heart lurches traitorously. "I don't want you to! For the past four years I've been just fine being nobody."

"No you haven't," he says in that calm but conclusive way that raises my hackles.

"And how would you know?"

"You've been good at hiding. Exceptional, even. But I'm close to being done retracing your steps. I should have a pattern of your movements by the end of the day. From what I can already see, you've been busy being far from nobody."

Oh God. "What the hell are you doing that for?"

The look he sends me this time asks why I'm even bothering. I raise my eyebrows in return. He shrugs. "I'm curious as to what you've been up to. Who you've been seeing. You can save Betty a considerable amount of effort by telling me now."

My gaze flicks to the server tower sitting silently in the corner of the room. "Betty? You're still naming your computers?"

"They work better when I do."

The urge to roll my eyes washes over me. I realize I'm softening toward him and take a sharp breath. "What I've been up to is none of your concern."

He stares at me for a handful of seconds and then draws his hands down his face. I catch the strain of weariness on his face, and that softening threatens again. I kill it stone-cold. "You look exhausted. If you let me go, you could get some sleep."

He laughs and shakes his head. "Don't waste your breath trying to find a way out, baby. But it'll do fucking wonders for my disposition if you came to bed with me. I'd love to finish what we started by the front door."

"Not gonna happen."

"Then I'll have to rely on caffeine. Nala, can you organize some coffee?"

"Right away, Mr. Knight." I jump at the robotic voice that filters in through invisible speakers. "Coffee, black, will be ready in five minutes and seventeen seconds."

"Seriously, enough of this. I have a job, Killian. I haven't missed a day's work in four years."

He returns to his desk and taps a few keys on the keyboard. Tension surrounds him like a damn aura. "You're going to miss this one. And the next foreseeable ones."

"Not showing up will only draw attention to my absence."

He taps a few more keys. "I don't give a flying fuck."

"I could be a fucking brain surgeon with back-to-back surgeries to perform for all you know." My teeth are clenched so tight I wonder how I can speak through them.

That earns me an amused twitch of his gorgeous lips. "You were too squeamish to apply a Band-Aid when I cut myself once, re-member? You'd pass out before you went anywhere near anyone's brain with a scalpel. Try again."

"I'm seriously rethinking my decision not to shoot you. I need to go to work, Killian."

He bats that response away. "Why? Money isn't an issue for you. Hell, I would've found you much sooner if you'd gone on a wild spending spree. So you're not working out of necessity."

He's right. The agency we worked for made sure we were well compensated. Not to mention the chunk of money I have that I don't deserve sitting in the bank.

"No, it's not the money."

"Then tell me, what's the great pull to this job?"

I don't answer immediately because I can't find the adequate words to describe the Punishment Club to him. He stops typing and turns to face me. Eyes riveted on my face, he slowly walks toward me. When he reaches me, he leans down and breathes in slowly. It's a control-gathering mechanism I recognize from our past.

"Think carefully before you tell me the draw is another guy, baby."

Chapter Seven

BLACK WIDOW

Fuck that noise. I'm not stupid enough to tug on that particular tiger's tail. Even if my reluctance is partly my loyalty to Axel. I could toss out his name, but I don't think he'd welcome the sort of attention Killian would send his way if I do. Killian once hacked and froze a guy's bank account for a week because he grabbed my ass in a nightclub.

Not that Axel can't handle himself. It's just that he's fully engulfed in a turbulent situation of his own that will earn me a black mark if I give him another to deal with. And as unlikely as I would've considered such a friendship a couple of months ago, in a few short weeks I've grown to like Axel's girlfriend, Cleo. She won't thank me either if I unleash Killian on them.

"If your silence is designed to drive me crazy, you're succeeding. Care to put me out of my misery?" The question may sound cajoling, but his voice rumbles with warning.

"I like my job. Does that count?"

"Not when your life could be in danger because of it, no. But tell me about it. I still want to know what you've been up to."

"I work at a…club. An adults-only club."

The dangerous gleam in his eyes intensifies. "Interesting," he responds. "And your role there is…?" he asks indolently. Only the tic in his jaw and the tension whipping through his body tell a different story. As does the light of warning flaring in his eyes.

I purse my lips and answer only because it'll save me from further interrogation later when Betty spits out the info she uncovers. "I'm the manager."

"And what does a manager at an adults-only club do? *Exactly*?"

"Come on—"

"Remember the one we attended in Moscow? And Shanghai?"

I remember. Sex on tap for anyone who wanted it. Given by every employee in the club. For a discreet but handsome fee, of course. I shudder that his mind has gone there. "Killian…"

"There were rules, but if I recall, they were fairly negotiable with the right incentive."

Anger spikes my blood. "Fuck you. This isn't that sort of club. I'm not that sort of manager."

He exhales, and a sizable amount of his tension eases. "Glad to hear it. That doesn't give me the whole story though."

"And you're not going to get it." I head for the door.

"Where the hell do you think you're going?"

"To get my things. And maybe start screaming my head off if you don't let me out of here."

He chuckles. "I'd love to see this new, hysterical part of you."

I reach the living room and search for my stuff. Recalling that I didn't see my backpack here or in any of the rooms he showed me, I whirl to face him. "Where are my things, Killian?"

His breath catches. "Fuck, you have no idea how good it is to hear you say my name again. You know what would be even better?"

"Whatever it is, keep it to yourself. I don't want to hear it—"

"Hearing you gasp it again when I slide my cock inside that tight, little cunt. Remember how much I loved the way the decibels build the closer you get to coming right up until you scream?"

The burn is immediate. Like a flash fire from a gasoline tank, it detonates in my pelvis and spreads wide and merciless, destroying every coherent thought in its path. I fight it with everything I can muster. "Jesus, you're as maddening as ever."

He prowls closer. I retreat until something stops me. A quick glance shows it's the sofa. We've circled back to the beginning.

"And you're so sexy and so fucking gorgeous I'm wondering how I'm still on my feet when just looking at you rips my insides out."

"You can't say things like that!" I'm this close to turning into the hysterical woman he mocked a minute ago.

"Why the fuck not?"

It's that grain of bewilderment in his tone that kills me. Killian was never shy about expressing his interest, sexually or verbally. He's the master of dirty talk in and out of bed, and unfortunately for me, I found out that I grew stupid every time he unleashed that particular talent.

His nonsexual emotions are a different story. Despite our volcanic and oftentimes obsessive interactions, he never once told me he loved me. And I've never asked if he did. I was never brave enough to find out. Perhaps I knew that, without it, everything we had was just a flashy neon sign in a deserted playground that would lose its sparkle eventually, making it easier to walk away from.

Or perhaps it could've been because the last man who told me he loved me turned out to be a liar, a cheat, and a whole load of other things I don't want to think about right now.

Killian stops before me and reaches out to slide his fingers through my hair. "The only way you're leaving here is if I'm coming with you. And for that to happen, I need to be one hundred and ten percent sure that it's safe. For *that* to happen, we need to hang tight for Betty to do her thing. A few times over."

"That's absurd. And I'm not taking you to work with me."

His touch on my hair is gentle. Soothing. "Okay. Then we're staying put. Now we can keep fighting or we can go to bed. I haven't even started to take the edge off this insane need for you. I'm not sure if I ever will. Kissing you only made me crave you more. But if that's the only offer on the table, I'm good to go again."

He's wearing me down. It's another skill of his that's achieved brilliant results in the past. I watched him use it in the field, watched him wield that and his killer Irish charm on women. He's never used it this hard on me before, probably because I was such an easy conquest he didn't need to. But now I'm poised on that familiar knife-edge of calling *fuck it* and throwing myself at him.

All-night sex with Killian. The first time it happened, I stupidly believed it was a one-off thing. He quickly proved me wrong. The unrelenting ache between my thighs urges me to let him prove me wrong again. And again.

My head feels like it weighs a ton when I force myself to respond in the negative. "I can't just not turn up to work. He's not going to buy that something's not wrong."

He goes still, and the fingers in my hair turn that little bit punitive. "He?" he breathes warningly.

"Axel. My boss."

"Why won't he believe you?"

Because he saw beneath my surface within moments that first time years ago, when the need for numbness drove me to Viper Red, the edgy, alternative nightclub in Harlem also owned by Axel. "Because I have a meeting with him at midday. A meeting I arranged. I can't just not turn up."

"Then call in sick."

"I'm not sick. Besides, he won't believe me."

"Why not? Will he come looking for you? Do you warrant special treatment or is he *that* caring a boss?"

"Maybe I do. Maybe not."

He just stares at me, and I know his focus has shifted from me to work on a different threat. Axel.

I groan and curse under my breath. "Fine. Give me my phone. I'll call and put it off."

The speculation doesn't wane even a fraction, although his hand drops from my hair to capture my hand. He tugs me after him back to the study and hands me a black phone that looks like it belongs in sci-fi movie. "It's encrypted. Just in case."

I take the phone and dial.

"Put it on speaker," Killian commands, a second before the call is picked up.

"Rutherford." The name is snapped in typical Axel Rutherford fashion. At this time of the morning, the likelihood that I've disturbed his horizontal playtime with Cleo is very high. He doesn't sound pleased.

"It's me, B." Killian lifts an eyebrow at the name. I ignore it. "I need to cancel our meeting this morning," I say briskly before he can say anything the man in front of me might misinterpret.

A knot of silence. "Why?"

"Something's come up. I might need tonight off too."

Further silence. "I see. Everything all right?" There's tension in his voice now, not dissimilar to Killian's when he's suspicious. I glance furtively at Killian, and his eyes are narrowed in gleaming speculation.

Shit. That's all I need—two alpha males butting heads over me. My grip tightens on the phone. "I'm fine. I'll reschedule and let you know."

"You do that."

"Bye." I hang up quickly.

Killian takes the phone from me and stares down at it for a moment before he looks at me. "You want to discuss him now or later?"

"I want to discuss him never. You got what you wanted, me as your prisoner for the next twelve hours. After that I'm outta here. But if you think I'm going to use that time to play catch-up, you're sorely mistaken. I'm going to bed."

He trails me to the guest bedroom and firmly wedges a foot in the door when I try to shut it in his face. "Sorry, sweetheart, the door stays open."

My exasperation has reached epic proportions but it's been a long night, so I simply drop my hand from the frame and stalk away to the huge bed dominating the room.

"Any chance of a good-night kiss?" he drawls.

"Does my knee between your legs count?" I snap back.

He grimaces but stays leaning in the doorway, and shit, even the way he angles that hot body is so gorgeous that I want to curse long and hard.

He waves a hand toward the adjoining bath and dressing room. "Fresh toothbrush and other stuff through there. If you need anything else, come find me."

I remain silent by the bed, exhausted but feeling as if I could still go ten rounds. The fact that I want nine of those ten rounds to involve his cock inside me is not an admission I welcome very easily, even to myself.

He doesn't say anything either, and we stare at each other for a full minute, the past chewing up the ground between us like a force five tornado.

His fingers find his back pockets, and he rocks on his feet like he's straining to stay away. "It's so fucking good to see you again, baby." His voice is rough, raw, and insanely sexy.

He probably doesn't expect me to respond. And I don't. Most likely because I don't know how much more of his presence I can take without screaming for a repeat of everything he did to me earlier. And more. After another minute, he gives me that sad smile again and walks away.

A popped balloon has nothing on the way I wilt onto the bed. I'm alone for the first time since Killian exploded back into my life. My heart hasn't stopped hammering, and a huge part of me already strains with the need to see him again.

I'm reeling from fresh shock ten minutes later when I emerge from the dressing room. The *other stuff* turned out to be a closet full of clothes that looked suspiciously like the ones I left behind in his various residences during our time together. Everything down to the saucy underwear that was our thing for a short while.

My hands are shaking when I draw back the covers, get into bed, and pull them up to my chin.

Jesus. I'm nowhere near ready for any of this. I'm especially not ready to tell Killian that someone from our past already found me three weeks ago.

Chapter Eight

KILLIAN

Sheer exhaustion is the only thing that manages to knock me out the moment my head touches the pillow. But even in sleep, my subconscious can't stop frantically spazzing with the knowledge that she's finally here under my roof. It's that frenzied restlessness that jackknifes me awake three hours later.

I don't even try to stay away. I wore sweatpants to bed instead of sleeping in the buff so I wouldn't need to get dressed when I woke up. I don't bother with anything else before I leave my room and make my way down the hallway.

In the early hours of the morning while she was knocked out, I disabled the bedroom lock and made sure there was nothing in the room she could use to keep it shut. Nothing that would keep me out indefinitely anyway. She's resourceful so I don't count anything out. Except maybe the likelihood that she would sleep in the guest room in the first place rather than in my bed.

We have a lot of shit to wade through. Do I think half of our problems can be worked out in bed? Fuck, yes. But I'm willing to do things her way. For now. As long as she concedes to a few things.

I push on her door and breathe a sigh of relief when it silently swings open. She's lying facedown, her hair a jet-black stream over one arm. A few heavy tendrils lie across her forehead and temple, partially barring her face from me. My fingers itch with the need to smooth them back, but I see enough cheek and mouth to be momentarily satisfied. I lean against the door and content myself with just staring. For now.

The covers have slipped down around her waist, enough for me to see that she slept in her tank top and the panties she had on last night, instead of using the dozens of night things I supplied her with. I let that go and trace the rest of her stunning body before tracking back up to her face.

Her eyes are open, and she's staring at me through a veil of hair. "Are you going to stand there all day staring at me like some creep?"

I laugh at her caustic but sleep-sexy tone. God, how I've missed that feistiness. Knowing she found her voice with me adds a little extra kick to my obsession that I won't deny is extremely heady. She broke out of the hideous suburban mold Matt tried to stuff her in and shed a few skins once she left Arkansas. And with each layer of her new, true self exposed, I fell deeper under her spell. "You're supposed to be asleep so I can creep in peace."

She rolls to her side, pushing her hair back from her face. The strap of her top slips, and I get an eyeful of her naked shoulder and slope of her breast. My temperature spikes, and the morning wood I woke up with doubles in size.

"I thought it was a dream," she murmurs almost to herself.

"Which part?"

"All of it."

"Want me to reenact some of the good bits for you?"

Her gaze meets mine and then drops to the hard-on tenting my pants before she looks away. "No thanks," she snaps before she sits up. Although she turns away, I see her gaze dart back to my cock before she pulls up the covers. "Did you want something?"

"Besides you?"

She rolls her eyes. "Killian…"

Now that I'm satisfied she still wants me, I decide to leave the subject of fucking her alone for a little while, hard as it might be. But there's something more urgent on my mind. "Tell me more about Axel Rutherford and his clubs."

Her beautiful eyes widen. "How did you know about the other…? Right. Betty."

I nod. "She came through earlier than I thought but you were asleep, so…"

Her fingers play over the design on the covers. "I told you, he's my partner-slash-boss. I run his club for him but…"

"But?"

"I sort of came up with the concept, so I get a percentage of the profits."

I nod, fold my hands under my arms, and ask the question that's been burning a path through my brain for the last five hours. "Why does he call you B?"

I get pursed lips before she answers. "Because it's my name."

"Explain."

"He calls me B, short for Black. As in Black Widow."

The tension that whips through me is itching to be let free. I struggle to contain it but I still need several beats for the red haze to die down. "Let me get this straight. You were using your code name in public?"

She tenses at my harsh tone. "My *partial* code name. My field name was the Widow. Our code name was Knight Widow."

"I haven't forgotten. But that name isn't a million miles from the name you're using now. You think that was wise?"

"It kept me under the radar for four years, didn't it?" she returns.

I have to concede that. Until her slipup, she'd succeeded in hiding in semi-plain sight. Like I've done all these years. But I'm still pissed.

Faith. The Widow. B. Black Widow. Whatever she chooses to call herself and however she disguises herself, she belongs to me. Only me.

"And he never asked your real name?"

"He didn't care. Which worked out brilliantly for both of us."

I only realize I'm moving toward the bed when I step on her discarded yoga pants. My gaze doesn't shift from her face. "What else worked out *brilliantly* for you?"

"He didn't give me endless grief like you are right now, for starters."

"Good for him. What else?"

She drives her fingers through her hair in a display of irritation. The lift of her braless tits momentarily banks my anger. But only for a moment. Because I learned a long time ago that I'm capable of being turned on by and furious with the magnificently beautiful woman glaring at me from the bed.

"Let's cut to the chase, shall we? You want to know if I'm fucking him?"

The thought drives me to the edge, figuratively and literally. I lean down and brace my hands at the edge of the bed. My fingers curl into fists with the quiet fury that tells me I won't react well if she answers yes to my question. "Are you?"

"No, I'm not."

My fists unfurl. "Did you ever?"

Her nostrils flare. "I learned my lesson that sleeping with one's boss or partner isn't the best idea in the world."

I ignore that. "Doesn't answer my question."

"No, I didn't *ever*."

I straighten. But the knots inside me won't ease. "Why does he talk to you as if there's something between you?"

She raises one eyebrow. "Wow. Paranoid much?"

"Don't fuck with me, Faith."

Her breath sharpens, and she pales a little. "I told you not to call me that."

"What do you want me to call you? *B*?" I snarl the name.

"Call me whatever you want, but not…that."

My gaze leaves her face, taking in her dark, dark hair, her beautiful but more sculpted face. Her stunning but less curvy body. A part of me concedes she doesn't look like the woman I knew. The Widow was a softer version of the woman in front of me. Faith was an even softer version of the Widow.

Black Widow possesses a savvy wisdom I want to explore and an edge I want to test. The notion that I don't have to pull my punches the way I did with Faith tweaks a part of my psyche I've blacked out for a long time.

But whoever she is, she still owes me answers. "There's more. I'm waiting, baby."

"There's nothing between us! He's...he's been through some shit. Don't ask me for specifics because I don't know. Plus..."

"What?"

"He has a sketchy past. I'm sure Betty informed you."

I nod. "His family is the last of the East Coast Irish mob. Father was involved in a war crimes investigation a while ago?"

"Yeah, but from what I can tell, Axel's not part of that life anymore. He was in the army though, and not just the fun parts."

"He told you this?"

"I looked into him a little bit before I decided to go into business with him. I may not be in the game anymore, but I can still do a basic search without leaving a trail. Anyway, there's nothing between us because he's involved, *seriously* involved, with someone else. So whatever you think you heard on the phone, it's all in that crazy head of yours."

I shrug. "Guess we'll find out soon enough."

"What does that mean?"

"Betty's almost done formulating a safe route for us to get from here to your Punishment Club with minimum detection."

She frowns suspiciously at me. "A few hours ago you didn't want me to leave, and now you're champing at the bit to get me to work?"

I slip my hands into my pockets. Her legs have crept out from beneath the covers, and it's all I can do not to reach out and caress them. It's a huge strain to drag my gaze from her smooth calves. To stop myself from testing if the backs of her knees are still supersensitive. "You're right. You've taken the day off but you can't just not turn up after that. You've just told me you work for a guy who has mob and army connections. He may not have been curious before, but I know what I heard in his voice. He knows something's up. I prefer to look him in the eye and see for myself whether he's a threat or not. So once I have a few more contingencies in place, you'll be good to return and properly hand in your notice. But we'll need to move fast after that if—"

"What are you talking about? I'm not giving up my job."

I stifle the urge to tackle this argument in a completely different way. My cock is certainly urging me in that direction. "I took care of the CCTV photo of you, but it was still out there for at least half a day. For all you know, Galveston has it too. You know what happened to the rest of our former team. How long do you think you can stay under the radar in a club with over six hundred members? Especially looking the way you do?"

She glares harder. "Looking the way I do?" she parrots.

My gaze travels over her body, the urge to taste killing me. "Yeah. Like fucking sex on legs."

"That's a seriously sexist comment."

"Well, I'd rather be the sexist asshole who keeps you safe. Deal with it."

With a growl of frustration, she throws the covers off and gets out of bed. "Do you even have a plan beyond tomorrow? Other than us being cooped up in here?"

The pressure in my groin intensifies, and my answer dries up in my throat at the sight of her bare legs and the flimsy panties hiding her pussy from me. My feet are moving toward her before my brain fully engages.

Her eyes widen, and she throws out her hands. "Killian, no!"

I stop in front of her, my breath not quite hitting home when I inhale. "Throw me a bone, baby. Do you have any fucking idea how hard it is for me to look at you like this and not touch you?" My voice is a rough growl that echoes in the space between us.

She backs away. "I…can't…"

"You so fucking can. Just stop fighting me for a second. Admit you've missed me as much as I've missed you. That you want to kiss me as much as I'm dying to taste your gorgeous lips again."

Her gaze slowly drops, as if she's fighting the urge, to my mouth. She licks hers, and my whole body tightens with the need to take what she's so stubbornly refusing us both. I barely manage to remain where I am.

"I can't start this with you again, Killian—"

"We won't be starting because we never ended."

Pain drifts across her face, and for the first time, that haunting that became so familiar in our last weeks together, the haunting that I tried to convince myself didn't exist, films her eyes.

"What we did was—"

I silence her with a finger on her mouth. "If you don't want things to get more fucked up than they are now, do yourself a favor and don't call what happened between us *wrong*."

The gravity of my words gets through to her. She flushes and looks away. Toward the dressing room. We both take a breath before she looks back at me. "You kept my things. Why?"

She's trying to distract me. I allow it for a moment and let my finger drop. "Too much effort to throw them away."

"Seriously, you have literally dozens of minions at your beck and call."

"*Seriously*. I tried to give them away. For some insane reason, I got into an argument with Debbie every time she pulled out the suitcases. The last time I tried, she point-blank refused and threatened to quit. And since she's the best housekeeper I've ever had, and I wasn't in the mood to do it myself..." I shrug.

"Well, you wasted your time bringing the clothes with you. My tastes have changed."

"I look forward to discovering the new changes for myself."

Her chest rises and falls in agitation for almost a minute before she shakes her head. "I'm not going to fuck you, Killian."

I breach the last few feet between us. Back her up against the wall. Just like I did last night, I lean in close and catch her earlobe between my lips. The sound of her breath hitching transmits straight to my cock. "That's fine. I'll do all the work. I have four years' worth of energy just dying to be expended. All you'll have to do is take it."

She makes another sound, a cross between a whimper of need and a growl of frustration. Then she dives beneath my arm and backs away quickly. "I'm going to the bathroom. I don't want you here when I come out."

I have to lock my knees not to follow. "Come to the kitchen when you're done. Breakfast will be ready in twenty minutes." At her wide-eyed surprise, I smile. "No, baby, I'm not cooking. We have company. So make sure you're wearing something other than that indecent thong and top. I'd rather not commit grievous bodily harm against the chef for catching a glimpse of you like this."

I walk out of the room before temptation pushes me to my breaking point. I ignore the sounds coming out of the kitchen and head back to my bedroom. My cold shower does pathetically little to help with my raging hard-on. It's only the thought of the danger in our immediate future that distracts my libido for enough time to get myself under control.

By the time I tug on my cargo pants and T-shirt, I'm no longer a hormonal embarrassment, although when I exit my bedroom and catch the faint smell of her shampoo, things get a little jerky again. I grit my teeth and head for the kitchen. She arrives a minute later. And stops at the sight of the man wearing an apron and tossing ingredients in a hot pan.

She looks from him to me, one eyebrow raised. I hold out her coffee. As she moves toward me, I can't help but stare at her body. She's changed into a pair of dark jeans and a gray T-shirt with a shiny black heart printed on it. The material hangs on her leaner figure, but all her perfect attributes are still very much visible. And still causing chaos in my body.

When she clears her throat, I drag my gaze upward to her faintly stained cheeks and the pointed look she's sending me.

"This is Mitch. He works for me."

Mitch looks over his shoulder. "Morning, ma'am."

She eyes the six-foot-five giant suspiciously. "Hi. He works as your chef?" she asks skeptically.

"Among other things. He can't tell you what those other things are though, can you, Mitch?"

Mitch cracks a small smile as he walks over with two plates. "No, sir."

"Why not?" she asks.

"Because I'll be forced to kill him, and I like having him around. He makes a mean omelet for starters. Here, try it." I cut a portion of mine and hold the forkful against her mouth.

She glares at me but is too polite to refuse in front of Mitch. She takes the offering and chews. "It's very good, Mitch."

His smile is a little wider. "Thank you, ma'am."

I grin at her grudgingly surprised tone.

"You'll see him from time to time. He may even attempt to become your shadow in certain situations. I'm sure you'll forgive him for his future transgressions."

That immediately draws a frown. "A bodyguard? No—"

"Hell, yes. Non-fucking-negotiable."

She inhales sharply at my tone. Maybe she knows she won't win this fight because she takes a sip of coffee before she speaks. "Can we talk about this?"

By talking she means fight, of course. "No, baby. We can't. But there is something we can talk about. Once we're done eating."

Her breath snags. My grin widens. "Not that. Trust me, I'm done talking about that. It'll be action from now on."

"Then what do you mean?"

"There's been another development. Betty's popped up with a couple more names."

She glances at Mitch, who is tidying up at the sink and then back at me. "He's in the wider loop, but I prefer to discuss this in private. Eat." I nod at her plate.

She doesn't protest, probably because she's hungry or because the omelet is that good. Either way, she finishes everything on her plate in silence.

"Want more?" I ask.

With a shake of her head, she pushes her plate away. "No, thanks. This was really great, Mitch. Thanks."

Mitch smiles. "You're wel—"

"Okay, don't overdo it," I snap. "It was good, but not that great." I stalk to the fridge and grab two bottles of water. "We're staying put this morning so I'll see you later, Mitch."

"Yes, boss." As he walks away to put our plates in the dishwater, she sends me a mocking glance.

"Nothing wrong with complimenting the chef, is there, Mitch?" she asks, avoiding my gaze as she takes one bottle from me.

Mitch opens his mouth to answer, glances at me, and stays silent. A minute later, he hangs up his apron and leaves the apartment.

"You're trying to bait me," I say as we leave the kitchen. "That's going to reap the exact results you claim not to want. I haven't stopped being jealous when you smile and make nice with other men."

Her steps slow, and her grip tightens around the bottle. When we enter the study, she stops, and we face each other in front of my desk. "Have you changed at all, Killian?"

I take a moment to answer. I want her to be in no doubt that I mean every word I say in response. "I foolishly thought that we could get through anything. Together. That what we had was strong enough. You leaving showed me I was wrong. You staying gone messed with my head. It took me a while to realize I'd taken us for granted. I'm not a good guy. But you want me and I want you. So this time around, I intend to do whatever it takes to make sure you don't leave me again."

"Did it occur to you that I didn't leave because of you? That I left because of *me*?" Her voice throbs with the depth of her feelings. Guilt. Remorse.

Some of that powers through me too. But never enough for me to deny wanting her. And therein lie our differences. She allowed her guilt to consume her. I buried it deep until it was nonexistent just so I could hang on tight to her. And I would do it all over again in a heartbeat.

I step closer and trail my hand through her hair. I take it as a good sign that she doesn't push me away. "Of course it did. But you don't get it, do you? You don't get to go off and live in your guilt on your own. If you want to face the past, we do it together."

"*If*? I can't just brush it away like—"

"Like I did?" When she refuses to answer or look at me, I slip my thumb under her chin and propel her gaze up. "It's okay. You can say it."

Her mouth works for a handful of seconds before she sucks in a breath. "He was your brother."

"Yes."

"He was my husband."

My gut clenches tight every time I'm forced to acknowledge that. "I would change that in a heartbeat if I had the power to. The fact that he had the right to call you his before you were mine drives me insane."

"Well, you can't change it! He was my *husband*, Killian. And we killed him!"

Chapter Nine

KILLIAN

Her words fall like deadly spikes between us. Her eyes are dark green haunted pools. I want to tell her the truth. *The whole truth.* But at what cost?

I have no problem speaking ill of the dead when they deserve it. But the chance that adding to her guilt will push her out of my reach? Fuck, no.

"You're wrong. We didn't kill him. You left him—"

"When he needed me the most."

I swallow the knot of fury that surges through my gut. "On the campaign trail, maybe. But nowhere else. We both know that. Tell me your marriage wasn't already over when we met. Tell me you didn't have divorce papers drawn up and tucked away in your underwear drawer ready to file."

She gasps. "How the hell do you know about that?"

"I'm a spy, baby. That's what I do. I went looking, and I found them. I don't mind admitting that was the fucking highlight of my second visit to your house."

She shakes her head, the weight of her remorse winning out against the outrage of my admission. Her lashes sweep down, and she swallows. "I may have been on the verge of filing those papers, but I was still his wife when we..."

"You didn't cheat on him. He was dead when we got together."

Her laughter is filled with bitterness. "And how quickly after that did we happen? Jesus, I fucked you at his funeral, and we both know I wasn't using you to lessen my overwhelming grief. How many kinds of bitch does that make me?"

"Who the fuck cares how you used me? I don't. You'd already said goodbye to him long before we put him in the ground."

"He wouldn't have been in the ground in the first place if he hadn't suspected something was going on between us. He wouldn't have been at the hotel, in that alley, if it hadn't been for us."

The door I keep locked on my guilt attempts to crack open. "We had dinner that evening, baby. That was all."

"That wasn't all, and you know it."

I sigh, take the water bottle from her, and put it next to mine on the desk. I stay silent to avoid corroborating that truth. We spent that evening barely eating and eye-fucking each other a dozen different ways across the table in the hotel restaurant. I have no idea what we talked about, or even if we talked at all.

The torture of not being able to touch her, of sitting opposite her with a hard-on the size of Texas, when all I wanted was to bend her over the table and fuck the shit out of her, had driven me seriously nuts by the time I put her in her car and sent her home to my brother. But my reason for staying at the Arkansas Grand Hotel was because of the connection to the op I was working on. The op that directly involved my brother.

Matt's call to me that night had been pure coincidence, but as usual, our conversation descended very quickly into taunts and insults and, on my part, a subtle probing into his activities that had raised his suspicion. Did I subconsciously intend for that to happen? For my brother to panic and seek out the man I was tailing in the hotel? Probably. I'm not enough of a saint to rule my soiled hands out of the equation.

"I knew he was tracking my phone. I didn't think he would follow me there though and get himself killed in a random shooting." Her voice is racked with pain.

It wasn't random. I swallow the words and pull her into my arms. There's no way I'm telling her Matt had been taken out by a well-aimed shot to the head in a merciless execution that may have been indirectly my fault.

I may have gotten used to carrying the guilt but I'll never be rid of it.

Because how the fuck do I tell her that I was on a covert mission when I visited my childhood home that day? A mission to find out whether Matthew Knight, my brother, was involved in the sex ring that involved several high-level members of the government.

When his name was first flagged by the analysts at Fallhurst, I had a hard time reconciling the above-average asshole of a brother I grew up with and Congressman Matthew Knight of Arkansas suspected of turning a blind eye to the bone-deep corruption going on under his nose. But even before I closed the file of intel on my brother, the seed of conviction was growing. I knew he wasn't above such heinous acts, although trafficking sex slaves, a disturbing number of them underage girls and boys, was taking things to a whole new level.

But the Knights were notorious for turning a blind eye if it would benefit them. Hell, I did exactly that when I clapped eyes on Faith Carson and decided she would be mine even though she didn't belong to me.

Randall and Patricia Knight, my much-esteemed parents, were the same. Both from a long line of families that preferred to be the money and power behind politicians, they thrived on manipulating the candidates they endorsed for their own gains. And they were wildly successful at it, right up until they were embroiled in voter-tampering charges. The convenient explosion at our luxury cabin in the mountains of Montana served the dual purpose of ending their lives and killing the rabid speculation as to their guilt before their case could go to trial. I never discounted the fact that they orchestrated their deaths much like they'd orchestrated their lives. Much like they'd tried to orchestrate mine.

Perversely, it was that tiny possibility of their innocence that propelled Matthew up the polls when he decided to run for a congressional seat six months after their deaths. Like the sleazy political animal he was trained to be, he'd changed the narrative of my parents' lives, spotlighted their hard work, and all but wept on camera for his loss. All the while knowing, like me, that Randall and Patricia never gave an inch unless there was something in it for them.

Matt learned to play their game before he was out of diapers. I blatantly refused. And earned myself a long stay in hell for it. In the middle of my junior high year, I went from private school to inner city public school without so much as a heads-up. My parents held a charity benefit for underprivileged kids, during which they self-effacingly shared their desire to be like the common man by sending their second child to a school in a dangerous, gang-ridden neighborhood. They didn't know that I barely escaped being knifed on my second day. Or that I eventually earned my safe passage to and from school by helping the gang leader build and maintain his burgeoning online porn business.

When my parents decided to go a step further and sabotage my college scholarship to MIT, I hitchhiked to Cambridge and camped on the dean's doorstep with my acceptance letter. He listened to my story with heavy skepticism but decided to give me a chance. I faked a résumé to land a part-time job so I could pay for my board, and I never went back home.

Matt took the option of tripling his hate for me for not being there when my parents were plunged into disgrace. I didn't lose any sleep over it. When I learned my parents had left everything they owned to him, I didn't lose any sleep over that either. In fact, except for the rare occasions when our paths crossed, I barely thought of my brother at all.

Until his name came up at the agency. Next to a prominent Arkansas businessman named Grant Carson. Faith's father. Another man whose true character she had no clue about.

I decide that bundle of emotional C-4 is best left to tackle another day. "He's gone, baby. We need to move forward with our lives. And I'll be damned if I'm going to let you deny yourself that life because you think what we did was wrong."

"You can't—"

I slam my mouth on hers. Because enough already. I've denied myself for long enough. Over four years apart and a whole twelve hours since she was back in my arms.

Like last night, the kiss is everything I dreamed it would be. And so much more. She attempts to resist me. Of course she does. Her mouth remains closed, and she struggles in my arms. I propel her against the wall, trap her with my body, and spike my fingers into her hair to hold her still. My tongue takes a glorious swipe across her lower lip. That's when I feel it. That hint of a moan. That tiny shudder that shakes through her. The faintest parting of her lips.

I swipe at her mouth again, and damn if that doesn't make my cock swell to epic proportions. The thought that I could blow my load just by performing this small act is both humbling and hysterical. I flick the tip of my tongue between the seam of her lips, and she shakes again. I keep up the pressure for a minute. Until her breath emerges in heavy pants and her thighs squirm harder against mine.

I raise my head the tiniest fraction. "Let me in, sweetheart," I rasp against her lips.

She makes a sound in her throat. A dying attempt to fight the inevitable. Her hands are still hanging by her sides, but her fingertips flutter against my thighs, as if she's resisting the urge to touch me.

"Touch me, baby," I urge. "Please. Dear God, I need you so much." I've never been afraid to beg. Not with her. Not when I realized very early on that it was a perceived weakness she could never resist exploiting. She may consider it a flaw. I consider it a strategy that gets me what I want.

I get what I want now as she gives a ragged moan and her glorious lips part to allow me entry. My racing heart slams harder as I taste her lips properly for the first time in a hellishly long time. We both gasp when our tongues meet, slide, and greet each other in a dance so heady that stars explode behind my closed eyelids.

The flutters along my thighs turn to grazes, and then I feel the imprint of her fingers on my pants. Testing. Kneading. Relearning everything she left behind.

I don't dare move or risk breaking this spell. But my cock demands closer contact. My mouth craves a deeper taste of hers. Fuck it. I grab her hips, tug her into me, and shamelessly rub the length of my cock against her belly. Her hot gasp feeds my arousal, and I roll against her again. That earns me a full-body shudder.

I pull back a fraction and stare into her semi-glazed eyes. "Feel that? It's all for you, baby. Take it. God, please take it," I plead against her mouth.

She continues to stare at me for a long moment. Then her hands move from my thighs to my hips. She reaches between us. I hold my breath. I plant kisses on her swollen mouth. And I hope. Her fingers drift higher to graze my fly.

Christ.

Once she decides, she doesn't beat around the bush. My button pops, and she takes control of my zipper. I fuse my lips to hers in a desperate, silent plea for her not to stop. She kisses me back as she slowly lowers the fastening.

My cock springs free. Eager and desperate. She takes me in her hand, and it's all I can do not to shout. "Yes," I groan instead, weak and useless as I pant for her. "Yes."

Her hand glides over me, warm and smooth and heavenly. I pump to meet the next downward glide simply because I can't help myself.

Her moan of approval makes me almost smile. Except I'm caught in the web of the magic she's weaving, helpless to her ministrations. I give her a minute to remember how I like it as she continues to pump me. "Harder," I command impatiently as I drop kisses along her jaw to the delicate skin beneath her ear.

She fists me immediately, knowing exactly what I want. I'm slick from the pre-cum drenching my swollen head. She catches a thick drop in her palm and spreads it over my length. Then she increases the rhythm. The sensation threatens to blow the top of my head off.

"Sweet Jesus…"

"Killian." Her voice is a husky, powerful siren's call that drags me from the sweet curve of her neck. I pull back a little until I can see her eyes. She's waiting for me, her stare as bold as the grip she's using to detonate my world.

"Fuck, you're so beautiful."

Her eyes turn a moss green and her nostrils flutter, but she doesn't say a word. Eyes glued to each other, we stare into our impure souls and breathe into each other as she pumps me faster, falling back into the rhythm she learned all on her own to drive me out of my mind. When my vision starts to blur, I blink hard. I don't want to lose sight of her gorgeous face, miss a moment of each breath she takes. "Yes, baby, just like that."

"Hmm…"

"Feels so good. Don't stop. Please don't stop…"

The weight of the climax bearing down on me threatens to disable me completely. My head drops forward. Our foreheads meet. Almost hypnotically, our gazes descend, and we watch what she's doing to me. She pushes my pants further down until she gets access to my balls. She cups them in one hand without slowing the strokes of her other hand. Expertly, she rolls me between her fingers, stretching and fondling, dragging me ever closer to the edge. My balls tighten, pulling upward in preparation to blow.

"Jesus, I'm going to come." My voice is almost indecipherable, my whole world focused on the beckoning rapture.

"Yes," she breathes, and pumps me harder, urging me on with hungry pulls I can't resist.

I capture her nape and fuse my lips to hers one last time before my world turns a lovely shade of purple bliss and I erupt like a fucking fire hose. I'm aware I'm shaking like a leaf and groaning like a fucking idiot. But I don't care. I continue to fuck her sensational hand until I'm utterly spent. My cheek slides past hers until my head rests against the wall. She rests hers on my shoulder, and we just…breathe.

An eternity later, I attempt to lift my head. "That was amazing. Thank you." I brush my lips on her cheek. She stiffens a little but doesn't pull away. Progress.

I want nothing more than to take her back into my arms, but I don't push my luck. I straighten, tug my T-shirt off, and use it to clean us up. I'm still semi-hard, and I catch her watching as I put my dick away.

"Come wash up with me?"

She nods. I walk her into my bedroom and through to the master bathroom. I throw my soiled shirt in the laundry and turn on the tap at the sink. I hate that she's washing my essence off her skin, but I'm a little more worried by her silence.

"You okay?"

She bites her lip, avoids my gaze in the mirror, and soaps her hands.

"Talk to me, baby."

Her mouth flattens for a second. "I'm not sure talking works. All we've done so far is fight and..."

"Make each other feel good? Yeah, I see how that's a problem."

She grimaces. "You know what I mean. We can't keep doing this."

"I beg to differ."

She stares solemnly back at me.

I sigh. "We've been off for a while. Rebooting is bound to have a few hiccups."

She flashes me an irritated glance. "I'm not one of your computers, Killian."

I hand her a towel to dry her hands. "No. You're way sexier than any of them can ever hope to be."

"I'll be sure to tell Betty that when we go back in."

"Shit. Please don't. I don't need her cranky. Not today."

She almost cracks a smile. Almost. She turns from me to hang up the towel.

"How about we call a truce and go keep our appointment with Betty?" I suggest.

"Okay."

We finish cleaning up and return to the study. She takes the seat next to mine and drinks from her water bottle as I fire up my air-gapped computer. An alert pops up on the screen. A single name jumps out at me.

"Fuck."

"What is it?" she asks.

I take a deep breath and reread the info. I don't want to alarm her unnecessarily. But the tension gripping my neck and the icy rage flooding my system tells me I didn't read the name wrong.

She moves closer. "Killian, what is it?"

Resigned, I turn the screen toward her. Let her see for herself. She gasps at the first name highlighted by Betty. She goes pale, and her eyes widen with shock.

"Is this intel correct?" Her voice is husky with disbelief.

"Yes. Paul Galveston passed through passport control at Dulles Airport six hours ago."

Her breath shudders out, and her gaze swings from the screen to mine and back again. "How can that be? I...I shot him. He's dead. He has to be."

I drag my hand across my face, refusing to let the unsettling news disturb me. "It's okay, baby. We'll deal with this."

"How? In the last twelve hours I've found out that two of our former team members have been hunted down, tortured, and killed. And now I find out the man who was behind it all, the man I thought I killed is still alive?" Her voice is shaking. Her whole body is shaking.

I reach for her. "Faith—"

She jerks away from me but doesn't rip into me for using her given name. "I thought I cut off the head of the monster. But nothing we did in Cairo worked, did it? God, it was all for nothing?" There's a new, peculiar note in her voice, way beyond the horror of discovering that Paul Galveston, one of the major players in the sex trafficking ring and one of the three men we were sent to Cairo to hunt down, is still alive.

I frown and watch her face grow paler. "No, it wasn't for nothing. We crippled their operation."

"Crippled isn't the same as dead. It isn't the same as definitively taking them out so they don't get a chance to peddle children again!" She turns her back, hiding her expression from me. "God, I've been hiding for four years while they've just carried on buying and selling children?"

"You can't blame yourself for this."

She whirls around to face me. "Did you know he was alive? Is that why you've been trying to keep me here?"

I rise from the chair and cup her chin. "If I knew he was alive, I would've hunted him down and ended him for what he did to you." The naked rage in my voice is abundantly clear. The moments after I found her covered in blood and the race to save her life after what Galveston did were the worst of my life.

She swallows, and her gaze moves back to the screen. "What about the others?"

Raj Phillips and Moses Black. Owners of Phillips Black, Inc. Millionaire shipping and export magnates by day, sex traffickers by night. Along with Galveston, the two men were the unholy trinity that comprised the US-based arm of a global sex trafficking ring.

Paul Galveston, the half-Egyptian son of senior senator Bernie Galveston of Arkansas, used his father's connections to smuggle girls from Morocco, Egypt, and Eastern Europe into the US via his private air charter business, with support from the shipping arm of Phillips Black. Legitimate contracts secured to send aid shipments via Europe to Africa were clandestinely used to ship sex slaves back to the US. That was bad enough to begin with.

What we discovered when we arrived in Cairo—that all three men, and whoever happened to be in the mood for it, freely availed themselves of their underage victims—gave Faith nightmares for a solid week.

And then things took a turn for the worse. "As far as I know, Raj is still on the run. But Black is dead. You have my word on that." I didn't miss my first shot. Or the three that followed.

Her lips thin in a grim line. "Galveston has to know he's on the watch list, but he's not even attempting to hide."

"His father is a powerful man. He still believes he's untouchable."

Her jaw clenches. "What if he's never stopped his activities? Can you find out?"

"Yes. Do you want me to?"

A wave of pain flashes across her face, and she shuts her eyes for a moment. "I want to say no, let the agency take care of it. But I can't. Killian...those kids..."

I walk over to her and slide my hands up her chilled arms to cup her jaw. "You don't have to deal with it. I can put us on a plane in the next hour, and make us disappear. Just say the word."

Her gaze returns to the screen. I watch steely resolve, and something else I can't quite define, settle on her face. "He needs to pay for what he took...for what he's done." Green eyes meet mine. "I want you to find out what he's up to."

The selfish bastard inside me that wants to keep her safe and all to myself groans at her decision. But the part that wants the Widow, his sexy, dynamic partner, back is elated.

I ignore the two emotions warring within me as I nod. "Okay, I'll work on it."

"What can I do?"

I caress her cheeks with my thumbs. "Nothing for now. You need to catch up on your sleep. Go rest. I'll come and get you if anything comes up."

She steps away, picks up the bottle of water, and heads for the door. With her hand on the handle, she pauses and looks over her shoulder. "Killian?"

"Hmm?"

"I'll need to brush up on my shooting skills. The next time I have him in my sights, I don't want to miss."

"If you want to brush up, I can make it happen. But you won't be getting anywhere near Galveston. Tell me you get that."

Her gaze drops for a moment. "I get that you want that reassurance. But...it looks like we both underestimated him, so—"

I shake my head. "No. He's mine."

"Why don't you find him first? Then we'll take it from there."

Her tone isn't argumentative. In fact, she's the coolest I've seen her since she's been back. I'm not sure if that reassures or terrifies me.

I find myself nodding. She walks out and leaves me standing there, staring after her. Unable to deny the gut instinct telling me that there's something more going on with her. Something I don't know about.

PART TWO
Backup

Chapter Ten

BLACK WIDOW

Cairo, Four Years Ago

"Wake up, baby. We're not landing for a bit, but if you want to check out the Atlas Mountains, now's your chance."

I keep my eyes closed, and I melt at the sound of Killian's voice and the kisses he's trailing over my bare shoulder. "Hmm. I'll get up in a minute. Have I told you how much I love going on assignment in your private jet?"

He crawls on top of me and redirects his kisses down my spine. "Not since I caught you eyeing my plane's tail fin like you wanted to hump it right before we boarded."

"Shut up. I was just checking out the new paint detail."

He laughs under his breath. "With your tits?"

"How is that even possible?"

"Well, you looked like you wanted to rub your tits all over it. I didn't know whether to be turned on or pissed off."

"Is that why you got me to rub my girls all over you instead?"

"Of course. Feel free to turn over and do it all over again," he invites in a decidedly huskier voice.

I turn over, stare up at Killian Knight, and my heart twists viciously with the power of what his face, his smile, and his body do to me. But my heart twists for something else too. The shame that lives under my skin. The regret for things I can't change. The certainty that my soul is damned forever.

But none of those condemning emotions stop my arms from sliding up and around his neck or prevent him from tugging the sheet from my body. His gaze drops to my chest, and I watch him swallow hard.

"Fuck, these tits." He leans on his elbows and cups them in his large palms. Reverently, he squeezes, molds, and plumps them before he sucks one nipple into his mouth.

They're not as big as they used to be when all I did was lunch and lounge, smile and squeeze myself into an effigy of what I thought I needed to be. The training I underwent in order to change my life has changed my body too. For the better, if Killian's visceral reaction each time he strips me of my clothes is any indication.

My back arches off the bed as he grazes my hard nipple with his teeth, and my nails scour his naked back.

"Killian?" I moan.

"Hmm?"

"I'm going to miss the mountains."

He raises his head a fraction, but his eyes stay glued to my breasts. "I'll take you there one day soon. We'll go by chopper, and I'll show them to you up close and personal. I promise."

His distraction is why he doesn't see my conniving smile a moment before I buck him off me and slither out of bed.

"What the fuck?"

I giggle, hurry to the bedroom window, and slide up the window shades. I barely have time to locate the majestic mountains before he's behind me, imprisoning me with one arm around my waist. When I wriggle, he curves his large body over mine. "Stay," he rasps in my ear. "Enjoy your mountains."

His tone suggests he's about to enjoy something else of his own. One hand recaptures my breast, and the other slides between my legs. We both groan at how wet I am.

"Are you still sore, baby?"

I bite my lip and nod. "A little."

"Okay," he replies a little reluctantly.

His hand starts to move away. I put mine over it. "But...I don't want you to stop what you're doing."

A puff of breath warms my ear. "Are you sure?"

"Mmm-hmm..."

He buries his head in the crook of my neck and breathes deep. "Thank you. I don't want to hurt you but I'm so glad I don't have to stop."

I don't admit to him that sometimes I like it when he takes me like this—when I'm uncomfortably sore and the pain is as acute as the pleasure. It makes accepting my happiness a little easier, my guilt a little less consuming.

He sinks two fingers inside me, and the snow-capped mountains in the distance turn into a hazy mirage. My head falls back onto his shoulder, and my knees weaken. I brace one hand above the window and the other behind his head and let him have me. He finger-fucks until I come and then replaces his fingers with his cock.

My already damned Catholic heart can't help but compare one Knight brother to the other and find the one I used to be married to severely wanting. Killian fills me up, both in mind and body, in a way Matt never did. Even holding still inside me now, the way he does each time he first penetrates me, draws fire from my toes all the way to my crown. I always thought toe-curling sex was a myth until I met Killian.

Now he slams inside me, and I rise to my toes, sublime pleasure sizzling through me. The plane catches a pocket of turbulence and dips, shoving me harder onto his cock.

My scream draws a groan from him, and then he laughs. "Shit, even my plane wants in on the action."

Despite the bone-melting bliss racing through me, I laugh. This is what he does to me. Laughter at inappropriate times. Mile-high sex with the clouds as our audience. Diving into sin and secrets with my eyes wide open.

A year ago, I wouldn't have even dreamed I was capable of this. But I've found out that life takes a turn when you least anticipate it. And my life has turned several times since Killian Knight walked into it.

Widow. Lover. Spy.

All three connected to the man who is now inside me, calling me beautiful, worshipping me as he gifts me with another mind-blowing orgasm before he finds his own.

By the time we land on the private airstrip just outside Cairo three hours later, I'm rested, relaxed, and ready to take on the monsters.

The villa rises out of the sunbaked desert like a shimmering apparition. Situated southwest of Giza, the location is remote and exclusive, the type of address that attracts the rich and famous in the mood for something different. A lush oasis in the middle of a stark wilderness is always a thing of beauty. But what has been created here is several levels above that. It's a jaw-dropping masterpiece.

Constructed entirely out of cerulean reflective glass, the single-structure property is sprawling, with several angled sides reaching up into the sky. It's hard to miss, but it's the rumors of its underground rooms that has put the residence named Amaris on the map of the bored, wicked, depraved, and decadent.

News that it's been rented for six weeks by Silicon Valley billionaire Killian Knight and his new girlfriend were circulated in the right places. Whispers of the exclusive-to-the-point-of-illegal parties we intended to throw for a select few achieved the right amount of buzz to attract our prey.

But the price of first contact with the sex trafficking players was high, even for a clandestine agency with an unlimited budget. It's the reason this operation was meticulously put together. It's the reason nothing can go wrong. If it does, the atrocities will continue. And I can't bear the thought of that.

Paul Galveston. Raj Phillips. Moses Black. The file on them is several inches thick, and I've learned it inside out and backward. I know everything there is to know about them, right down to their preferred brand of toothpaste. A necessary evil that has made my stomach turn ever since I learned the true depths of their depravity.

My relaxed state on the plane is nowhere in sight a day later as I sit through the last video-linked security briefing with my handler back in the US. It's six hours before our first meeting with Galveston and his allies tonight. I hide my sweating palms by sliding them over my denim-clad thighs. I know I don't succeed in playing it cool when Killian's leg gently brushes mine under the table. It's a whisper-soft touch but the message is loud and clear.

Pull yourself together.

I take a slow, deep breath. I can't afford to blow this. And for this case to get its final stamp of approval, I need to ace this last meeting. I grit my teeth and raise my gaze.

Eric Biggins, my handler, looks at me with the dead eyes of an agent who's spent far too long in the business and witnessed too many horrors.

"So, you all set?" he asks.

"Yes," I reply. Killian nods.

"The extras will arrive at zero six hundred," Eric confirms.

I swallow the rising bile and remind myself of the need to use honey to catch bees. "They're all over eighteen, right?" I blurt. "And they all consented?"

Eric, whose name I suspect is false, gives me a peculiar look. It's not the first time I've asked this question. And, unlike my previous assignment where I followed orders without question, I've probed the ins and outs of this assignment to the point where I run the risk of being insubordinate. But there's too much at stake.

"Fully verified," he answers after a few tense seconds, and sends a narrowed-eyed, *what the fuck?* glance at Killian. "And, no, they won't be doing anything they're not already doing in their regular jobs. With the exception of one or two of them. But you don't need to worry about that."

I open my mouth to question this new piece of information. Killian shifts in his seat. And because I know, again, that it's unusual for him—I've never known the man to fidget, ever—I decide not to push my luck, and close my mouth. He's trying to protect me. There are those who believe he's risking his career and safety by vouching for me for this assignment. I'm still relatively new to the game, and this operation has been a long time in its execution. If I fuck up, it won't be just my ass on the line. I can't do that to the team or to Killian, especially when I know why he went the extra mile for me on this occasion.

This mission is personal. Eric and a few others have been dubious about my motives from the start, but I've only confirmed my true intention to Killian. Well, it was more like he laid the evidence before me and I didn't deny it.

He knows I'm doing this for Julia. My sister.

"Faith?"

Shit. I spaced out for a second. I refocus to find both Killian and Eric staring at me. I nod briskly. "Got it. Thanks, Eric."

He looks a little skeptical, but he returns my nod and leans forward to disconnect the feed. I feel Killian's stare but I keep my eyes trained on the dark monitor.

"I'm sorry," I mumble.

He doesn't speak for a long time, and my skin tightens in mild panic.

"Look at me."

Double shit. Those three words never bode well for me. It normally precedes a chewing out or a super-intense fucking guaranteed to leave me a babbling wreck.

While I would much prefer the latter right now, I'm about to get the former. I grit my teeth and face him. The considerate lover who worships me is nowhere in sight as he stares, tight-jawed, at me. "What the fuck were you thinking, asking questions like that?"

"I wanted to be sure."

"No, what you were doing was handing Biggins the excuse he needs to throw you off this assignment. If you have questions, then ask me. Let me give you the assurances you need. Don't you trust me?"

My hesitation sends him rushing to his feet. The chair he was sitting in powers back and hits the wall of the secret room we're using as a communications base in the villa. "Shit, Faith, you're scaring the shit out of me. You barely slept last night, and you've been jumpy all day. Maybe I should think about pulling out of this op."

I surge to my feet too. "No! You can't."

Cobalt-blue eyes glare at me. "Like hell I can't. I'm your superior. I can do whatever the fuck I want."

I take a breath to calm myself. "You know I haven't been on board with using such young escorts at the party. But we've put months into it. We'd be stupid to pull the plug now."

"We've been over security a hundred times. They'll be protected. But if you can't trust me enough to get your head in the game, then there's no point. I'd rather we be stupid than dead. Maybe we need a few more weeks, just to get your head straight."

"No. Absolutely not. Weeks means more children, Killian. Sold to dirty assholes to ruin or worse. If I can't sleep now, you think I'll be able to function then?"

"Do you think I can sleep at night worrying that going in before you're ready can get you hurt? You think I'll be able to live with myself if something happened to you?"

"Nothing will happen. I promise. I just got a little off, that's all. I'm okay now."

He paces back and forth in the room. Rubs his hand over his stubble. "No. I can't risk you, Faith—"

"Please, Killian. I can do this." I keep my voice low and even. Getting hysterical now will lose me even more valuable ground.

He stares at me for an age. I force myself to remain still, knowing in my bones that, as much I want to employ other means to bring him around, trying to use sex to convince him will be the absolute wrong move.

He finally exhales. "We're going to spend the rest of the afternoon going over every single detail again. Get one fucking detail wrong, and we're getting back on the plane and going home. Got it?"

I nod.

His eyes narrow for another minute. Then he holds out his hand. When I reach him, he yanks me close and rakes his fingers through my hair. "I should take a belt to your tight little ass for worrying me like this," he mutters against my lips. "But you also happen to be the most intelligent woman I know. I need your A-game tonight, Faith. Please."

"You'll have it. I promise." I kiss the corner of his mouth in gratitude. He sighs and returns the kiss. It's whisper-soft at first. Then it isn't, because soft and cuddly isn't us when it comes to sex. Teeth nip, tongues duel. Fingers dig in and claim.

And then because he deserves a reward for sticking by me and because I'm utterly weak when it comes to him, I strip right there in our little communications room. And he bends me over his desk and shows me who's boss.

By the time our guests of honor arrive, my mask is in place. Arkansas born and bred means Southern hospitality was fully ingrained by the time I turned three. I learned to smile through killer migraines and foxtrot with giant blisters on my feet.

At my sweet sixteen party, I spent a solid hour laughing and gossiping with Heather Jane Fitzgerald, all the while knowing she'd fucked the boy she knew I had a huge crush on before coming to my party. Sweet revenge came by way of spiking her drink with two doses of Nana's extra-strong lithium tablets, thus ensuring she suffered three days of the trots. The get-well card I sent her was sealed with a kiss imprinted by my favorite pink lipstick.

Of course, these days the stakes are much higher. But still I smile and offer champagne to child rapists and allow myself to be hugged by Moses Black, the man who was filmed throwing the body of a boy overboard his yacht because one of his guests got too rough and accidentally strangled him during sex. I've thrown up twice since the party started two hours ago, each time after coming into physical contact with one of the men.

Despite my assurances to Killian, I'm finding it hard to keep it together when I want nothing more than to slide out the stiletto knife strapped to my thigh and drive it between Paul Galveston's ribs. Or grab the Glock strapped under the canapé table and shoot Moses Black in the face.

"Darling, come and join us for the fireworks."

My smile is flawless as I end my conversation with an aging rock star with an affinity for underage girls and join Killian and Raj Phillips. Killian is wearing a pristine white collarless linen tunic and black pants. The hair he's let grow a little wild and long brushes his shoulders, and with his bright eyes and designer stubble, he's easily the most breathtaking man at the party.

I take his hand, and we walk past the huge, sparkling pool to the edge of the landscaped garden that costs thousands of dollars a month to maintain. The pyrotechnicians are ready to begin. Our guests are all waiting with bated breath for the display that set the agency back another twenty thousand.

"I'm looking forward to the display," Raj says as he tosses back a mouthful of Angostura rum. "But I hope what comes afterward lives up to expectation. Just thinking about it has me harder than a priest next to a choirboy."

My vision goes black for a single second as he laughs darkly at his own sick joke. For a moment I wonder whether he knows. About Julia. About everything that happened nine years ago. The records were sealed because of her age. But I've recently discovered that if you have the right connections and you look hard enough, you can find just about anything. Jesus, is he toying with me? Do they know why we've invited them here? Does—?

Killian links his fingers with mine, pulls me to stand in front of him, and winds both arms around my waist. A second later, his mouth brushes my cheek. With my hair caught up and my dark orange cocktail dress designed to leave my shoulders bare, he has access to my neck and shoulders too. He takes his time to trail a few kisses there before he looks over at Raj. "Well, we've thrown a few of these parties, and we've never had a guest leave us unhappy before, have we, sweetheart?" he says.

I pull myself together, take a sustaining breath, and turn my head, carefully avoiding Raj's gaze, and look into Killian's eyes. "No, honey. Never. I hate to brag, but we have a very difficult time choosing who to invite these days. It'll break my heart if anyone here tonight isn't fully satisfied with what we have planned downstairs." I clench my gut and transfer my gaze to Raj. "We have everyone's taste covered. I assure you."

Raj's smile widens, and he all but rubs his hands in glee. "Fantastic."

I smile some more and dutifully gasp as the first set of fireworks rips through the sky. Since every one of the twenty-five guests invited knows what's coming next, the closer the display gets to its denouement, the higher the depraved sexual energy builds in the crowd. Once it's over and the applause dies down, all eyes turn to Killian.

He waits for a full minute, keeping them on tenterhooks while he kisses me. Then his gaze flicks over the crowd. "Sorry, folks, I don't like to miss a chance to thank my lovely woman for everything she does for me," he drawls.

Laughter is tinged with dark, fevered anticipation.

"Okay, we've kept you waiting long enough. Shall we head to the sin bin?" he asks.

Without waiting for a response, he takes my hand and walks me around the pool and back inside the villa. Our guests trail behind us, the three men who are the reason for all of this first in the group.

We reach the far end of the wide living room. Killian pulls down a glass panel in the wall and enters a code. A secret floor about the size of a door clicks and lowers three feet away. Subdued lighting illuminates the stairs leading down into the sublevel, which holds the same square footage as the floor above.

Again, Killian leads the way, his fingers linked with mine to help me down the stairs. When we reach the middle of the room, I take a beat to ground myself before I turn to smile at our guests.

"Holy shit," Moses mutters under his breath as he turns a full circle.

Every imaginable sex gadget and accessory, and some that are in prototype stages, is displayed in the room illuminated by strategically placed gold lights. The objective was to blow the minds of men who already think they know everything there is to know about sex.

"This is like *Eyes Wide Shut* meets *Space Odyssey* meets *Game of Thrones*. The sexy bits, not all that blood and gore shit," Raj expands as his gaze lights on a spank bench a few feet away and the scantily clad young woman sitting cross-legged on it. "Fuck me, I can spend a full week down here, no problem at all."

Paul heads for the nearest group of girls reclining in suggestive poses around the room. There are twenty women and five men in total hired for the event.

As predicted, all three men go for the youngest looking in the group. I'm still nauseated that this part of the op involved dressing them up to look and act like they were underage. It doesn't matter that they're carefully chosen escorts flown in from across Europe. Or that they are being paid handsomely for a night's work. I can barely bring myself to look at any of them.

But I have a part to play. I wait until all the guests are situated and busy with their chosen partners. The waiters, who are also part of the team, specifically here to ensure booze flows and the escorts are protected, ease my anxiety a little.

Enough for me to approach Paul and Raj. "Gentlemen, if you'd like to come with me. We have a further surprise for you. You can bring your new friends with you," I say with a perfect smile.

Paul tugs a girl after him, as does Raj. "Hey, Mo," he calls out to Moses, who's sprawled out on a lounger, about to unzip his pants, "keep it wrapped for another minute, would you? We've been invited to the inner *inner* sanctum."

Moses jumps up, hooks his fingers into the collars of two young men who were about to service him, and drags them after him. One of them stumbles, and my breath snags on a spike of anger.

"Easy, baby," Killian warns in my ear.

I'm shaking by the time we walk through the steel door at the back end of the underground room. This room is even more special. Red silk shibari ropes specially sourced from Asia hang from the ceiling. Gem-encrusted sex toys are laid out on black velvet cloth, and others hang on the walls.

"Fuck, yeah," Paul growls, eyes glinting with degenerate sexual heat.

"One week. Easy," Raj insists.

Moses instructs his boys to grab a bottle of Cristal each. "Come with me. I'll teach you a neat trick I learned in Tunisia last year." He barks out in laughter and heads for a double lounger.

Every bone in my body wants to crush these men into a messy, useless pulp. The latest intel that came through before the party started was that they met with suspected black market brokers to arrange another shipment of innocent children today. But despite the white-hot rage filling my veins, I have to remain calm.

Twenty girls per month ranging in age from fourteen to seventeen. Never older. Because apparently, sleazy old men can't get it up for legal girls. They're the reason I aced the three test-run assignments needed to prove myself, and the two I undertook as a fully trained operative. I did everything in my power to be considered for this mission. And no matter how I feel, I can't blow it.

My baby sister wasn't bought or sold, but she was still targeted by a man she trusted. A man who was more than three times her age and who should have protected her but instead molested her for four long, silent years. I watched her turn from a bubbly twelve-year-old into a pale, secretive, haunted shadow of herself. I watched my parents turn to the very man responsible for Julia's deterioration for help. And all through his systematic abuse of my sister, Father Michaels of the Holy Catholic Church of Northern Arkansas continued to preach goodness and mercy and forgiveness.

He stood over her coffin, prayed for her soul, and mourned the life she'd ended by her own hand as being over way too soon. And even after we found Julia's suicide note naming him as her abuser and he was caught with another child, he strenuously denied any wrongdoing. I spent the months during his trial for molesting a dozen other children filled with uncontrollable rage. And heaven help me, I even considered cold-blooded murder for the first time in my life.

My fight to ensure he stayed in jail for the rest of his natural life was what led me to Matthew Knight, an ambitious assistant district attorney looking to make a name for himself.

I mentally flinch away from thoughts of Matt and return to my unwanted reality. I hear a rip of clothing from Raj's lounger and a gagging noise from Moses's, and my fingers tighten within Killian's hand.

"Enjoy yourselves," Killian says. With a kiss on my temple, he steers me toward the door. We don't need to stay because the room is bugged. Each bottle of alcohol has been doctored with a modified strain of sodium pentothal, designed to relax their guard. We're still playing the long game but it doesn't hurt to lay a few more traps.

"Aren't you going to join in?" Paul asks, his eyes narrowing on Killian and then on me.

Killian's smile is pure arrogance bred from the fact that, in financial stakes alone, he's several classes above these men and doesn't mind showing it. "We just met today. Like a fine red wine, we prefer our associations to…breathe for a while, attain the right bouquet. Should we find that our tastes match, then we can take this to the next level. But don't let me stop you from enjoying yourselves."

Although Paul smiles at Killian, something moves behind his eyes that dances icy fingers down my spine. But Raj doesn't need a second prompt. He reaches for the blond girl in pigtails and dressed like an English schoolgirl, right down to the snow-white tights. I turn away in disgust, and thankfully Killian is there, a solid wall buffering me from the men responsible for my roiling emotions. He must sense Paul's suspicion because he changes his mind at the last moment and doesn't take me out of the room.

Instead he leads me to the farthest lounger and pushes me onto it. But then he positions himself so his body blocks the men from my view. His eyes convey nothing but sex and desire as he lowers his head and kisses me.

I know he's kissing me to take my mind, and eyes, off what's happening on the other side of the room. Even now, he's protecting me, while dealing with his own jealousy by staking his claim on me.

I don't mind. Kissing him takes away the nausea that hasn't abated since we walked down the stairs into this sleazy pit of immorality.

We wait until they're fully immersed in their orgy of booze and sex before we leave. We enter the main room and mingle for another two hours. And then, as per the invitation, Killian, in effortless arrogant-billionaire mode, ends the party and throws everyone out.

No one dares to grumble. Raj looks a touch disappointed, but he attempts to shrug on his clothes as he weaves his way drunkenly toward us. "We want to reciprocate your hospitality. Next week. We'll send a driver for you."

Killian looks over at me with an ambivalent look on his face. "Our schedule is pretty full…"

"Trust me, you'll like the kind of party we throw too. Maybe even more."

Killian smiles. "Oh yeah?"

Paul smirks and waves his hand around the room. "I like this, but I guarantee we can top a few things."

"It's not a competition," I say with a very bright, very false smile.

His eyes slide to mine. "Everything is a competition, sweet thing."

Killian's hand tightens warningly on my hip. "Now *that* is a throwdown I simply cannot refuse."

Paul laughs and slaps him on the back. "Good, good. So you'll come?"

Killian looks down at me. "What do you think, sweetheart?"

"Yeah, what do you think, *sweetheart*?" Paul's smirk widens as he raises his eyebrows at me.

I place my chin on Killian's shoulder and give a saucy smile. "I think they talk a big game, so I'm up for seeing what they've got," I reply.

"Great. It's a date. And this time you will join in. With everything."

I'm wrapped in chilled fury by the time their convoy of SUVs leaves the villa in a trail of dust. I can barely see my way through ensuring the escorts are fine and relatively unharmed. I leave Killian to supervise their departure, and I can't get into the shower fast enough. He joins me ten minutes later, and we wash away the vile stench of sleaze with sex and soap.

Then we head to the communications room to trawl through the footage. The memory of what was done to Julia sears me each time I look at Paul Galveston and his partners and the sick acts they're performing on-screen. Each time Moses's finger tightens around one man's collar and he laughs with sick glee, I want to throw up again. Then I want to hunt him down, rip his face off, and stomp on it.

"Baby, I can do this on my own," Killian says after an hour of watching the footage.

I shake my head. "No. We do this together."

He examines my face for a moment, then nods, and I pray I won't have to watch for much longer. My prayers are answered when Moses grabs one young man by the collar and cups his jaw. He turns his face one way and then the other, carefully examining his features. "How old are you? Really?"

The escort, primed to answer one way only, replies, "I can be whatever age you want me to be."

A very drunk Moses shoves him away. Raj looks over. "What's up, man? Something wrong with the merchandise?" he laughs.

Moses rests back on the lounger. "Something's off. He feels a little…overused."

My breath catches, but Killian doesn't look as anxious as I feel. Paul slaps his girl's ass and orders her to ride him faster. Then he looks over at Moses. "Rest easy, pal. When the shipment arrives in twenty days' time, you can take your pick of fresh meat."

Moses groans with filthy anticipation. Raj responds with a slurred shout.

Killian looks over at me and smiles.

We have a date to pass on to the team.

Chapter Eleven

BLACK WIDOW

Present Day

I don't know why I try to go to sleep after leaving Killian in the study. I can't deny that I want to block out thinking about Paul Galveston or any of the other slimeballs we met during our stint in Cairo. But there's no way I can relax with my mind churning with the news that the man behind one of the biggest sex trafficking rings in the world is still alive and breathing free air.

But more than that, the memory of how everything went so very wrong is the one thing I don't want to think about. Before Cairo, I thought the extra baggage of guilt Killian and I carried might just be bearable and, hell, even lessen once the past lost a little of its sharp sting. But it turned out karma was just getting warmed up. And, in hindsight, a part of me knows I deserve everything that went down in Cairo.

I jump out of bed and pace from one end of the room to the other, wishing I'd taken up Anwat's offer of another round of Muy

Thai when I had the chance. The buildup of restless energy is eating into my emotions and threatening to drive me out of my mind.

I want to punch something. Bad. Or have something punched into me. Like Killian's cock. The memory of how the sex was between us shivers through me, and I bite my lip to suppress a moan. I need some of that. God, do I need it.

"Can't sleep?"

I jerk around at his voice. Then twist back around in case he can read my impure thoughts in my face. "No," I snap.

He doesn't speak but I know he's still there. When I risk a glance over my shoulder, he's looking at the rumpled bed I vacated ten minutes ago. Electricity crackles hotter as his gaze returns to mine. "Wanna get out of here for a little bit?"

My eyes widen. "What? Really?"

"Don't get excited. We're just heading to the rooftop."

Although I deflate a little, the thought of getting out of the apartment, stunning though it is, is very welcome. Because the only other means I can think of to alleviate my anxiety is with sex. The sheet-clawing, hair-pulling, sweat-drenching kind. And I've already indulged in way more than I need to in the twelve hours since Killian exploded back into my life.

"Okay."

He nods and leaves my room and returns a minute later with my running shoes and leather cap. He's wearing a cap too but his feet are bare. The memory of how much he loves walking around with no shoes knots a ball of raw emotion inside me. I gird myself against it as he waits for me to put my things on. We head to the front door, and I wait while he goes through the rigmarole of the entry code, handprint, and retina scan he told me about last night. When I roll my eyes, he smirks at me. "Yeah, it's a fucking pain, but you're worth it."

I say nothing. He repeats the process again when we reach the outer foyer, which turns out to be as equally stunning as the apartment. And when we enter the elevator, he removes a key from his pocket and slots it into a panel before hitting the button for the rooftop.

"You had all this done in the last four days?" I ask.

"No. I asked Betty to find me a building with security-paranoid tenants. You'll be shocked at how many there are in this city. This was the best of the bunch. I only needed to modify a few things."

The elevator spits us out into a glass enclosure. This time he only needs a code and thumbprint to release the door.

We step out into the mid-afternoon sun. I lift my face to it, close my eyes, and breathe in deep. I feel Killian's gaze on me, but I don't look at him when I open my eyes. Instead, I take in my surroundings. It's beautifully landscaped with tall shrubs, weaving vines, and large boxed plants that have a distinctly unweathered look about them. The soil also has a newly churned smell.

"These are new too?" It's not really a question. And I have an idea why he's transformed the rooftop into a lush garden when he smiles and points a finger upward.

Surveillance drones. Satellites. To a normal person, the extra precaution he's taking by filling the roof space with cover-giving foliage would sound like a tinfoil-hat-wearing kook babbling about conspiracies and Big Brother watching. But I know in our case that it's all justified. Even more so now with the threat Galveston poses and the possibility that he might have the same image Killian used to find me.

I push thoughts of him away for now. There'll be time enough to deal with him once Betty locates him. Instead I look around. There's a brand-new barbecue grill that looks large enough to cater for several large families. A cooler sits on a table next to it. And beneath a row of potted palm trees, low seats with fat white cushions have been arranged around a large center table. The space is huge, much bigger than the one I transformed not too far from here. But they both have the same serenity, which is hard to come by in New York City unless you're insanely loaded. Suddenly, I'm hit with a bout of unfamiliar nostalgia.

"I have a rooftop just like this."

He's trailed me as I wandered through the garden and now stares at me, a touch of surprise in his blue eyes. "Yeah?"

I nod. "At the Punishment Club. It was just an unused space before. I designed it and turned it into a relaxation spot…away from the main club." I don't know why I'm telling him this. It's not like we were ever in that get-to-know-each-other stage or will be anytime soon. We went from forbidden fruit to torrid lovers without pausing to take a breath. Then added the dangerous ingredient of international espionage to the mix right up until it all blew up in our faces. Then I took the only option available to me and ran like hell.

He tucks his hands beneath his arms in that effortlessly manly way that makes his thick biceps flex. It's all I can do not to stare and salivate like a horny idiot. "I'd like to see it one day," he says.

I press my lips together because I want to blurt out that I'd love to show it to him.

"So…punishment club?" he asks with raised eyebrows after a pulse of silence.

I jerk out a shrug. "Seemed like a good idea at the time. I just had no idea how much it would take off."

He nods. "The concept is certainly interesting."

"Not really. There's a hell of a lot of guilt going around."

"And has it helped you?" he asks after another minute passes.

I stiffen a little. "It's not about me."

"Why the hell not? You created the place. And you've cared about it enough to stick with it for four years."

"It wasn't just for me."

He frowns. "For Axel? So he's reaping the benefits of all your hard work?"

There's a pulse of annoyance in his voice that I'm not going to acknowledge. I get the feeling that his irrational jealousy won't disappear until he sees Axel and Cleo together and witnesses for himself how those two react around each other. Talk about fucking combustible. But I also think about the punishment rooms we reserved for ourselves when we first opened the club.

Axel has a chair and a bank of TV screens.

Mine has a bed and a box with a single photo tucked inside. Sealed four years ago and never opened.

I carefully neutralize my features. Killian was always a master at reading me. The secret in that box is one he doesn't need to know. Maybe I'm punishing him too the way I've been punishing myself by not telling him. But that particular punishment is primarily mine to bear. My secret to keep.

"Axel is not an issue, Killian. Seriously."

His jaw flexes. "So you keep saying, baby. But I'm having a hard time dealing with the fact that he's had you for four years." He stays me with a halting hand when I open my mouth. "Yeah, maybe not sexually, but still. Four years. I barely had you for one. So you have to get why I go a little nuts when you mention him."

Huh. I never thought of it that way. And the more I think about it now, the more I realize that, had I thought of any woman with Killian in the same way, I probably would be feeling less than ecstatic too. "Well, technically, I didn't mention him. You did."

His eyes narrow. Before we disintegrate into another fight, I walk over and drop down into one of the cushy seats. He follows and sits next to me. Above us, the canopy of miniature palm trees shields us from the sky, but enough sunlight filters through to warm my face.

I close my eyes and tuck my hands behind my head. "I could really do with a beer."

"Are you trying to avoid another fight with me?" he asks.

"Yes."

He sighs, and I hear him move away. Half a minute later, he returns. "Here."

I open my eyes, and he's holding out a cold Bud Light. "Thanks." I take it from him and gulp down several mouthfuls.

He keeps looking at me without drinking from his own bottle.

"What?"

"When did you start drinking beer?" he asks.

I tense a little, and my gaze shifts from his. "A while back." When I was on a downward spiral into my own hell-based drama.

"What aren't you telling me, baby?"

God. A whole lot. But this one I can admit to without feeling as if what remains of my soul isn't being ripped out. "You were forced into therapy. I…found other means to…exist."

He looks into my eyes, and we both silently admit that, while I was the one to leave, it wasn't easy for me either. "Booze?" he asks.

I nod, feeling a tiny cathartic release I don't really deserve for that admission. "For a time."

"And the other times? Drugs?" he probes.

I shake my head. "No. I listen to a twenty-five-year-old CEO cry for three hours straight about how he wants to bang his fifty-five-year-old secretary because she looks like his high school teacher. Or a fitness instructor who flogs himself because he can't get over accidentally killing his neighbor's dog."

He shakes his head and takes a long swig of beer as his gaze hovers contemplatively in the middle distance. "So the club wasn't totally a punishment for you. It was partly your savior," he observes quietly.

The bottle starts to slip from my fingers as shock pummels me.

His stunning eyes return to mine, seeing far too much. I must look as poleaxed as I feel because he caresses my cheek with a finger. "It's okay, baby."

I jerk away. "It's not okay. And you don't know what the hell you're talking about." But I strongly suspect that he does. Jesus.

Killian Knight wouldn't have risen to the high rank he did at the Fallhurst Institute, all while maintaining his normal nerdy billionaire existence, if he wasn't clever. Although he's never taken the test, his IQ is estimated to be insanely high. Right in this moment, I resent his ability to turn all that high-mental-quotient brain and blue-eyed, mind-scrambling face on me.

A beep from his pants pocket saves me from defending myself further. Or providing answers to the myriad questions I see brimming in his eyes.

He pulls out a sleek gadget and looks down at the screen. He scrolls through whatever information is displayed and then glances at me. "Wanna take this field trip a little further?"

I inhale in surprise. "Where?"

"Betty has mapped out a route to the club with the least amount of functioning CCTV cameras. And another route to your apartment." He looks up at me. "Which one do you want to hit first?"

"My apartment," I respond immediately. "I can't go to the club dressed like this."

"We'll have something to eat first, then we'll go. Okay?"

"Okay."

"Great." He puts the gadget away and nods to the cooling bottle in my hand. "Finish your beer."

* * *

We eat an early dinner prepared by Mitch, and this time I wisely don't make a comment about how great the steak and salad are. Afterward, Killian disappears into his study for half an hour. I use the app on my phone to check the footage from the security cameras I placed at vantage points around my apartment building.

I'm relieved when nothing jumps out at me.

The other ghost from my past is keeping her distance. After three weeks, I'm beginning to wonder if our meeting was just a freakish coincidence.

Except there's no such thing. Wasn't that what Killian drummed into me the very first day of training? I think of that black site in Virginia with a mixture of awe and guilt. I loved the training, putting my brain through hell and my body through worse. I loved the clandestine meetings with Killian in the woods behind the facility even more. I discovered that being fucked against a tree, while seriously uncomfortable for my back, was still one of the hottest things I've done. And it was great while it lasted.

Until we were busted.

By her.

I frown now and shake my head. Her call out of the blue, after two years of silence, scared the shit out of me. But what scared me even more was running into her three weeks ago at the club. I was certain it wasn't a coincidence until I found out she was there to see Axel. She hasn't contacted me again. Because I told her to leave me alone? Yeah, when did she ever listen?

"Something's wrong. What is it?"

Holy shit. The questions don't stop coming. I stash my phone and roll my eyes at Killian. "Other than my need to get out of here?"

"Don't give me that," he snaps. When I remain mutinously silent, he points at me. "I'm going to get it out of you. You know that, don't you?"

Sadly, that's what terrifies me. "Have at it. I'm going to have fun watching you try."

There's no half-joking comeback this time. He's all business as he folds back the sleeves of his dark blue shirt, worn over black pants. He's run a brush through his hair at some point in the last half hour. I note its shoulder length. I note his designer stubble. Hell, I notice everything about him. And the package that is Killian Knight does something to my breathing that I'm sure scientists would have a field day with when I drop dead from the effect.

"Are you ready to go, or are you happy to stand there eye-fucking me all night?"

Heat singes my cheeks. I want to walk over and punch him. Then climb him and wrap my body around his the way I used to love doing.

Jesus. Get a fucking grip.

I yank my backpack—which had miraculously made an appearance when we returned from the roof—off the sofa and stalk down the hallway.

He follows, and we leave the apartment. The downstairs lobby is just as stunningly beautiful as what I've seen of the rest of the apartment building so far. It's also completely empty, which is strange for such an upmarket place.

I wonder whether it's by design or luck and then roll my eyes at myself. No such thing as luck.

The second we hit the street, Killian places his hand in the small of my back and hustles me to the black SUV parked on the curb. Before we slide into the backseat, I notice another SUV idling a few meters away.

Mitch is behind the wheel of ours, with another guy in the passenger seat. "That's Linc. Say hi, Linc," Killian says.

The burly man is almost a carbon copy of Mitch, save for the fact that he's black and his head is completely bald. He turns and offers me a courteous smile. "Evening, ma'am."

Killian doesn't offer my name, and I realized he didn't with Mitch this morning either.

"Hi," I reply.

We merge into traffic. Killian is back to fiddling with the gadget in his hand, and I look out to get my bearings. Upper East Side, four blocks from Axel's apartment. I keep that nugget to myself.

We don't talk for a few streets, until I notice what's happening with the stoplights.

I glance over at Killian. He's busy working away at his little gadget. I frown. "Are you doing this?"

"What?"

"You know exactly what I mean."

He raises his head and looks over at me. "You're talking about the lights? I remember you mentioning how it drove you nuts when you're at a stoplight and it turns from green back to red in like five seconds."

My eyes widen. "Yes...and?"

His smile turns into a grin and he waves his little gadget at me. "I found out that it drove me nuts too."

"So..."

His eyebrows waggle. "You stick with me and it'll be green lights all the way, baby."

What the fuck? "I'm pretty sure that's illegal."

His smile evaporates, and iron-willed Killian is back. "So is tampering with CCTV cameras, but I'm absolutely sure I want you off the streets pretty fucking damn quick. If the cost of that is a few hundred people being three minutes late to wherever they're headed, I'm completely okay with that."

We make it to Gramercy Park in less than twenty minutes. I'm thinking this is what heads of state must feel like when traffic stops for them as I get out and walk into my apartment building. It may have been illegal, but shit, I could get used to it very fast. I don't tell

Killian though. He'll probably gift wrap the algorithm for me in ten seconds.

And what's wrong that? a tiny, mildly exasperated voice asks.

A hundred different reasons. I'm reminding myself of what those reasons are when I approach the door to my apartment. Before I can insert my key, Killian's arm slides around my waist and pulls me back into his body.

"Hang tight for a second," he says. "Can I have your key?"

I want to refuse, but Mitch and Linc are standing in front of my door. And I get the feeling I won't be let through it until Killian does whatever security check he intends to do. I hand over the key. When they disappear inside, I step away from Killian.

"I have my own security, you know."

He nods, but his eyes remain in the doorway. The two bodyguards return a couple of minutes later. "All clear."

I purse my lips and refrain from saying what's on my mind as they position themselves on either side of my front door. We enter, and I'm shutting the door behind me when Killian inhales sharply.

"Jesus. What the fuck is that?"

Chapter Twelve

KILLIAN

There's a pole in the middle of her living room. One that looks uncannily like... *Shit*. I can't get my mind around it. Raw, carnal images war with unwanted scenarios in my brain. I drag my gaze from the solid steel column to where she's standing. Pink heat creeps into her face. But still she's fierce as she replies, "Exactly what it looks like."

A stripper pole. Fuck me. "Why?" I hear the gravel roughness of my voice, caused by arousal and suspicion, and I'm not even a little bit ashamed of either.

"Because I wanted one." Her voice suggests that's the end of the conversation.

Except it so isn't. Unless she wants me to go apeshit. Which I'm half a second from unleashing. "Faith..."

Something in my tone must alert her to the paper-thin veneer I have over my control. Or it's my use of her name. The name she seems to now detest.

Her gaze meets mine for a second before it slides away. "I was trying a few things after I moved in to keep me from going stir-crazy. I couldn't go running or join a gym. The sounds of a treadmill drove my elderly neighbor nuts, so I had to come up with some-thing else. The pole seemed like a good idea at the time. It's grown on me."

The red haze recedes, and impure thoughts rush to the fore. I turn back around and stare at the pole, picture her sliding against it. My cock responds eagerly.

"Don't get any ideas, Knight," she snaps.

"Too fucking late, baby," I reply, but I still can't look away from the pole. God, I'd kill to have her dance for me right now.

I glance over at her. She shakes her head definitively, muttering under her breath before heading for a short hallway. A moment later, a door slams. My very turned-on attention returns to the pole, and my imagination runs wild with what I could do to her against it. Hell, what she could do to me. Her super-toned body is perfect for it. My hand sneaks over my crotch, and I touch myself with all the finesse of a virgin nerd. I pinch the head of my cock in the vain hope of stopping this killer hard-on that feels like it's going to slay me, but all I can think of is Faith with her legs wrapped around the steel pole or hanging upside down from the top while taking me into her mouth and sucking me off.

Sweet Christ.

I whirl away before I do something really uncool, like come in my pants. I take a deep breath and properly take in the rest of her apartment. My raging erection throttles back as I look at her things, as I stare at the space she's lived in for four years without me.

I still don't really know why she fled from me after the nightmare in Cairo. But in light of our immediate problem, I have to let things lie for now. But that conversation is coming. Soon.

Besides a very comfortable-looking set of sofas and a stylish rug, there's the usual TV and entertainment center, a couple of potted plants, scented candles, a wool throw, and a bookcase filled from top to bottom with spy novels. Wait, not all. I spot a book of erotica, and my eyebrows spike. I really shouldn't touch it. I shouldn't...

I'm flicking through the book for the third time when I hear the click of heels behind me. I place a finger in the well-thumbed page on multiple orgasms and turn around.

"Killian, I've been…"

Whatever she's saying is drowned out because…holy fuck. My breath punches out of me and I swear I see stars. "Jesus, baby. Muay Thai, pole dancing, and now you walk out of your bedroom looking like that? Do you want to give me a fucking heart attack?"

The black see-through lace shirt she's wearing is covered by a tightly zipped-up corset that makes her waist look ten inches wide. The effect is a lush, mouthwatering, hourglass magnificence that I know I'll kill for because I've already done it once. And that's even before I take in her straight hair, the very provocative bangs resting on her brows, and the fuck-me red lipstick on her luscious, fuckable mouth.

"This is how I…" She stops suddenly and looks warily at me.

This is how I dress for work. I do my very best not to think about all the times horny assholes and dirty bastards have seen her like this. But no matter how much I try, my blood simmers with the jealousy that has been a part of me since the moment I set eyes on her.

I'm making sure she quits that fucking job if it's the last thing I do. It might be because that heart attack I talked about seems very likely with each passing second.

I drag my eyes from that vulgar little triangular gap between her legs, lovingly cradled by soft leather, up the flare of her hips to the tits I'm dying to see, to touch, to taste again. She takes a deep breath, and my cock screams in agony.

"You were saying?" My voice sounds like I've swallowed a fucking porcupine, and I don't even give a shit.

"That…umm, I've been thinking."

"So have I."

Her gaze goes to the book in my hand before darting back to my face. The book about sex that she's read a lot of times if the dog-ears are any indication. "About our Galveston problem, Killian. Not the stripper pole…or whatever's going through your mind."

I return the book to the shelf. Something else to discuss later. If she's taken an interest in bondage or tantric sex or deep-throat blow jobs, I certainly want to know about it. "Trust me, sweetheart. You don't wanna know what I'm thinking right now," I reply, but the mention of our mutual enemy sobers me up long enough to take a deep, cleansing breath and focus my mind. "Okay, let's hear it."

She walks toward me in stiletto boots, and it's all I can do not to find the nearest rope and tie her to that damn pole. I shove my hands into my pockets instead.

"We have six hundred members at the club. And another couple of thousand names of potential members we've turned away because they were either batshit crazy or their proclivities were more suited to another type of club. Or behind the locked doors of a jail cell," she adds with a tightening of her red lips.

I drag my attention from her mouth. "You kept the records?"

She nods. "I have it on a thumb drive at the club."

"Okay, we can cross-reference their names with the list of sex clubs and brothels or anyone associated with sex trafficking minors. If anything pops up, Betty can do a deeper dive."

A shaft of pain crosses her face. "We thought with Moses and Galveston dead, we'd done enough for Fallhurst to dismantle the rings." She exhales heavily. "But now we know Galveston is alive and possibly still active."

"We have to assume they plan to revive the sex ring. Killing the agents could just be revenge for Cairo, but they probably wouldn't be disposing of the team if they were planning on retiring anytime soon." I sigh. "We'll focus on the usual shipping angle and maybe border patrols. We need to look at whoever's now in charge of Phillips Black. Could be there are people within the company who knew about the trafficking. Or Raj could still be pulling strings from wherever he's hiding."

"You think we can get a list of their employees?" she asks.

"I can make that happen."

She nods. "Okay."

She turns to leave the room, and my eyes immediately drop to her heart-shaped ass and the pin-straight hair brushing the top of it. "Fucking hell," I mutter under my breath.

Her back stiffens and her stride falters for a millisecond, but she keeps walking. When she returns clutching a small purse, I'm massaging my nape purely so I don't massage the ache in my cock.

"I'm good to go."

"Great." My voice is still strained. Hell, my whole body is strained. I don't know how much longer I can go on like this. Still, I man up and follow her out the door.

The route Betty plotted to Hell's Kitchen and the Punishment Club gets us there in record time. Faith enters a code, and we drive into an underground parking garage.

She eyes Mitch and Linc when they exit the SUV and follow us to the elevator. "They're staying here, right?"

I let my eyes speak for me.

"Killian, I can't bring bodyguards to work with me," she protests.

I push the button for the elevator. When it arrives, I gently guide her inside. "Nonnegotiable."

She swears under her breath and glances at the two giant men crowding the small space with us. There's an evil light in her eyes that tells me she has payback on her mind. "Well, I hope you boys don't mind being the center of attention. Friday nights are...extra-special nights, and with those endless muscles, you're prime bait material for tonight's program."

A muscle jumps in Mitch's cheek, but Linc remains as unflappable as ever. I don't reassure them, because they're grown men, and also because my own temperature is already too high from watching her walk from the car to the elevator in those tight leather pants and sky-high heels. "Be nice, sweetheart."

Her glare tells me she's not in the mood. "I'm just giving them fair warning."

I see what she means the moment we walk into the main reception area. Wall-to-wall skin is the name of the game. It's not exactly BDSM, but there's no effort to hide the lurid activities going on right there in the open. And this is just the ground floor.

Every muscle in my body clenches tight. Before I know it, I'm sliding my arm around her and backing her up against the nearest wall. I plant my hands on either side of her head and crowd her with my body. "Tell me again that you don't get involved with any of this shit." I sound like I'm hanging on by a thread. And I feel it.

Her eyes narrow. "Seriously? Not now—"

"Yes, fucking now. I'm one goddamn heartbeat from throwing you over my shoulder and taking you the hell out of here. So if you want me to let up, answer me."

She puffs out an annoyed breath. "Nothing sexual. Ever."

I release my pent-up breath, and then I ask one of the many questions that's been eating at me. "And that book in your apartment? The one on erotica? Any reason you've taken an interest in that kind of thing?"

She blinks up at me through her sexy bangs, and slave that I am, my cock jumps. "How do you know I haven't always been interested in…the more adventurous side of things?"

"The way we fucked was hardly vanilla, baby," I point out. "But I'm more than happy to step things up for you if you need it."

Her green eyes turn a shade darker, and her breathing intensifies. "Let me go, Killian. I need to go organize a special pass for your guys or they won't be allowed upstairs."

My temples begin to throb. "And what's upstairs?"

"Let me go, and I'll give you a tour."

I'm not sure I want a tour. In fact, the only thing I'm sure of is that I want her out of here, like yesterday. But I drop my hands and step back.

"Lead the way."

We walk past naked and nearly naked bodies in all shapes and sizes. The stench of sex is in the air, and it's like they're all waiting for some sort of sign to begin a giant orgy. I catch a couple of cougars eyeing Mitch and Linc. To their credit, the two men are holding their own. Or rather staring straight ahead and pretending none of the skin flick in front of them is happening. Courage under fucking fire. It's why I pay them the big bucks, I guess.

We approach another, quieter reception area. The attractive black girl behind the desk smiles at Faith. "Hi, B."

She returns the smile with a small one of her own. "Hey. Is Axel around?"

"He just got in. He's in his office."

"Thanks. Can you sort two passes for me, please?"

The receptionist nods and slides two silver cards through a portable machine and hands them over.

We get in another elevator and go another couple of floors. "This area is for gold and platinum members only. From here, you need a card to access every floor, but the silver cards only get you to the fourth floor. After that, you either need to be a member or have a special invitation." The level where we exit has the same theme going on as downstairs but with less people and more sophistication.

It's also clear that these regulars know Faith. She nods at a few people and exchanges words with a few more. I exhale the breath locked in my throat when I notice that her acknowledgments are friendly but professional. Still, enough already. We stop at a well-stocked bar, and she orders a drink—a Hine on the rocks—for me. My jumpy senses settle a little. She hasn't forgotten my favorite drink. Our fingers brush as she passes me the glass, and I watch her lips part as she takes a rushed little breath.

Before I can comment on it, she nods at her bodyguards. "I can't take them back to Axel's office. They'll have to stay in the bar."

I've clocked where the exits are and where any potential threats may come from. And the Glock resting against my spine is a reassuring presence. "Fine."

Surprise lights her eyes. I smile, toss back my drink, and slide the empty glass on the counter. We leave the reception area and walk through a surprisingly brightly lit hallway. "This is the newbie floor. We keep things less...heavy around here." She points to the monitors by each door. "And we also keep an eye on everyone in the first few weeks."

Some of the monitors are dark, and some are full-color playback of what's going on behind closed doors. I'm not interested in watching other people have sex so I keep my eyes on my woman. "So that Burning Man sex tent scenario downstairs happens every Friday?"

"Pretty much."

"That looks more like sin and less like punishment."

She smiles. "Not everyone likes baring themselves in front of strangers. Not everyone enjoys being touched by another human being. There's a redhead in the group downstairs whose therapist recommended the club for her anxiety. God knows why. I tried to talk her out of it but she insisted. That's not technically a punishment but I made an exception for her, and it seems to be working, so..." She shrugs.

I'm quietly impressed. Not enough to kill the need to get her the fuck away from here ASAP though. Whatever she started this club to prove, it's time for her to move on.

We tour the second floor but I decline going any further. I don't need to see what's going on on the upper floors. I get the idea. We take the elevator back down to the basement and walk through a set of security doors marked *Private*. She stops in front a plain-looking door but seems reluctant to enter. "This is my office."

I raise one eyebrow. "Unless you have a naked guy chained to the wall in there, there's no reason for you to be nervous. If you do, you're about to be in a world of hurt."

She rolls her eyes and enters the code. The latch springs open, and we step inside. She walks across the gray carpet, her gaze darting to mine as she discards her purse.

A large antique desk and chair sit beneath a large window. The usual office accessories of sleek computer, stationery, lamp, coat-rack, and, because she loves them, a few potted plants are scattered in the usual places. There's a large, comfy sofa with cushions and a woolen blanket next to one wall. Through a partially opened closet, I see several changes of clothing, more blankets, and a couple of pil-lows.

Besides the worrying thought that she may have slept here at times instead of going home, there's nothing out of the ordinary. And yet she still looks nervous.

It takes a moment for the light bulb to go off in my head.

This has been her domain for four years. A concept she's taken from inception to mega-success. Her very own stake in something solid where she didn't have one before. I took her from housewife to spy, but she was still in my world, playing by my rules.

Faith Carson will kick ass in whatever area of life she pursues. But everyone needs to be told they're doing a good job. Especially when they're expected to leave behind the thing they've created at short notice.

Shit. I don't regret my decision to force her hand on this, but I feel a little bad for being a complete bastard about it.

I walk over and slide my hands over her shoulders. "Regardless of my reservations about all that nakedness going on upstairs, I'm seriously impressed with what you've done here, baby."

She relaxes a little and even manages a smile. "Thank you."

I nod. Then look around some more. There are no personal items, save for a letter opener with the letter *B* inscribed on it. While I commend her for keeping her cover under wraps and ensuring her safety, I'm still a little disturbed by how effectively she's erased her past. She could walk out of this room and no one would know she was ever here. And because that suits my purposes right now, I'm not too upset by it.

"You wanna grab the thumb drive?" I ask.

She nods slowly and walks over to a safe behind her desk. She removes two thumb drives before she locks it.

I breathe a little sigh of relief. "We good to go now?"

She shakes her head. "In a minute. I need to see Axel first."

Chapter Thirteen

KILLIAN

In another life, Axel Rutherford and I could've been either best friends or bitter enemies, depending on whether I chose to have him in my life or not.

We'll be neither because I don't intend to give him a chance to stake a claim either way.

It could have something to do with what I heard—and immediately detested—in his tone when he spoke to Faith on the phone last night. It was...proprietary. As if he believes he owns a piece of my woman. From the hour I spent investigating him while Faith was sleeping, he comes across like the ruthless, possessive type, so I know that conclusion isn't without merit.

The man who rises from the desk when we enter his office confirms that conclusion. I may be an arrogant bastard where she is concerned, but he looks like a possessive asshole. And that doesn't bode well for either of us.

Besides, he's got that brooding-face-and-intelligent-eyes shit going on that women eat up.

Take the brunette sitting on the sofa, for example. There's a fevered intensity in her eyes when she looks at him that would've bordered on the uncomfortable had I not recognized it in myself whenever I look at Faith.

Axel's gaze, however, is not on his woman but on me.

"B, I saw you on the monitors. I could've dreamed you said you wouldn't be coming to work tonight."

"Yeah, so I changed my mind."

"Fair enough. And is there a reason you're turning up to work with an entourage? Did you change the club's policy again without letting me know?"

"What do you care, as long as we're turning a profit?" she demands.

"You're right, I don't. But I still want to know why you need two SUVs to come to work."

He's still talking to her but his gaze stays on me. Direct. Non-threatening but the promise is there. In fucking bucket loads. I let loose a feral smile of my own, close the gap between us, and hold out my hand. "Killian Knight. That's probably my fault."

"Axel Rutherford." We shake hands, and his eyes narrow after a beat. "You're the tech guy who invented that thing…What was it? A super-microchip?"

I nod. We lock imaginary horns for a few more seconds, and I get the feeling my other skills are not unknown to him. After another beat, he cocks his head at Faith, still without taking his eyes off me. "Does she belong to you?"

Her face stiffens, and her cheeks flush adorably. "What the fuck, Axel?"

My lips twitch. Okay, so maybe I won't devise ways to destroy Axel Rutherford just yet. "I belong to her. It's easier for both of us if we put it that way."

Axel's shrug suggests he considers it the same difference. I don't argue with that. We study each other a moment longer before he focuses his attention properly on Faith. Whatever he senses makes his jaw flex. "Everything okay?" he bites out.

I hold my breath. She toys with her bottom lip for a bit. "I need to take some time off."

Axel folds his arms. "Hell, no. Request denied."

I shove my hands into my pockets so no one sees them ball into fists. Throwing punches will only delay us getting out of here. "She wasn't really asking," I say, very much aware my voice is granite-hard.

Axel's gaze swings back to me. "Wasn't she? I could've sworn—"

"Since no one's bothered to introduce me, I'm Cleo McCarthy." The brunette rises from the sofa and joins us, smiling at Faith.

"Sorry, Cleo," Faith mutters. "I seem to be caught in the middle of a dick-measuring contest."

Cleo attempts a smile, but it doesn't quite make it through the strain on her face. "Trust me, I get it. I was hoping to see you today." Axel's gaze swings to Cleo, locks, and stays. The look they exchange is furnace-hot but charged with something volatile. Whatever's going on between Axel and his lover—and I have no doubt they are—neither of them are giving a quarter.

Kinda like what is going down in my own life.

"Yeah, something came up."

Cleo nods. "Yes, Axel told me. Well, I'd love to have another lunch sometime."

Faith bites her lip, and Axel's gaze sharpens.

"Leave her be, Cleo," he drawls. "Looks like she's got bigger problems to deal with."

Faith glares at him. "I can speak for myself, thanks." She turns back to Cleo. "Not sure when I can. I'll call and let you know, okay?"

Cleo nods, and even though she tenses a little when her gaze flicks to Axel, she smiles again. "Of course."

Faith glances between them and frowns. "Is everything okay between you two?"

"Mind your own business, B," Axel replies.

She rolls her eyes. "Cleo?"

"We were having a...disagreement," Cleo says.

Axel smiles. "Not true. We were done disagreeing. She'd just seen the error of her ways and was just about to make friends again. Weren't you, sweetheart?"

"In your dreams," Cleo snaps, but I feel the charged longing behind her words.

"Since my dreams are all about you, too fucking right."

Thick silence settles over the room.

I clear my throat. "Can we move this along?"

Axel's gaze stays on her for another moment, and then he nods. "Now that that's settled, sure. You were saying?" he drawls to no one in particular.

"Leave of absence. Unspecified length of time. Starting right now," I repeat.

Axel rounds his desk and hitches one thigh over the corner. "Hell of a time to drop this on me, B."

I try not to grit my teeth and realize I'm still not okay with the name he's calling her. "It wasn't planned," I offer. "But it can't be helped."

He absorbs that and shrugs. "Well, if she belongs to you and you need to do this, then—"

"I swear to God, you say that again, and I'll punch your lights out," Faith snaps.

Enough of this shit. I walk up behind her and slide my hand under her hair to cover her nape. "You. Belong. To. Me. We're doing this. Deal with it and let's get it done," I growl in her ear. "We're wasting time as it is."

Her lips part but she doesn't say anything. After a moment, she exhales softly. I give her a quick squeeze, let go, and step back.

Axel's brows spike, and he shakes his head. "Fuck me, I never thought I'd see the day."

Faith throws him a glare. "Oh, whatever. Screw you, Axel."

He rises and strolls over to his girlfriend. He stares down at her for a moment, drifts a finger over her mouth, and then turns around. "Fine, if you need to go, go. I have things to do, especially now that you've dropped this pile of crap in my lap."

"Don't be melodramatic. You'll barely notice I'm gone."

"You're a fucking pain in my ass, B, but I'll notice," he says.

Now that I have evidence that Axel is obsessed with another woman who *isn't* Faith, I choose not to let his words affect me too much.

"Jade will step in until you get one of the managers from your other clubs to fill in. The one at Viper Red should be fine," she says.

I raise my eyebrow. "Jade?" I ask, although I don't give a fuck who Jade is. But information is king, and gathering intel, no matter how useless it seems, is ingrained in me. Besides, I'm still one hundred percent sure that Faith is keeping something from me, so every fact is vital.

"She's the receptionist downstairs. She's started filling in on my days off, and she's been great so far. I see no reason why she can't step in for now."

Axel nods, but his gaze and hands are moving over Cleo. "Great. Glad that's sorted. Now if you'll excuse me…"

"One more thing." I look at her but Faith hesitates. "Tell him, baby."

Axel gives us his attention. "Tell me what?"

She holds up the thumb drives. "I also came to give you a heads-up that I'm taking a copy of the client list with me. And the list of the applicants whose membership we refused."

Axel doesn't seem particularly disturbed by the news, but his hands drop and his gaze turns vigilant. "Okay…what the hell do you need that for?"

I shake my head before she can speak. "We'd rather not say. But it's important that we have it. All of it."

Charged silence pulses in the room. It's to his credit that he judges the situation and gets what's at stake. Not that it would've mattered in the long run. Hacking the club's database will be child's play if Axel decides he wants to be precious about it. But it's easier and time efficient if we don't have to.

"Fine," he says. He reaches into his pocket, takes out a card, and holds it out to me. "If you need anything else, give me a call."

I take it from him. "Thanks. If I can ever return the favor, let me know."

Axel strolls forward and stops in front of Faith. Everything inside me tenses. He fucking better not be thinking about doing anything like touching her. Or, hell, kissing her. His eyes narrow on her face for a moment. "Take care of yourself."

She nods.

He turns to me. "Anything happens to her, I'll fuck you up."

Okay, fair enough. "Anything happens to her, I'll let you."

"Oh my God. How the hell do you hear yourselves over all this chest thumping?" Faith snaps. I almost feel sorry for her. Almost, because I know I'll pay for the testosterone bombs we're throwing around her. "If you're done with the bromance and the cock swinging, I'm going to leave now," she snaps impatiently.

Axel opens his mouth.

She holds up her hand. "You better not be about to use pansy-assed words on me, Axel."

"Fine. Get the hell out of my office, B."

She looks over at Cleo, and, contrary to her sharp words to Axel, Faith's face softens for a moment. They share a smile, and she turns and leaves the room. I follow her back into her office. As suspected, she gives me the cold shoulder as she unlocks a safe built into the wall and grabs whatever else she needs. When I hold out my hand, she silently hands over the thumb drives, and her gaze sweeps over the office.

"How much longer do you need to stay? Do you need to do anything else?"

She shrugs. "No. I can leave anytime I want."

"Well, let's make that right fucking now, shall we?"

Perhaps she's putting a brave face on it, but I'm still disturbed that she doesn't throw so much as a fond, lingering look at the room before we walk out and she shuts the door behind her.

Was that how easy it was for her to walk away from me in Cairo? One moment she was unconscious, hooked up to machines with her life hanging in the balance. The next she was gone. The hours I spent wondering if she was dead were the worst of my life. The faintest trail in the form of missing funds from our joint agency expense account was the only way I knew she'd planned to leave me.

The discovery that she'd planned her exit meticulously left me stunned for days. It's the reason I know I can't let down my guard around her.

Her gaze slides to mine as we enter the elevator. Whatever she sees in my face makes her avert her eyes.

We stop at the bar to collect a stoic-looking Mitch and Linc. Five minutes later we're back in the SUV.

"I want to go back to my apartment," she says.

I shake my head. "Not gonna happen. Your security is shit."

She glares icy fire at me. "My security is absolutely fine."

"How do you know? Has it ever been tested?"

She frowns and shakes her head.

"Your surveillance is pretty adequate, I'll give you that, but all it'll take is a good kick to that front door of yours and it's over. So, no, you're not going back there. Besides, we're not living in two separate apartments. Not while there's a threat out there. Once this is all over, we can discuss it."

She exhales long and slow. "Fine. What about my things?"

"Already taken care of."

Her eyes widen. "What?"

"I said—"

"I heard what you said, Killian. I'm just wondering if we're going to make it to tomorrow without me severely maiming you."

I smile for the first time since we left the club. I feel a little lighter. But I'm pretty certain that's not going to last very long when the vehicle bounces over a pothole and her body moves suggestively with it. The sight of leather and lace against her skin is driving me nuts. "You're more than welcome to try."

She catches the change in my voice and swallows. "How…" She clears her throat. "How wide are you going to search for Galveston?"

I let her change the subject pulsing between us. For now. "He went straight to his father's house in Georgetown when he landed. So Galveston Senior is still very much involved. How deep is yet to be determined. We already know there's a connection between the contracts he brokered for his son to start delivering aid to Africa and the trafficking picking up sharply. But the Galveston family has doubled its airline outfitting business in the last two years. So it could be they don't need the shipping angle any longer. We never managed to get any actual eyes on what the insides of the planes look like, so we don't know if they're building secret compartments to transport their cargo or whether they're bribing officials to look away. Or both."

Her brows pleat. "We're talking officials from over a dozen countries. That's a hellish undertaking to check everything."

After a beat, I nod. "Yes." It hasn't escaped me that asking my supercomputer to do all this searching is a monumental task. Not to mention the fact that the human angle is vital for any investigation. Without boots on the ground, there is only so much we can achieve.

I reflect on that as we arrive at my apartment building and head up in the elevator. Mitch and Linc come with us but step out one floor below.

She raises her eyebrows but doesn't ask for an explanation, and I don't give her one. She walks out ahead of me when we exit the elevator. The way she sways her hips and deliberately drums her fingers on her thighs as she waits for me to open the door tells me I'm getting a little payback for what happened in Axel's office. I'm mildly sweating by the time I disable the alarms and let us into the apartment.

"I'm going to change," she says the moment we walk in.

"I think that's a good idea," I reply as I cross over to the bar. "Can I fix you a drink?" I throw over my shoulder.

She gives a slow, uncertain shake of her head, and a tiny twitch of puzzlement crosses her face. I suspect she's feeling a little off-kilter. Well, I'm feeling like my balls are about to fall off from the constant pressure she's putting them under. So, I guess we're equal.

Her footsteps fade away as I pour a shot of Hine, knock it back, and pour another. This one I nurse as I walk to the wide window and look out over the stunning view of New York City at night. I shove my hand into my pocket and encounter Axel's business card. I take it out and stare at it. There's no job title or business address, just his name and telephone number embossed in gold on a black background.

The man's military history isn't a secret. Combined with his family's mob history and the kind of work he does now, he'll probably be the right person to sort out our manpower issue. And if he partnered with Faith for four years without once questioning her background, then he most likely can be trusted to be discreet.

I return the card to my pocket. Something to think about, maybe, but not right now. The other items in my pocket, the thumb drives, demand priority. I take another sip of cognac and head to my study. I download the information and feed it into my specialized search code, expanding the parameters to include every possible scenario I can think of.

Then I sit back in my chair, rolling the glass between my fingers. I don't want to go to bed. Not without her. And with her in a pissy mood, it's going to be a fucking long night.

My cock doesn't get the message though. It throbs and jumps when she appears in the doorway. She's still wearing those fucking control-shredding leather pants, but the lace top and corset have been swapped for a white tank top. Without a fucking bra. Jesus.

The memory of her gorgeous breasts in my hands, of her luscious nipples in my mouth, is as vivid as ever.

She nods at the monitor. "Anything?"

I shake my head without taking my eyes off her tits. Even from across the room I can see her nipples reacting to my scrutiny.

She walks over, rounds the desk to my side, and sets her tight little ass down on the edge of it. Her body doesn't brush mine, but my every sense is attuned to her. She reaches over and plucks the glass from my hand and takes a delicate little sip.

"You're in a mood for payback. I can tell," I mutter, my tongue thickening just from the smell of her skin.

Her eyes gleam green fire at me but she doesn't answer. She takes another sip and slowly glides her tongue over her lower lip.

"Which part upset you most?" I press. The earlier we get my sins out in the open, the quicker I can get my punishment.

"Oh, let's see. The whole 'you belong to me' thing."

I nod. "Okay. Anything else?"

"The general taking-over part."

"I see."

"Oh, and the not believing me about Axel bit too. That ticked me off big-time."

"Uh-huh."

She sets my glass down and traces the lip with her forefinger while staring at me with one eyebrow cocked. After a minute, her eyes narrow. "Well?"

"What, sweetheart?" I ask gently.

"Don't you have anything to say?"

I rescue my glass from her finger-seduction and down the rest of the shot. "Sorry I didn't believe you about Rutherford."

Her cute little chin juts out. "That's it?"

"I'm not going to apologize for telling him that you belong to me. You do. Just as I'm yours. You just don't like hearing it."

She huffs out a breath. "And why do you think that is?"

I shrug. "I could tell you but you'd just get madder at me. And I *really* want to get on your good side."

My gaze, drawn like magnets, returns to her tits and the saucy pebbles of her nipples. She allows me to watch for a couple of minutes before she stands and paces a few steps to the window.

Her body framed against the glass like that, and with her back to me, I can't help but stare some more, at her ass cradled by the skintight leather. My breath hisses out and my cock strains against my fly. Christ, I'm definitely going to need to jack off if I have any hope of sleeping tonight. For a second, I contemplate the to-hell-with-it approach to getting inside her, but then I remind myself that, even though it feels like a fucking decade, she's been back in my life for just over twenty-four hours.

She raises her arms above her head and rises up on her toes in a slow feline stretch. Then her fingers sink into her hair. She plays with the silky strands, twisting and bunching them before she shakes the heavy weight down her back. The ends fall precisely on the rise of her sweet butt and pull my gaze back to that part of her body and that naughty little triangle between her legs.

Still perched on her tiptoes, she slowly swivels around to face me, displaying her supple body in all its curved and sleek glory.

My fingers grip the armrests. Saliva fills my mouth, and my whole body throbs with raging need. "Baby…" My voice is a hoarse plea.

She looks over, eyes at half-mast, and she gives me a bored yawn. "I'm going to bed. Good night, Killian."

My head slams back against the seat, and I shut my eyes. "Fuck." Five minutes after she's gone, I'm still breathing like I've run a damn marathon. I've debated with myself, tried reasoning with my steel-hard cock to no avail. My fingers fumble with my fly. I'm ready to give myself some desperately needed relief when Betty cock-blocks me with a series of sweet chirps from her mainframe.

I drag my eyes open and stare at the screen. At first I'm not sure what I'm looking at. And then it becomes clear.

Fucking hell.

Chapter Fourteen

B

I have no one to blame but myself for not being able to sleep. I could've taken the high road. Or ignored everything Killian said in Axel's office.

Instead, I had to goad him. Now I lie in bed, the ache between my thighs an ever-expanding balloon of agonizing need that shrieks for attention. I toss onto my side, the other reason for my insomnia staring me in the face.

I left my box back at the club. I couldn't very well retrieve it with Killian dogging my every footstep, hovering closer than my shadow. And since I don't know if or when I'll be returning, the anxiety that's been eating away at me is escalating.

I toyed with calling Axel when I came to my room earlier, but after witnessing the nauseating male bonding between him and Killian, I can't trust that he won't let something slip if they ever meet again.

An instant later, a twinge of discomfort snags at me for distrusting him. He trusted me enough to let me take care of him when he visited his punishment room. I trusted him enough to let him look in on me when I visited mine, although I haven't done that for a long time now. I've allowed other people's need for absolution to suppress my own, despite my every intention of keeping the box close so that I'd have a constant reminder. Since I spend...spent more time at the club than at my own apartment, I thought it better to just leave it there.

Now, the possibility that I might not have it close for a while burns me with acid guilt. It's what propels me out of bed at four in the morning when I finally give up hope of sleeping. I need to get it back.

I grab my phone and send Axel a quick text.

He's already awake or my message has woken him. Either probability doesn't please him.

Axel: Can you tell the time, B?

My anxiety is too high for me to indulge in our usual derisive banter.

Me: My box from my room on the sixth floor. I need it delivered. Discreetly.

The bubbling cloud shows he's replying to my message.

Axel: Sure. Name time and place for delivery.

Relief punches through me.

Me: Thank you. I'll let you know. I owe you.

Axel: Lunch with Cleo when you're done sorting your shit out. For some insane reason, she likes you.

Me: Deal.

With that taken care of, I smile a little to myself as I put away my phone. Axel is much farther gone about Cleo than he lets on. What I know of his baggage suggests it's as heavy as mine. But he's dealing with it. Whereas I vacuum-packed my guilt, swapped sensible Mary Janes for fuck-me Louboutins, and very rarely looked back until the past slammed into me three weeks ago.

Shit, something else I need to tell Killian.

I turn over, and the sheets tangle between my legs. With one problem taken care of, Killian is front and center of my mind. And in front and center of that is the memory of the erection tenting his pants when I left his study. The thing was fucking huge. Gloriously ready and available. I felt actual pain when I shut the door behind me. The slickness between my legs now tells me I'll be feeling it for a long time.

Unless I give in. Take what he claims is mine. The temptation is unrelenting. But what I fear more than fucking Killian again is becoming addicted to the *us* that should never have been in the first place.

I lost everything even before we hooked up the first time.

I lost what little was left when I went off script and severely jeopardized our mission. Killian doesn't know it, but I have nothing left to give.

We thought we covered our tracks well when I packed my bags the day after Matt's funeral and claimed I needed time and distance. But my friends and family knew. Disapproval turned into harsh judgment. Then into rejection. I didn't give a shit. High on my giddy little adventure, I flipped everyone that mattered the bird on my way to my new, exciting life. And even broken and battered as I am now, I don't think I want to go back. That part of my life is behind me. Besides, I don't deserve forgiveness. I'm irreparably altered, and I can't bear to see the evidence of that change in others' eyes.

The last time I saw my mother, she stared at me with sad, condemning eyes. "It's a mercy your sister isn't here. She always looked up to you. God knows what she would think of you and what you're doing now."

I didn't tell my mother Julia was partly the reason I embraced my new life. But I hated my mother for saying that. Because I would give anything for Julia to be alive, just so she would learn from my example and not make the same mistakes.

Thoughts of my sister propel me from bed and out of the bedroom. I'm still wearing my tank top and panties, and I don't stop to throw on any more clothes. It's a reckless little move with guilt and temptation flowing in my blood like the headiest drug. But fuck it. My damned soul could do with being a little more damned. Maybe then I'll embrace my doom and get some actual sleep.

I hear the rapid clacking of a keyboard, and I don't hesitate to push the study door open. The light from the monitor reflects his stupidly gorgeous face. Although it's clear he hasn't been to bed yet, or his night has been as shitty as mine.

He looks as wrung dry as I feel. Against my will, my earlier irritation over his possessiveness dissolves. Yes, I want to fuck the living shit out of him, but I also want to cradle him in my arms, caress his forehead with soothing fingers, and watch him sleep the way I used to. But then his eyes meet mine. And tension whistles through me.

"Hey."

"Hey," he responds. Sizzling blue eyes take in my semi-naked body before returning my gaze. The memory of his hoarse plea from earlier rams into me. But I can tell the mood is gone for him. Or at least temporarily cloaked by something else. I find out a second later.

"While you were sleeping Betty coughed up something else. Anything you wanna tell me?"

I frown, start to shake my head, and then grimace. Damn. Busted. "Maybe."

He exhales and drags his hands down his face in that calming technique that tells me he's fighting the need to punch something. "Baby, you're really testing my last nerve—"

"Okay! She found me."

"Just so we're clear, who found you?"

"Fionnella Smith. Or at least that's what she calls herself now." An innocuous name that hides so much more.

Killian snorts. "Do you mean who I think you mean?"

I nod.

He cracks a hint of a smile. "She always had a warped sense of humor."

"I didn't think it was funny."

"I know, baby."

My heart jerks at the endearment, and I hate myself for loving it so much. "I wish you'd stop that," I grumble. Just because.

"I can't help it," he says simply, the same way he did when he stated earlier that I belonged to him. Killian's possessiveness is in-grained. Sometimes I wonder why I bother fighting it.

"Try," I suggest, perhaps a little desperately.

He just stares at me. His eyes tell me he doesn't want to, and my heart drops a little because I know in that moment I'm in deep trou-ble. That's always been our problem. We couldn't help ourselves, and, ultimately, we didn't want to. We discovered our weaknesses in each other, and we ruthlessly exploited them.

"How did she find you?"

"She called me a month ago, on my cell. Then, three weeks ago, she just turned up at the club." I don't mention Cairo and what Fionnella did for me that day. It has nothing to do with what's hap-pening now. I hope.

"Fuck."

"Yeah. Who the hell is she, really? What's her role at Fallhurst?" When I first met the woman calling herself Fionnella Smith, I thought she was a handler. But she wasn't. None of the team knew what her true role was. Or those who did weren't prepared to di-vulge it.

"I asked a couple of times. I was stonewalled. I stopped asking."

"And she didn't tell you who she was?"

Killian shakes his head, a wry smile curving his lips. "I was too busy playing the nerd to be concerned too much about her name. Plus her evasion tactics are legendary."

I shudder. "She scares me with all that smiling and all that...joy."

Killian chuckles. "Yeah, her boundless joy scares me too."

We share a grin. His gaze drops down my body. His eyes heat up, and the laughter evaporates.

"This was important. And you didn't tell me," he accuses with a low, deep voice after a moment.

A tide of guilt rises inside me, and I shift my gaze to a point over his shoulder.

"Look at me."

I clench my gut hard before I can comply with his command.

"You said Axel knows who she is?" he asks.

I shrug. "Well, she was there to meet with him. If they knew each other beforehand, they were pretending otherwise that day."

"You know why she came to see him?"

I hesitate. I don't want to breach Axel's trust.

"Faith…"

Every time he says that name…*my* name like that, it's like a lightning rod to my system. A jolt designed to drag me back to who I was. Who I can never be. "Dammit, don't keep calling me that—"

"I'm not going to call you 'B,'" he says with a finality edged in steel. "Your name is Faith. You'll always be Faith to me. End of story. Now tell me why she was there to see Axel."

"He has his own punishment room. He has his own ghosts. I think she was there to help him slay a few of them."

He stares at me for several seconds and then nods. "Did you ask him how he knew her?"

I frown. "I told you. We don't have that sort of relationship."

He sighs. "Okay, we'll assume that was what she was there for, but why did she call you before?"

"She didn't tell me," I reply.

Cobalt-blue eyes hook into me. "She didn't tell you, or you didn't give her a chance to?"

I've entertained that possibility since the nightmare started unfolding yesterday. But Fionnella, as sprightly and maternal as her demeanor conveys, was always a nebulous character. And the impression she left with me, that I owed her one after Cairo, has always lingered in the back of my mind, although it was never vocally expressed. I'm not ashamed to admit that her phone call out of the blue triggered wild panic. And that head-in-the-sand position I adopted is biting me in the ass now.

"I didn't give her the chance to," I admit to Killian.

He nods, accepting my explanation without censure. And something soft and vulnerable gives way inside me. God, it's not fair, what he does to me.

I leave the doorway and walk closer to him, even though the

more sensible thing would be to go back to my room and put more clothes on. "How did you find out?"

"I got Betty to back trace surveillance in the streets around the club. There's footage of her around the time you mentioned. She wasn't trying to evade the cameras." He stares at the picture on the screen and shakes his head. "Although, fuck me, what the hell is she wearing?"

I join him at the desk and stare at the familiar figure on the monitor. "Yeah, she turned up looking like a bag lady. I think she gets a kick out of it."

He relaxes in his seat. "You didn't happen to keep the number she called you on, did you?"

I shake my head. "Nope, there was no caller ID. And since I didn't want her to reach me in the first place, I didn't ask for her number. I even disposed of my phone and bought another one the next day to make it more difficult for her." A wasted effort, it turned out. My eyes narrow. "Are you thinking of contacting her?"

He shrugs. "I don't want to waste time on her if she's not pertinent to what's happening now."

"But…you think she is." It's not a question.

Another shrug. "I have a feeling we'll find out soon enough."

Chapter Fifteen

B/FAITH

We stare at the monitor for another few seconds, and then my gaze shifts to the one on the far left. There's a picture of Paul Galveston on one side of the screen, and an image-recognition software program running on the other. Behind the images, lines of code race up in dizzying motion.

Poor Betty is working her digital fingers to the bone.

My gaze darts to Galveston, and I can't stop the shiver that races through me. Killian's fingers trace down my lower arm to circle my wrist.

"Hey, we're going to get through this shit. Okay?"

Although I nod, I can't look away from the screen. The memory of aiming my weapon, and squeezing the trigger, rises up like an unstoppable nightmare before my eyes. I should've gone for a head shot, the way I'd been trained to. Why the hell didn't I?

Because when it came to it, I wasn't a killer? I silently shake my head.

From the first moment I stepped into the gunroom at the Fallhurst Institute, I felt at home. Cradling my first gun turned me on. The power. The danger. I've blocked it all out. But now the stinging memory returns. "Am I a horrible person, Killian?"

He jerks in surprise. "What?"

I wrap my arms around my middle and move away to the window. My unsettled gaze bounces over the skyline before I turn back to him. He's swiveled around in his chair and is watching me. "I shot him, and I didn't even feel bad."

His beautiful eyes turn to ice chips. "Why the fuck should you feel bad for defending yourself against an asshole who was coming at you with the intention of doing you harm? Who ended up doing you harm?"

I shake my head. "But I shot him. In the chest. I watched him bleeding out. We were in the middle of a fucking desert. How is he still alive?" I know my questions are irrational, but I can't help myself.

"The motherfucker stabbed you. You'd lost a lot of blood and were struggling to stay conscious. Your aim was probably off. You can't blame yourself."

My gaze veers away but I still feel his slowly trace down my body. A minute passes.

"Show me the scar," he says thickly.

I freeze, and my heart starts hammering. "What?"

"At the hospital, they said they were having a hard time stopping the bleeding because your wound was deep. It was why you slipped into the coma. I've never seen it. Will you show it to me?"

I shake my head. "It's not very pretty." And it's intensely personal. More than he will ever know.

"I have some not very pretty ones too. Let's compare," he tosses out jokingly. Except I know it's not a joke. The look in his eyes is deadly serious.

This is my cue to leave. Return to the safety of my bedroom. "You first," I murmur.

He immediately pulls his T-shirt off, leans forward, and points to the inch-wide raised scar on his lower back.

"I know that one," I say. A shallow knife wound sustained in a back-alley fight in Croatia on his second assignment. I have caressed it many times while I explored his body. Kissed it while he slept.

"Come here," he says. I walk over to him. He takes my hand and guides it to the base of his skull. He holds my finger against a raised three-inch bump. "Stitches from a tire iron that wanted to be intimate with my brain. From a guy whose truck I tried to steal when I got stranded in Minsk. He wasn't very happy."

My lips twitch, but the smile doesn't quite make it. "You're a billionaire who invented a chip to make rockets go faster or something. You didn't think to just buy the truck?"

He shrugs. "He wouldn't take a bank transfer or my Audemars Piguet watch, which he thought was fake. Carrying cash on that op wasn't really encouraged, so my options were limited. It was steal the truck or walk fifteen miles to the nearest rendezvous point in three feet of snow. I chose door number one. Turns out I wasn't great at hot-wiring a vehicle in the middle of a blizzard."

My fingers trace the scar. "When did it happen?"

He hesitates before answering. "Two years ago."

I've thought about it over the years, whether he continued being an operative or not. I even imagined him with other partners. Other women. I'm not sure how I feel about having the confirmation.

As if he reads my mind, his gaze tracks and snags mine. "It was supposed to be an easy, solo, two-day mission. In and out, picking up a laptop a team member was forced to leave behind when they had to get out quickly. The data on the laptop was too important. I was in the mood for a change of scene so I offered to go."

He doesn't owe me any explanation. But fuck if the tightness in my chest doesn't ease with relief. My fingers drift over the scar and over his warm scalp. I continue to gently massage, the joy of running my fingers through his hair a hypnotic pleasure I can't seem to stop.

When my fist slowly clenches around a thick clump, he makes a sound under his breath.

"Baby, you know we're not going to last much longer like this, don't you?" he says in a guttural, barely discernible voice.

"Yes," I answer simply. Because every second since that moment in the park last night has been leading up to this. It was the first thing that terrified me when I heard his voice. It's what terrifies me now as I use my hold on him to tilt his head.

Our eyes meet. His upper body is bare. I know every inch of it. "Show me more."

A definitive shake of his head. "No, it's your turn."

"I have only one."

"Then show me something else. We can get to that last if you want."

My breath catches. This is happening.

I trail my fingers through his hair, taking my time to rake my nails along his scalp before drawing them down his neck and across his wide shoulder.

He hisses under his breath, and his eyes drift shut for a moment, as if he's absorbing and imprinting this contact into the very fiber of his being.

I love touching Killian. Something happens to me when we touch. It's a chemical thing that defies logic. So I don't fight it. He lets me play, down over his chest, between the crevices created by his impressive six-pack. He hasn't let himself go in the last four years. Not one little bit. Sleek muscles bunch beneath my fingers, and I actually feel him shake the lower I go.

"Stop fucking torturing me, baby. Show me what I want to see," he growls, his urgent demand hot against my cheek.

My hands reluctantly fall from his body. I shouldn't feel this mild panic about undressing in front of him. But I'm suddenly nervous about exposing myself completely to him. Perhaps I know that there will be no turning back this time. No abbreviated session we can fool ourselves into thinking doesn't really count. Or maybe it's that little nugget of doubt that suggests he won't like this new, thinner, maybe lesser, version of me.

But then I look down into his eyes, and all I see is the same out-of-control fire that's raging inside of me.

"Now, baby."

I go to draw my top over my head, but at the last moment, I change my mind. Instead I pull my arm through one strap and then the other. I don't deny that the slide of the cotton against my skin turns me on. I hook my fingers in the bunched-up fabric and slowly pull it down over my breasts. Lower lip caught between my teeth, I hold my breath and raise my head.

One look is all it takes to reassure me that Killian is as turned on by this version of me as he was by the old version. "Move your hair over your shoulder, let me see you properly," he commands.

Even the act of shoving my hair over my shoulders turns me on.

When my top half is fully exposed to him, he rolls his chair closer and settles his hands on either side of my hips. His face is level with my breasts, and his fevered eyes are riveted on my hard pink nipples.

"Fuck, they're even more beautiful than I remember."

"My girls?" I shakily joke.

"My beauties," he rasps. Keeping his hands on the desk, he leans forward and gently blows on one nipple. The sensation powers down my body straight to my pussy. He repeats the action on the other peak, and I feel myself getting wetter.

"God, you're exquisite. So goddamn beautiful." The reverence in his voice is so deep and pure it draws a helpless moan from my throat. "I'm going to taste you now. Would you like that?"

I inhale, and my head bobs in an eager nod.

Hot blue eyes dart from my chest to my face, his avid gaze absorbing my every reaction. "Lean forward, baby. Squeeze your tits together with your arms for me."

My heart flutters wildly as I comply. His request is a new one to me. In the past, he liked me to cup them for him. Now they feel extra-heavy, extra-sensitive as he moves that last excruciating inch and draws his tongue across one tight nub. We both groan. My eyes squeeze shut, and I feel like I'm drowning in fiery pleasure as he begins to lap at me. His tongue and my nipple are the only points of contact, and that is the most incredible, spine-melting feeling.

"Killian," I sigh, unable to stop myself from articulating what he's doing to me.

"So good, baby. So fucking good," he growls around my nipple.

He transfers his attention to my other needy breast and creates the same insane magic before sucking it hard into his mouth. My ass grinds on the desk, my pussy desperate for relief against the ache clamoring deep inside.

I throw my head back, eager for more of what he's doing. The helpless noises rising from my throat trigger an insane reaction in him. His ministrations turn even more ravenous, the suction on my flesh turning almost painful as he gorges on me. As the moan rips through me, and my hips undulate faster.

"Are you fucking my desk, sweetheart? If I keep doing what I'm doing, are you going to come all over it?"

He shouldn't be able to make me blush. The things we've done with each other, to each other, should erase all embarrassment. And yet heat flows up my neck into my face. Because I feel like I'm on the edge. As if another swipe of his wicked tongue will set me off.

He pulls back a little and stares at me with wild eyes. "I asked you a question. Your body's on fire, and you're pumping those hips in that fast way you do when you're so close. Should I keep kissing your gorgeous tits? Do you want to come on my desk or on my cock?" he asks as he swipes his tongue between my squeezed-together breasts.

I have to swallow a couple of times before I can answer. "On…on your cock."

He groans long and deep. "Shit. That means we need to relocate. And…I don't want to. Not just yet." He turns his head to the side and sucks hard on one nipple.

Pleasure rains sweet fire on me. "Oh God!" The balloon of craving between my thighs threatens to burst wide open. The heavy petting against his front door yesterday barely took the edge off my insane need. It's building up again, wilder, fiercer. I know it's going to annihilate me. "Please…"

"Does it hurt, sweetheart?" he whispers hotly against my skin, and even the hot puff of his breath threatens to send me over the edge.

Desperate, I squeeze my thighs together. "Yes!"

He stands and yanks me off his desk. My eager arms and legs circle his shoulders and hips. He stumbles when my hot sex snuggles his rigid cock.

"Jesus!" His forehead rests against mine, and he breathes deep. When he raises his head, his face is a mask of barely-held-together control. "Hang on just a little longer, sweetheart. I'm not going to fucking blow my load propped up against the wall like a damn schoolboy this time. Much as I loved that hand job, the next time I taste heaven again will be in that tight, beautiful pussy."

"Hurry. Please. I need you so much."

His face slackens with an emotion that scrapes me raw deep in my heart. "God, Faith, I've waited so damn long to hear that." His voice is filled with pain and joy, longing and hell.

I bury my face in his neck when he starts to move again. My eyes prickle, scaring me even more…throwing me back to the last time I truly wept. That memory has no place here, and yet where else can it belong but right here, between the two people who created it, even if one of them has no clue about it?

My heart squeezes as I hug my secret close.

My baby.

The precious child I lost when Paul Galveston drove a knife through my womb.

A sound rips through the room. Battered. Mournful. A wounded animal in its death throes. It's torn from what remains of my soul.

Killian stops dead in his tracks. "Faith? What—?"

I shamelessly rub my damp sex against him. "Don't stop. Please. The bed, Killian. Take us to bed."

The scent of my arousal explodes between us. His breath shudders free, and he resumes walking. He can't see me like this, so I call on every ounce of composure I can find. The moment we reach the bedroom, I spike my fingers through his hair and fuse my mouth to his. More than an eager participant, he devours my lips as he makes a beeline for the bed.

The landing isn't smooth or sophisticated. We tangle and roll and fight not to break contact. His teeth nip at me, and my nails dig in where they land. I'm still wearing panties, my top is bunched around my waist, and he's still wearing his pants. To undress we need to separate. Neither of us wants to.

"Sorry, sweetheart," he mumbles against my lips.

"What...?"

The sound of my panties ripping answers my question. He pulls the tattered scrap of satin from me without breaking our kiss. A soft rush of air between my pussy lips sends a shiver of anticipation through me. He rolls us over so I'm on top and growls against my lips, "Unzip me, baby."

I don't need a second prompt. My shaking hands delay the task a little longer than I want, but it helps that he doesn't have boxers or briefs on beneath. His cock springs up, hot and heavy, and oh so gloriously hard into my hands. We both groan as I eagerly pump him from root to tip.

He finally tears his mouth from mine to grip my shoulders and hold me a little distance from him. We both look down at what I'm doing to him. "Christ, you do that so good," he says through clenched teeth.

"You feel amazing."

"And you look insanely gorgeous. And hungry. Do you want me?" he demands raggedly.

"Dying, Killian. I'm dying for you."

"Show me," he responds.

I nudge him between my thighs and tease his length with my wet sex. We both shudder. He looks up into my eyes, and we accept that we're at the breaking point.

"Inside, darling. Put me inside you now," he pleads.

"Yes."

He holds me up, his strength effortlessly sexy, and I position him against my core. He releases me, and I sink down, sheathing him tight and hot and spine-meltingly magnificent.

There are no words to describe the alchemy of our coming together. No words to express the bruising perfection of Killian's thick cock inside me. So we don't bother to find them. We stare deep into each other's eyes, breath suspended, absorbing the awe and majesty of it. Beneath me, he trembles from head to toe. My hands frame his face, his jaw, his neck before, unable to resist, I lower my mouth to his.

His hands finds my hips, lock me down, and he pistons inside me with a superb roll of his hips. We're both shameless voyeurs, finding indecent pleasure in watching what our bodies do to each other. So, inevitably, we part again to stare at the perfect synchrony of pussy and cock.

"I've dreamed of having you like this again, watching you take my cock with your beautiful tits bouncing in my face." He tilts his head up and catches one nipple in his mouth. "God, I'm fucking these tits the first chance I get. Then I'm eating your sublime cunt again. After that, that tight ass you've been torturing me with is mine."

Everything I crave. "You sound like you have a list in mind," I gasp through the thrusts.

"You have no fucking idea." The words are a strained mess, punctuated by vicious thrusts inside me. Each one knocks the breath out of me and shoves ecstasy into me. I knew I wouldn't last long. And while I mourn it being over for me way too soon, the storm approaching is one I've waited so long for. I want to be drenched to my very marrow. Then wrung completely dry. "Killian…"

He catches the warning in my voice. He kicks his pants away, and with a twist of his body, rolls me over onto my back. Muscle memory kicks in, and I raise my legs just as he shoves his arms beneath them. My butt is elevated off the bed and the next thrust drills into me, sparking stars across my vision.

"Killian!"

"Jesus!" His jaw is clenched tight, and sweat beads his forehead.

Fire races up from my toes, and I let loose the scream scrambling through my vocal cords. His thrusts turn lightning fast and drive me up the headboard. When my head begins to bang against the wood, I don't give a shit.

I'm coming. Dear God, I don't think I'll survive the aftermath.

"You will. It'll be fucking earth-shattering. But you will, baby. And it'll be so good. I promise."

My eyes widen when I realize I spoke the words aloud.

I see his strained smile. And then my eyes roll. Bliss, unstrained and blindingly powerful, surges through me. My cunt spasms with extra-enthusiastic vigor.

Above me, Killian tenses. "Fuck, you grip me so tight! Shit, I can't hold on," he gasps, and then I feel his lips brush mine. "Open your eyes, beautiful. I need you to watch with me."

I drag my eyes open, watch his cock push inside my eager pussy, and ripple through my orgasms. Each time he emerges slicker, our pleasure is heightened. He supports me with the sheer strength of his lower body, keeping us locked together as we fuck each other straight into paradise.

We collapse back onto the bed in a mass of boneless limbs, incoherent words, and cum. He gathers me into his arms, and I drape myself over him, spent and useless.

After an age of gliding his hand through my hair, Killian exhales heavily. "God, Faith, that was beyond beautiful."

I nod around the panic creeping into my heart.

His other hand drifts down my back. And encounters my top. He chuckles. "We never got around to taking this off."

"Hmm."

"Let's take care of that now."

A thought attempts to shove its way through my sex-hazed brain. But it never makes it. Killian pushes me back against the pillows and drags the top up my body. I weakly fight free of it just as he hisses.

"Fuck!" I keep my eyes closed for one more vain second. Because I have to open them, look down, and see what he's looking at.

The puckered, angry-looking skin is just below my navel. Only an inch and a half across but it's deep, and even though it's completely healed, I experience a lingering pain whenever I touch it. The doctor described it as phantom pain. I call it the guilty reminder of the consequences of reaching for the forbidden.

I exhale shakily when Killian's fingers caress it reverently. His face has lost its healthy, vibrant color, and his jaw is set in concrete. He shakes his head a couple of times, visibly battling his fury. "God, baby, I'm so sorry."

"It's...I..."

Words I can never utter stay locked in my heart as he lowers his head and grants me an anointment I don't deserve. "We'll find the bastard. I promise. We'll find him, and I'll put him down."

The vow is deep and solemn. He touches the scar one more time with his hands and then with his mouth.

Then he worships his way up my body.

And I fight back tears for the second time tonight.

Chapter Sixteen

FAITH

I wake up from a sleep fractured by sublime dreams and ominous nightmares to find Killian sprawled on top of me, elbows on either side of my shoulders and his hands cupping my breasts. I gladly abandon my anxiety to bask in the sight of the gorgeous, sexily disheveled man availing himself of my body.

"Having fun?"

Gorgeous blue eyes lift to mine, and their sparkle is the most beautiful thing I've seen in a while. He grins at me, and I change my mind. That smile is definitely the most beautiful thing.

"I tried to but I couldn't resist. You looked so exquisite lying there all supple and mouthwatering."

Of all the things to wake up to, this is far from the worst-case scenario. It's been a long time since I've been worshipped like this. And I'm weak enough to want to bask in it for a little while. Before the danger and the crap and the secrets force us into an unavoidable reality. "How hard did you try?" I ask, tongue firmly in cheek.

His lascivious grin is second hottest only to the lazy swirling of his tongue over my nipples. He continues his ministrations for another minute before he climbs up my body to fuse his mouth to mine. We kiss for a couple of minutes before he pulls away.

"Good morning," he drawls.

"Hi," I reply.

Then he rocks his hips and hot steel rod against my thigh. "Get the picture now?"

My breathing truncates. "Which part of my body is that for?"

The hands still fondling my breasts pinch my nipples in a rolling action that's mind-blowing. "Your choice. I'm putty in your hands."

I laugh. "I had no idea putty came in titanium."

His mouth returns to my breasts. The absorption on his face is a triple threat to my heart. "I'm still yours to do with as you please," he mumbles without lifting his head.

Predictably, my racing heart trips over itself. I look around his bedroom, vaguely taking note of everything I missed last night. His MIT sweatshirt is draped over a recliner. An elaborate puzzle sphere I have no hope of ever solving sits on his nightstand next to the tray containing the collection of watches he never travels without.

And, of course, he has a laptop close at hand. Killian hasn't stopped being the right amount of messy, nerdy, and sophisticated. More and more, I'm getting the picture that he hasn't changed much at all.

But I have. So much. I went seeking retribution in Julia's name. And ended up damaged beyond repair, with blood on my hands. It wasn't easy walking away the first time. It won't be easy this time either.

I refocus to find his eyes on me. He hasn't stopped what he's doing to my breasts, but his eyes are growing speculative, a part of his mind bypassing thoughts of sex to decipher what's going on in mine.

I close my hands over his, and he pauses, his gaze inquiring. Without speaking, I shift back on my elbows until I'm halfway up the headboard. Fluffy pillows support my lower back, and I'm in a prime position to offer him what he wants. I slowly squeeze our hands, and my breasts, together.

"This was number two on your list, right?"

He freezes for a second. Then his eyes go from sparkling to gleaming with intent. All signs of mirth leave his face, but he continues to lick me in wider circles, making the globes of my breasts and the valley in between wetter.

I let go to grip the top of the headboard and let him have his way. After a minute, he rises and prowls slowly toward me to rest his knees on either side of my rib cage. With his long, disheveled hair falling around his face as he looks down at me, his sleek muscled body, and the huge cock bobbing excitedly over my breasts, he's a wild and beautiful beast. I don't get a chance to look to my fill. He leans down and glides his tongue over my upper lip, then my lower. When I open, he slides inside, curling his tongue around mine in a dirty kiss that leaves me breathless.

That's when he pulls away and mutters against my mouth, "Cup them for me, baby."

My hands drop to my breasts. I hold them together, the air snagged in my lungs as I watch him draw his hips back before sliding his hot, velvet-smooth cock between the snug globes. Like so many sexual acts, I had my reservations about this before I met Killian. I never figured how doing this would actually get me off. He opened my eyes in more ways than one.

I groan at the sexy sensation of his dick sliding against my skin. His broad head hits the soft underside of my throat, and I raise my gaze to gauge his reaction.

His mouth is open, thick puffs of air rushing out with every forward thrust. He's barely started, and yet he's already so into it his face is flushed and his thrusts have hit that familiar unrelenting rhythm that suggests it'll take an earthquake to move him from his purpose.

"Fuck. You look incredible," he rasps, his gaze shifting from my face to my breasts and back with almost feverish urgency. As if he can't get enough of the visual stimuli.

I squeeze my breasts tighter, closing my flesh even firmer around him.

"God, yes!" He pumps harder, faster, his balls slapping against my abs. He looks so awesome, feels so good, I can't look away.

He braces one hand against the headboard and drifts the other over my breasts, teasing the already sensitive nipples even further. A rush of wetness explodes between my thighs, and I squeeze them together to contain the sensation. My hips undulate in time with his, my pussy clenching and unclenching around the phantom cock I wish were inside me.

"How do you feel, baby?" he demands thickly.

"Hot. Aching."

"You wanna come with me?"

My head bobs. "Hmm…yes."

He holds two fingers against my mouth. I suck on them and wet them for him, and he returns them to my boobs. Without losing the tempo of his thrusts, he begins to squeeze and tease my nipples. Incredibly, sensations pile high, a hundred arrows of heat singeing me from brain to nipple to pussy.

Delicious shivers wrack my body as I crest the peak. "Killian… oh…"

He pinches my nipples to the point of pain. My tiny screams seem to be a trigger to my body to let go. My hips jerk off the bed as my orgasm blindsides me.

I hear a hiss and a curse. Then hot spurts drench my chest and neck. Above me, Killian's groans go on forever, truncated by guttural praise for me.

Once again I'm a boneless mess, fully sated even though I haven't been penetrated. When he lifts off me, I moan with the loss of his delicious weight, but my happy haze doesn't wane too much. I watch him walk away, his toned and ripped body a feast for my eyes.

He returns with a warm, damp towel he uses to clean me up. When he's done, he slides into bed and gathers me close. We drift back into sleep, then wake up, fuck again, and then take a shower.

We emerge to the smell of brewing coffee, and my stomach growls.

Killian grins at me as he pulls on a pair of jeans. "I'll get Mitch to whip us up some breakfast."

I nod. "And then what?" Now that I don't have the Punishment Club to worry about, the thought of sitting around waiting for whatever evil is lurking to jump out and grab me pisses me off even more.

He strolls over to me and slides his fingers into my hair. Firm thumbs pitch my head up so our gazes connect. "Let's see what Betty's got, and we'll come up with a plan. Sound good?"

"Yes."

I look around for my top, but it's nowhere in sight. Neither are my panties. I look over at Killian.

"What?" he asks.

"Where are my clothes?"

"I put them in the laundry in my dressing room."

I frown. "Why?" I've never seen him pick up after himself, let alone after me. The times in between assignments, when we were at his Malibu mansion, Debbie, his housekeeper, slavishly looked after him. The other times, it fell to me, or whatever manpower our roles allowed, to cater to his messiness. When I had to do it, I didn't mind. It was the tiny bit of my old life I couldn't and didn't want to shed.

He shrugs now. "It's no big deal."

I raise an eyebrow at him. He sighs, takes my hand, and tugs me out of bed. Together, we walk into his dressing room. Only it's not just his things hanging up in the closet and stacked up on the shelves. A good selection of my clothes is neatly piled next to his.

His arms slide around me, and he lays his chin on my head. "Don't hate me, but I just wanted to see your things next to mine, the way we used to have them."

My breath shudders out of me. "Killian…"

"Don't make a big deal out of it, baby. They're just clothes," he says in my ear.

I turn in his arms and look into his eyes. "They're not just clothes. And you know it." He's playing dirty, sinking his claws into me.

He looks unrepentant. "They're here now. And you'll be sleeping in my bed now, so it makes sense. And it saves Mitch from getting his eyes ripped out if he accidentally catches sight of your gorgeous bare ass."

He throws the joke out but his gaze is watchful. I can fight him and insist my clothes are returned to my room, or I can let it go. I've already spent the night in his bed. I intend to spend a few more while we grapple with whatever it is we're dealing with. When the time comes for me to leave, I won't be taking my clothes with me anyway. The only things I'll need are the clothes on my back, and my box.

The thought of the box, and everything it entails for me, puts things into perspective. "Okay, you win this round," I concede.

His eyes narrow warily. "What's it going to cost me?"

I turn around and head for the stack of casual clothes. I select a dark gray sleeveless tunic dress that falls to mid-thigh and pull it on. "A drink on the roof tonight."

"Deal."

I open a drawer to look for my panties and find his designer-labeled boxers instead.

"Over here." His hand on my waist guides me to a similar set of drawers two closets over. He pulls it open, plucks a pair of peach lace panties from among the pile of lingerie, and almost reluctantly hands them over. "I love taking them off you, but I won't mind if you don't wear them at all."

"Let's not get poor Mitch's eyes into trouble with an accidental flashing, shall we?"

One corner of his mouth lifts. "Touché."

I finish dressing and while I pull a brush through my hair, Killian tugs on a powder-blue T-shirt that does incredible things to his eyes. I can't help myself; I ogle him through the mirror until he catches my eye.

"You keep looking at me like that, baby, and we'll never make it out of the bedroom."

The front door buzzer sounds, and that takes care of that. Killian looks almost regretful and a little irritated by the interruption. But we leave the room. Since Mitch is waiting at the door, Killian goes to let him in while I head to the kitchen.

They enter a minute later, and the bodyguard-slash-chef is holding a grocery bag that contains French bread, among other things I can't see.

"Morning, ma'am."

"Hey, Mitch." I slide the second cup of coffee I poured to Killian. He accepts with a smile and a peculiar light in his eyes. I realize I'm sliding into old habits and mentally kick myself.

"What can I get you to eat?" Mitch asks as he ties the apron around his waist.

"Scrambled eggs is fine."

"Or eggs Benedict with a waffle on the side with strawberries and cream on top?" Killian suggests.

I salivate as I glance from him to Mitch. The burly man, who should look out of place in the kitchen but weirdly doesn't, nods. "It'll be ready in fifteen minutes."

"I'll have the same, thanks," Killian says.

The older man nods again.

Killian takes my arm, and we leave the kitchen. I glance at him on the way to the living room. "Where did you find Mitch?"

"My very expensive, very temperamental rental car broke down on a remote road in the middle of the KwaZulu-Natal. He and Linc found me. Which was great because I wasn't looking forward to sleeping in my car for the third night in a row. Aston Martins are great to drive, but they're pretty crappy as hotel rooms."

"You were on another assignment?"

"No, I was chasing a lead that turned out to be another dead end."

In the living room, we head to the wide sofa I woke up on two days ago. He pushes me down at one end and sits next to me.

"What lead?"

He looks at me without speaking and sips his coffee. My breath catches a little. "Me?"

His gaze turns a little sad, a little disappointed at my surprise. "I told you, I never stopped looking. You once mentioned you wanted to visit South Africa. Nancy, Betty's older sister, threw out a description that matched yours, so I went to look. You, or rather the woman who was supposed to be you, turned out to be a vineyard owner's wife from just outside of Stellenbosch. They invited me to stay for a few days. I had nowhere else to be, so I took them up on their offer. It's a beautiful part of the country. We should go back there sometime."

This time it's my heart that catches. I can't make the promise, so I drink my coffee. Killian stays silent for another minute. "Anyway, I thought I'd take the scenic route back to Johannesburg. KwaZulu-Natal is beautiful too. Not so much the vast areas without cell phone reception."

"What were Mitch and Linc doing there?"

"They didn't feel like sharing that with me. And I didn't ask. But I checked them out when I got back home. Turns out they were ex-military. We kept in touch. When I attended their wedding and found out they were both out of work, I offered them this gig."

"They're married?"

Mitch walks in then, and a small smile curves his lips. "Coming up on two years."

"Congratulations."

"Thanks, ma'am. The food's ready."

"Thank you. And please, call me…" I pause, and my gut clenches tight. The name I threw away a long time ago crowds the back of my throat. But I'm not worthy of it. I feel Killian's sharp gaze on me. "Never mind."

We head back to the kitchen and eat breakfast in near silence. I compliment Mitch's cooking skills again, ignore the dark look Killian throws me, and get up to pour us some coffee. When we're done and once Mitch leaves, we wander into the study.

The gadget Killian carries hasn't beeped, so we don't expect to find anything when we get there. With nothing to do and too much time on my hands, my mind probes forbidden territory again.

I shouldn't ask. I know I shouldn't. "Where else did you look for me?" I blurt.

Killian walks over to where I'm standing with my back against the glass wall. Behind and below me, mid-morning rushes past in New York City.

Up here, I experience the slow passage of time like dull thuds of my heartbeat. Killian's hands circle my waist, his thumbs sliding back and forth in lazy curves beneath my breasts. "Costa Rica, Jaipur, Mexico, London. Twice in New Jersey. Twice in Ireland. And all over California."

"Not Arkansas?"

Something passes over his face. A shadow. A secret. I recognize it because that shadow lives in me too.

"Your life there was over. I helped you sever the ties, remember?"

The breath I take is tinged with pain. "Julia's grave. Is it…is she…?"

He kisses me softly on the temple. "The money we paid for it to be tended and freshly flowered has another twelve years to go. I kept an eye on it. She's fine."

Tears prickle my eyes, and I swallow hard. "Thank you."

He lowers his head and presses his lips to mine. My arms creep around his neck. We kiss long and deep. Enough for some of the sadness to fade before he lifts his neck.

"I wish I'd met her."

My heart turns over with love and sadness for what I lost. "She would've liked you. But she probably would've liked Betty a whole lot more."

He tilts his head. "She was into computers."

I nod, the memories of my sister, the way she was before evil touched her, rushing through my mind. "She was so smart, always taking things apart and putting them back together just to see how they worked. She talked my parents into buying her a laptop for her birthday…just before…" The pain builds back up again, but this time with the impotent rage that accompanies the thought of a precious life cut far too short.

Killian's hands cradle my jaw. "I'm sorry, baby, I didn't mean to drag this up for you."

I shake my head. "It's...okay. The reminder is good."

He frowns a little. "Is it?"

"It helps me deal with a few things."

"What things?" he probes.

A different memory slides into focus. It's not one I like dwelling on. Probably because while my head knows it was wrong, the fire of vengeance burning in my heart remains satisfied with what I did. "Sometimes, when I think about what we did—what I did at Paul and Raj's party—"

He stiffens. "It wasn't officially sanctioned, but it was necessary."

I nod. "But when I think about it, I think of Julia. And I think that if only she'd told me. Or if I'd followed my instincts when I felt something was wrong, like I did with that man at the party, she would still be alive, you know?"

"Faith..."

"I killed a man, Killian. Someone who wasn't even part of our official op. I shot him in the heart. And I never looked back." It was my first, and it wasn't premeditated, and I knew then that it would become one of the many nightmares that would never let go of me. But there was an acceptance in the moment I pulled the trigger that has scared me ever since.

Killian's hold tightens, forcing warmth into me. "He was raping a child for his own sick pleasure. I know you enough to be certain that walking away would've fucked you up even more."

"But wasn't that what the training I underwent was all about? For me to remain rational in such circumstances? But I didn't. I jeopardized everything."

"No. You don't know that for a fact."

"You suspected our cover was blown or that they might be leading us into a trap. And I wouldn't let you pull us out. What if that's the reason Ted and Shane were eventually found and killed?"

His jaw turns granite-hard. "Stop it. The op may not have gone according to plan, but we shut the assholes down."

"*Temporarily*. Paul Galveston is still alive. Which means the sex trafficking is still going on."

"That's not on you."

His reassurance attempts to lessen my guilt. But inevitably, pain and despair rise again. I missed the one shot that could've ended this. And I have to live with it.

Chapter Seventeen

FAITH

Cairo, Four Years Ago

Two hours before the second phase of our op gets under way.

The last time I met our targets, I was sick to the point of throwing up. Only it turns out my nausea is more than just acute disgust with the three men who head the sex trafficking rings.

Last night, while going through final preparations, it finally dawned on me that it may be something more. Something life changing. Hell, as if my life hasn't changed enough already.

Since then, I've done the calculations thirty ways to Christmas, and I can't find another explanation for my nausea or my no-show period except for the fact that I'm knocked up. A clandestine search on the Internet for dates shows I may be about seven weeks along.

Sweet Mother of Mercy.

If I believed God listened to me anymore, I would say a prayer. For what, specifically, I don't know. But I would say a blanket one anyway. Except God and I haven't been on the best of terms since he abandoned my baby sister to the vile hands of one of his supposedly trusted flock.

I haven't forgiven him for that, and I don't think I ever will.

So I swallow the familiar Sunday school prayer verses that attempt to rush past my guard, and double-check my Ruger for the seventeenth time. It's a comfortable weight, and the three-inch barrel makes it compact enough to sit in my purse without attracting too much attention.

"Are you ready?"

I turn from the bathroom mirror to face Killian.

My op partner. My lover. The father of my child. It's a transition I haven't had time to make room for. Not with the insane roller coaster my life has been twisting on for the last six months. Not when we were so new. I search his beautiful face, analyze his sexy grin. I think of his serious alpha side, and his protective side. His razor-sharp intellect, and his killer body.

Everything about him checks the box for lover, and someone I can trust to have my back in the field.

But father?

From what Matt said about him before we met, I expected a selfish billionaire asshole with a heavier dose of the sexist traits his brother displayed so carelessly toward me. Or worse.

But I learned very early on to take what my now-deceased husband said with a bucket of salt. And that was before I found out his true intentions in marrying me. I was the poster woman for his campaign. The photogenic, law-abiding, churchgoing citizen from a respectable middle-class family, who just happened to have a dead sister.

Matt's good looks and trustworthy vibe brought in the needy suburban housewives and easily charmed grandmothers. My deep love for my dead sister and my campaign for stringent laws for sex offenders opened the floodgates for the sympathy votes.

I stood by his side and watched him win his congressional seat by a landslide.

And then the lies, the contempt, and the long absences in DC started. Rumors of his affairs with his female staff hurt at first. But then, weirdly, the pain went away. By the time Killian turned up, I was over the initial shock of being blindsided, yet again, by a situation I never saw coming.

Where anger and grief had fueled my path on Julia's behalf, cold calculation and the solid reality of divorce papers reassured me when it came to Matt. I intended to serve the papers at a time when it would cause him the most damage. He'd used my sister's precious memory as a stepping-stone for his career. And just like I'd done to Heather Jane Fitzgerald when I was sixteen, I was going to pay Matt back for his betrayal.

Only he got it worse. My intention was to punish him. I never wanted him dead. He would still be alive if Killian hadn't shown up and turned everything on its head.

"Faith? Are you okay?"

I focus on Killian. We've fucked more times in the last six months than I've had sex with anyone since I lost my virginity at eighteen. And yet, there are so many things I don't know about this man. He never talked about his parents save to say they never loved him and he grew not to give a shit. Which, loosely translated, meant he thought they deserved everything they got in the end. Would he be a great father? Or even an okay one like my father was before my actions drove a wedge between us?

And what about me? A newly trained operative with a child? And, hell, do I even want this child?

Yes. My certainty on that front is unshakable.

"Baby, what's going on?" Killian's sharp voice slices through my thoughts.

I push everything to the back of my mind, especially that last bracing, definitive answer that produces even more questions, to deal with later.

"Nothing. I'm sorry. I spaced out for a bit, imagining you wearing nothing but that tunic for me later."

His eyes gleam with predatory hunger. "Oh yeah?"

"Hmm, I have visions of ripping it off you the way you've been ripping my clothes off lately. I'm going to need a new wardrobe soon if you keep that up, by the way."

He closes the gap between us and places his hands on my hips. I toyed with wearing either traditional attire like what Killian is wearing or going with my favorite designer. My black Alexander Wang dress with the slightly flared skirt won out.

"I'll buy you a dozen new wardrobes for the privilege and pleasure of getting you naked at the quickest opportunity."

"Wouldn't it be more cost effective for us to move to a nudist colony?" I joke as he pushes his face into my neck.

He stiffens against me for a moment and then slowly relaxes. "I'm not going to start the evening by thinking homicidal thoughts about even the possibility of anyone else but me seeing you naked."

I'm still getting used to the blunt instruments that are Killian's jealousy and unbridled possessiveness. I'm also getting used to the fact that it gets me shamefully wet when he goes all primitive alpha on me.

Would he be the kind of father to prowl his front lawn with a loaded shotgun to deter boys once his daughter turns sixteen?

God, what the hell am I thinking? I don't even have official confirmation yet, I have zero idea how he feels about fatherhood, and we're in Cairo on a dangerous assignment, currently en route to what we both suspect is a sex party involving underage kids.

Thoughts of the evening ahead sober me up enough to drag my head from the clouds. Killian's eyes meet mine, and his features turn serious too.

He takes my hand, and I shamelessly cling to him as we leave the bedroom, and the villa.

We travel in a convoy of two SUVs because his cover of obnoxious, ostentatious billionaire is perfect for the extra security we have with us at all times. Our trip takes us deeper into the desert. The farther we go into the barren landscape, the tenser we both get.

Fifty minutes later, we arrive at the property that looks suspiciously like a hotel. The armed guards at the towering gates trigger another layer of apprehension. I clutch my purse a little tighter and thank God for Killian's reassurance of GPS trackers on both our clothing and vehicle. Our drivers are part of the team and can provide additional backup if needed. But despite all of that, I've been trained to accept that whatever can go wrong, will go wrong, and to adapt quickly.

Although I don't know how to adapt to the fact that, as we drive under a series of elegant arches into the heart of the hotel, all I can think of is the new life inside me and the risk I'm already exposing him or her to.

More grim-faced armed guards greet us when our vehicle eventually stops. Several more SUVs and rough-terrain Jeeps are lined up on the drive.

We walk through a series of corridors, and I force myself to focus and create a mental image of the landscape. Maybe I need to get Killian to create an app for that for our next assignment.

Another mosaic-tiled corridor brings us out into an open courtyard filled with sharply dressed guests. Mostly men, I note, with another shiver of discomfort. Besides the handful of women sipping cocktails, the only females are the entertainment, mainly scantily clad belly dancers.

I'm clocking exit points when I spot Paul and Raj coming toward us.

"Killian, Faith. You made it."

Handshakes are exchanged. I try not to stiffen when Paul leans over to brush kisses on my cheeks.

"We said we would," Killian responds coolly, his arrogant billionaire persona fully in place.

"And we're honored by your presence," Raj adds with a wide smile. He's already halfway to getting drunk, and possibly high as well, if the slight slur in his speech and the rabid glint in his eyes are any indication.

Like before, Paul's eschewed his motherland's attire for a sharp gray suit with a white open-necked shirt. Raj is dressed casually in a white shirt and white palazzo pants. And Moses, who joins us a few minutes later, is a cross between the two.

Champagne is offered along with caviar and truffle-topped blinis. For the first time, I get to try the technique of pretending to drink without actually taking a mouthful. I catch Killian doing the same.

"Is this a hotel?" he asks, looking around.

Paul nods as he walks us around the lamplit courtyard. "As yet unopened. It belongs to an associate of mine. He ran into a couple of financial snags that pushed back his schedule. I'm helping him out by paying him to throw a few parties here. It's perfect for entertaining, don't you think? I like the…exclusivity."

"Absolutely," I concur, but his interest remains on Killian.

"Come, I'll give you the tour. Show you where you'll be staying tonight."

Killian and I exchange glances. "We weren't expecting to stay the night." His tone suggests he's not on board with the surprise move.

"Nonsense. It's an hour's drive back to your villa. That sort of journey isn't recommended once you've partied like we intend for you to party."

"That's why we have chauffeurs," Killian replies with a tight smile.

"I'm sure they will appreciate being given the night off too. Or are you one of those billionaire assholes who craps on everyone who's not as wealthy as him?" Paul says with a smile that doesn't reach his eyes.

I stiffen.

"Whoa, let's hold the insults until we've gotten past the canapés, okay?" Killian's voice is coated with chilled steel, and the arm around my waist tightens fractionally.

Paul makes an offhanded gesture of contrition. "Come on, I was just kidding. Besides, who the fuck is going to call you out on who you crap on? Being a billionaire should automatically give you that right, if you ask me."

I take a slow breath and talk myself down from the urge to throw my champagne in his face.

"But, hey, you came here to have fun, am I right? The true fun doesn't start until half of these assholes here go home to their vanilla beds. So"—he slaps Killian on the arm—"you two are staying. End of discussion."

He struts off, and I see the tide of fury wash over Killian's face. Luckily we're a little distance from the other guests, so no one witnesses his silent rage or how quickly he gets himself under control.

"I want to rip that fucker's throat out."

"I want to cheer you on while you do it," I say under my breath.

Killian pulls me closer. "We can leave right now if you want."

I really want to. But isn't this what I've been fighting for since Julia died? For some sort of justice for innocent children?

"No, we can't. If what he's planned is happening when most of the guests are gone, we have to stay."

"There's no need for both of us to stay. I can get the team to take you back to the villa. I'll stay and see this through."

Again the temptation to say yes is so strong that I have to swallow to suppress it. "I signed up for this. I can't just leave because the bastard sickens me. I'm staying."

His gaze probes mine for a long moment. "You're sure?" he asks me.

"I have to be." I came here to do a job. I have to see it through. For Julia's sake.

He nods. Then, in a move we practiced countless times during my training in Virginia, I shield his body while he dumps half his drink in a potted plant, and he does the same for me.

Halfway through the evening, Moses and a man dressed in an embroidered tunic, fez, and toga pants join us. "This is Mahmoud. He'll be your butler for the duration of your stay." His dark gaze swings between the two of us. "Now, Paul promised you a tour, but he's otherwise engaged so you got me. Shall we?"

We've no choice but to go with him. I block him out as he goes through his spiel about the property. I do wonder why they're even bothering until he nudges Killian's arm. "We were thinking, if you wanted to branch out into real estate, this could be a gold mine once the airstrip and helipads are put in place. It's far enough away to offer the sort of exclusivity certain types cream themselves for, know what I mean?"

Killian shrugs. "It certainly has...something."

Moses nods enthusiastically. "Paul is working on a deal with the guy who owns it to take it off his hands. We'll let you know how it goes."

"You do that." Killian pauses a beat. "I thought you were in shipping though?"

Moses makes a face. "The company basically runs itself. I'm in the market for more exciting adventures." He nudges Killian again.

Luckily we arrive at a private courtyard, directly in front of a small swimming pool. Four square pillars denote the sides of the self-contained apartment, which is an equivalent of a Moroccan *riad*. "This is your residence for the night. Great, isn't it?"

Killian nods at the two guards standing on the flat roof balcony. "What's with the armed guards?"

Moses grimaces. "We've had a few gatecrashers in the past. Motherfuckers from the government who have sticks up their asses about everything. The guards are an early warning system."

We make the right noises all through the remaining tour. Moses delivers us back to the party and goes off to chat with Paul. Galveston looks over and gives a two-fingered salute. And we carry on like that throughout the evening until the so-called vanilla guests take their leave just after midnight. Then we're led to giant wooden double doors.

Just like last time, Raj can barely contain himself. "No flashy underground bunkers here, Knight. We just deal in quality raw materials."

Paul throws it open with an arrogant flourish. My heart hammers in dread and futile rage as I step forward.

The place is set out in an *Arabian Nights* theme. Had this place been anywhere else on earth, I would've been impressed by the art and beauty etched on the walls and scattered around the room. But the human displays on the tables stop my breath and threaten to bring up my lunch.

The live bodies laid out are completely naked, the food displayed on their various parts making no attempt to hide their genders. My stomach roils violently. Killian's hand touches my back.

"Easy, baby. They're not kids," he mutters in my ear.

My breath rushes out of me, and I force myself to look closer. Sure enough, they're young, but very early twenties young as opposed to kids.

Before my relief can sink in, Moses finds us, another bottle of champagne dangling from his fingers. "So what do you think of our starter platters?" he says with a lewd grin.

"Impressive, but nothing I haven't seen before."

"Fuck, you're a tough guy to please. Well, wait till you see the main course."

Killian makes a show of looking around. "Don't see anything that floats my boat yet."

"You had your inner *inner* sanctum. We have ours."

Twenty minutes later, we're escorted into another room and introduced to the sickest depravity of them all. "So, what's your poison?" Raj asks.

Killian drapes his arm around my shoulder and lets loose a conceited smile. "A good host carefully investigates their guests' likes and dislikes before inviting them to a thing. You got close, my friend. Really close, but you fell at the final hurdle. I'm worth nine billion dollars. That's a heck of a chunk of change to jeopardize for the sake of getting caught on camera indulging my…interests. And yes, I know there are cameras in this room."

Moses's face drops, and he shakes his head. "You're paranoid—"

"No, I'm not. On this occasion, I'm going to choose not to be offended. You go ahead and enjoy yourself. We're leaving."

He steers me toward the door but not before I catch a glimpse of a middle-aged man dragging a half-naked girl into his lap. I clench my stomach against the need to vomit and fight a greater urge to stalk over and rip her out of his arms. Killian eyeballs the guard blocking the doors, and I close my eyes when I hear Paul Galveston shout Killian's name.

"No," I mutter fiercely under my breath.

"It's fine, baby. Trust me." His supporting arm stays around my shoulders, and he turns us around.

For the first time since we met him, Galveston looks less than the cocky bastard he projects. "Look, Knight, believe it or not, this wasn't about you. Some of the guests here like to take back digital souvenirs." He shrugs. "We didn't want to disappoint them."

"Fine. So don't disappoint them," Killian replies evenly.

Paul rubs his middle finger across his brow. "Stay the night anyway. Mo mentioned some other business ventures we want to discuss, right? We're really interested in bringing you on board the real estate project."

Killian offers him a bored look without answering.

Galveston's lips twitches in a mean little sneer before he catches himself. "Let's offer you a sweetener to make you stay."

Killian looks around the room. "Sorry, I've lost my appetite."

"Fuck, you're a tough customer, aren't you?"

A shrug.

"Will you give me…us until tomorrow to make it up to you?"

Killian takes a few moments to think about it. Then he looks down at me. Nothing in his face gives away his true emotions, but I feel turbulence whipping through him.

"Fine."

Paul cracks a triumphant smile. "Good man." He whistles for one of the guards. "He'll walk you back to the residence. I'll see you in the morning."

I can barely hold it together long enough to walk back to our rooms.

The moment we shut the doors, I whirl on Killian. "How did you know?"

He raises his finger to his mouth like he's caressing his lower lip, but I get the *hold on* signal. He quickly searches the room, peeking behind paintings and underneath lamps, before he walks over to me, his jaw clenched in fury. "Because shit bags like Galveston thrive on that sort of crap. He'd like nothing more than to have me on tape and in his pocket for life," he growls.

I can't stop shaking. "Why don't we just call the local authorities? God, Killian, those kids."

He cups my shoulders. "It's too late. If we act now, we'll blow our cover. I promise, the moment we leave here in the morning, I'll make the call. There are ten kids in that room, but there are hundreds more out there. We can't just scrub the op because we still don't know *where* the shipment's coming in. And we can't monitor all the ports at once even with a date in mind. The port of Alexandria alone will take a huge amount of manpower to stake out. Tomorrow may be our only window to try and get a further advantage." He presses a kiss to my forehead. "Hang in there, okay?"

I give a wretched nod. I excuse myself to go the bathroom, where I throw up the contents of my stomach. I suspect Killian thinks I'm vomiting because I'm disgusted by what we witnessed. While that's partly true, I let him believe that's all of it.

And during the night, when I get up for the third time to throw up, I accept that maybe I'm not cut out for this spy shit. At all.

Maybe turns into a definite *yes* a handful of hours later when I get up to vomit for the fourth time, and the smallest sound ends up blowing my life apart.

* * *

KILLIAN

I feel the center of my gravity shift in my sleep. It's not a spy thing warning me of danger. It's an emotional klaxon shrieking at me that something's not right.

Sure enough, when I roll over and reach for her, Faith's not next to me. I'm not prone to panic. Danger, faced cold, almost always has a better outcome than a knee-jerk response. But both knees are in full jerk mode before my feet hit the floor.

I try to reason with myself, but my heart is not buying the shit my head is feeding it. There may have been a murderous light burning in her eyes each time we spoke of what's going on a few rooms away, but she wouldn't risk the kids by doing something stupid—like attempt to free them on her own. I know how much this mission means to her.

Still, my skin tightens with dread as I tug on my clothes and head out into the living room. We both thought sleep was out of the question when we halfheartedly went to bed. But somehow we managed to snatch pockets of sleep. When I last woke up half an hour ago, she was right there, next to me.

But she's nowhere in sight now. Instinct makes me reach for my Glock and tuck it against my thigh as I open the door and step out into the private courtyard.

The soft lapping of the pool and the hum of the pump are the only sounds disturbing the air. I bypass the pool, noting that the two guards are absent from the rooftop. I don't know whether this is a good or bad thing, so I shove it to the back of my mind for now.

The front door to our private residence is ajar.

Okay. Fuck.

I take a breath to calm my racing heart and try not to think of all the scenarios that could unfold. None of them are good. Faith mostly likely wouldn't have gone after our enemies by herself, but neither would she have gone for a walk in a place like this, on a night like this. Unless...

I slam a lid on my thoughts long enough to remember the layout of the hotel. We entered through the south gates. The party was held in the east wing. Our residence is west.

I take the corridor leading east. The faint sound of music tells me the party is still going on. I swallow my distaste and quicken my steps. That's when I hear it.

The first gunshot is clear and drenches me with ice-cold dread. The second and third follow a split second later. All three come from behind me.

I spin around and sprint back the way I came, past our residence and down the west corridor.

I burst into yet another courtyard. It takes precious few seconds to comprehend the scene before me. A man I don't recognize is lying facedown in a pool of his own blood. Another man, whom I identify as Paul Galveston when my brain kicks in a second later, is lying next to him. He's also covered in blood.

And Moses Black is standing over her. My Faith.

She isn't moving. And as I watch, Moses raises the champagne magnum in his hand, high above his head.

"You bitch," he snarls. "You worthless, fucking bitch."

He starts to swing the bottle. I don't hesitate. My first shot hits him in the back of the head. He goes down, his body barely missing Galveston's as he crumples into a heap.

When I reach him, I pump three more bullets into his chest for good measure. But my focus is on her. Faith.

And the blood.

Jesus. So much blood. My knees hit the ground beside her. "Faith? Faith! Talk to me, baby." My voice is a shaky mess.

The tiniest moan signals she's alive. Her eyes are shut but her lids quiver. I don't allow myself to be relieved because we're in the middle of fucking nowhere, and...hell, the blood.

"God, baby, hold on." My hands shake as I lift her up and cradle her. I'm probably making every goddamn mistake in the book by moving her, but my mind is blank to anything else but the fact that she may be bleeding out. Dying right here in my arms.

I hear footsteps behind me, and I swivel around, my finger already on the trigger.

"Don't shoot. It's me!"

The moment I recognize Shane's voice, I turn back to her. "Faith, can you hear me?"

The barest murmur and a whimper of pain. A fevered search of her body shows the blood is most saturated at her stomach. I tear off my tunic and press it to the area.

"Mr. Knight? Sir, we need to go!"

"Come here. Keep pressure on her stomach," I snap at Shane. My voice is calmer now, every inch of my focus trained on her.

I hear footsteps. Shouts from nearby. I shield Faith with my body and raise my gun.

"It's our team, sir. They're waiting in the next courtyard. The vehicle is outside," Shane says. "But we need to go now."

I don't need a second prompt. I carefully pick Faith up, craddling her in my arms.

We tear across the courtyard and through a gated archway to emerge on a dirt road. My driver is behind the wheel. Shane, the analyst I tried to block from coming on this mission on account of his age, yanks open the back door. We pile in, Faith clutched tight in my arms, and the driver steps on the gas.

The team member in the passenger seat turns around. "Mr. Knight, what are your orders?"

I don't raise my gaze from Faith's face. Each blink, each puff of air she exhales is essential to my sanity. "Call the nearest hospital. Tell them we're on our way. Call the extraction team, report what's happened, and tell them to send a chopper to meet us at the nearest possible rendezvous point with a doctor on board. And tell them to send the authorities to get those kids out of there."

He nods and gets on the phone immediately. The helicopter intercepts us five miles away.

At the private hospital in Cairo, the medical staff whisks Faith away from me and into surgery. And I endure the longest hours of my life. I'm ten paces from turning into a raving lunatic when the doctor enters the room. Words fall from his lips but only two register.

She's alive.

She's alive.

I take my first full breath in forever. I must ask to see her because he leads me to a private room at the end of a long, quiet corridor. And beneath a jumble of tubes, intravenous needles, and blankets, my heart lies, pale and breathing and beautiful.

I make different, drastic plans in the four days she stays in her coma. On the fifth, the doctor updates me with news of her improvement. He thinks she should wake up in the next twelve to twenty-four hours. And she can go home in about a week. I leave her side and return to my hotel to make my report to a stone-faced Eric Biggins and to deliver the news that I'm leaving the agency.

Twenty-nine and retired sounds like the beginning of an excellent novel. Maybe that will be the title of my memoir. I make even more plans before I return to the hospital.

When I sit on the side of her bed and take her hand, her eyes flicker behind her lids. I sense that she's awake. But she doesn't answer me when I talk to her. She doesn't open her eyes.

She's not ready to face reality yet.

That's fine. We have all the time in the world. When the doctor convinces me to go and get some sleep, I reluctantly take his advice.

I shouldn't have. It was hands-down the worst move I ever made.

Because in those hours I was asleep in the hotel two blocks away, the reason for my heartbeat walked out of the hospital and left me behind.

Chapter Eighteen

KILLIAN

It's been five days. Betty is being unusually coy about spitting out any actionable intel. It's either that or our enemies have covered their tracks better than we expected, because every bit of information she finds—from flight manifests to bank records—is over four years old. She's not having any luck either with the surveillance. It almost seems like Galveston allowed himself to be picked up on camera at Dulles Airport as a silent fuck-you to us before disappearing.

I don't want to think he's that tech savvy, but the very real evidence that he's alive shows he has the resilience of a cockroach. Add to that his substantial family money, and the guy could cause real problems if we're not careful.

I watch Faith leaf through a coffee table magazine on bicycles—bicycles, for fuck's sake—then drop it to pace the living room. I need to have a word with Linc about buying better reading material. The sunlight catches her raven hair as she pauses in front of the window. The combination of her hair, my long-sleeved white dress shirt she tugged on earlier, and her reddened lips gives her the look of a naughty angel. An angel who deserves to spread her wings, not be held captive in my gilded prison. Even if it's for her own safety.

The roof garden has lost its appeal. There's only so much fresh air you can inhale a quarter of a mile up on a rooftop before it becomes old. I toy with the idea of taking her back to bed. *That* never gets old.

But we finished fucking an hour ago—one of those epic marathons that reaffirms life but leaves you drained. For like five minutes when you haven't had sex in four years.

I'm raring to go again but my baby needs a little recovery time. The cocky bastard in me hides a satisfied smirk when I catch her tiny wince as she changes direction. I like leaving a mark on her, but I love leaving one inside her even more. I love the thought that she feels me with every step she takes.

But right now, I hate the restlessness I sense in her. It's not from waiting on Betty. It's not from being thrown into limbo wondering what's out there. It's something else. That same something she wears like an invisible cloak. The secrets that shield her from me.

It pisses me off. But I suppress the need to pry the secret from her and rise to intercept her. "Want to watch a movie with me?"

She swivels on her heel and stares up at me, hands propped on her hips. "I love watching fast cars and things blowing up every two seconds, but I've had my fill of that for now, thanks."

"Okay, you can pick the movie this time."

"And have you grumble all the way through the subtitles?"

"If you can blow me while I eat your pussy, we can find a compromise between Swedish documentaries and high-octane car heist movies."

She rolls her eyes. "Only you will make that correlation."

I take her hand and drag her back to the seat. She leans her elbow against the back of the sofa and rests her chin on her arm. Her hair falls forward, and I can't help myself; I slide my fingers through the silky curtain.

"Hey, I have time to make up and a very dirty mind to appease."

Her green eyes peer at me through her bangs. "Tell me about Costa Rica," she says.

The request isn't unexpected. She's asked me about London, Ireland, and every place I went looking for her. But Costa Rica brings up bad memories I don't want to recall. "I'd really rather fuck you."

She stares at me for a long moment. "Something happened there," she murmurs.

"Something always happened where I went. I fell deeper into hell whenever I left without you."

She blinks and inhales shakily. "Tell me about Costa Rica, please."

My gaze falls to her sexy lips. I want to kiss her, wild and hard enough so she forgets her questions. She feels the power of my want because she sucks her bottom lip into her mouth. I like that too.

But...Costa Rica. "Same story. Close but no cigar." I laugh and shake my head. "If you ever decide you want a movie made about you and need body doubles, I can find you a dozen doppelgängers. Easy."

"Please, Killian."

My chest tightens, and a spurt of anger comes with it. "You're asking me to bare my fucking soul to you while you keep yourself from me. You think I don't notice you've been doing that?"

Her features tighten a little, but she sighs. "No, I know you do."

"And...? That's all I'm getting? Your acknowledgment that there's a problem?"

She attempts to stare me down. "For now. But I still want to know."

Irrational. Bold. Greedy. I can't even fault her for it. I feel the same way about her.

I jerk to my feet, my turn to pace to the window. My turn to feel like my skin is too tight to contain me. Memories of Cairo and her leaving me at the hospital have been replaying with alarming frequency for the last couple of days. Each time I see her scar, each time I brush my lips over the inch-and-a-half gash that nearly killed her, I'm thrown back to that night and the long, dark hours that followed.

I was going to change everything for her. I still would in a heartbeat. But she has to want it too. I'm done fighting for us on my own.

So. Costa Rica. I stab my fingers through my hair. "I'm not sure why that time was the worst. I guess there's only so much failure anyone can take. But when it turned out not to be you, I went a little off my head. I just wanted to...forget for a while."

Her eyes turn dark, and she flinches back a little. "Okay."

I stop and raise one eyebrow. "Okay?"

"You don't need to tell me who you fucked or—"

My bark of laughter earns me a glare. "You think I fucked to forget?"

"Don't laugh at me, Killian."

I approach, sit back down, and glance over at her. "Or what?" I taunt because, fuck it, I need more. So much more than she's giving me.

She rises on her knees and crawls over to me. The buttons left undone and the shift of cotton over her skin remind me she's naked underneath my shirt. The clothes we threw on were only so we could raid the fridge mid-morning. "Or I won't let you do whatever you want to me later."

Her words transmit straight to my cock. Yeah. Okay. So I'm a fucking slave when it comes to her pussy. And every other inch of her body and soul. But I'm a little resentful that this is all it takes. Which is why I stop myself from stripping her right this very second and gorging myself on her. From the pulse beating at her throat and the hardening of her nipples, she wants that too.

Too fucking bad.

I rest my head on the seat and close my eyes. "My Costa Rican guide warned me about the places not to go after a certain time of night. But the taste of failure and half a bottle of tequila racing through your bloodstream has a way of making those sort of warnings less...pertinent."

She inhales sharply. "Jesus, Killian," she whispers.

"I went. I stumbled on an underground cage fight club. It seemed like a good idea at the time to get involved."

"No..." I hear the pain in her voice, and perversely, it soothes me a little.

"My guide found me four hours later, minus five thousand dol-

lars and my favorite vintage Rolex. I did manage to gain two fractured ribs, a chipped tooth, and multiple bruises though."

"Oh God."

"Yeah. It wasn't one of my stellar moments."

She doesn't speak for a handful of minutes. And I'm not in the
mood to think about the past, so I keep my mouth shut and my eyes
closed.

"I'm sorry."

I open my eyes. God, even with that mournful look, she's beyond
beautiful. "Are you?"

She nods. "I didn't think you would look for me for that long…"

I close my eyes and laugh again because it's all so absurd, the
inevitability of my craving for her and her inability to fully comprehend it.

She doesn't rip into me for laughing at her this time. Instead I
sense movement, and then I feel her breath on my face. "I'm sorry,"
she whispers again.

I shake my head. "More. I need a fuck-load more, baby."

"Yes." She's closer. I smell her. A lethal cocktail of gorgeous female, shampoo, perfume, and the trace of my cum somewhere
inside her.

Her lips brush butterfly wing kisses on my neck and my jaw. I
clench my teeth against the pathetic urge to groan. A second later,
firmer kisses on my collarbone and a slow, hot lick on my skin draw
the air out of my lungs.

One hand slides over my abs, her nails leaving a trail of fire as
she teasingly tugs up my T-shirt. I don't readjust my position to help
her pull it off. This is her show. This is her working for it. I need
a little of that to keep me sane. So I let her. She manages to draw
the bottom over my head to wedge behind my neck, and my whole
front is revealed to her.

Her breathing truncates as she trails a finger from my throat to
the waistband of my pants. "God, you look so hot."

I'm on fucking fire, just from the sound of her sexy, husky voice
alone. "Keep going. Tell me what else you like."

Both her hands rest on my chest, and I feel her drawing even closer. A whisper of her breath over my ear. "I like the way you jerk against me when I dig my nails into your skin."

She follows her words with a demonstration, and I reward her with a head-to-toe spasm.

"I love the way your skin tastes, firm and a little salty." An open-mouthed kiss follows on my pecs just above my nipple.

Holy hell. I want to drag my eyes open and get a visual hit of what she's doing to me, but I'm already rock hard, treacherous drops of pre-cum already staining my pants. My hands curl into the sofa. "More."

Her lips drop an inch lower, right over the disk of my nipple. "These nipples are so sensitive, aren't they? They pucker so eagerly for me."

"Dammit . . . Faith."

She wets my skin, blows on me, and then flicks her tongue so damn saucily over my eager flesh. My whole body clenches in agonized pleasure, the groan I've been fighting tearing itself free of my control. She licks me just as avidly, as greedily as I do to her tits every chance I get.

"God, that feels incredible."

"I love the way your voice goes gravelly and low when you're turned on, like you can barely form the words," she croons against my skin. Her filthy mouth trails lower, her kisses getting hungrier, dangerously hotter.

My arms vibrate with the need to touch, to claim. But I love what she's doing more. When her teeth nip the area just below my navel and she frees my button, I can't take it anymore. My eyes fly open, and the stunning visual of her beautiful face, her glorious hair, her hands on my body stills everything inside me.

Fuck me, I'll never get over what this woman does to me. She sinks her fingers into my waistband on either side of my hips as she raises her siren eyes to me. Her eyes tell me she wants me to help ease my pants off. I don't raise myself up to help her because I crave that little fire that will blaze at me in three . . . two . . . one . . .

There it is. With a burst of energy, she yanks extra hard on my pants, just enough down my thighs for my overeager dick to spring out. Her nostrils pinch with her sharp intake of breath, and her lips part hungrily. She seems to be having a hard time dragging her gaze from my cock.

"Tell me," I croak.

Stormy eyes blink up at me. "You look like a superhot centerfold."

If I could summon my brain to work that way, I would probably say something clever. Instead: "Your centerfold," I stress.

Her head bobs once. "Mine." Her chin nudges my throbbing dick. Stars float past my vision.

"More," I beg.

Fingers still hooked in my pants, she crouches between my legs, lowers her head, and pulls the broad crown of my cock into her mouth. My back bows as untrammeled pleasure rips through me. "Shit, baby, your mouth!"

She pulls at me until I pop from her tight suction. My balls tighten at that insanely filthy sound. "You want more?" she asks as her tongue flicks against my opening.

"What the fuck do you think?" My voice is a useless jumble of noise. But she doesn't really need to hear me. The warm cavern of her mouth enfolds me once again, and I'm thrown back into the sweetest hell.

Eventually her hands leave my pants, to take hold of my straining balls. The perfect trifecta of sucking, pumping, and caressing drives me to the edge in pathetically little time. The hands balled into fists at my sides fly up to sink into her hair. My hips rise to meet her suction, and I hit the back of her throat with less than gentle finesse. She groans, and I curse because this, her taking me like a champ, draws me even deeper under her never-ending spell.

"Jesus, Faith. I'm going to drench that gorgeous mouth."

Her gaze rises from my crotch to my eyes, and I glimpse the encouragement. She needs me just as much as I need her. In this moment, she is a slave to the promise of my release.

"You want it?" I ask.

She barely lifts her mouth from me to groan, "Yes," before she is sucking me deep again. My fingers tighten a little unmercifully in her hair, and I push down. She trembles wildly against my hold.

"Stay," I growl.

She lets go of my pants and lays her palms flat on either side of my thighs. The submissive pose, the power she hands me, breaks me completely, as she knew it would. I come hard, thick and endless, feel her gag, watch her swallow. She is everything. And I die just a little bit, knowing I may not be her everything.

I vaguely recall my hands falling from her hair. I am a useless mass of sensation when she climbs up my body to sit in my lap, to snuggle her face in my shoulder and hug me tight.

"I'm sorry that happened to you in Costa Rica."

My eyes drift shut, and my hands crawl around her to hold her tight, but I don't have the words to respond. Slowly I feel her tense. Her head pops up, and I can feel her reading my face. I don't hide my turbulent emotions.

And when she returns her head to my shoulder, we both know that the tectonic plates of our dynamic have shifted. I experience the briefest moment of panic, which subsides into acceptance. We're headed where we're headed. And whatever the outcome, it is now unstoppable.

Chapter Nineteen

KILLIAN

The next day threatens to become a carbon copy of the previous one. This time, dressed in khaki shorts that lovingly cradle her ass and a black T-shirt, she does that bunching and twisting thing with her hair while she stretches up on her toes. When she makes a return trip from the window, I look up from my tablet and crook my finger at her.

"You're restless," I say, setting my gadget down. "I have a suggestion."

Her eyes darken a touch, and although she licks her lips, she shakes her head. "We can't fuck all day every day, Killian."

"I'd love to prove just how wrong you are, but that wasn't what I had in mind."

Her shoulders slump a little. "Okay…what?"

"You wanted to polish up on your marksmanship."

She nods eagerly. "Yes."

"Great. Mitch and Linc will be here in fifteen minutes."

Her eyes light up. "We're going out?"

"Yes, we are." My gaze drops to her long, bare, beautiful legs. I imagine dozens of guys looking at them. "You going to change?"

She rolls her eyes. "It's the middle of summer, Killian."

I wrestle with my jealousy and drag my gaze back up. "I reserve the right to be a total asshole to any bastard I catch looking at you."

Her gorgeous mouth lifts, transforming her face from jaw dropping to mesmerizing. "Ditto," she replies.

It takes my addled brain a beat to get her meaning. My frown gets a laugh. A rare sound that I've missed too damn much.

"What, you think guys are only interested in me? Check online. You have a ridiculous fan base. Your TED Talk on coding six years ago has over ten million views, and the comments will make you blush."

I walk over and link our fingers. I know I shouldn't ask, but the words fall out anyway. "Did you ever check online for me?"

Her gaze drops, and she shakes her head. "You would've found me."

Damn straight I would have. The atmosphere threatens to sour again so I drop a kiss on her mouth and release her. "Better hustle. We have a ways to go."

She leaves the room, and I double-check our destination one last time. When she returns, her hair is tied back, her leather cap is in place, and she's already wearing sunglasses. But her feet grab my attention. She's wearing dark, sky-high wedge-type shoes that make her legs look even longer. And the tilt of her chin tells me she's prepared to argue with me if need be over them.

Fuck. I put my cap and shades on and grab the portable gadget to keep an eye on Betty. She's taking too damn long. Her algorithms might need tweaking a little if she hasn't produced results by the time we return.

Mitch and Linc are waiting outside the elevators when we exit the apartment. My respect for them notches up another level when their eyes remain above Faith's neck. Gay or not, they're red-blooded humans, and her bare legs are insane enough to attract the types of looks that drive me to the brink.

We hit the ground floor, and I catch her hand to slow her down as Mitch heads outside. A moment later, Linc nods. We leave the building and turn left.

Faith looks around for the SUVs. When she doesn't spot them, she flicks a glance at me. "Where are we going?" she asks in a low voice without breaking her quick stride.

"The next block."

To her credit, she doesn't ask any more questions. Not until we're in another building, heading up in the elevator. "We're not driving."

I shake my head. "No. Too many cameras and traffic lights to mess around with. I didn't want to risk it."

She looks up at the red elevator numbers. "But...what are we doing here? This building doesn't have a gun range."

"No, but it has something our building doesn't. A helipad."

Her head whips to mine. "We're flying? And where are we going exactly?"

"Uniondale."

She frowns. "That's miles away."

"It has the least amount of surveillance in the area. And it was also the only shooting range I could get to at short notice that won't attract too much attention."

She takes it all in and nods. When we exit, I catch her gaze clocking all the entrances and exits, where potential danger might lurk. Although the gun range will supply us with a selection, we're both armed, and I've seen her run in heels so I know she can take care of herself. But still, I remain on high alert as we climb the flight of stairs that'll take us to the roof and the helicopter.

My pilot is the same driver who picked me up at Teterboro. Like Mitch and Linc, he has skills over and above the ordinary. Between us, we have an impressive selection of weapons to defend ourselves with. Which means fuck-all if our enemy is still hiding in the shadows.

It might be time to stop the wait-and-see approach and step into the light.

I turn to watch Faith's face, wondering how she'll take it. Her gaze is on the large, gleaming metal flying machine sitting twenty feet away.

"Sweetheart, stop making eyes at my Sikorsky." I don't particularly keep my voice down.

She flushes but her chin kicks up. "But she's just so beautiful. I want to pet her until she purrs."

I grin. "I'm almost tempted to get you to do that so I can watch. But we have an audience. So get your pretty ass on board."

The large aircraft is divided into two sections—seating up front for the pilot and copilot. Six seats in the main soundproof area at the back made up of three club chairs and a long bench seat. I help her into the back, and Linc and Mitch join the pilot up front. Mitch settles in as copilot.

Faith chooses a club chair instead of joining me on the bench seat. I allow it because I can still reach her if I want to. Plus, sitting opposite her this way, I can cop an eyeful of her stunning legs whenever I want.

She uncrosses and recrosses those very legs a minute later as we lift off. "Your horns are showing, Mr. Knight."

"I fucking hope so. Those legs are driving me nuts."

She flushes again, a little deeper this time, and I wonder how she'll feel about spending the journey in my lap, specifically riding my cock.

A firm head shake before I get the chance to voice my thoughts. "Forget it, Knight. I'm not letting you distract me from my first chopper ride across New York."

I lean back and cross my ankles. "Even if the view is much better from here?"

Her gaze drops to the growing bulge in my pants, and her nipples begin to pucker. "Yes," she squeezes out tightly after a tense few seconds.

I allow myself a deep chuckle. "Okay, baby. If you say so."

"I do say so. You're not as irresistible as you think, you know."

My mild contentment evaporates in a heartbeat. "Yes, I kinda got that from the four-year absence."

A shadow crosses her eyes. She looks away from me for a second, at the view I have zero interest in. I wait for her. But when she looks back she doesn't speak for a long while. "Killian…"

"You're going to have to tell me sometime. So how about you tell me now?"

Her throat moves in a slow swallow. "You were right. I shouldn't have been on that op that night in Cairo. I should've listened to you and gotten my head straight first. Or backed out altogether and let another team take care of those bastards."

My jaw grits against the need to deny that. But I've had a long time to analyze it. "I was in charge. The final decision fell to me. I wanted you with me so I ignored my instincts."

A weird acceptance settles over her face. "So you didn't think I was ready either?"

"You aced every operation prior to that one, but in hindsight, you weren't ready for one that struck so close to home. Not at that time, no."

A breath shudders out of her. "God, I fucked up so badly."

I lean forward and take her hands in mine. "No, you didn't. You wanted to save those kids and make things right for Julia. I wanted you to have that bit of peace, so I closed my eyes to the many pitfalls in the operation. Extra backup for a start. And constant surveillance on the assholes. Hell, a couple of drones watching them, and few discreet tags wouldn't have been amiss either. But the biggest mistake was deciding to stay the night. That was my call."

She shakes her head and pulls her hands from mine. "We both made the decision to stay. I should've woken you up when I heard that boy scream. But…I had my gun. I thought I could handle it. "

My fists clench but I don't say anything. I get the feeling she needs the cathartic release of replaying that nightmare.

"The bastard…he was dragging the boy down one of the corridors. God, he couldn't have been older than ten or eleven." She shudders.

I call fuck it, release her seat belt, and scoop her up into my arms. Although she accepts my touch and comfort, she's miles away. Too far away. "The bastard had his arm around the boy's neck and his other hand…" She takes a deep breath. "I told him to let him go. He replied in Arabic. I didn't understand but I didn't really need to. He was drunk, and he was laughing as he…groped the kid. The look in their eyes, utter fear and…depravity. I just couldn't…"

"It's okay, baby."

She shakes her head. "He said something to the boy and dragged him into the courtyard. The boy…he was terrified, Killian. It shattered me. I raised the gun. When the man saw it, he tried to use the boy as a shield. I think I lost my mind a little. I just pulled the trigger. I was trying to save the boy, but even shooting his attacker the way I did was so stupid. God, I didn't even think that I could've hurt him."

"You didn't. Your training kicked in. Your aim was perfect, and you got the bastard in the carotid."

"What happened after that is hazy, but I remember Galveston…standing over me. With a knife…"

Ice slides down my spine at the thought of how much worse everything could've gone while I was asleep. "Enough, Faith. You don't need to relive every second of it. The Egyptian authorities got the kids out of there. All of them. The boy's name is Sayeed. He was stolen from his family home the week before but he's fine today because of you."

I let her absorb that for a minute. But her ragged expression doesn't alter. "When I woke up in the hospital…" She pauses, and I freeze because this is the first time we're talking about this.

"Yeah?" My voice is a low croak.

"I was horrified. I'd killed two people in cold blood. And the terrifying thing was I knew I would do it again."

I rub my hand down her arm, my brain firing with all the questions I want to throw at her. "Doesn't explain why you left."

She stays quiet for so long I think she's not going to answer. "I didn't trust my judgment. I'd taken two lives with little remorse when I'd been trained to tackle just such a situation without endangering life. I was on the wrong side of emotional."

"There is…was a debriefing process for that. And I would've helped you get through it too."

"But you…you were part of the problem," she says in a bleak little voice that flays me.

Jesus. "What?"

She exhales heavily. "You…you overwhelmed me with…everything."

I stiffen and can't quite catch my breath, but I don't defend myself. Because I can't. The magnitude of my obsession staggered me too. The only problem was that I wholeheartedly embraced it. Immediately. Whereas she fought it. And is still fighting it.

"I'm not blaming you for any of it, Killian. I enjoyed being overwhelmed."

Right. "But you didn't trust me to take care of you. Not when it counted."

She winces. "No. Don't you get it? I didn't trust myself to make the right call when it needed to be made."

"What the hell does that mean?"

"I took matters into my own hands, and two people died. Well, I thought Galveston was dead too." Her mouth twists in bitterness. "But I couldn't even get that one right."

"So your answer was to leave me without so much as a fuck-you?" Four years of anger pulses through my voice.

Her lowered gaze shutters even further. My instincts blare that I'm only getting partial disclosure. "That's not everything, Faith. Is it? What else happened? Did Galveston touch you? Did he do anything—?"

She pales, and I want to kick my own ass for throwing out the unthinkable possibility.

"No. At least I don't think so other than…what he did with the knife." She takes a slow, steady breath. "Please, Killian, let this be enough."

"*Let* it? Why?"

"I fucked up. Badly. Leaving was the only way I thought was right to make amends."

Fury pounds through my veins. "Well, you thought wrong. You put us both through hell. How the fuck does that make anything right? And what was your intention? To hide away forever? Going from the club to your apartment and back again? What sort of life is that?"

She pulls away from me and wraps her arms around her middle. "What would you recommend then? I buy an island in Hawaii and spend the rest of my life sunning myself and drinking mai tais?"

I catch her chin in my hand. "Can the outrage. I know you're hiding something more. What the hell aren't you telling me?"

Her mouth quivers. "Can't you just accept that this is the way it has to be?"

"Fuck no. You know me better than that."

She yanks herself from my grasp. "I'm sorry, but the bottom line was that I didn't want to be a spy anymore, and I was afraid you would talk me out of it. Getting away from you was the only option."

"Faith—"

"I couldn't risk the possibility that the next person to be killed would be you!" Her lips are pressed together in a tremulous white line.

My gut clenches at the words.

The percentage of the Fallhurst Institute's agents returning unscathed from the field was impressive. It was one of the first statistics I checked out before agreeing to join. But there were casualties too. In that line of work, it's inevitable. So I know the risks she feared were real.

I search her face. I see that she believes it.

And yet…

Chapter Twenty

KILLIAN

Before I can probe further, the chopper banks to the right. I look out the window and see our destination. The building is a single-story, shingle-roofed structure with a simple sign that announces its purpose. There is a single pickup truck parked at the front, and as we descend, a figure emerges from the front.

I turn back to Faith. Her attention is fixed on the property too. But I know that she is aware of my scrutiny and is avoiding me.

For now, I swallow the questions crowding my brain as we fly over the T-shaped property and land in a clearing about a hundred yards behind the building.

We disembark in silence. Mitch and Linc head off in opposite directions while Rob, the pilot, remains close by. His loose-limbed stance belies the fact that he's on high alert, and I scrutinize the tree line too.

Linc returns first. "All clear," he says.

We duck under the slowly rotating rotors and head for the side of the building. The truck is heading down the driveway, its taillights blinking once in the trailing dust before it disappears. Mitch pulls the keys out of the front door and holds it open. "We have the place to ourselves until six p.m."

The smell of gunpowder and cleaning oil hangs in the air when we enter. On the towering wall behind the long counter, a vast array of firepower is displayed, from hunting rifles to submachine guns. Mitch locks the door and pockets the keys while Linc moves behind the counter to pull out a large tray holding boxes of ammunition. On the counter itself, ten different types of pistols are laid out on black velvet cloth.

Faith pulls off her shades and baseball cap and looks around, noting the near-complete silence. "You arranged for the place to be empty?"

"It wasn't that difficult. Today was turning out to be a slow day, apparently. And the owner was properly incentivized." I hold up two weapons. "Glock or Smith and Wesson?" She used both during her time at the training facility, although after that she switched to the more compact Ruger.

Her gaze drops to the weapons. I spot a tiny wave of uncertainty fluttering over her face. Our conversation in the chopper flares up between us. "Whatever happened before, Faith, we are in this now. You said you wanted to be prepared. So pick a weapon."

She points to the Smith & Wesson. I hand it to her butt-first before I grab the two boxes of bullets. Mitch walks us down a hall-way and uses the set of keys in his possession to open another door. He throws a switch on the wall, and the large space where the actual range is located lights up. The worn Astroturf muffles our footsteps as we move along the row of cubicles that make up the shooting gallery. Faith picks the one dead center, and I take the one next to her.

"Need anything else, boss?" Mitch asks.

"No. We're good, thanks."

He nods and hands over two pairs of protective earmuffs and goggles before he leaves.

Faith calmly feeds the bullets into the chamber and slams it with a confident kick. But as her finger moves over to flick off the safety, I see her tremble.

I put my own gun down and step up behind her. My intention was to keep up the pressure of my interrogation when we were alone, get her to give up the last piece of whatever the fuck she's holding so close to her chest. But the timing sucks right now. I'm willing to bet that, before she held the gun on me in the park last week, the last time she held a gun was back in Cairo.

I had the dubious benefit of a deep debrief to help me deal with that nightmare. She hasn't. Unless she's holding back about that too.

I stash my angst, and I cup her shoulders. "Hey, it's okay."

Another shudder runs through her body. "No. It's not." The answer is definitive enough to make my pulse trip in apprehension.

"Tell me what's going on. What are you feeling?"

The gun wavers in her hand, and she lays it down on the wooden slab in front of her. "That I can't bear the thought I'll have to point a gun at someone again in the near future. That I'll have even more blood on my hands."

My fingers tighten. "I'm going to fight like hell for that never to happen. But if it has to, do you want to be prepared or not?"

She turns and locks her green eyes on mine. A mixture of defiance and irritation swirls in their depths. It's not the look I crave to see on her face, but at least the bleakness has receded. After a moment, her jaw flexes.

"I hate it when you make a good point," she says.

I lean and whisper in her ear, "I know. I tell you what, the person who gets the most dead-center shots gets to dictate how the rest of the evening goes. Deal?"

The barest hint of a smile turns up her lips. "Are you sure you're prepared for that level of ass-kicking?"

My gaze drops down to her legs, and even though my senses are still raked raw with everything she said in the chopper, my basest instinct is still very much alive and kicking. "I'll happily take whatever punishment you dish out if it involves using those legs on me."

Her eyes turn a darker shade of green, and her nostrils flare delicately as she inhales. I swear I catch a hint of gratitude in her eyes before she turns and reaches for the gun again.

I place her earmuffs over her ears and step back and put mine on. "Remember your training. Breathe."

She nods and steadily raises her gun. The first shot explodes from the muzzle and goes wide, nipping the bottom edge of the target. "That doesn't count," she snaps.

I bite the inside of my cheek to keep from laughing and remain behind her. "Am I putting you off, baby?"

"You wish," she says, but she catches her lower lip between her teeth in concentration as she lines up another shot. This one is closer to the target. The next one is even better.

Yep, she was rusty, but she's quickly finding her feet again. I move to my cubicle and grab my gun. I fire three in succession, each hitting the bull's-eye. The next two stray an inch or two to the left. But the last rounds hit dead center.

She glances over at me as the target reels toward us. "That was a stupid bet," she mutters.

I laugh under my breath. "Best of five?"

Her lips purse. Then she nods. "You're on."

I win the first set. She challenges me to a second set. I win that one too. We take a break while I fetch more bullets. She's drinking from a water bottle when I return. A few drops slide down the corner of her mouth, land on her chest, and disappear between her breasts.

My GI Jane fantasies roar to life. She reads me loud and clear, and the bottle in her hand quivers as she lowers it. "Killian...what—"

"I'm going to buy you some dog tags," I promise, my voice thick with arousal. "You're going to wear them between those beautiful tits. I'll get you some combat boots too. Those scuffed-up ones with the thick heels. You'll wear just the tags and the boots, with your hair tied up like that and those naughty bangs teasing your eyes. And you're going to sit on my face for a solid hour. You can come as many times as you want."

A visible tremble rakes her body, and she swallows hard. "And...after that?"

I walk slowly over to her, pluck the bottle from her fingers, and take a long drink. "I'm tying that long hair around my arm, and I'm fucking you from behind…in both holes…until one of us passes out."

She sags against the wall behind her. I catch her around the waist and pull her back up and hold out the bullets. "You ready to go again?"

Her eyes narrow. I laugh and earn myself a punch in the arm. "Just for that I'm going to kick your ass this round."

And she does, and the one after that, by fractions of an inch. But, because I'm the selfish asshole who wants what he wants, I pull out my ruthless streak and win the next four rounds.

She yanks the earmuffs and goggles off in annoyance. "I still say it was a stupid bet."

I discard my gear and enter her cubicle, my eager gaze seeking out and finding what I crave. "Stupid or not, I believe I have a prize coming to me."

She slowly looks over her shoulder at me. "And what's that?"

"You know what the sight of that ass in those shorts has been doing to me for the last four hours?" My voice is as thick as the needy bulge growing in my pants.

Her lips part on a quick little pant. The sound of it wraps around my cock and squeezes tight. "I asked you a question. Do you?"

She raises her chin. "I'm not a mind reader."

I smile. Her breathing accelerates even more. "Maybe not, but you're a body reader. What's my body saying, sweetheart?"

She makes a show of scrutinizing me from head to toe, her eyes lingering in places that set me on fire. Her gaze snaps back to the front. Her fingers flutter over the items laid out. "Killian, we can't."

I step up to her, pressing my crotch against the culprit responsible for my current state. "Tell me you don't want this bad boy inside you. Tell me you don't feel this insane hunger that's killing me."

The tiniest nudge of her ass against my crotch. But it spells her doom. "I do. But we can't do that…here."

The simple admission after so much resistance is almost my undoing. I bend my knees and settle myself firmly against her until I feel the globes begin to cradle me. "Baby, don't fuck with me. I dictate how this goes, remember? I won fair and square."

A saucy smile lifts the corners of her mouth. "Okay. I'm yours. Tell me what you want."

I want to fall on my knees and shout hallelujah. But I can't risk not being able to stand if I do. I straighten and trail the backs of my fingers down her arms. "Leave those hands where they are. Grip the edge if you have to, but they leave that shelf and I'm starting again."

Her breath hitches. "Starting what?"

My mouth whispers over her smooth cheekbone, the smell of her skin so intoxicating that I want to devour her. "You'll see. Now face forward and do as I say."

Her hands grip the edge of the wooden slab.

I circle her trim waist with my hands, tighten my hold, and rock my hips against her for a second before I glide my hands down to grip her ass. My touch is less than gentle when I squeeze. A hot little moan leaves her lips.

I kick her legs apart, wide enough for me to kneel between them. Then I reach around to the front and open the button on her shorts. A tug of the zipper and the offending material keeping her from me drops to snag on her hips. The sight of her very skimpy thong stupefies me for a minute. "Fuck, baby, you're so lucky I didn't know you were wearing this before."

"W…why?" she stutters adorably.

"Because so far, those tiny scraps of lace you wear cover your ass. But on the day we decide to go out, you wear two pieces of string?"

I bring my hand down hard on her left butt cheek. She yelps, and her whole body shakes. I follow my spank with a bite, and her knees give way. A moment later, her scent hits my nostrils.

"Fuck, I can smell you." I spank her right cheek, and I'm rewarded with the same reaction. With the same wave of heat from her pussy. "God, you're a filthy little thing, aren't you?" I take another bite. "Aren't you?"

"Y…yes."

I yank down her shorts until her widened stance stops them at her calves. But I have more than enough to work with. I pull her thong up between her butt cheeks until her pussy strains against the material. When she tries to rock against the friction, I spank her again.

"You're not allowed to get yourself off. Not until I'm good and ready."

Her moan is half protest, half surrender. I tug again, and again, and watch with rapt hunger as she gets wetter.

"Look at me."

She glances at me over her shoulder. The sight of her stormy green eyes through her bangs adds a layer of steel to my dick. How the fuck is it even possible for me to be this hard just from that alone?

"Do you want to come?"

Her cheeks flush a deep pink, and she nods. "Please."

"I can't wait to hear you repeat that word sometime soon, when you're on your knees." I tug again, and her eyes flutter.

The next tug is much harder, designed to rip the material keeping her from me. It gives way with a snap.

"Oh God."

I pull the scrap of fabric away, tuck it into my back pocket, and sink to my knees. A tap on her ankle, and she raises one leg. I pull the shorts off, keeping her legs adequately parted, and spread her cheeks.

The sight of her glistening pussy and swollen clit drenches me with a need so strong I feel like I'm going to pass out just looking at her. "God, Faith, you have the most gorgeous cunt."

She trembles harder, probably from my raw language. Or from the use of her name.

"Faith," I test again.

Another shiver. But no protest. I save that piece of info and part her wider. Her beautiful butthole reminds me I haven't taken that incredible pleasure yet. Something else to savor soon. Unable to resist another second, I drag her back and flick my tongue against her puckered flesh.

"Ahhh!"

Beneath my hold, her thigh muscles spasm wildly, and her next breath hisses out. "Feel good?"

"Yes," she moans. She rocks back against me, and I push my tongue deeper into her. "So good."

I'm not sure how much longer I can hold on. Still circling her sphincter, I drag my middle finger through her soaked pussy. Back and forth until she's whimpering.

"Killian…please…"

The plea is too much for me. On the next pass, I slide my finger inside her pussy. Her hungry channel immediately closes around me. Her hips begin to pump, cheeky little strokes at first. Then, when I add another finger, she increases the tempo. I can't find the words to berate her because the picture she creates of her plump ass, her arched back, and the rope of her hair swinging back and forth is so intoxicating I don't mind. I finger her harder, faster, pushing my tongue deeper into her ass.

Her breathing turns ragged, her hands white-knuckled where she's gripping the wood. The only thing I'm missing in this incredible picture is the vision of her tits bouncing with her movements. But then she gives a little pre-orgasmic scream.

"Oh…oh God, I'm coming," she gasps.

"Fuck, yes," I encourage hoarsely.

Her back bows tighter as if her spine is the string that connects her pussy to her brain. Her contractions begin to gather pace, tightening and releasing my fingers. I've felt her come many times, but this is still the most incredible thing. Greedy for more, I crook my finger inside her, searching for that sweet spot that turns her wild. There it is. She bolts up onto her toes and screams louder this time. An instant later, I feel her sweet essence drench my fingers.

My free hand flies to my crotch to tackle my zipper, the need to be inside her—now—pounding painfully through me. She's still twitching through her sublime orgasm when I ram my cock inside her.

She screams and starts to come all over again. Holy fuck. I lock my hands on her waist and hold still, fighting against the muscles relentlessly milking my cock, determined to make me her slave.

"Faith. Oh God, Faith…"

She rocks back against me, slamming her ass against my groin. And because I'm too fucking far gone, I meet her halfway. We pound into each other, our breathing frayed and desperate, the only thing real for us the unique bliss that is ours alone. I want to fuck her forever, until the whole world stops turning. But the ferocious fire barreling up my spine and shooting into my balls tells me my time is limited.

But hell, I'm taking everything I've got. "Fill you…I'm going to fill every inch of your cunt with my cum." I pound her harder, until I swear I feel the edge of her womb on my next thrust.

"Yes! Killian…" My name is a long, strained moan that pulls my balls right up against my cock.

I grit my teeth for one last futile second. And then I erupt. I throw my head back and succumb to the indescribable pleasure sucking me deep into the most glorious abyss. But I don't remain there for long. The world tips upside down, and I'm flying, cresting wave after wave of bliss as her orgasm lengthens mine.

My legs shake and threaten to give way. I sag against her body and wrap my arms tight around her.

"Shit. Shit. God, Faith. I…I…" *Love you. I've loved you since the second I saw you.*

The words remained locked in my throat. Why, exactly, I don't know.

I don't know whether she suspects them or not. We just remain, bowed and spent over the wooden slab, until reality returns in the form of the smell of gunpowder and damp Astroturf.

Reluctantly, I pull out of her. I tug her thong out of my back pocket and clean us up the best I can. Her pussy is still damp, and my cock is still wrapped in her cum. But I don't give a damn. I don't care if the whole world knows we've just fucked. I drop a quick kiss on her pussy when I pull up and zip her shorts. She rewards me with one last shudder.

And just because I can, I kiss her mouth long and deep. When lift my head, she presses her fingers to her lips. "Every time..."

"What?"

"Every time I think it won't get any better, you make it amazing," she murmurs, her voice a little stunned.

I'm not surprised when the words pull at my chest, instead of pumping up my ego. I want to lay every promise of her every desire right there at her feet in this shitty little shooting range. I don't. But a little bit of my apprehension recedes.

I brush my knuckle down her cheek. "Stick around, baby. I promise I have more to give."

She smiles, but I catch that shadow again and turn away before it ruins my relative calm.

I gather the weapons, and we head back onto the main floor. Mitch and Linc are by the door, talking in low voices. Rob is leafing through a copy of *Guns & Ammo*. He discards it when he spots us.

"You ready to head out, Mr. Knight?" he asks.

I nod and hand the guns over to Mitch, who replaces them in their glass vaults. I leave them to lock up, and escort Faith back to the chopper. Five minutes later, we lift off.

She's sitting next to me on the bench seat, her head tucked against my shoulder. I'm not sure whether it's the sublime sex or the fact that my instincts tell me we've reached saturation point, but I slide my fingers into her hair and gently tug her head up.

"I need to know, Faith. Everything."

I watch as her mouth quivers and her eyes slowly fill with tears. My badass lover, who once drop-kicked two Bulgarian thugs without breaking a sweat, is crying.

"You'll hate me."

My heart turns over. "No. I won't." The conviction in my voice is total.

Her eyes widen. "Killian—"

"I'm not a fucking saint. There are some things I won't find easy to live with, but I will *never* hate you."

A tremulous smile curves her lips but doesn't make it to her eyes. "A blanket pardon would be great right about now."

I cup her chin and press my mouth to hers. "We will work toward it, if we need to. But you're telling me. Tonight."

Her eyes turn a darker shade of moss. After a beat, she nods.

Something gives inside me that leaves me weak with relief. I nudge her back against me, and we watch the denser outskirts of New York State give way to the bright lights of the Big Apple.

We're five minutes out from landing, when Miniature Betty beeps in my pocket. For a moment, I'm startled, having momentarily forgotten about the other dangers hanging over us.

Faith tenses against me as I lift the gadget and hit the requisite buttons. She's dislodged from my side when I jerk upright.

"Fuck!"

"What's wrong?"

"Betty's spotted a ninety percent likeness of Paul Galveston."

Her breath catches. "Where?"

"The Algonquin in Midtown."

"He's here? In New York?"

I nod and scroll through the rest of the information. My blood turns ice-cold. "She backtracked his movements."

"And?"

"He was on the Upper East Side two hours ago."

"That could mean anything. Or nothing." I hear the hope in her voice. But the fear is stronger.

Both emotions run through me as I keep scrolling. The last nugget sends my world into free fall.

"What is it, Killian?"

I hit zoom on the image and show it to her. Her stunned gasp echoes my emotions.

"That's...Fionnella."

I scrub a hand down my face. "Yes."

She looks closer and spots what I've already seen. "Is she...? Oh my God, she's in our...your apartment," she remarks in a shock-dulled voice.

"Yes," I confirm.

Her hand is shaking when she sets the gadget down. "What…we can't just leave her there…can we?"

"When I saw Galveston's location, I was going to instruct Rob to change course and fly us to Teterboro. My plane is waiting. I could fly us anywhere else in the world as long as we're not in the same city as this fucking bastard…"

Her gaze drops to the gadget. "But we can't."

"No. This isn't a coincidence. I think we need to see her. Find out what this is all about."

Half an hour later, tense silence rules the penthouse living room as we stare at the smiling woman seated across from us.

"So, I'm sorry to be the bearer of un-fun news, but you've had almost a week together. The honeymoon is over, kids. It's time to get back to work."

PART THREE

Burn

Chapter Twenty-One

KILLIAN

I'm a lot pissed and puzzled about how Fionnella bypassed my security without triggering any of my alarms. "We don't work for you. Hell, we don't even know who you really are."

Her gaze shifts from Faith, where it's rested for far too long, back to me. "You never worked for me, handsome. That's what made us so great together."

Faith's fingers dig into mine, and I know she's getting pissed with Fionnella. We have enough unknown quantities to deal with without this strange woman dropping into our lives now. Coupled with the ridiculous ease with which Fionnella's breached my security and doesn't seem sorry about it, Faith looks like she's seconds from tackling the older woman to the ground. I would probably let her, if only this weren't another shitty moment sent to fuck up my aim to lock down the woman I love.

"Are you going to tell us who you are?" I snap.

Her gaze shifts back to Faith and stays, and it's my turn to experience the charged tension. "She knows who I am, don't you, B?" Fionnella says.

Faith stiffened.

Enough of this shit. "That's not her name, and you know it. And yes, she's told me about your little visit to the club," I tell her.

Fionnella shrugs. "That was a happy coincidence. My call to her before that, however, wasn't. If she hadn't thrown her hissy fit then, maybe we wouldn't be in this mess."

"Watch it," I snarl.

For some reason, that makes her smile wider. Her gaze drops to our clasped hands, and she nods in satisfaction. "You're still nuts for each other. That's great. Although it took you a while to wise up, didn't it?" Again she redirects her question to Faith. The undercurrents whizzing through the room fry a few more of my nerves.

"Just tell us why you're here," Faith's voice is whisper-thin and edgy.

"Paul Galveston."

We both tense. "What about him?"

"You know he's reared his ugly little head up from the swamps. So do we."

"We? So you work with us at the Fallhurst Institute?" I ask.

She smiles at me. "Does it matter who I work for?" Before I can answer, she continues. "In case you're wondering why, it's because you found her." She nods at Faith.

"What are you talking about?"

"He's been waiting for you to lead him to Faith. I tried to warn her three weeks ago after her little mishap with the camera on East Fifty-Third Street."

I spring upright, unable to sit still with the knowledge that a shit storm is headed our way. "Jesus, how the hell did you know about that?"

"Does it matter? I know. He knows. We need to deal with it."

"Do you know he's here, in New York City?"

Fionnella nods. "Yes. Well, he was a few hours ago."

I frown. "What's that supposed to mean?"

"It means he may not be in New York any longer. Whatever he came here for may be done."

"Enough with this *Murder, She Wrote* crap. If you know something, tell us," Faith snaps.

She smiles at Faith. "All in good time, dear," she replies in a perfect imitation of Jessica Fletcher.

"So Galveston may or may not still be in New York City. Are they planning something? What about Raj Phillips?" I demand.

Her brown eyes gleam before she waves my questions away. "Raj has been dealt with. He's no longer a problem. Galveston is our main concern now."

"Why does he want... Why is he looking for me?" Faith asks.

Fionnella's gaze is almost sympathetic. Except the steely directness is hard to ignore. "The guy you killed in Cairo was a sleazebag. But he also had an unholy trinity thing going for him that made him a key player in Galveston's operation."

"Who was he?" Faith asks.

"He was the shipping minister. He was also Galveston's distant uncle through his mother's side—don't ask me to give you a genealogy lesson. And he was a minor royal of some sort. Word got out about where and how he died. Caused all sorts of ripples in all sorts of circles."

I scrub my fingers through my hair. "Shit."

She nods at me. "Yes, they weren't very happy with his nephew Paul. But because of his connections, he managed to avoid a trial and imprisonment, but they weren't about to let him go scot-free. Galveston's been off the radar because he spent a little time under 'house arrest.'" She makes quote signs with a grin. "They tried to release him last year, but we pulled a few strings to extend his stay until his father stepped in with a bigger sweetener than we could afford."

"So the senator is still involved, despite knowing what went down in Cairo?" I ask.

"Yes, up to his eyeballs."

"Then why haven't you arrested him? Why didn't you arrest Galveston the moment he stepped foot back in the US?" I demand.

"It's not that simple. If it were, I wouldn't be here."

"Bullshit. He tried to kill her." I nod at Faith. "Have him charged with attempted murder."

Fionnella's smile dims, and she all but rolls her eyes at me. "Don't be naïve. Exposure like that won't be sanctioned by anyone at the agency."

"*Ex*-agency. I...we don't work for them anymore," I tell her.

Fionnella raises her eyebrows. "Right. I heard the rumors to that effect, but let's leave that for now. Faith, you can't just walk away. There are protocols you need to go through. The uncoupling doesn't happen just because you wish it."

"I'll sign whatever they want. I was there for less than five minutes anyway," Faith says.

Fionnella remains silent for a long moment. "But you made an impact, in a good way. Before Cairo anyway. Are you sure you—?"

"She's sure. We're both sure," I interject. "Can we get back to Galveston?"

"Sure. You want to know why we can't just scoop him up? Because we still don't know the intricacies of his operation. And we've confirmed that it's still going on. It's a much smaller operation than it was before now that Black and Phillips are out of the way, and thanks to what you did in Cairo. But it's only a matter of time before Galveston expands again. Especially now that we're sure that he has—" She pauses as the buzzer on the door sounds, and stares at me with a question in her eyes.

My apprehension ramps higher. Mitch or Linc wouldn't interrupt unless it was important. As in life-or-death important.

Faith jerks forward in her seat too. "Killian..."

I lean down and brush a kiss on her forehead. "It's okay, baby."

Fionnella's gaze shifts from Faith to me. "For what it's worth, your security is impressive. Whoever's out there will have a tough time entering if they're not on your approved list."

Faith glares at her. "Everything's a laugh riot to you, isn't it?"

Fionnella smiles serenely back. "No, not everything," she murmurs softly.

I puzzle over the odd note in her voice as I walk out of the living room and head to the door. I push a button to display the camera's view outside. It's Linc.

I hit the intercom. "Everything okay?"

He holds up a small envelope to the camera. "This was just delivered for you downstairs. We've checked it out. It's a thumb drive with no incendiary components. But it's encrypted, so we don't know what's on it."

"You should take that."

I jerk around at Fionnella's voice.

She and Faith are standing six feet away from me. Christ, I wish I weren't so averse to strangling annoying women. "Not until you get Faith the hell away from here," I snarl at her. Although my instincts tell me she's on our side, I get the feeling she's more on Faith's side than mine.

More fucking secrets.

"You're right. My bad. Come on, B."

She's yanking my chain with that B thing. I know it. All the same, my teeth grind as I wait for them to return to the living room, and then I go through the security measures to open the front door.

Linc looks a little concerned as he hands me the envelope. "Is everything all right, sir?"

"I have no fucking idea. Do me a favor and get my pilots on standby, would you? And tell Mitch we might need to leave at short notice. Oh, and get the guys outside to be extra-vigilant."

He nods briskly and hurries away.

I turn over the plain white envelope in my hand. Then I slide my finger under the flap and upend it. A plain black thumb drive falls into my hand. It looks innocuous enough, but anonymous deliveries never bode well. Not in movies and most definitely not in real life.

I examine it closely as I walk back into the living room. The women are standing at the window, speaking in low voices. Faith stops and tenses as I approach. Fionnella's gaze rests on her for another moment before she sends me that Sunday-school-teacher smile that makes my gut clench.

That is until she sees what's in my hand. For the first time, her affable expression drops, and she looks a cross between angry and resigned. "Oh, dammit."

"What?"

"That looks familiar."

I examine the stick closer. "Probably because it's a cheap, seven-dollar thumb drive. You can get them anywhere."

"But not what's on it. Unless I'm hugely mistaken, and I really hope I am." But she doesn't sound hopeful.

I look over at Faith, and her face is as haggard as I feel. The vise around my chest tightens. I don't regret chasing her down but, Jesus, if all this shit is happening because of me...

"Well, we're not going to find out just standing around," Fionnella says. "I have a laptop—"

"So do I."

She shakes her head. "Use mine."

"Why?"

Her smile attempts a resurrection. "I have a feeling you'll react a certain way once you see what's on there. It's better you don't leave digital bread crumbs."

"Fuck, do you ever just speak plainly?" My question emerges in a near growl.

"All the time. You just don't want to hear me now because you're pissed I broke through your precious security. And you feel a little threatened about my familiarity with your woman."

My breath hisses out of me. "Jesus..."

"You wanted plain. Now you have it." She nods at the drive in my hand. "We're wasting time, son."

"Give me your laptop," I manage to say through gritted teeth.

She returns to the sofa and yanks open a large, tattered purse. The machine is compact, but even by my standards, it's hugely impressive. She braces it on her arm, lifts the lid, and inputs strokes too fast for me to follow.

Faith walks toward me as I take the laptop and insert the drive. I wish there was a way to shield her from whatever's coming. My gut tells me it won't be pretty.

It's not.

Fionnella curses under her breath as the picture of a bloodied face materializes on-screen. I look at Faith, and she's deathly pale as she stares at the man.

"Who is he?" she asks.

The picture pans out to show the figure tied to a chair. Nothing about the plain, dark room looks familiar. But my skin crawls.

"That's one of Fallhurst's agents," Fionnella responds. "He was supposed to be on assignment in Boise, Idaho. He didn't show up. That was five days ago."

Faith shudders against me. "Oh God."

I put my arm around her shoulders. As she curls into me, the dots connect with a blinding flash.

My gaze locks on Fionnella. "Wait. This is how you found out about Ted and Shane, isn't it?"

She nods. "Yes. Two agents killed in two different countries are bad enough. A third one so soon after the first two—"

"You have a mole," Faith blurts.

Her lips purse, and she nods again. "That's why we can't just scoop up Galveston and toss him in the darkest black site hole. Not until we find out who's feeding him the information."

"Because whoever it is will just continue..."

We're absorbing the discovery when the sound of a gunshot rips through the speakers. Our gazes return to the screen as the agent falls off the chair and lands in a dead heap on the ground.

"No!" Faith's voice is a ragged sob.

"Shit," Fionnella mutters.

I bite back a curse and keep my gaze fixed on the screen, looking for any clues that might help us down the line. But nothing happens. The camera stays on the dead body as a voice that sounds like Galveston's, and yet not, filters through.

"That's three for three, Knight."

My puzzled gaze darts to Fionnella.

"Black, Phillips, his uncle," she elaborates.

My breath punches out of me. Fuck. But a moment later, a tiny wave of guilty relief goes through me. If he considers us even, then Faith is safe.

His next words chew through my relief like acid on flesh. "For my part, since I'm still alive, despite your girlfriend trying to make it otherwise, I'm prepared to negotiate. Fifty million dollars in exchange for letting bygones be bygones and leaving your precious Faith alone."

Everything inside me freezes, even while I calculate how quickly I can make that happen.

Fifty million dollars for Faith. The woman I love. I'd pay it a hundred times over.

Fionnella hits *pause* on the recording and shakes her head. "Don't even think about it, son."

My teeth grind. "Well, luckily it's not up to you."

"Yes. It is."

I laugh. "How the hell do you figure that?"

"You really don't want to find out."

I crack a smile of my own. The gall of this woman. She's half my size, and I can break her into little pieces without losing too much sleep. "Try me. Really," I encourage softly.

Her eyes harden to frozen lakes. "Have you told her you didn't just happen to stop by to visit brother dearest that day five years ago? Does she know you went there to investigate him?"

Chapter Twenty-Two

KILLIAN

Faith gasps and flinches away from me. Her eyes are wide pools of dread and growing anguish. "What?"

I kill the panic crawling up my spine. "What the fuck are you doing?" My teeth are clenched tight enough to make my jaw hurt.

Fionnella ignores me and turns to Faith. "And you, *B*? Did you tell him that I was the one who helped you get away from him in Cairo?"

It's my turn to flinch. My turn to be sucker punched so hard that I think my lungs may never work again.

But our Sunday-school-teacher-turned-torturer isn't done. "Does he know about—?"

"Stop it! What the hell do you want?"

The raw demand in Faith's voice sobers Fionnella. She plucks her glasses off her face and absently cleans them with the corner of her sleeve. Her grimace is laced with contrition when she glances at us. "Look, I'm sorry. I don't want to wreck your happy little bubble. I really don't. But giving that a-hole what he wants isn't the answer.

Also, keeping secrets never ends well, so I suggest you two deal with that. Later."

I drag my gaze from Faith's, my heart sinking at the suspicion and agony I see in her eyes. I know that look is reflected in mine.

So many fucking secrets. Will we get the chance to make things right?

"What. Do. You. Want?" My voice is an icy blade that cuts through her bullshit.

Fionnella slides her glasses back on. "Say no to the demand," she says briskly. "Let him think you're the arrogant, asshole billionaire he imagines you are. Hell, take it a step further. Taunt the heck out of him."

"For what fucking purpose?"

"To lure him out. He's desperate. We need him to make a mistake. Tip his hand as to who the mole is."

"You want to risk Faith's safety to catch your mole? Are you out of your goddamn mind?"

"Killian—"

"Hell, no," I snarl before Faith can voice whatever unacceptable argument she's about to offer.

She says it anyway. "Think about it! Sleazebags like Galveston are the worst kind of traffickers. They're addicted to their product. You give him the fifty million, you'll be jump-starting his operation again. He'll throw bigger parties than the one he threw in Cairo, with more children. He'll bribe more people to look the other way. You may protect me, but you'll be condemning countless more people to hell."

Fionnella nods approvingly. "What she said."

Jesus. Their twin truths grab and lock into me. No matter how much I reject it—because dear God why would I readily put her in harm's way?—I know denying Faith this will haunt her forever. Possibly even end us, if our secrets haven't done that already.

But still I shake my head because the idea of letting Galveston within a mile of her is unthinkable.

Fionnella leans down and hits the *play* button again.

Galveston's voice filters through. "And you personally owe me too, Knight. Don't think I don't know that you pulled that little stunt in Cairo three years ago. You have forty-eight hours to get me my money."

The screen goes black.

"What does he mean by you owe him? What little stunt?" Faith demands.

I glance at Fionnella. Although I get the feeling she knows, she keeps her mouth shut. For once. I shove my hands into my pockets to keep them from punching something. As confessions go, this one isn't so bad. "I bought the Cairo resort through a dummy corporation six months after the incident. A few months after that, I burned it to the ground."

Faith's mouth drops open. "You what?"

I shrug. "It wasn't hard. A gas explosion, it was reported. It's in the middle of nowhere. By the time the firefighters got there, it was gone."

"What about the agent?" Faith asks into the silence. My heart twists at the ragged pain in her voice. A glance shows her lips pinched in a thin, white line. She's blaming herself for this.

Fionnella doesn't reply.

"Are you just going to leave him...wherever he is?"

"There's protocol for this kind of thing," she replies evasively. "It'll be taken care of."

Faith goes even paler.

"Are we done here?" I snap.

"Not until I have your word you won't act...irrationally—"

"You have my word that I won't pay a single dime in the next twenty-four hours. That should give you time to come up with a plan that suits me and keeps Faith out of danger. If you don't, all bets are off."

I can tell Fionnella's not happy with that, but there's fuck-all she can do. Although I don't put it past her to try. "You told your guy to put your pilots on standby. Are you staying put or are you going somewhere?"

The decision I toyed with on the way back from Uniondale solidifies. "You seem to have compromised my security, so there's no point remaining here. Besides, leaving town will create the impression that we're spooked. That should work in both our favors before we make a plan one way or the other."

Her frown deepens. "At least tell me where you're going."

I want to ask why she's bothering to ask since she'll probably find us anyway. But I want her out of here more than I want to argue with her.

"We're going back to LA."

She looks over at Faith, whose face is set in a tight mask. Then she nods. "Okay, I'll be in touch."

She leaves, taking the thumb drive with her. I don't mind. Every frame and word are seared into my brain. I don't follow her either. She let herself in. She can let herself out.

Besides, I have a much bigger problem confronting me right now.

I watch Faith move to the window, her arms hugging her middle. "Aren't you jumping the gun, assuming I'm coming to LA with you?" she asks with her back to me.

We have a lot of shit to get through, but the issue of her safety isn't one of them. It never will be. "I told you I wasn't letting you out of my sight before I knew for a fact that you were in danger. You're out of your mind if you think that position is about to change now that we have confirmation."

She whirls around and stares at me with dark, bruised eyes before stalking out of the living room. I follow at a slower pace. She's stripped out of her shorts and top and is heading to the bathroom when I reach the bedroom. I stare, unable to drag my gaze from her beautiful, naked body. Primal instinct rises to the fore as I track her to the bathroom.

I lean in the doorway and watch her gather her hair on top of her head. She ignores me as she steps into the cubicle and turns on the shower.

Okay. We're fighting in the shower. I strip too and follow her in.

She smells of her usual intoxicating scent and also faintly metallic. Gunpowder residue from the shooting range. God, was that just a few short hours ago? It feels like a lifetime has passed since we made the bet that got me where I craved most to be. Inside her.

The place I yearn to be now. "Baby, don't shut me out."

She whips around, and the pain in her eyes slays me. "I want to know. What she said...is it true?"

"Faith—"

She shakes her head. "Tell me about Matt. Please. Why...why did you really come to Arkansas?"

I grit my teeth. I don't want to talk about my brother. I really don't want to talk about him while the woman he had but didn't deserve is naked and almost in my arms. But it looks like we're doing this. "His name popped up when we were investigating Galveston. Nothing to do with the actual trafficking as far as we could tell, just...He was mixed up in sleazy deals. He was desperate to get into Washington. He thought he could buy his way in."

"So you came to what? Spy on him?"

I hesitate and then go for broke. "Yes. And your father."

Her face leaches of color. Her mouth drops open, and she sways. I reach for her but she holds up her hands. "My father?" she whispers.

I sigh. "His name popped up too, but it turned out to be nothing in the long run."

She slowly shakes her head. "My God. You came to spy on my family," she says numbly. Then she tries to slip past me.

I catch her by the shoulders. She tries to knock my hands away again but I hold on tighter.

"Let me go, Killian."

"No, we're talking this out. Right here, right now."

Stormy eyes stare at me, shock and pain building. Then she deflates. "Did he...Matt didn't die in a random shooting, did he?"

I shake my head. "No. He died because he funded his campaign with laundered money from people who later wanted favors he couldn't deliver on. One of them was connected to Galveston."

She shudders and squeezes her eyes shut. "Oh God. Why didn't you tell me?"

"You didn't love him. You were divorcing him. What I didn't know was that you blamed yourself for Matt's death. Not until last week."

Her eyes pop open. "So before last week you thought I was the heartless bitch who didn't care about why her husband was gunned down in an alley?"

"Of course not. Don't put words in my mouth. I didn't think you needed the extra burden of knowing he was involved in shit like that especially when I knew you felt guilty about us."

She shakes her head. "What about me? Were you there to spy on me too?"

I take a deep breath. "Yes. But it became clear you weren't involved."

"Is that why you recruited me? So I could help you spy on my husband?"

"I recruited you because you were intelligent. And fuck it, because I wanted you away from Matt. I wanted you with me."

Silent tears fill her eyes. The sight of them slashes my insides. "Baby...God, I'm sorry."

A wretched sob rips from her. Desperation builds until I stop her tears the only way I know how. By putting my mouth on hers, absorbing her pain inside me. She shivers against me, her whimpers growing louder as she fights me.

Fuck that. "I'm not letting you do this," I mutter fiercely against her lips.

She fights me harder. Steam and agony and guilt rise around us. Sharp nails dig into my sides. My mouth still fused to hers, I step forward and pin her against the wall. The torrent from the shower hits us both over the head, soaking us. I push my tongue into her mouth, feel the helpless slide of hers against mine. Another whimpered protest breaks free. Nails dig in harder. Her nipples pebble against my chest a moment before she plants her hands on me and pushes with considerable strength. I give her a little leeway up top, but from the waist down, we're fused together. My cock is cradled by her belly, and that's where I want to stay.

"Let me go, Killian." Her voice is ragged with pain and arousal.

I smile because my answer is easy. "Never. Not even when I'm dead."

I start to lower my head. She pushes harder. "No. I'm not letting you fuck me better."

I drop my forehead against hers and say desperately, "Okay, then let me fuck you senseless."

Her deep shudder resonates within me. "No," she says, but her voice is weaker. Less pain, more arousal.

"Yes," I stress. I slide my hand down one supple hip, down her thigh to her knee. And I hook my arm beneath it and lift her leg high.

She reads my intent, and her breath hitches. "Killian…"

"Please. Take me. Put me inside you," I plead against her lips.

The hands still braced on my chest stay for an interminably long minute. Then they diverge. One heads up to curl around my neck, pulling me down to meet her angry kiss.

The other heads south, past my groin to curl around my aching cock.

"Yes," I groan, helpless in her hold.

"We're going to burn for this."

"Then we'll burn together."

"Oh God."

"I'm dying for you, Faith. Take me."

She pumps me urgently, almost furiously. Then she positions me against her pussy and brushes my crown through her wet heat. My knees sag. I'm already seeing stars, and I'm not even inside her. I kiss her as I hitch her leg higher and lower my body. And then, because there's nothing more magnificent than watching her take my cock, I lean back and watch as I slide into her tightness.

Slow. Excruciatingly steady so she feels every inch of me. So her mind shifts from what is wrong between us to everything that's right.

She watches me fill her up until her eyes flutter and roll. Until her whole body shakes with the transcendental power of it. "Oh…"

"How can something this beautiful be wrong, Faith?" I whisper hoarsely against her mouth. I pull out and push back in, and her whimper turns into a sweet moan. "Tell me."

"I...oh God."

I wanted to pound her senseless, until every shard of pain is re-placed by mind-numbing pleasure. But this...this spiritual union is so much more. Her head comes up, and her eyes meet mine.

I love you, I want to confess. *So much.* But the fear of it being rejected stays my tongue. She's reeling from discovering why I was really at her birthday party five years ago. There are so many other layers we need to unveil before I have a hope of knowing how our future will pan out. I can't add these three little words—no matter how much I want to—to the mix. Not just yet.

So I tell her with my body. I lift her other leg, brace them over my arms, and push deep, deeper until I feel the edge of her womb. I stay there for a blinding moment, trembling, because inside her feels like home, but right there feels like the sweetest heaven.

Her belly quivers as she clenches tight around me. "Killian... you're so deep," she whispers in a hushed voice.

"I'd go deeper if I could," I whisper back. "Wrap myself around your soul."

She stares at me, and her eyes begin to fill again. I let her cry, let whatever demons are chasing her spill free. She sobs against my shoulder when she comes. I kiss her deep as I stroke that heaven-made spot again and find my own sublime release inside her.

Afterward, in subdued silence, she lets me wash her, and then I wash myself. Damp-haired and barely dry, we tumble into bed. I pull her close and hold her tight. Our agitated hearts pound against each other in weirdly soothing matched beats.

At some point, we fall asleep.

When we wake, she slides on top of me and braces her hands on my chest. I grip her hips and deliver the pounding I promised. Again her climax ends in tears. When she collapses against me, I caress her sweaty body for minute, and then I reach for the phone.

She doesn't protest when I arrange for us to fly out of New York in the morning.

After four long years away, I'm taking her home.

Whether she stays is another matter altogether.

Chapter Twenty-Three

FAITH

"We need to expose you to the mole. Sooner rather than later."

I see the rage that fills Killian's face at Fionnella's words. Since she turned up at the house in Malibu, every word she's uttered rubs him the wrong way.

He's nowhere near okay with any of this. Keeping me safe from Galveston is a worry for him, but ultimately it's not an insurmountable problem for Killian Knight. I know he'd spend every cent of his considerable wealth to fortify me against even a hint of harm if he could. No. He's doing this so I can find some peace from knowing no other children will suffer at the hands of Paul Galveston. He's doing it for my sister's sake.

He rises from the sofa and prowls around the living room. I know how hard it was for him to make the call to Fionnella to say we were on board.

I love him for that. Hell, I love him for everything. Good and bad. But I don't know if my final secret will break us or not.

And I'm too chicken to find out.

What happened with him in his bathroom back in New York City two nights ago altered things for me. The revelations have allowed me to hope that things might not be so dire after all.

The knowledge that Matt didn't die because of me and the illicit desire I felt for his brother helped a great deal. But that burden has been replaced with the heavier one of keeping the loss of our baby from Killian.

Despite his contentment that I'm back here in California with him, I see the shadows in his eyes when he watches me.

"The only way to do that is to integrate you—temporarily"—Fionnella adds hastily when Killian whirls around from where he's standing gazing out the floor-to-ceiling window of his Malibu mansion—"into the agency again. We will do it under the guise of you getting your long-overdue debrief, followed by you taking your official exit protocol tests. We'll drop a few hints that you two are planning a long absence with destination unknown. The forty-eight hours have passed. Galveston knows by now that you're not going to pay the money. Hopefully that will light a fire under the mole's ass."

"And then what?" Killian bites out, his folded arms bulging with his restlessness.

Fionnella looks around at the vast property that sits on its own wide bluff in Malibu. The nearest property is a quarter of a mile away, and every imaginable measure has been taken throughout the mansion to ensure my safety, with Mitch and Linc managing a staggering team of fierce-looking mercenaries around the clock.

"You're not exactly sitting ducks in this house, so I doubt he'll make a move here. If we feed him the information that you'll be heading overseas soon, he'll most likely choose then to make his move. But it won't come to that. We've developed a slightly more sophisticated way of placing digital bread crumbs on the agency's system. We'll find whoever it is before the information gets to Galveston, son. Trust me."

Killian's tension doesn't ease even a fraction. I rise from the sofa and walk over to slide my arms around his waist. He immediately pulls me closer, brushing his lips over my cheek and then the corner of my mouth. My reassuring smile pulls a deep exhale from him before he redirects his attention to Fionnella.

"When does all this bullshit start?" he asks.

Fionnella smiles and swipes a finger across an ancient-looking tablet. "Tomorrow morning. Nine a.m. You have an appointment with one of our specialists. You'll be there for a few hours. A car will pick you up at—"

"No, I'll bring her myself," he says.

The older woman's lips purse, but then she wisely nods. She's gotten what she wants, and she knows not to push the issue. "Okay."

Fionnella slants a glance at me. One I hold for a second before I let my gaze slide away. I'm not ready to answer the questions she's silently shouting at me.

We walk her to the door, and she gives us another blinding smile before she climbs into the SUV that looks like it can withstand a nuclear bomb.

Killian doesn't hold back when he slams the door behind her. "I don't like this," he breathes against my neck.

"I know."

"The variables are too many. I hate gambling your safety on possibles and maybes. It's ten kinds of fucked up."

"Yes."

"Stop trying to humor me."

"Okay."

We stay like that for a minute. Until his hands tighten convulsively on my waist. "Fuck, I want to throw you into the chopper and head for Van Nuys right now. We could be in the fucking Amazon jungle by morning. Or a cave in Iceland. Let me buy you a cave in Iceland? You won't need any clothes. I'd drape you in bearskin rugs to keep you warm, but you'll be naked underneath. Naked, and all mine," he croons against my ear.

A decadent shiver runs through me. "I'll think about it. But after we do this. Okay?"

"Dammit. I can't deny you anything. You know that."

I drag my fingers across his tense torso, reveling in the shiver that ripples through him. "I think I'll go for a swim. Join me?"

I'm trying to take his mind off tomorrow, and he knows it. "That depends."

I peer at him through my bangs and blink innocently. "On?"

"Indoor pool or outside?" he asks with a definite husk to his voice.

"You choose."

Fierce blue eyes scour my face, my breasts, my legs. "Indoors. Meet you there in five minutes?"

I nod. He takes a few extra moments to release me. I strut away with a sexy sway I perfected for the Punishment Club, knowing his attention is riveted to my body. I'm not proud of myself. For the last two days, I've relied on sex to delay the inevitable and to cope with what's happening. Sex with an edge of desperation on my part, and of worry on his part, sure, but sublime, heart-wrenching sex never-theless.

I walk through the stupidly large, marble-floored living room, my gaze sweeping over the incredible views of the ocean.

The first time I saw the spectacular mansion, I jokingly called it his Iron Man house. Killian's boyish grin told me that was the ex-act reaction he'd wanted. Turns out Tony Stark is secretly my genius lover's favorite comic-book hero. Go figure.

I hurry along a wide, glass-bordered hallway into the massive master bedroom. The California king is rumpled from our activities before, and with Debbie, Killian's housekeeper, having been given the day off, it's going to stay that way till tomorrow. I smile as I pick up his discarded T-shirt from the floor on the way to the dressing room, that little act of taking care of him lifting my heart.

The bigger, baser act of really taking care of him leaves me a little breathless as I tug my short sundress off and head for my lingerie drawer. The swimsuit is part of the closet of clothes I left here four years ago. My heart tumbles over again at the thought that Killian really has kept everything I left behind.

I select the blue bikini because it reminds me of Killian's eyes.

And also because it's super-skimpy to the point of indecent. The first time I wore it, he made me promise to only use it for our private, indoor pool.

I secure the strings, slip my feet into six-inch red-soled platform shoes, and catch my hair up in a loose bun. The shoes are impractical as fuck, but what the hell. After a light application of gloss, I leave the room. I smile as I head for the pool, and then I realize...I'm *happy*.

I stumble to a stop, and slide a shaky hand over the pulse racing at my throat. God.

What kind of person am I? Using sex to cover my sins and daring to be happy about it. *We'll burn for this.*

Those were my words to Killian two days ago, but no. My lover is above guilt. Whereas my hands are soaked in guilt and blood.

"Your five minutes are up."

I jump at the voice transmitted into the room from hidden speakers. I drop my hand, swallow the angst raging inside me, and walk out of the room. Another curved corridor with even more fabulous views takes me to the stairs that lead down one level to the blue-tiled pool.

He's reclining on a lounger with his arms tucked behind his head. But I'm not fooled by his relaxed stance. I feel his tension from across the room, and when he turns his head a moment later, I'm seared by razor-sharp hunger. His gaze moves lower. And he jerks upright.

"Fucking Christ." His chest expands and contracts rapidly, and were I not confident of his prowess, I'd fear he was about to have a heart attack.

I walk over to stand before him and let my own gaze drift over the wide expanse of his bare shoulders and torso. "Hi."

When his gaze falls to my legs and his eyes turn molten, I don't fight the illicit thrill that worms its way through me.

"What the fuck are you trying to do to me?" he croaks.

I give him a little smile even though I want to smile wide, tell him I love him. I can't yet, not until he knows everything. "Is one of those for me?" I nod at the two drinks sitting on the table next to his lounger.

His hand shakes as he picks up one cocktail and hands it to me. I provocatively wrap my lips around the straw and suck, reveling in the sharp hiss it draws from him.

After a long swallow, I place the glass on the table and carefully step out of my heels. "I'm going to cool off. Are you coming?"

He swears again as vivid color slashes his cheeks. "Go. I'll watch."

I nod and swivel on the balls of my feet. I feel his scrutiny on every inch of my body as I walk to the shallow steps leading into the pool. I swim with my head above water, and my unhurried breast strokes take me from one end of the pool to the other. I sigh at the heavenly sensation of the silky, warm water on my body.

Halfway through my second lap, Killian rises and prowls to the edge of the pool. He's making no effort to hide the huge erection in his shorts, and the ever-pervading hunger between my legs flares to life. By the time I complete the third lap, he's sitting on the first step, his legs half-submerged in the pool.

"Enough, baby. Come here."

I swim over to him, dropping onto all fours when I reach the bottom step. The water laps against my breasts. His gaze heats up fiercer, and he swallows hard.

"Closer. Please."

I move higher, until my upper body is out of the water and I'm between his parted knees. "Release your hair," he commands roughly.

When I comply, he reaches forward and tunnels his fingers through my hair. "You're the most beautiful thing I've ever seen. The most precious thing in my life. Tell me you know that?"

My heart shakes with the depth of what I feel for this man. Everything inside me wants to scream it. "Oh, Killian."

His trembling hand moves over my neck, my collarbone, my breasts. "God, I need you. So much."

"Tell me what you want," I offer.

His eyes darken dramatically. "Everything."

I nod, even though I know he means more than my body, and I know I can't give him that. Not just yet. I lean closer until I can place my mouth against his. He deepens the kiss immediately, his ingrained need for control threatening to take over. He growls when I pull away but groans when my lips trail over his neck. Then lower down his torso.

Breathing heavily, he watches me as I nip and lick my way down to the edge of his shorts. He leans back on powerful arms and raises his body. I yank at his clothing, and his cock springs free. Hot and thick and heavy, it drives the need to tease from my body. With a moan of desire torn from my soul, I wrap a fist around him and draw him deep into my mouth.

"Yes! That's it, baby. You have the power. Take it. Take it all. I'll go wherever you lead me. Anywhere. Anytime."

The things he says. Tears that lately seem to hover just below my surface spring into my eyes.

His thumb gently brushes my cheek as a tear slips free. "I'm yours, Faith."

Emotion moves through me as I take him deeper into my mouth, letting my actions show him I'm his too. I draw on every past experience to drive him out of his mind, not stopping when he frantically tears at my bikini top and pulls apart the strings holding my panties. The second I'm naked, he enters the pool and takes up position behind me. Between one breath and the other, he slams deep inside me. My scream echoes over the water, before bouncing back into us.

"God, I love hearing you scream for me."

He slams harder, and my throat sears with my louder scream. Killian fucks me with ferocious purpose, driving the message home about how much I mean to him. And I take it all, heart, body, mind, and soul. Tears spill freely from my eyes. And I'm at the point of throwing in the towel and taking the selfish way out—of confessing love before confessing guilt—when he rears up suddenly and shackles me in his arms until I almost can't breathe. Can't move. He throbs inside me, his cock beating as fast as his heart. "Promise me one thing. Please. Faith. Just one promise."

"Yes," I gasp.

"That you won't use what's happening to leave me."

Shock drenches me. "Killian—"

"I'll never ask for anything else. Just tell me you'll never leave me again."

My heart shrivels a little because I know whether I stay or go may be out of my hands. So I give him the promise I can. "I'll stay for as long as you want me to."

The brutal shudder that wracks him is the start of his intense release. I'm right there along with him. He croons beautiful words in my ear, worshipping me with his body as I succumb to my own bliss.

We spend the rest of the day wrapped in each other. As I fight the sleep that inevitably takes me, I make my own silent promise. That I will fight to stay by his side if I have to.

Chapter Twenty-Four

FAITH

The Fallhurst Institute is tucked away in the Santa Barbara hills. It's designed to look nondescript, at least from the outside. There are no barbed wire fences or armed patrols warning people off the land. The single, tasteful sign is painted in a harmless blue and white. At the front desk, two smartly dressed receptionists wear headsets and offer professional smiles to anyone who strolls in, and the two bodyguards patrolling the large foyer carry their weapons discreetly.

But the moment you enter the elevator, you know you're not in Kansas anymore.

We hold still for the infrared body scan before Killian slides a silver keycard through a slot and punches a code in the panel where the elevator floor numbers are displayed. The doors close, and the smooth descent into the bowels of the earth begins. There is no LED display to tell us how many floors we've navigated, and a slight feeling of claustrophobia creeps over me.

He looks over at me. His eyes are warm but his smile is tense. "You okay?"

I attempt a smile back despite my own tension. "That cave in Iceland sounds great right about now."

He brushes his knuckles over my cheek. "Just say the word, baby."

My heart fills to bursting. Then dips beneath the weight of my secrets. "It's been three days, and you haven't asked me about Cairo. Why I let Fionnella help me."

His hand drops. His body goes rigid, and he faces forward. After a moment, he gives a self-deprecating laugh. "You wanna know why? Because I'm fucking terrified."

My eyes widen. "What? Why?"

"Because you're one of the toughest people I know. And if you're having a hard time telling me why you left me, then it's something big. I thought I could face anything. But the thought of losing you once you confess is killing me. So I'm choosing to bury my head in the sand for now."

My mouth drops open, his explanation making such sense to me that I want to hug him. Then I want to beg for forgiveness on my knees for what I'm doing to us. What I can't undo right this minute in this cold, clandestine place. Because the elevators doors are opening, and a tall, thin man with sharp hazel eyes is waiting for us. His clothes are bigger than his frame and his pallor screams low-level analyst hunched twenty-three hours over a computer.

"Mr. Knight. Miss Carson. Welcome back to the Fallhurst Institute. My name is Scot Scarsdale."

I have no idea who he is, but I nod in response.

We walk down a series of slate-colored corridors with closed doors on either side until we reach the last door on the right. "Your assessment consultant is waiting inside for you, Miss Carson. Mr. Knight... would you like to come with me?"

"No," he says.

Scot frowns. "You can't go in there with her."

"Then bring me a chair. I'll wait out here."

"Uh... I don't think that's protocol."

"Fuck protocol. Is Fionnella Smith here?" Killian snaps, his eyes narrowing mercilessly on the increasingly uncomfortable-looking man.

Scot's frown deepens. "Who?"

Right. Of course he has no idea who we're talking about.

Killian's jaw tightens. "A chair. That's all I need. Now, Scot."

"I'll have to speak to my supervisor—"

The door behind us opens. The redhead is drop-dead gorgeous, right down to the superbright gray eyes, long lashes, and the twin dimples that appear in her cheeks when she spots Killian and smiles.

"Killian...Mr. Knight. This is an unexpected pleasure." She glides past me, her pencil skirt swishing silkily, and holds out her hand in greeting.

Killian's look of surprise turns into a smile. "Lisa, what are you doing here?"

"I was called in on a case." Her gaze shifts to me, reluctantly. "I'm guessing you're my nine o'clock?" she asks with a perfectly plucked, raised eyebrow.

My nod is jerky and cold. I can't help it. She reminds me of Heather Jane Fitzgerald with her fake warmth, perfect teeth, and boyfriend-stealing body. "I'm Faith Carson. You must be Mrs. Channing."

"It's *Miss*. I'm single," she adds. While staring right at Killian. I want to punch her in the face. After a moment, she lowers her gaze demurely. "Come on in, please." She stands aside to let me in and then immediately turns to Killian. "Can I help with anything?"

I'm expecting him to repeat his request for a chair. Instead he shakes his head. "Scot was just about to escort me to level seventeen, weren't you?"

Scot runs a shaky finger inside his collar. "Uh...I'm only allowed up to level ten."

Killian holds up his keycard. "Luckily, I am. Just point me in the right direction. All these corridors look the same to me."

"Yes, of course. I can do that. Right this way, sir."

"Good to see you again, Lisa," Killian says with a nod and a smile.

"You too. I'll be here all day. Feel free to stop by." She points to a small light bulb at the top of her door. "If that's red, it means I have someone in with me. If not, I'm wide open."

I bet you are.

"I might just do that," he replies. I stare in astonishment as he walks off without a second glance at me.

I'm still reeling when she shuts the door behind her and turns to me. "Miss Carson, please take a seat. According to my notes, you've been…away for four years? Make yourself comfortable. We have a lot to get through."

For the next three hours, she probes every inch of my first and second assignments with the agency, jotting down my reactions and responses when I was under pressure.

"Why are you taking notes?"

She looks surprised. "For assessment of your fitness for future missions, of course."

Right. She doesn't know I'm quitting. "Okay."

Her smile is quick and tight, not slow and seductive like the one she gave Killian. I shift in my seat when another arrow of jealousy lances me.

At midday, she calls a halt to the interrogation. I can't leave her office fast enough. Scot is on his own when I exit Lisa Channing's office. He escorts me into the lobby and hurries away as Killian straightens from the pillar he was leaning on and crosses to me.

We walk outside in silence and get into the SUV we drove in.

"Why did you just leave me there?" I blurt even though I swore somewhere between the second and third hours of my assessment that I wasn't going to acknowledge it.

He reaches over and takes my hand, drawing it into his lap. "Because I know the way she operates. Any sign of something between us would've meant another day of probing questions."

I frown. "But doesn't she already know about us?"

"She knows I had a thing with the Widow. She'll probably figure it out eventually, but I wanted to save you the hassle. I want you to be done with her and the whole damn place as soon as possible. Okay?" He raises my hand and kisses my knuckle.

As an explanation, it's pretty decent. And yet…

I'm still seething by the time we roll through the gates of the Malibu mansion. Dinner consists of scrumptious quesadillas prepared by Debbie and a bottle of chilled white wine. But my appetite is nil.

I give up halfway through, and I toss my napkin on the table. "I'm going to take a shower."

"Want some company?"

I shrug. He joins me anyway. Works magic on me with his hands and mouth. By the time we leave the shower, my mood has improved.

Except the next day is just as bad, and the day after is worse. For starters, I go to Lisa Channing's office alone after Killian disappears with Scot the moment the elevator doors open.

The moment I sit down, she starts grilling me about Cairo, and specifically about Killian. About how long we were involved. I'm waiting for the question on how long we fucked, each time we fucked, when the door opens and the subject of my interrogation for the last four hours walks in.

Lisa jumps to her feet, her dimples making an appearance despite the slightly puzzled look on her face. "Killian…hi…umm, we weren't quite done."

"Really? My apologies, I must have gotten my wires crossed. The light outside your door was off."

Her eyes widen. "Was it?" She struts a little too close, her arm brushing his when she walks past him to peer at the light. "That's so weird. I didn't turn it off."

He shrugs, his gaze resting on me.

Lisa walks back into the office, her hands gliding over her lean hips in a subtle move that draws attention to her assets. "Well, seeing as we were at a natural break, Miss Carson, I think we'll leave it here for today."

I stand up and grab my purse. "Great. Cannot wait for tomorrow." The snark in my voice is hard to contain. I head for the door before I do something unfortunate. Like shoving the cactus sitting on her desk somewhere very painful.

"See you around, Lisa," Killian says.

"Oh, I thought you came to see me?"

I grit my teeth and tell myself to keep moving. But I can't help it. I swivel to watch Killian.

"I came to escort Faith back upstairs."

Lisa's gaze darts to me for a moment before she raises an eyebrow at Killian. "You two came together?"

He slides his hands into his pockets. "Yes." He leaves it at that.

Lisa stares at him for a long moment before she smiles. "Next time, then."

"Sure thing."

I contain myself until we're in the elevator.

"*Sure thing?*"

His hands leave his pockets, and he crowds me into one corner of the small space. "I came to save you. Don't I get any credit?"

"No," I snap. God, I hate being jealous. I hate the nastiness it spikes through my bloodstream. I shake my head. "*Sure thing*," I spit again. "She was questioning my motives and my ethics. Can you believe her?"

He lowers his head. "Sorry, baby."

I pull away. "So, is she a genuine redhead?"

His eyebrows knot for a couple of seconds before his eyes widen. Then he laughs.

"Fuck you."

His laughter deepens. "You're jealous."

"Fuck you."

He stops laughing and pushes his groin against me. "Not in the elevator, baby. We don't have enough time."

"I'm glad you find all this hilarious."

"God, I can't wait to get you in the car."

"Nothing is going to happen in the car."

He slides his middle finger into his mouth in a shockingly sexy, slow lick that immediately drenches my panties. Then he holds it in front of my face. "This finger is going into your pussy the moment we're in the car. You can clench that tight cunt around it while you ask me your questions."

My breath snags in my lungs. We're the most real with each other when all the bullshit is stripped away. And sex is the most effective way to go about doing that.

"Or you could just answer the question now?"

He lowers the hand that promises pleasure, and my mood plummets with it. "I ought to spank the shit out of you for even suggesting that I'd fuck my shrink."

"Because you draw the line at sleeping with your coworkers?"

"You will forever be my one exception. The only woman for me. How many times do I need to repeat that?" There's an edge of exasperation in his tone.

"She's clearly hot for you," I say, and hate myself for my inability to leave the subject alone.

I don't know what I expect him to say to that, but the elevator reaches the ground floor, and we step out. His hand slides around my waist, uncaring of the glances we attract as we walk through the foyer to the limo idling at the curb. Killian chose not to drive today after traffic delayed us getting home yesterday. Instead we flew by helicopter halfway and Mitch drove us the rest of the way.

I get in the back and shift to the far side, noting that the partition between us and the front seat is up. Killian dives in after me and grabs me the moment the door shuts. A second later, we're sprawled across the seat. "Where were we?"

"Nowhere," I blurt.

He holds his finger against my pursed lower lip. "Open."

"No."

"Jesus. Your stubbornness is a huge turn-on, I give you that. But goddammit, we'll be at the chopper in fifteen minutes, so maybe shelve the attitude for now and let me make you come? You can fight with me some more when we get home."

"I don't—" The rest of my words are lost when he reaches under my dress, yanks my panties aside, and rams his finger inside my disgustingly wet pussy.

He exhales harshly, and his head drops against my neck. "God, I knew you'd be wet," he says.

"No, you didn't."

"You think I don't know this body? That I don't know what makes you sigh and what makes you scream?" He crooks his finger, and pleasure blazes through me.

"Ahhh…"

"I love that you're jealous, baby, but I don't want you twisted to the point where it comes between us. Got it?"

I grit my teeth and stay silent.

He adds another finger, doubling the pleasure, but then stills. "I need an answer, beautiful. 'Yes, Killian,' will be fine."

When I attempt to shift my hips, he uses his body to restrain me. My frustrated growl draws a laugh. "Now, Faith. And look at me when you say it."

I slowly open my eyes and meet his cobalt blues. And fall deeper in love. "Yes, Killian!"

His blinding smile stays with me all through the fantastic orgasm that he gives me.

Which is a good thing to have in my memory bank. Because only less than a day later, my world turns a darker shade of gray.

Chapter Twenty-Five

FAITH

It starts with Killian walking into the west living room a few hours later, where I'm watching the spectacular early evening view over the Pacific. One look at his face, and my heart begins to pound.

He paces back and forth a few times before he resolutely faces me. "I told myself I wouldn't ask because, frankly, I'm not sure how I'll handle it if the answer doesn't go the way I want it to go. But the alternative, the not knowing, is killing me."

I exhale. I have a strong suspicion of what he's going to ask. This has been a long time coming. I'm stunned that, with our history of questionable obsession, he's remained silent on the subject for this long.

"Killian, it's—"

"I need to fucking know, Faith. Did you fuck someone else when we were apart?"

"We weren't apart. We were over."

"Bullshit. You knew this would be inevitable. The only way we'll ever be over is if we're dead. Answer the damn question."

"No."

His jaw clenches. Hard. He paces to the end of the room and back, digging his hands through his hair. "I can't accept that."

"You'll have to."

"Why the fuck do I have to?"

"Because if I give you an answer, then I have the right to ask a question of my own."

He freezes for a second, then gives me a tense nod. "That's fair enough."

"How do you know? You don't know what I want to ask."

"I'll answer any damn question you want, Faith. Just answer mine first."

The power I'll be handing over in that reply stays my tongue for a full minute. And he grows paler by the second. By the time I open my mouth, he looks sick. "I've changed my mind. I don't want to know."

"Killian—"

A tortured breath shudders out of him. "It's fine, Faith. Forget it." He stalks off to the far side of the room, his fingers laced over his neck as he stares out the window. He's not seeing a damn thing. I know this because his eyes are darting crazily over the horizon while ripples of anguish shake his body.

I walk over to him. He tenses, as if he doesn't want me to touch him. If he could, he would physically reject me right then. But our connection is hardwired to accept each other, for better or worse. I contemplate my own question and the answer I'll receive should I be brave enough to voice it.

Please, please, please.

I tighten my arms around his waist and rest my forehead between his shoulder blades. "I didn't sleep with anyone," I murmur.

His whole body seizes up like he's been shot. His arms drop and he whirls to face me. Cobalt-blue eyes scour my face, probing my every expression. "Repeat that. Louder."

I lay my hand on his chest. Feel the heart hammering beneath the thin layer of cotton. "Before you arrived in New York, I hadn't had sex in over four years. Except with my vibrator."

Beneath my touch, I feel his heart miss a beat. He remains

statue-still for another charged second before he exhales raggedly and staggers back against the window, pulling me into the circle of his arms. "Jesus Christ, Faith. I don't know what I was thinking, putting myself through that. But God, thank you!" He plants a kiss on the top of my head and hugs me tighter. "Thank you."

"No problem," I murmur, my own fear beginning to mount.

He continues to kiss and mutter words of gratitude in my ear, whatever residual emotions left by the demons slowly leaving his body. While I sink deeper into my own hell.

Lisa Channing and her little show of lust triggered my own questions. Questions that are killing me to keep inside.

Just ask him!

I open my mouth, but my vocal cords refuse to work. Or maybe I don't care as much as he did. Bullshit. I care. But maybe I don't need to know just yet. Tomorrow would be fine.

I pull away from him. He raises my chin and kisses me before releasing me. With a wide, increasingly smug, cheese-eating grin. I turn away sharply.

"I'll...I'll go check on dinner," I mutter, and I hurry, cringing as I go. Debbie will throw me out of the kitchen in two seconds flat. But at least I'll have two seconds to deal with the brutal anguish raking through me.

The thought of Killian sleeping with anyone else...

God.

True to form, Debbie glares at me when I walk into the kitchen. Like how I feel about Killian, she's madly jealous about her kitchen.

"I just need some water."

She intercepts me with a bottle she produces out of thin air. I sigh, take it from her, and escape through a series of connecting doors to an atrium filled with climbing vines. I'm taking deep breaths to calm myself when I sense him behind me. I slowly turn around.

He's lounging in the doorway, hands shoved in his pockets, eyes fixed on my face. "You never asked me your question."

I shake my head. "It's fine. I'm good."

"Bullshit. You look as miserable as I felt five minutes ago."

I can't deny it so I shrug.

He steps toward me. "Faith."

I back away. "I said I'm good!"

"I jacked off. A lot. To images of you. To the memory of you. And it helped at first. Until it didn't."

Oh God. "I'd really prefer not to know—"

"Then I decided to torture myself even more by saving it for special occasions. On your birthday. On the anniversary of the first time we kissed. The first time we fucked. That time you cried when I took you to the top of the Eiffel Tower. Things like that. I'm a sick bastard, I know." He laughs. "But at least it gave me something to look forward to."

I know I'm standing there with my mouth open, but for the life of me, I can't shut my gaping hole.

"But there was never anyone else, sweetheart. The thought didn't even cross my mind. You're the only one for me. I'm hooked on your beautiful face, your exquisite body, and your sweet, tight, gorgeous pussy."

Words that will never make it into poetry history books, but they move me enough to evoke tears. I'm a blubbering wreck by the time he crosses the room and snatches me into his arms. I cling to him, muttering incoherent words as he trails kisses all over my face. His hands are busy too, gliding down my body to cup my ass in a firm, carnal hold. "As for this incredible ass, I get fucking stupid every time I look at it," he confesses in an almost mournful voice.

My tears turn to laughter. He smiles and then laughs too.

"Well…" I deliberately pause.

He raises his eyebrows. "Well, what?"

"I'm kinda stupid about you too."

His eyes darken, and his features slowly tighten. "All of me?" he asks with a new tension that speaks to the enormity of my answer and what it'll mean to him.

I swallow the lump in my throat and take another step onto the path of no return. "Yes, Killian. All of you."

He tilts my head up, staring deeper into my eyes. His nostrils pinch on his next breath. "God, Faith. I should be used to the world shifting beneath my feet when I'm with you, but every time I think I'm adjusting, you make me lose my mind even more." He lowers his head until his mouth is a whisper from mine. "Promise me you'll never stop."

It's an easy promise to make. "I'll never stop."

He seals our lips with a deep, fervent kiss that goes on until we're both breathless. When we part, he rests his forehead against mine. "I wish I could take you out tonight. I want dinner by candlelight somewhere special, followed by dancing. Followed by all-night fucking somewhere equally special."

I want to tell him that being with him is special enough, but I feel a little like a fraud, only baring parts of myself to him when he deserves the whole. So I keep my mouth shut and let him kiss me again.

When we part, he drifts one finger over my mouth. "Can I make a date with you, exactly the way I want, for after this shit is over?" he asks.

Tears prickle my eyes, and my smile is hopelessly shaky as I nod. "I'd love to. But in the meantime…" An idea slowly blooms, and my heart races for a completely different reason.

Killian's gaze narrows. "Hmm?"

"We can have a version of that, here at home, if you want?"

"*If* I want? Of course, I want."

I let loose a sultry smile. "I'll need a couple of hours."

He nods after a moment. "I'll get Debbie to delay dinner."

"No, it's fine. I'll take care of it. You go play with your computers."

"I'd rather play with you, but…okay." He links our hands and walks me to the kitchen. Then he leaves me to talk to Debbie.

Once the housekeeper establishes that I'm not there to invade her territory yet again, she gets on board with my request. The Thai-food dinner she had planned is scrapped in place of Killian's favorite.

"He prefers the Sauvignon Blanc with the lobster. Shall I chill a bottle to go with it?" Debbie asks with a smile.

"That'll be perfect."

Her smile widens. "Leave it to me. I'll dig out the nice tableware. Where would you like me to set up? The north terrace or the south?"

I mull over the question for a few seconds. "The south terrace, please."

"Good choice. There's a perfectly balanced view of sea and stars from there at that time of night."

I raise my eyebrows, and she shrugs. "What? So I'm a hopeless romantic."

My laugh is a little more carefree, the belief that Killian and I may just get through this after all settling a little deeper. "Thanks, Debbie. I appreciate it."

Debbie bustles around the kitchen, a new excitement quickening her movements. "You're welcome. I'll have to step out to the store to get some fresh candles. The ones we have are a few years old…" She pauses for a second, and her smile dims as she glances at me. My smile slips a little too as the subject of my absence threatens to spoil the mood. It couldn't have been easy living with Killian while I was in hiding. A second later, she walks over to the peg by the wall and grabs her purse. When she turns around, her smile is back in place. "I won't be long. If you need anything else, just leave me a note."

With a smile of gratitude, I leave the kitchen. My heart skips a few beats at the thought of my plans. Two hours isn't a lot of time. I hurry toward the suite of guest rooms, where the contents of my apartment were relocated when we got here. The bigger items were left behind at my request, but if I know how Killian's mind works, the stripper pole will be with my belongings.

It's the first thing I see when I enter the room. I grin and then bypass it to rummage through storage boxes until I find the other items I need.

I pick the guest bedroom closest to the south terrace, which also happens to contain a spectacular bed, an awesome view, and very little else. The wide bed frame is made of a single, sleek piece of oak that curves into a headboard that extends halfway to the ceiling. The design draws the eye to the ceiling itself, where a large, rectangular mirror reflects my image back to me.

I catch the banked excitement and nervousness in my eyes. I've dealt with countless clients with weird requests over the years. And yet I'm more nervous about this than I ever was about anything I did at the Punishment Club. I lay the outfit on the bed and set up the pole in front of the bed. I take a couple of swings to test out its sturdiness before I leave the room to return to the master suite.

A leisurely bath and the process of readying myself for Killian relaxes me a little. But my nerves kick up again when, an hour later, I throw on a robe and return to the guest bedroom. The intercom that connects every room in the house is located next to the bed. I walk over and press the button for the study.

"Killian?"

"It's about time. I'm going out of my mind," he growls. "What are you doing in the south terrace bedroom?"

Despite my nerves, I grin. "It's a surprise."

"You're calling because you want me to come over now though, right?" he urges impatiently.

"Not yet. Can you come in fifteen minutes?"

He stays silent for a beat, and I know his patience is straining. "Okay. But this better be fucking good."

I glance over at the pole. "It will be." I take my finger off the button and hurry through the final preparations.

By the time he turns the handle and enters the room, I'm in position.

He freezes in the doorway, looks from my face to the pole to the floor-length cloak hiding my outfit, and back again. He takes a few more steps inside. His breathing alters, turning a little uneven. Without taking his eyes off me, he holds up a bottle of vintage Krug champagne and two glasses. "Courtesy of Debbie," he murmurs in a low, gravel-rough voice.

I nod.

He stops next to the bed. "Would you like a glass?" he asks.

"Not just yet. But go ahead and pour yourself one."

He takes a deep breath. His mouth works for a moment before he drags his eyes from me long enough to set the glasses down and deal with the foil of the champagne bottle. While he's busy doing that, I allow my gaze to drift over him.

He must have taken a quick shower after my call. His hair is damp, and his feet are bare. The tailored pants he's wearing aren't belted, and his black silk shirt is completely unbuttoned. The sight of his ripped torso makes my stomach flutter.

The cork pops, and I jump. My gaze returns to his face, and his mouth is pinched tight as he pours the frothing liquid into the glass.

He flicks a glance at me. "Sure you don't want one?"

I shake my head. "No, thanks." I nod at the bed. "Make yourself comfortable."

He eyes the bed and then my dark red cloak and mutters, "Fuck," before he drains the drink.

He discards the glass and steps onto the wide bed. With his gaze still pinned on me, he slowly slides down the headboard into the pile of pillows. "I'm not going to survive this, am I?" he mutters under his breath.

I smile, say nothing, and press a button on the remote in my hand. Low, throbbing music starts on hidden speakers. Another button diffuses the lighting in the room except the one above my head.

Killian watches me like a hawk, his hands on his thighs. As the sound of "Earned It" filters through the room, I toss the remote away and reach for the fastening on the cloak.

The second it drops, Killian jackknifes on the bed. "Jesus!" His voice is little more than a strained, shaky growl, but the effect of it burns straight through me. "Shit…Faith, you look…God you look…" Killian stops and shakes his head.

My outfit consists of a black leather bikini and a garter belt attached to full leather riding chaps. But the bikini bottom is a thong, and the chaps connect to six-inch, red-soled stilettos. As for the bikini top, one wrong move and the girls will pop out.

The rabid look in his eyes drives me to distraction. But I have a performance to give, so I press my siren-red-painted lips together, attempting to ground myself as I wrap my hands around the pole behind me. "It's not GI Jane, but—"

"Fuck GI Jane," he snarls thickly. "This…holy fuck, baby, is so much better," he croaks.

I offer him a smile. "Then lie back and enjoy, Killian."

For a moment I think he's not going to do it. The look in his eyes tells me he wants to rush over and claim me. But the music is wasting so I slide down the pole, widening my legs as I sink onto my heels.

With another curse, Killian drops back onto the pillows. His eyes flick to the mirror above me for a second before they return, a little wilder. I slowly rise again, circling the pole before I take a firm hold and swing myself in a wide arc.

He sees the back of my outfit for the first time, and a hiss breaks free. One hand reaches for the thick erection pulsing beneath his fly. He grips himself through his pants and gives a strangled groan. I complete another arc, wrapping my legs around the pole before letting gravity draw me down. Through my bangs, I watch his breathing worsen, his lips parting as he struggles for oxygen.

I step away from the pole with my back to him, rotate my hips in a slow circle clockwise and then counter-clockwise before I lean over to grab the pole again. With my legs planted a few feet apart, the position gives him full view of my ass and the shadow of my sex.

I dip my torso even lower so I can watch him from between my legs. His fly is halfway open, and his lower lip is caught firmly between his teeth.

I'm a little nervous about my next move, but I fight the unease and pray my Muay Thai has conditioned me enough to do it. I plant my hands on the floor and kick up my legs. I maintain the handstand for a brief, blessed moment before I scissor my thighs around the top of the pole. When I feel stable enough, I pull myself up and wrap my arms around the steel. I'm so pleased with myself that I undulate my hips against the metal, simulating the ride I'd rather be performing.

"So beautiful. God…so beautiful…" His voice is barely coherent.

"Do you like it, Killian?" I tease.

"I'm going to fuck you so hard," he promises raggedly.

The heat of his words makes me wetter. The penultimate chorus of the song warns me I'm running out of time. Still undulating, I extend

my legs and tighten my thigh muscles for more stability and then release the pole to pull on the strings of my bikini top. The sensation of
my breasts spilling free is so arousing that I cup them and moan.

"Christ, Faith, I…can't take it…"

I glance over at him, the man I love, and the look in his eyes tugs
at the very heart of my emotions. I have so much to make up for,
and for the first time, I attempt to pray for a second chance I don't
deserve.

He groans, and my attention refocuses on him. He's flushed and
his cock is gripped in his hand. Time for a little deliverance.

The music is ending. I take a hold of the pole again and nod to
the nightstand as I glide back down. "A present in the drawer for
you."

He doesn't move for a moment. Then he throws an arm out to
tug the drawer open. Unsteady fingers scramble inside and emerge
holding the bottle of lube.

Turbulent blue eyes find mine, and he swallows hard. In silence,
I tug at the side fastening of my thong and pull the leather from my
body, leaving me in the garter, chaps, and heels. I'm naked where it
counts, and I can't wait to be owned.

Raising my arms, I grip the pole above my head. "Come and get
it, big guy."

Killian vaults off the bed, kicks off his pants, and then prowls toward me. When he reaches for his shirt, I shake my head.

"Keep it on, please." There's something dark and wildly sexy
about his long hair and open shirt. He's already on the edge but I
want him even wilder.

When he reaches me, he sets the bottle down by my feet. Then
he cups my boobs, urgently thumbing the peaks as he thrusts his
tongue into my mouth in an almost brutal kiss. After a minute, he
raises his head. "Do you have any idea what you're doing to me with
that body? That sensational mouth?"

My gaze tracks his magnificent body to the stiff, veined cock.
"Some," I murmur.

He kisses me again for a longer spell before he transfers his attention to my breasts. He licks and sucks them till they're raw and beyond sensitive. Until the slickness between my legs coats my inner thighs. He smells me and curses. "If I go anywhere near that pussy, I'm fucked. Turn around. Keep your hands on the pole. Don't let go."

Need drenches me as I obey. "Yes."

His hands frame my hips and tugs me backward until my ass cheeks cradle his cock. He pumps his hips a couple of times, groaning through the tortured bliss.

"I can't wait to be inside that tight ass, baby."

My hands shake with the effort to contain my emotions. "Hurry, please."

He reaches for the bottle. In the next moment, warm oil dribbles on my lower back. I hear the bottle hit the floor again, right before his hand glides the lube to where he needs it. The touch of his thumb against my butthole zips electricity through me.

My wild trembling draws a rough sound from his throat. His hand leaves my waist to grab one breast as the other continues to caress my puckered hole. The sensation of him tugging on my nipple as he applies pressure on my back passage is like nothing I've felt before. But I know a greater pleasure is coming.

His thumb slips past the tight ring, and the burn lights up my whole body. "Argh!"

"Fuck, you're so tight," he growls as he glides his slick digit in and out of me. His other hand continues to work my nipple, and I feel the first rumblings of an orgasm.

"Jesus, you're going to come just from this, aren't you?" he asks in a voice draped with more awe than I deserve.

"Killian…"

He leans close and brushes a kiss on my jaw. "I need more time with that beautiful ass or I'll hurt you, baby. So if you need to come now, go for it. But I'm taking a piece of that action too."

He rams his cock in my pussy a split second later. The sensation of his double impalement rips my orgasm from me. "Oh…oh God!"

"Yes!" he shouts through gritted teeth.

We both shake as I spasm endlessly around him.

"I need you, baby. So bad. I'm sorry...," he whispers in my ear.

He withdraws from my pussy, and then I feel his broad head against my ass. He's slick from my cum and the lube, so the burn of him entering me is slightly minimized. But then he pushes deeper. And I lose sensation in my legs.

"Killian!"

He catches me around the waist, withdraws for a second, and then drives deeper. I scream as pleasure and pain crack dual whips over my spine.

"Fuck! So good...so damn good," he groans.

I'm reduced to screams and moans as he penetrates me with ever-deeper thrusts and beautiful words of worship. His hands caress every inch of available flesh as he drives into me. Just when I think I can't take any more, he rams deep and stops.

"I can't hold on much longer, baby."

I moan an incoherent answer.

"Watch, Faith. I need you to watch."

It takes a moment to remember the mirror. Slowly, I raise my head. Meet his gaze in the reflection above us. Dear God, what a sight we make. Me, gripping the pole, with my legs splayed wide. My love, with his wild hair and wilder eyes, owning me with his cock fully wedged in my ass. Decadent. Beautiful. Together.

"You see how amazing we are together? How impossible it is for me to ever let this go? To take a breath without you?" he demands roughly.

"Yes, I do," I reply simply because it's the same way I feel about him.

He stares into my eyes for an eternity. Then his head drops to my neck. "Good. That's so good. I'm going to come for you now."

He withdraws and slams back inside me half a dozen times and then starts to unravel. I watch it all unfold in the mirror before my own climax hits again. We're struggling for breath when it's all over. Somehow he manages to lift me and stagger with me to the bed without breaking contact.

"I'll give you whatever you want if you promise me this outfit every Sunday for the rest of my life," he croons in my ear as he caresses my chaps-clad thigh.

My laughter coincides with the sound of the intercom summoning us to dinner. We both groan.

"Shall I get her to box it up for later?" Killian suggests.

I reluctantly shake my head. "We can't. She'll hate me."

"I'll write it into her employment contract that she's not allowed to hate you."

"No."

He snuggles into my neck for a moment and then reaches out to hit the intercom. "Twenty minutes."

"Sure," Debbie replies happily before Killian turns off the intercom.

"Her timing sucks. I'm in heaven, and I don't want to leave," he complains.

I reach back and caress his cheek. "I'm sorry."

He sighs again and disengages. We both groan. It takes a moment for me to adjust to the emptiness I feel in body, heart, and soul. When I turn my head, Killian is watching me.

"I feel it too, baby," he murmurs.

We lie like that for another minute before he undresses me completely. Still in silence, we go and shower. I wear the robe I used before, and Killian puts his clothes back on.

As promised, Debbie pulls out all the stops to make dinner magical. The risotto appetizer is sublime, and the lobster thermidor main course is served with creamy garlic mashed potatoes and salad. We feed each other until we're stuffed and then give in to a bowl of Killian's favorite ice cream.

Over the last glass of wine, we watch the moon over the water and the stars in the sky. And as I lay my head on his shoulder, I dare to utter another prayer. This time for more than a second chance. I pray for a lifetime of chances with the man I love.

Chapter Twenty-Six

FAITH

But again, God wasn't listening. Only I don't realize it until it's too late.

Mellow from my awesome night with Killian and fully steeped in the belief that we can overcome our challenges, I sail into Fallhurst the next morning with a spring in my step and tolerance in my attitude. Lisa Channing can bring it on. And she attempts to.

I stop shy of telling her Killian and I fucked our brains out the night before and then twice this morning before we left the house. I may be feeling smug and confident, but I'm above rubbing the poor woman's face in it. With any luck, after today, I won't need to see her again, and neither will Killian.

It occurs to me then that my future, after this nightmare is behind us, is wide open. Unless Killian wants to relocate to New York, I'm most likely done with the Punishment Club. Axel won't be happy, but what the hell...

Which means I have to find another vocation. I have enough money to open another nightclub here in LA. Or if not...

"Miss Carson..."

The job of *wife* sounds great.

"Miss Carson?"

Except I haven't been asked yet. But…Killian loves me. Right?

"Miss Carson!"

I blink and focus on Lisa. "Please," I say with a smile, "call me Faith."

A bolt of shock charges through me. It's the first time I've said my own name in years. It's the first time I've acknowledged it without feeling a little sick inside. I'm not the same person I used to be. But, through Killian's eyes, I'm beginning to accept that I'm not the total monster I thought myself to be either.

Sure, I've done things that I'll have to live with. Taking a life, no matter how vile that life was, has eroded a part of my soul I'll never get back. As for Matt, I've accepted that he threw me away long before I met Killian. That I lusted after Killian before I was technically free is something else I'll have to live with. The only hurdle to face that fills me with fear is confessing my carelessness with the one precious life I should've protected with everything I had.

"…So unless there's anything else you want to talk about, I think we're done here."

I swallow, grab my purse, and rise from the chair. I need to find Killian and tell him every last secret in my soul. No time like the present. "No, I can't think of a single thing."

Lisa Channing nods and closes her file. "I'll make my final report and hand it in next week. You'll be contacted after that."

I'm sure I won't be, but who cares. "Great. Thanks."

"Would you like me to get someone to take you back upstairs, or is Mr. Knight coming to get you?" She says his name without the interest I've heard previously.

Either she's accepted that she has no chance with Killian, or the come-on I witnessed was all in my head when I was feeling on less stable ground.

Whatever. I can't wait to put everyone and everything to do with the Fallhurst Institute behind me.

I glance at the clock in Lisa's office and notice I've only been here an hour. Killian and I thought I would be longer, so we made plans to meet at midday. I can't call him because cell phones aren't allowed past reception.

"No need. I'll see myself out," I say to Lisa.

She walks me to the door but hangs back when I pull it open. "Goodbye, Miss Carson."

I nod and leave the room.

The man walking toward me isn't Scot Scarsdale. But he's a clone from the same army of analysts. His badge clearly says so, as does his pasty smile and wire-rimmed glasses.

"Miss Carson, Mr. Knight asked me to come check on you. He wants you to know he'll be a while."

"Well, I'm done now."

"Okay, I can either escort you to the seventeenth floor or you can go up and wait in reception for him."

"Can you take me to him, please?"

"Of course. If you'd like to come with me?"

I smile, my impending freedom suffusing me with happiness. "Sure, lead the way." We enter the elevator, and he slides his keycard through the slot. We ride for a few floors in silence. "Are you allowed to tell me what goes on on the seventeenth floor, or will you have to kill me?"

His head snaps to me, and his eyes widen for a moment. "Oh. No, it's nothing like that. I mean...it is...Well, what I'm saying is, level seventeen requires top clearance, of course, but—"

I reach out and lay a hand on his sleeve. "Hey, it's okay. I was just messing with you."

"Oh." He looks down at my hand for a second, a hint of a frown creasing his brows. When I drop my hand, he shrugs. "Well, I'm used to that."

The bitter snap to the words prickles my skin with cold disquiet. It's enough for me to hurry out of the elevator when we jolt to a stop.

I haven't been to level seventeen before, so I don't know what to expect. But I'm sure it shouldn't look like an underground garage with industrial-size steel pipes twisting and turning in a maze of metal. I take a few more steps into the large space and then turn around.

My blood goes cold.

He's pointing a gun at me, the black muzzle gleaming pure menace. Shock holds me still long enough for him to punch a couple of buttons on the elevator panel before stepping out. I rush forward when the doors start to shut.

"Stop," he commands coldly. "I may be just an analyst, but I went through some training to get this job. Six feet, I believe, is the space I need to keep between us to stop you from attempting to disarm me before I shoot. I'm not ashamed to admit that I know you can kick my ass, but trust me, if you come any closer than the requisite six feet, I'll shoot. Now turn around and let's go."

Heart shaking, I swivel back to the maze of pipes. "Where are we going?"

"For now, straight ahead of you."

I force my feet to move. After about two hundred feet, I glance over my shoulder. He's maintaining the six feet that keeps him out of my reach. "What's your name?

He shakes his head. "Don't bother trying to establish rapport. It doesn't matter. Nothing matters now."

The finality in his voice sends another cold shiver down my spine. "You're the mole."

His pale skin goes even paler. "You know."

"Yes, but whatever you've done, it's not too late to make things right."

He makes a creaky sound that is a poor imitation of laughter. "You know what they do to people like me in jail?"

"Why? What did you do?"

His head bows for a moment. I slow my steps but then his head snaps up, and he slows down too, keeping the exact distance between us as before.

His fingers grip the gun tighter. "I really don't want to shoot you, Miss Carson. Turn left, please."

I follow another set of steel pipes. "Where are we going? At least you can tell me that?"

"I don't know. I just have to deliver you to him, that's all."

My heart drops to my feet. "Him? Paul Galveston?" I ask over my shoulder.

He nods.

"You don't have to do what he says. Help Killian…Mr. Knight and me instead. We'll—"

"Look at me. Tell me what you see," he says.

I stop and take a closer look at my captor. Everything about him reeks of despair. The no-hope, finite kind. I don't have the courage to voice that because that will also seal my fate.

"Exactly," he says softly.

He jerks the gun, and I start moving again. Toward the dark green door a hundred feet in front of me.

Nothing good lies on the other side of it. I know that in my bones. Ten feet from it, I stop.

"You need to open the door, Miss Carson."

I shake my head. "No."

"I'm sorry."

I glance over my shoulder and see he's much closer now. And his hand is already raised. I kick him in the gut, and he flies backward. The gun is knocked from his hand, and he wheezes as he struggles for air. But he doesn't stay down for long. My heart drops when he scrambles for his gun. I stumble backward as he stands. He's still breathless, but there's a desperation about him that chills every cell in my body.

Whatever Galveston is holding over him is powerful enough for him to want to see this through. I don't wait to see if he'll shoot me so I take the only choice I have. I grasp the door handle and yank it open.

A shadow looms in front of me, blocking out the sunlight.

"Hello, beautiful."

Fear smashes through me. Galveston.

I don't see the Taser coming, but I feel it jam into my ribs and hear its sickening sizzle as it electrifies my nerves.

Blinding pain explodes stars across my vision. I'm falling. Falling. Then I sink into nothing.

Chapter Twenty-Seven

KILLIAN

The light is off outside Lisa Channing's office. And I'm not responsible for dismantling it like I did last time when I wanted to get Faith out of here. That thought seeps the first drops of ice into my bloodstream as I walk down the hallway.

Still…panic is counterproductive. There could be a perfect explanation for the light being off and Faith still being inside.

Yeah, right. She may have calmed down about Lisa Channing, but I'm willing to bet she'd rather walk the soulless corridors than spend an unnecessary minute with Lisa.

I knock and throw open the door without really waiting for a response. Lisa Channing is sitting behind her desk, typing up notes.

Her eyes widen when she sees me. "Killian! Is everything okay?"

My frantic gaze darts around the office. My gut grows colder when I don't spot Faith. "Where is she?" I ask.

She frowns. "Miss Carson?"

"Yes. Where is she?"

"We finished our session forty-five minutes ago. She left to go and find you."

No. God, *no*!

I rush to Lisa's desk and scoop up her phone. My finger shakes as I punch in the number. "This is Killian Knight. Is Miss Carson upstairs? Okay. I need you to lock down the building. Right now. Yes. This. Is. A. Code. Fucking. Five!"

I slam down the phone as an alarm starts to blare. Then I pick it up again and redial. "Mitch, Faith is not here...Yeah, she could still be in the building. Or she could be gone. She finished her session forty-five minutes ago." Mitch swears, and that uncharacteristic sound drives a knife deeper into my gut. "I hope to God I'm overreacting, but I need you and Linc to search the area. I'll call back in ten minutes."

I end the call and round on Lisa.

Her eyes are wide. "What's a code five?" she asks.

"It mean the woman I love is in danger. And if anything happens to her, I swear to fucking God—"

She cowers back from me, and I realize I'm yelling. I clench my fists and force myself to calm down. "I'm sorry. But I need you to tell me exactly what she said to you before she left and who she left with."

"We just...I told her the session was over and asked if she wanted me to get someone to escort her. She refused and said she would come up and find you yourself."

"Did Scarsdale fetch her?"

"I don't know. I didn't go to the door."

I close my eyes for a second. "I need your computer."

She glances over at the monitor. "The work is confidential—"

"I'm not interested in reading your patients' files. And I wasn't really asking," I snap as I head for her desk. Thankfully, she vacates her chair and moves out of my way. "I want to find Faith before the asshole who has her gets farther away."

I snatch the phone as I jump behind the desk. The moment the call is answered, I snap, "Get me the surveillance feed for Lisa Channing's office. Inside and outside."

She gasps, but I ignore her. The shocking discovery that the Fall-hurst Institute has her sessions under surveillance is for others to deal with. My main focus is finding Faith.

"No, send it to her workstation," I respond to the analyst's question. The feed pops through ten seconds later. Another minute later and I have a face. I turn the monitor toward Lisa. "Who is that?" I demand.

She stares at the man Faith is talking to and shakes her head. "I don't know." I drag the monitor back and tap out the code I need to snatch the information. It takes three minutes, but each second feels like a lifetime. When I'm done, I jump up and race for the door.

"Killian?"

I glance over my shoulder as I pull the door open. "What?" I demand through clenched teeth.

"I...hope you find her."

I don't respond. I just turn around and race down the hallway.

Hope has no place here. Only the solid reality of Faith back in my arms will suffice. I can't lose her. Not when I only just found her again. Every day since that moment in the park in New York City, I've looked at her and asked myself how I managed to get through the past four years. The simple truth is that I don't know how.

But what I do know now, what blazes a searing path through my soul, is that, this time, if I lose her, I won't make it.

* * *

My rational brain tells me to return to level seventeen, where all the cool, supersecret gadgets that I'm helping the government use to spy on our enemies are located. But my gut propels me to reception, and specifically the box where our cell phones are kept while we're in the building. I snatch Faith's and mine, collect the other gadgets I never leave home without, and head outside.

My phone blares as soon I step out of the sphere of scrambled signals that blanket the building. The vise around my heart clenches tighter. "Galveston."

"This is the second time you've let me down, Knight. I really hope for everyone's sake that there isn't a third."

"Where is she?"

"She's safe. Did you really think you could disrupt my life and get away with it?"

"It's really me you want. So why not come after me?"

He laughs. "There you go again, thinking I'm stupid. I really shouldn't have let you two walk out of that party that night in Cairo. Raj was all for concluding our business before morning. I said we should wait. I regret that decision deeply."

"This is about Faith, Galveston. No one else—"

"This is about what I say it's about," he interjects. "But okay, for now, let's discuss the fate of your woman. There are so many possibilities. I can sell her to a sheikh in the Middle East. Or I know a band of brothers in a certain kingdom who will cream themselves for a woman like your Faith. For some absurd reason, they like their wares a little used. They might feed her the odd drug or two to keep her subdued, but I guarantee you she'll rule their harem in no time. Or I can simply chop her up into little pieces and feed her to the sharks on my next trip abroad. It really is all down to you. You hold the power, Knight. How about that?"

The gadget in my hand emits a little beep. For the first time since this nightmare started, my heart beats with something other than solid dread. "Put her on the phone, Galveston."

He hesitates long enough to drag my attention from the gadget. "I can't."

I don't want to follow my thoughts down that stark road. But I need to know. "Why not?"

Again he hesitates. "I don't want to start our relationship with lies, so I'll come clean. She's out cold."

Pain and rage sucker punch me. "You hurt her?"

"It was just a little zap. She wouldn't have come quietly. But she barely felt a thing, I assure you."

A red haze crowds my vision, and I have to fight to stay conscious. "I'm going to kill you," I vow in a voice I barely recognize as mine.

He chuckles. "Let's not make such dire promises to one another. Your woman already tried once and failed. Now if I were the eye-for-an-eye type, I'd pay her back in kind."

My grip tightens around the phone. "You already tried to kill her once, you asshole. You touch a hair on her head, and I'll hunt you down to the ends of the earth."

"You won't need to go to all that trouble. My terms are simple. Seventy-five million in return for your Faith. Agreed?"

"Agreed," I respond immediately.

"Excellent. This time, I'm going to demand a quicker turn-around. You have until six p.m. Account details will be on your phone in the next minute."

The line goes dead, and my world turns to ash. The sound of an engine turning over finally drags me from the depths of hell. I look up as Linc screeches to a halt in the SUV. Mitch pulls up in the limo seconds later. They both exit.

"Sorry, sir. We saw no signs of her," Mitch says.

"It's fine. I know who has her," I reply calmly.

They exchange glances. "This Galveston guy?" Linc asks.

I nod and hold up the gadget. "And I have her location."

"Okay. We did find someone else though."

"Who?"

He holds up his phone. It's the same guy Faith was talking to outside Lisa's office. Except now he looks very dead. "We think it's the mole you mentioned. The gunshot wound looks self-inflicted."

I stare at the picture for another second before I dismiss it from my mind. "We're leaving. We'll call the institute on the way. Get them to deal with it. And Mitch, mobilize the rest of the team. Leave one man behind at the house to look after Debbie. Get as many men as you can on the chopper. The tracker I put on Faith is still moving. Give us a call before you leave the house. I'll give you the final location."

I round the hood and climb into the SUV. Linc jumps into the passenger seat. I hand him the gadget, and he inputs the coordinates into the satellite navigation as I step on the gas and accelerate out of the Fallhurst Institute parking lot.

"You're sure it's her?" he asks after a few minutes.

I nod. "I put a tracking device in her clothes."

He stares at the green dot for another minute. "If he sweeps her for bugs—"

"Trust me, I know," I snap through gritted teeth. The very real possibility that I might lose the only lifeline that connects me to Faith throbs with each heartbeat.

I try to focus on the road and the twenty-seven miles that lie between us as Linc pulls out his phone and calls the agency with news of the dead agent's location.

The moment he hangs up, my phone rings.

"Yes?"

"I see there's been a development." It's Fionnella Smith.

"Yes. Your plan failed. Spectacularly. Your mole managed to get his fucking hands on Faith. And now Galveston has her."

"Damn. Listen, son, I'm—"

"No. I don't want to hear it. We tried it your way. It didn't work. We have nothing more to discuss." I hang up and tighten my grip around the steering wheel.

"We'll get her back," Linc mutters.

"Fuck yeah, we will." We ride in silence for another couple of miles.

"They've stopped moving," Linc says as he taps the coordinates into his phone.

My gaze drops to the dot. "Where is that?"

"According to the address, it's an abandoned group of buildings that used to be attached to an old municipal airport south of the Santa Ynez Mountains. And…"

"What?" I snarl.

"It still has a functioning airstrip."

My stomach turns liquid. But I still stomp my foot harder on the gas. The vehicle shoots forward. Linc grips the bar above his head with one hand and dials Mitch's number with the other.

Through the roar in my ears, I hear him relay the address to Mitch and tell him we'll be there in nineteen minutes. I shave three minutes off the time, and we roll through the barbed wire gates just before midday. I slow the vehicle to a crawl as we scan the area.

All the buildings and equipment are covered in years' old decay. Except for the small airplane sitting at the end of the tarmac.

It hasn't taken off yet, and the green dot is within touching distance. Twin streams of relief well through me. Only to drain away when I see the Jeep racing toward the plane.

I abandon all attempts at stealth and step on the gas. There are two large hangars and half a mile between us and the Jeep. Too far. God, she's too far away.

In a small plane like that, Galveston could take off within seconds.

"Shit." Linc draws his weapon but keeps it on his lap.

"If you shoot her by accident, I'll kill you."

He nods. "I'm aware of that, sir. This is going to be tricky though."

I clench my jaw and milk every last ounce of horsepower from the SUV. It's still not enough as I watch Galveston leap from the Jeep and drag Faith after him toward the plane.

Three men jump from the back and aim assault rifles at us.

"Sir," Linc mutters.

I keep my foot on the gas.

"Sir, you need to stop."

"They won't shoot me. If they do, Galveston doesn't get his money."

"I understand. But—"

I engage the brakes at the last possible moment and screech to a halt a couple of feet from the Jeep's bumper. Rifles cock when I throw open my door and step out.

Galveston turns with one arm across Faith's shoulder and a gun aimed at her head.

God.

"I knew I couldn't trust you," he sneers.

I ignore him. My gaze rakes over Faith, the chill inside me flooding me in waves. "Baby, are you okay?"

She nods, but I see the pain in her eyes. I look closer and see the deep bruise on her temple. My fists clench at my sides.

"You're not leaving with her, Galveston. Not today. Not ever."

He laughs. "How the fuck are you going to stop me? You're outnumbered, and outgunned. Transfer the money to me right now, and you can have her back. Or I put a bullet in her head."

I hear Linc speaking softly into his phone but I keep my gaze trained forward. A minute later, he steps out too.

I take another step toward Galveston and his men. "You hurt her, and you die today. Let her go and I just might let you get on that plane and take off. Those are the only guarantees I'll offer you."

"Fuck you, Knight."

I shrug. "Decide quickly; you're running out of time."

"What the hell are you talking about?"

I nod at the fast-growing speck on the horizon, but I address the men with the assault rifles.

"Those are my guys in the chopper heading toward us. My guy Linc here has instructed them to block the runway and not allow your plane to take off. I don't know what Galveston is paying you to help him kidnap my woman, but here's my deal. I'll pay each of you one hundred thousand if you drop your weapons right now and step over to my side of the party."

The men exchange quick, startled glances. Then predictable greed lights up their features.

Galveston's mouth drops open. "What the fuck? Don't listen to—"

"His name is Killian Knight. You probably don't know him, but it'll take only a minute to look him up," Faith adds. Then she sends me a little smile. "He's an amazing guy."

I nod. "I'm an amazing guy with a few dollars to play with. One hundred thousand. No questions asked. All I want is my girl back, safe and sound. Tell them, Linc."

"Yep. He has money to burn for days. All he wants is his girl back."

The sound of rotors approaching grows louder. "Which one of you is the pilot?" I shout.

The man to the farthest right jerks his chin at me.

"I'll pay you double if you step over here first."

The chopper is hovering low enough for them to see the six men on board, and the guns they're wielding. Galveston's men waver for another five seconds before the pilot drops his rifle. The other two follow immediately.

"You fucking sons of bitches," Galveston snarls.

He points the gun at his pilot. Faith immediately drives her elbow into his gut. His gun goes off, but I don't turn to see where the bullet hits because my heart stops as I watch Galveston redirect his gun toward her.

But I hear Linc's curse and hiss of pain as I leap forward. I reach for the gun tucked into my pants. I drop to my knees, take aim, and shoot at the same time Faith pivots and knees Galveston in the balls. He doubles over and grabs at his jewels as blood erupts from his shoulder.

I'm not a fan of kicking a man when he's down, but I barely stop myself from cheering when Faith delivers a roundhouse to his head that sends him sprawling on the tarmac. "That's for tasing me too, you motherfucker!"

I can't deal with the fact that he tased her right now. If I do, I'll probably shoot him again. I stop long enough to kick his gun halfway across the runway before I scoop her up in my arms.

"You're safe. God, you're safe."

She wraps her arms around me and buries her face in my neck. One of us is shuddering. The other is shaking. I don't care. She's alive.

Somewhere behind us, the chopper lands. Minutes later, sirens rip through the air as local law enforcement arrives. Through it all, I clutch her harder, and she weeps against my shoulder.

"It's over," she mutters.

"Yes." I sweep her into my arms and head for the chopper. We pass a couple of cops kneeling over a cuffed Galveston. His shoulder is wrapped in a thin bandage but he's still bleeding.

There's a little harmonious justice in knowing that Faith's bullet in Cairo caught him in the right shoulder and mine caught him in the left. Still, I stop anyway to deliver my last piece of advice.

He glares at me as I smile.

"Congratulations, you've just become my pet project. I'm going to devote a considerable amount of money to make sure you stay in prison for the rest of your life. If I hear that you're attempting to gain parole, I'll pay a few skinheads to make sure you don't leave prison with your balls intact."

He pales further but keeps his mouth shut as I walk away.

"I can't believe we nailed him," Faith mutters.

I grip her tighter. "Believe it. He had you in his fucking clutches. That's not something I'm going to forget quickly."

"God, I'm sorry."

My teeth grind against the last traces of fury riding me. "We'll discuss proper safety protocols later. After I get you home and spend the next month holding you in my arms."

Hers tighten around my neck as I step into the chopper. The blades start to rotate.

"Just a heads-up, baby. Linc is coming with us. He was shot."

Distress darkens her eyes. "Oh God."

"Galveston's bullet grazed him but he'll be fine. He's already planning the many ways Mitch will wait on him while he's recovering."

When Linc steps into the chopper, her tears fall harder.

I hold her all the way back to Malibu. Somewhere along the way, her tears stop, but her eyes remain shadowed. She doesn't speak when I undress her and wash her clean. The tears start again when I make love to her.

And as she falls asleep in my arms, I can't erase the hollow feeling that I may have jumped the gun a little when I thought that our troubles were over.

Turns out they weren't. With seven little words uttered the next morning, I'm plunged back into hell.

"I need to tell you about Cairo."

Chapter Twenty-Eight

FAITH

I blurt the words before I lose my courage.

He shakes his head. "No. You don't. We've been through enough—"

He stops talking when I pull away from him, get out of bed, and pull my clothes on. After a moment, he dresses too, although his gaze never leaves me. He follows me to the living room. I sit on the sofa but he remains standing, his hands braced on his hips.

"She was sitting at my bedside when I woke up. Fionnella. She said she was there to help me, in whatever way I wanted. But that I needed to think carefully whether I wanted to go back to doing what I was doing. With you."

Fury sparks across his face. "What the fuck—?"

"She was right. I've always been the sort of person who picks an interest and devotes everything to it until I know it inside and out. I aced being a spy because I wanted to be with you, and I wanted to stop the traffickers. For myself and in my sister's memory. Take those things away, and I was useless."

"You were not useless. A touch reckless at times, but never useless."

I exhale. "Maybe not but I let my emotions blind me to every-thing else. And being with you in that role conjured up a hell of a lot of emotions. I didn't wake you when I heard the scream because I was terrified you might get hurt. Or worse. But a true partner would've. That was what we were there for, to support each other. The sort of work you did, the odds of that happening again, was too much to risk…"

He rubs his hands over his mouth and jaw, pacing for a full minute. Then nods. "So you left. Okay. I don't fully accept it yet, but I'll get over it someday." He starts to move toward me. "Can we get on with our lives—"

"There's more," I blurt.

He freezes again, pales a little, and grabs the back of his neck. "Okay. Let's—"

"Mr. Knight?" Debbie steps into the living room.

His head jerks up. "What is it?"

"Um…you have a visitor."

His eyes narrow. We don't need more information to know who it is. Sure enough, a moment later, she walks in.

"Jesus. You have got to be the fucking definition of bad timing," Killian snaps.

Fionnella smiles. "Bad Penny Smith. That was my nickname back in the day."

"Bullshit. Your name isn't even Fionnella Smith."

She sends him a droll stare. "Have you been running Betty ragged trying to find out information about me?"

Killian shrugs, his face still a hard, slightly pale mask. "And I thought I made myself clear when I said we're done? It's barely nine a.m., and I've had my quota of shit news for the day. Partly thanks to you, I hear."

I feel Fionnella's stare, and a moment later Killian's, but I can't move, can't think. Shit, I can barely breathe. Because it turns out, she didn't come alone. At least not to me. The box she's holding ab-sorbs every inch of my attention, freezing me from the inside out.

"Well, you've already done the hard work. I just thought I'd fill in a few more blanks to put everything to bed once and for all."

"You could've called."

"Where's the fun in that? The mole was a mid-level analyst with a gambling problem. Which Galveston encouraged. And a predilection for child pornography, which Galveston nurtured and transitioned from online to real life. While he made sure to get it all on tape for blackmailing when needed."

"Jesus, how did he make it past Fallhurst's vetting process?" Killian demands.

"You'll be surprised what people can hide when they put their mind to it."

I flinch because I know the comment is directed at me. "Is that it?" I force myself to ask, when everything inside me wants to rush across the room and snatch my precious box from her.

"Well, Galveston is singing like a canary in the hope of a reduced sentence. We're compiling a list of names that'll guarantee the sex ring is shut down once and for all."

A piece of my heart that's been ripped open since Julia's death is soothed on hearing the news. I'll always mourn for my sister, but at least I can take heart in knowing I've righted some wrongs in her name.

Killian paces for half a minute before he comes to crouch in front of me. "So we're done here?" He throws the question over his shoulder, but his bewildered gaze stays on me.

Fionnella hesitates for a moment. "Yes."

I sense her coming toward me. My eyes plead with Killian. He sees it but he doesn't understand. Not until Fionnella sets the box in my lap and pats my shoulder.

"It's time, darling girl. Unless you want to keep running for the rest of your life, it's time."

She leaves the room and the house. My heart has stopped beating. I'm sure of it. Or maybe I can't hear it over the noise of everything I've ever wanted exploding right before my eyes.

Killian crouches before me, his own breathing locked somewhere in his body. He knows. Not what exactly, but he knows.

Eyes turned a desolate blue move from my face to my lap and back again. "Tell me what's in the box, Faith."

It takes a few tries to get my voice to work. "I'm sorry…"

His mouth compresses and he waits.

"Every reason I gave you was true. But…this clinched it for me."

"That's the *more* you mentioned. Isn't it?" he asks roughly.

I nod.

His hands tighten almost painfully on mine. Then he charges to his feet, takes the box from my lap, and opens it. He stares for an age. Lifts the single picture from its silk bed. When the box drops he doesn't pick it up. Neither do I.

"We made this…" His voice is bleak, a pathetically pale imitation of itself.

"Yes," I whisper.

He stares down at the sonogram. Shakes his head and groans. "Oh God, Faith. How could you not tell me? We created this together."

My heart breaks in two. "We created it, but I lost it. I put it in danger and had it ripped from my belly because I thought I could take on a monster by myself."

"God…" he repeats again. The picture shakes in his hand. "You should have told me," he rasps.

"No, you didn't deserve to bear the burden. Don't you see? It ripped me apart, and I'd only known I was pregnant for a day. If I'd told you when you asked me if I was okay…right before we left the villa, maybe things would've turned out differently. Instead…everything fell apart, and I chose to be the only one to bear the burden instead of two people suffering."

"What about the other side of it? What about two people *healing* together instead of broken and apart?"

"How can I heal? How the hell do I come back from something like this? I forgot my training and telegraphed my vulnerability to Galveston. He didn't know I was pregnant until I *showed* him. I put my hand on my stomach and fucking pointed to him that I was pregnant. He saw, then he just went for our baby!"

The sound that rips from him is so viscerally savage that the very air turns to ice. He staggers away from me, falls into the chair, and drops his head in his hand.

"I don't know, but losing each other on top of that? Was it worth it?"

I shake my head in despair. "I didn't think we should have been together in the first—"

"Bullshit!" His head snaps up, and his eyes are wild and red-rimmed with the volatility of his emotions. "I'm fucking tired of hearing you say that. It's an excuse you hide behind to wallow in your suffering, and it's got to stop."

He's angry. He's incandescent in fact. "The timing was a little off, I accept, but I would still have craved you whether I met you when I was twelve or one hundred and fucking twenty. I was made for you! Don't you see that?"

I keep my mouth shut. We wallow in our fresh agony, our breaths snatched for the sole purpose of sustaining our lungs.

Then, slowly, he lowers his hand and the picture clutched in it. "How far along were you?"

"About seven weeks."

He swallows hard. "Was it a…the sex…"

"It was too early to tell. But when I think of…I feel it was a girl."

"Where did this come from? Why did Fionnella have it?"

"I…I left it at the club. In my punishment room. I asked Axel to keep it for me. He must have given it to Fionnella to bring to me."

"So she knew about the baby." There's a thick vein of bitterness in his voice.

I nod. "The moment I woke up, I asked about the baby. She was there. She told me the doctors hadn't been able to save it, but they'd saved me a…the picture."

My confession hasn't been good for my soul. Every inch of me is in tatters. And my worst fear, that Killian would suffer too, is written all over his face.

He presses the heels of his hands into his eyes without letting go of the picture. After an age, he drags himself to his feet and holds out his hand to me. I take it because I can't not.

He leads me through our bedroom and into the dressing room. Without letting go of the photo, he searches through my things and lays out black denim, a white top, and my favorite leather jacket. He pushes them toward me. I yank off my dress, and while I'm putting the clothes on, he goes to his side of the room and puts on similar clothes.

We both put our boots on, and I follow him out of the room. Through the living room and down the stairs to the third level below where his semi-underground parking garage holds six cars, three SUVs, and two motorcycles.

He walks over to a gleaming shelf, takes down two helmets, and walks over to the custom Ducati Diavel. When I reach him, he silently hands me a helmet. I take it and put it on. He picks me up and places me on the second seat, and then swings his leg over to sit in front of me.

He tucks the picture inside his jacket, next to his heart, and then looks over his shoulder. "Hold on." The command is rough and low.

I'm terrified of the savage pain in his voice more than I'm terrified of riding on a powerful motorbike. The furthest I got during my training was a glorified scooter. But I trust him. So I lean forward and slide my arms around him. His stomach clenches tight for a moment before he guns the engine. And a moment later, we vault out of the garage and down the driveway.

The Californian coastline is ruggedly beautiful. The late morning sunshine is sublime. Three full minutes after imagining that I'll fall off the bike to a horrible death, I'm a complete convert. I mirror his leans through the curves, and it feels like we're one person. Except there's an ocean-wide chasm between us. Over a dozen times, tears fill my eyes, and I'm ravaged by Killian's pain. A dozen times I blink them away and cling to the man I love more than I want my next breath. We ride for a solid hour without stopping or speaking.

When we eventually stop, it's at a barren bluff with the wind whipping around us and not a soul in sight.

He rips his helmet off, and I see he's fighting his emotions too. He opens his mouth but I speak first.

"I'm sorry, Killian. So sorry. The way we met…I didn't think I deserved you. So when I had to give you up, it killed me, but I felt like it was what I had to do. But…"

The hand holding the helmet drops to his thighs. "But?"

"I don't want to let you go. I want to fight for you. Whatever I need to do, just tell me, and I'll do it. I want you, Killian. Every day, every night, and in between. I love you. So much. I love you."

His breath rushes out, and he drops the helmet. He bends over and braces his hands on his knees. Eyes squeezed shut as he just breathes in and out.

When he straightens, his eyes are wet. "We're going to make another baby," he declares in an emotion-rough voice.

Totally not what I was expecting. "What?"

"You fucking heard me. We're going to make another baby. You're going to give birth to a healthy, beautiful baby girl who looks just like you. She'll be the most gorgeous thing in the world. And we're going to be happy. End of fucking story!"

My jaw hits the ground. And while I'm completely and utterly flabbergasted, he strides over to me and yanks me off my feet.

"I love you. You are everything to me. I will never let you go, and you, dear God, you will promise me right now, unequivocally, that you will never leave me."

"I promise. A million times, I promise. I love you. Forgive me."

"I forgive you. And I love you too." We kiss and kiss and hug and cry. We roll around in the dirt and find ourselves again.

Hours and hours later, when the twilight closes around us, I lift my head and look into his brilliant blue eyes. "I'm ready to start on the baby right now if you are."

And right there on that windy bluff, we start our lives.

DID YOU MISS AXEL AND
CLEO'S STORY?

PLEASE SEE THE NEXT PAGE
FOR AN EXCERPT FROM
BLACK SHEEP.

Chapter One

FUCK BYGONES

AXEL

Childhood sweethearts.

Even way back then, I despised the term. There was nothing childlike about what I felt for her. Even less was the implied sweetness of our connection. But we let them smile and label us as they pleased. All the while knowing and relishing our truth. She was pure sin, and I was the devil intent on gorging myself on her iniquities.

I lived for it. For her. The sexy, hint-of-sandpaper voice that could bring me to my knees. The limpid blue eyes that paralyzed me. The killer curves that made me want to destroy every other boy or man who dared to look at her sixteen-year-old body.

At nineteen, I was fully cognizant of my obsession, was aware that it was a live grenade destined to blow me apart one day. But I was ready to die the first time I looked into her eyes. As long as I died in her arms.

I should have known my end was near the day she called me by her special name.

My Romeo.

She called me that the day I took her virginity beneath the stars on the beach of our families' adjoining Connecticut properties.

My Romeo. As if she knew we were doomed. Perhaps she knew *I* was. Perhaps she'd known of the plan all along. Or she hatched it the day my father enrolled me at West Point. The day he embraced his grand and greedy plan to fatten his bank balance from war instead of just from common mafia mongering.

The irony was that I was the only fool in the piece. I may have accepted my role as Romeo, but her name wasn't Juliet.

No, the devil's siren went by the name of Cleopatra McCarthy.

And when it came right down to it, Cleopatra McCarthy was only too happy to watch me burn in the flames of my obsession. Happy to watch me die.

Childhood sweethearts. Fuck that.

Whatever we felt for each other was as old as dirt, filthy as sin. What I feel for her now is…too fucked up to name.

So now I watch her. She watches me.

Strangers. Enemies. Our hate sparks between us like forked lightning. Bitter, twisted. *Alive.*

There may be a wide dance floor between us and the sound of jazz funk blaring through the speakers inside the walls of XYNYC, my New York nightclub, but we may as well be cocooned in a little bubble of our own, merrily breathing in the fumes of our hate.

Eight years is a long time to drip-feed yourself poisonous might-have-beens. But I'm more than comfortable in my role of rabid obsessor.

I lean back, elbows on the bar, ignoring all around me except the woman tucked away in my roped-off VIP lounge. The elevated lounges offer a clear view without obstruction. The short black dress clings to her hips and upper thighs leaving her legs bare, the halter neckline and her caught-up hair displaying lightly tanned shoulders and arms.

The glass of vintage Dom Pérignon champagne in her hand hasn't been touched. Not a single inch of her voluptuous body has moved in time to the music, even though music is…*was* a great love, once upon a time. Even after all these years, I retain residual resentment that I had to share her with Axl Rose and Dave Grohl, watch her body twist in ecstasy that wasn't induced by me.

A waiter offers her a platter of food. She shakes her head and takes a step toward the black velvet rope that blocks the lounge. My bouncer steps in front of her.

She glares at him.

Without glancing my way, she reaches into her tiny purse for her phone. She sets her glass down, and her fingers fly over the screen.

My own phone buzzes in my pocket. I'm not surprised she has my number. Any member of my family could have obtained it by illegal means and given it to her. I take a beat before I pull it out and read the message. "I've been coming here almost every night for two weeks. You have to talk to me sometime."

I glance up, make her wait for a full minute before I reply. "Do I?"

Her nostrils flare lightly. "He wants an answer."

My mouth twists, and I swear the impossible happens, and I hate her even more than I did one second ago. "What are you now, his messenger?"

Her gaze flicks up to me before she shrugs, her bare, slender shoulder gleaming under the pulsing lights. "You've ignored all his emails and your brothers' calls."

"They're spineless assholes."

"Are you going to talk to me?"

"No."

"Then why keep me here?"

"I told you the terms of admittance. You come of your own free will; you don't get to leave until the club closes. That's in two hours."

"This is ridiculous, Axel."

My stomach knots just from seeing her type my name. "Then don't come again."

She looks up. Our eyes meet across the dance floor. Her hatred washes over me in filthy waves. I want to roll around in it. She holds my stare defiantly for a minute before she lowers her head to her phone again.

"It's not that simple. Please hear me out."

Again my stomach clenches, but this time it's accompanied by a crude little jerk in my pants that grabs my attention. "Please? You begging now?"

Annoyance flickers across her features. Her thumb hovers over the screen for the longest time. Then my phone buzzes. "Yes."

I didn't expect that. The Cleo I knew never begged unless it was to plead for my cock inside her. My mind circles around why she would do so now, and my erection hardens. A few crazed seconds later, I decide it's safer for my sanity not to know, and I settle back into sublime hate. "Too bad the first time I hear you beg has to be via text. Answer's still no."

"Axel, this is important. Let bygones be bygones and hear me out. It won't be more than five minutes. Please."

I'm doubly pissed off that I can't hear her say that word. I've waited a long fucking time to hear it. I'm even angrier that I can't cross the distance between us to ask her to repeat it. I put everything into the two words I text to her. "Fuck bygones."

It may be a trick of the light, but I swear she feels my new level of rage. Her lips part in an inaudible gasp as she reads my reply.

Turning away, she stalks to the private bar in the lounge. The waiter nods when she murmurs to him. He slides a shot glass across the counter and reaches for the premium tequila sitting on the shelf behind him. He pours. She picks it up and raises the glass to me before she downs it in one go.

I stride to the edge of the dance floor, hating myself for being concerned about the consequences of what she's doing. Then I remind myself that it's been years since I witnessed Lightweight Cleo topple over after one shot of tequila.

All the same I watch her, narrow eyed, as she downs another shot before heading for one of the velvet booth seats. There is the tiniest weave in her walk, and I have to clench every single muscle to stop myself from charging across the space between us.

The simple, undeniable truth is I can't.

Because of Cleopatra McCarthy, my life exploded in a billion little pieces. Pieces I didn't bother to put back again because I knew the exercise would be futile.

So for over eight years, I've lived with this new, permanently-altered-for-the-worse version of myself. A version I'm not in a hurry to reassess or remodel. A version that keeps me steeped in the obsidian fury that fuels my existence.

I stay on my side of the divide because to come within touching distance of her is to succumb to the carnage raging inside me. After all this time, I should have enough of a hold on myself to smother the compulsion.

I don't. If I did, I would've stopped her from stepping foot inside my club the first time she turned up.

But even worse than the control I sorely lack is the fact that I'm a glutton for punishment. Hell, it's the reason I run the highly successful and exclusive Punishment Club. In the handful of years it's been open, I've made over twenty million dollars in membership fees alone. Who the fuck knew there were crazies out there like me seeking to be exposed to the very thing they hate the most?

I derive a little perverse satisfaction from the fact that I'm granting them an outlet, even while I'm unable to find one for myself. I accepted my fate a long time ago. What haunts me can only be cured one way—by the moment I stop breathing.

"Macallan. Triple. Neat."

I reel back my thoughts and turn at the sound of the deep, raspy voice.

Quinn Blackwood.

He's not exactly a friend but there's mutual respect and acceptance of the otherworldliness inhabiting our blackened souls. It's what drew us to each other when we were placed in the same group for a brief time at West Point. Although Quinn never served, we kept in touch and ended up owning several nightclubs together, XYNYC being one of them.

Like me, he doesn't need the income. Like me, this place is one of many outlets for the demons that haunt him.

I make sure Cleo is still seated and return to the bar.

I watch Quinn knock back a large drink in one ruthless gulp. "You know there's a better blend in your VIP room, right?"

He slams the glass on the counter with barely suppressed violence. "Too far," he replies.

We're roughly the same height so, when he shoots me a glance, I'm well positioned to see the hounds of hell chasing through the jagged landscapes of his eyes. I don't flinch. I welcome the horde like kindred spirits. Our souls have endured more than enough to last us several lifetimes, and we both know it. "That bad, huh?"

His jaw clenches as he takes a breath. "Worse."

"Need any help?"

A dark shadow moves over his face, and he shakes his head. "It's done. I have what I need."

I don't press him for more information. Ours is not that kind of relationship.

I catch movement from my lounge, and my gaze zeroes in on my nemesis. She's risen from the sofa and leans against the railing once more, the untouched glass of champagne again in one hand. The bodyguards are once more alert, and a few of my errant brain synapses attempt to be amused by the glare she sends their way. "If you need anything else, let me know," I say absently, unable to take my eyes off the woman whose presence looms as large as the Sphinx before me.

I sense Quinn following my gaze, then returning to me. "Looks like you have a situation of your own that needs taken care of."

"Yeah." My voice feels as rough as it sounds. "Fucking tell me about it."

He doesn't nod or smile. Quinn Blackwood rarely smiles. But then, neither do I. Another thing we have in common. "Anything I can do, let me know," he says.

No one can help me with this. "Thanks," I say anyway.

He asks questions that bounce off the edge of my consciousness.

I shrug. I nod. I respond. But throughout, my senses are attuned to the other side of the room.

I barely register him stalking away. I click my fingers, and Cici, one of my waitresses, sidles up to me. I relay instructions, and she leaves, but not before she smiles in a way that ramps up my irritation.

I can't think about that now. I have more than enough to deal with tonight.

Four lounges from Cleo's, Vardan Petrosyan, the New York head of the Armenian mob, is downing expensive vodka like there's a drought coming. His unsavory presence sticks in my gut like a rusty blade, but since he's one of the many devils I've struck a deal with, I have to tolerate his company for as long as necessary.

He's been here going on two hours. I've ignored him for most of that time. Any longer and I risk pissing him off.

Men like Petrosyan demand fear where they can't achieve respect. I feel neither, and he knows it, but he's also aware I need him more than he needs me right now. So we both pretend I feel the latter.

I make my way to where he sits with his entourage. His minders stand in my way for the extra second it takes to make their point before they step aside.

The mob boss has a tall, slim blonde perched on each thigh. They both glance at me as I approach. I ignore them and focus on the short, stocky man with boxy features.

When he finally removes his wandering lips from one of the women's cleavage, Petrosyan stares at me with dead black eyes, a cold smile sliding across his face. "I was beginning to think you forget about me," he tells me in broken, heavily accented English.

"I wanted to catch you when you were feeling soft and mellow," I reply.

He barks out a laugh. "Nadiya, he thinks I'm soft and mellow. Do *you* think I'm soft and mellow?"

The blonde on his left immediately shakes her head.

"Feel free to check; let's make sure, ya?" he encourages.

She happily obliges by groping him brazenly. "No, Vardan, you are hard…everywhere."

He chuckles, his eyes a touch colder. "You see, my man, you waste both our time."

I take a breath and force a deferential nod. "My apologies. Do you have everything you need?"

He stares at me for several seconds. "No, not everything. But it is nothing that a little...negotiation cannot satisfy, eh?"

I've been expecting this—the obligatory extortion that happens every few months. Normally, I head it off by stating a few facts and figures, namely that I'm paying almost double market value for the service Petrosyan is providing me. This time, I don't.

Cleo's persistent visits are evidence that my plan is working. The fracturing Rutherford kingdom is developing even more cracks. And I'm willing to pay dearly for that.

"What do you want, Petrosyan?"

His expression doesn't change, but sensing a victory, he immediately turfs the girls off his lap. Once they've drifted off, he stands, adjusts his shiny suit, and rises up on the balls of his feet. But nothing can disguise the fact that I'm a foot taller than him.

"I want for you to tell me what you're doing with all the product you buy from me, for start. It's not ending up on the street or in clubs, I know that for fact," he says.

"And like I told you when we started this...partnership, it's none of your business." Although I owe him no explanation, I don't relish the idea of telling the mobster that every ounce of heroin I've procured from him for the last two years has been flushed down the toilet. That this isn't about taking over my father's business to make money for myself but to ensure the Rutherfords have zero business by the time I'm done with them. And if by doing so, I help take a few hundred kilos of drugs off the street...I mentally shrug.

Petrosyan's jaw flexes, but he nods. "Okay, then let's talk *our* business. Economy is in toilet. I need to raise prices—"

"Two hundred thousand a month. Fifty thousand dollars more for the same deal."

He looks off to the side, pulls on his cuffs, and then his fish eyes dart back to me. "I am thinking a cool quarter million has nice ring to it, no?"

"Fine. Deal. Are we done?"

Surprise livens his eyes for a few seconds before his gaze turns speculative. "You must really want to...how you say, shank it to my former business partner, hmm?"

"Yes, I must really want to *stick* it to him."

The turn of phrase baffles him for a second then he gives up in favor of confirming that I've really folded and given him a one-hundred-thousand-dollar price hike after a two-minute negotiation.

Now that he's satisfied, I turn to leave.

"I would sleep with gun under my pillow if I had someone like you for enemy," he states.

I look over my shoulder. He's watching me carefully. Trying to read the unreadable. "Then it's a good thing we're friends, isn't it? And you do sleep with a gun under your pillow."

He laughs. "Well, for you, I would make it *two* guns."

"You keep your end of the bargain, and you will never need to."

He catches the warning in my voice, and the laughter fades. "You keep up payments, and we won't have problem." He clicks his fingers for his girls.

Our battle lines redrawn, I return to the bar in time to spot Cleo raising a nearly empty champagne glass to her lips. My jaw clenches. Added to the two shots of tequila, I'm uncertain what the result will be. So I sharpen my focus with an even more vicious blade. Everything falls away as I saturate myself with her presence.

Every breath. Every blink.

I catch the moment her hips sway, ever so slightly, to the throbbing rock anthem.

The move resonates through me like the cuts of memory's blade. In an instant, I'm thrown back to the bedroom in the pool house I claimed the day I turned eighteen. It was the single thing I requested when my mother asked me what I wanted for my birthday. The need to distance myself from my father had grown into a visceral, unbearable ache. My mother saw it. She granted my request, despite my father's firm refusal. It was most likely what earned her the black eye two days later.

I don't know because I didn't ask. It would've been useless to do so anyway. She would've lied. And I was too selfish, too thankful for the mercy of not having to live under the same roof as my father, to rock the boat.

So I claimed my tiny piece of heaven in hell. And it was there that Cleo danced for me for the first time. Where we celebrated a lot of *firsts*.

That particular memory flames through the charred pits of my mind. I don't fight it. Like the fleeting moments of pleasure and pain, it will be gone in an instant, devoured by the putrefying cancer that lives within me.

Sure enough, it's gone from one heartbeat to the next, and I'm left with rotting remnants of what once was.

"All taken care of, boss."

I snap my head to the side. Cici's standing next to me. Her gaze slides over me from head to toe before it settles on my face. She's wearing that special *do me* smile she's worn since she started working here six weeks ago. I made the mistake of fucking her as part of her interview process. I shouldn't have. I could pardon myself by making the excuse that her presence in my office that day coincided with the first call in three years from Ronan, my oldest brother.

Ronan. Daddy's boy through and through, right down to the pansy-assed ring on his left pinkie.

Like one hundred percent of our interactions, that call hadn't gone well. So I needed an outlet. It was either a fist through a wall or my cock in a pussy. I chose pussy. I refuse to make excuses for that choice. Because what's the point of having a black soul, of making choices that leave your hands permanently soiled in evil, if you don't fucking own it? But I do admit to a modicum of regret. She's not the first employee I've fucked, but usually I'm a little more circumspect with my choices. My blinding rage prevented me from seeing that ill-disguised, you-fuck-me-I-own-you light in Cici's eyes until it was too late.

Now, irritatingly, ever since our one encounter, the ever-growing stench of possessiveness clings to her every time she's in my presence.

She sidles closer now. "Is there anything else you need?" she says in a low, intimate voice. "I couldn't help but notice that both you and your friend are wound up tighter than a drum tonight. I...I can help relieve your stress...if you want?"

In the next minute, she'll find an excuse to touch me. I'm slammed with the smell of cheap perfume and shameless arousal. Because my senses are wide open and raw, I take a deeper hit than I normally would. Which makes me direct more anger at her than I know is warranted.

"Cici?"

"Yes, boss?" she responds with a breathy eagerness.

"Fuck off and do your job," I snarl.

She recoils with shame and turns red-faced toward the bar.

"Jesus, twice in one night. You'd think I have a disease or something," she mutters under her breath as she busies herself collecting a drinks order from the bartender.

I feel no remorse when she walks away in a huff. I don't give a shit what's got her ass in a vise or who else she's hit on tonight. Under normal circumstances, her feelings matter very little to me. Tonight, I care even less.

When she moves away, I exhale and glance at my watch. On Tuesday nights, the club shuts at three a.m. It's almost one. Two more hours to go.

I brace myself before I raise my head.

It does absolutely nothing to buffer the potency of Cleo's stare or the effect of the evil little smile I see playing at her lips when our eyes hook into each other.

She's under my skin, where she's lived for seventeen years. And she knows it.

Fifth Harmony's "Work" blasts from the speakers. The hard beat and dirty lyrics produce a lusty sway of her hips. The look in her eyes and the movement of her body are almost dichotomous. Her eyes tell me she hates me. Her body beckons me with the promise of transcendental lust.

I should retreat to my office where I can watch her from the relative safety of security cameras. Or walk the other upper and lower floors, greet a few VIPs who would love a personal acknowledgement from me.

Fuck that.

I stay put and nod tersely at a few regulars who are brave enough to breach the no-fly zone around me. When my bartender slides a glass of Scotch to me, I pick it up and down it.

Cleo and I play the staring game until she reaches for her phone once more. She toys with it for a beat before her slender fingers fly over it.

My blood thrums harder as I take my phone out and read her message.

"Stop this, Axel. Be a man. Come over here and talk to me."

My cheek twitches in an imitation of a smile. "You're not senile, I hope, so you wouldn't have forgotten that I don't rise to dares. Or taunts."

"Dammit. What do I have to do?"

Those six little words send all the blood fleeing from my heart. It turns harder than stone, and my vision blurs for several seconds. I cannot believe her gall. "You're eight years too late with that question, sweetheart."

Her head snaps up. She's breathing hard. She shakes her head. I'm not sure if it's denial, disbelief or a plea. It's probably none of those things. It wouldn't be the first time I've attributed a benign sentiment to her actions only to be shown the true depths of her traitorous heart.

My phone buzzes again. This time there's a single word on my screen.

"Axel."

A whispered caress. An entreaty. A demand.

It's a thousand other things. All wrapped in sugared poison. I push away from the counter, despising the knots in my stomach and the steel in my cock. I feel her gaze on my back as I stalk through the door next to bar that leads to my office.

Shot after shot of adrenaline spikes through my bloodstream until dark, volatile sensation drenches me to my fingertips. My office door slams behind me, and I throw the bolt, as if locking myself in will prevent my growing insanity.

Already I want to tear the door off its hinges and rush back to the bar. I force my feet the other way and throw myself into my chair. High on the wall, the screens reflect the various areas of the club. My eyes zero in on her. I don't even fool myself into thinking that she's as defenseless as she looks. Her skin may look satin smooth, but it's coated with steel armor.

Deliberately, I shut off the feed to that camera and activate my phone. As I type, I silently urge her to accept my words.

"You're free to leave. Take me seriously and Do. Not. Come. Back."

As I power off my phone, the full extent of my weakness cannons through me. I don't want her to come back, and I don't want to hear her out for one reason alone.

She's here because of my father.

She's here on behalf of the man I hate more than anything else in the world. The man who made sure that, at nineteen, I would never have the option of redemption as long as I lived.

For a few years, I thought he would be satisfied with helping the devil stain my soul. But no. He's still after me. He's used his sentries in the form of my brothers, and now he's pulling out the big guns. I give him kudos for sending Cleo. With each visit, I've felt my edges crumbling away.

Despite everything I feel for her, I've tortured myself with the urge to give in. To hear that voice up close and personal. To smell her. Touch her.

Is her skin still the softest satin I've relived in my dreams?

Jesus.

I crave all of it even when I know it will be the last straw once she speaks the words she's been sent to deliver.

The Rutherfords and the McCarthys.

Once unlikely allies turned bitter enemies. Two dynastic families with feet firmly entrenched in underground crime. Drugs. Girls. Racketeering. Extortion.

Murder.

Between the two of us, we changed the course of our families' destinies. And I intend to change it even more. I intend to annihilate the Rutherford name until there's nothing left.

In a family of cold-hearted black sheep, I, Axel Rutherford, am the blackest. Abundantly despised by my three brothers, actively hated by my father.

She was the golden princess. Put on earth to test every single one of my hardened edges. And I happily burned away every last one for her.

But my reward wasn't forever with her.

Instead she turned away from me. And crawled into my father's bed.

Acknowledgments

My thanks to the usual suspects who make this writing journey a heady ride:

My Minx Sisters, you know who you are. You keep me sane when I need to be and happily join me when I need to go nuts!

To Helen Breitwieser, my agent, for your awesome support and enthusiasm for this series!

To Alex Logan, my editor, for your brilliant insight into making this story the best it can be. Thank you so much.

To all the bloggers, reviewers, Goodreads readers, Facebook groups, and Twitter and Instagram followers who selflessly share my stories, I love you all hard. Thank you for all you do.

Finally, to my wonderful husband and kids. Thank you from the bottom of my heart for every single moment of love and support you lavish my way and for your enthusiasm for what I do. I couldn't do this without you.

About the Author

Zara Cox has been writing for almost twenty-five years but it wasn't until nine years ago that she decided to share her love of writing sexy, gritty stories with anyone outside her close family (the over-eighteens anyway!). This series is Zara's next step in her erotic romance–writing journey, and she would love to hear your thoughts.

You can learn more at:
ZaraCoxWriter.com
Twitter @ZCoxBooks
Facebook.com/Zara-Cox-Writer